CHIA JOO MING won the Singapore Young Artist award in 1993 and participated in the Iowa international writing program in 1995. He was also writer-in-residence in the Chinese program, Nanyang Technological University, in 2014. Chia is a three-time recipient of the Singapore Literature Prize. He is currently a senior executive sub-editor in *Lianhe Zaobao*, Singapore main's Chinese-language newspaper.

Exile or Pursuit is his first novel translated into English.

SIM WAI CHEW is a professor of English literature at Nanyang Technological University, Singapore. He obtained his BA from the University of East Anglia and his Ph.D. from the University of Warwick. He has research interests in Singapore literature and culture, Postcolonial literature and theory, Sinophone studies, Comparative Literature, and Southeast Asian studies. He has published a monograph on the work of Anglo-Japanese author Kazuo Ishiguro and co-edited a collection of essays on British-Asian fiction. He has also co-edited a collection of Singapore short stories. The broad theme of Southeast Asian writing as an alternative theoretical locus to metropolitan discourse inspires his research and creative work.

CHIA JOO MING

EXILE OR PURSUIT

A Novel

Translated by

Sim Wai Chew

BALESTIER PRESS
LONDON · SINGAPORE

Balestier Press
Centurion House, London TW18 4AX
www.balestier.com

Exile or Pursuit
Original title: 放逐与追逐

First published by Balestier Press in 2019

A CIP catalogue record for this book is available
from the British Library.

ISBN 978 1 911221 17 3

EXILE OR PURSUIT

1

CHIU-YUN

1

The year it all started, Hok Leong had just entered secondary two. A new student joined their class. Her name is Lin Chiu-yun, the form teacher said. She's from Indonesia. From now on—everybody—please help her out as much as you can.

Hok Leong's tentative memories of school life began more or less from that period.

To welcome the new student, the teacher clapped his hands, willing everyone to join in. Hok Leong felt that this was a tad unsophisticated but was prepared to go through the motions. He raised his hands and was about to bring them together when suddenly he heard his name.

"Hok Leong. Your Chinese is pretty good. You should help Chiu-yun."

The boys in the class started to hoot. Hok Leong felt embarrassed and put his arms down.

Teacher wanted him to start immediately the next day. Hok Leong should come half an hour earlier to school, meet Chiu-yun at the library, and go through the material covered in class, he said.

Teacher must be sleeping, Hok Leong thought to himself. He had to help out at his father's food stall every day. There was no way he could come early. Even if he did he'd rather play football with the boys. How could he help the new girl?

Hok Leong did not respond to the teacher. His classmates continued to laugh uproariously at his discomfort.

The next day Hok Leong did not come early to school. He forgot about the task given to him. In fact he was late. His father's won ton noodles stall enjoyed extremely good business that morning. Even for him, it was a tough job getting away. Who had time to help the new Indonesian classmate with her school work?

2

Hok Leong's main impression of life before secondary two was the switch in the medium of instruction. In primary school, maths and science classes were conducted in English. In secondary school that all changed. The maths tests in secondary school were actually Chinese language tests. Although his Chinese was good, he couldn't understand the question paper and failed all the tests. He asked his classmates—how did they know that one question meant "add up" the figures, another meant "subtract"? "Idiot," his classmates said. "Jia-Jian-Cheng-Chu, He-Cha-Ji-Shang," they chanted, repeating the sing-song mnemonics that they had learned in class to handle the matter.

Hok Leong didn't understand the mnemonics and continued to fail the subject. It was also much later that he memorised the Chinese names for the chemical elements: Potassium-Sodium-Calcium-Magnesium-Aluminium, Zinc-Iron-Tin-Lead-Hydrogen, Copper-Mercury-Silver-Platinum-Gold. These were also couched in mnemonic form.

Apart from Chinese and Physical Education, Hok Leong failed every subject in secondary one. When he received his report book at the end of the year there were two words in it: "Provisional Promotion." Father, who was illiterate, asked him, "Did you pass"? Hok Leong didn't know how to reply. "Should be, I guess. Teacher didn't say that I had to repeat secondary one," he said.

Elder brother was two years older than him; elder sister a year older. Both had lousy grades. Elder brother had to repeat a year and ended up in the same level as elder sister for secondary three. Although they were from different schools, the schooling outcomes were similar, it could be said. Hok Leong had another sister, younger than him by two years, who fared better with her grades. Going by school results, Hok Leong ranked number two in their home, so his parents didn't scold him too much.

Apart from not having the time, Hok Leong also didn't ask father for permission to leave early because he figured father wouldn't believe the reason given, namely that he had to help a fellow student. In all probability, father wouldn't accept that. He would be shocked that Hok Leong's ability to tell lies had deteriorated by that much. Hok Leong's so-called good Chinese was obtained from reading martial arts novels and had nothing to do with academic ability. Why else would he obtain such poor results in Maths? Hok Leong didn't know if teacher was serious about the task given to him. How could he help the new Indonesian girl? He couldn't very well ask her to read martial arts novels, right? Hok Leong had started reading Chinese newspapers when he was in primary four. On the subject of martial arts novels, he liked "Duke" Wei and the character known as "little fish." He fantasised about penetrating deep into a remote forest so that he could find some skilled kung-fu master to challenge and fight. His elder brother had several martial arts novels that he refused to share with Hok Leong. His brother treated them like gold, as if they contained all manner of esoteric secrets.

Mother hated it when she saw them reading such works. She said it distracted them from school work. Like father, mother was illiterate. She didn't know why people read books.

You either *know* something or you *don't know* something, she said. If you don't know, reading about it won't help. Take, for instance, his Chinese. His Chinese was good because he was good in it. Even if he didn't read much, he'd be good in it. For the rest, even if he read a lot, it'd be useless. It wouldn't be of use to him.

3

Hok Leong forgot that he was supposed to help the new girl from Indonesia, but the girl didn't forget. During the recess period she walked up to him and asked, "Why didn't you come earlier today?"

Hok Leong was about to go to the canteen with his friends. He had forgotten about the matter and stood there, nonplussed. His friends waited for him. He didn't say anything. There was no time. His friends yelled at him to hurry up. He continued on to the canteen, not minding in the least. But half way there he began to worry. What if the girl told teacher about his oversight? What would happen if she did that?

The girl didn't tell the teacher. The next day, when everybody took the opportunity in between classes to visit the toilet and let off some steam, the new girl saw him in the corridor and repeated her question: "Why didn't you come earlier today?" Hok Leong wanted to tell her: My father is a hawker. I help out at his food stall every day before I come to school. Sometimes I'm late for school because of that. Who has time to help you? To get such a long message across he needed time, but standing in the corridor he didn't have it. And he was afraid that his friends would tease him. So he shortened the script. "I don't have time," he said. Then he left.

When he returned home that day, he decided that he had better ask his mother. From next week onwards we have extra tuition on Mondays, Wednesdays and Fridays, he said. We need to get there half an hour earlier. "What kind of tuition?" his mother asked. "Chinese," he replied. He didn't say that he was helping to coach someone *in* Chinese. He believed mother was like father. If he told the truth, she'd find it hard to accept, suspecting that for some reason his ability to tell lies had deteriorated. He hoped mother wouldn't give permission. He could give that as an excuse to the teacher.

His mother mumbled something under her breath. Eventually she said yes. She would tell father about it. Hok Leong's elder brother and sister were both in the morning school session. If Hok Leong didn't go to the hawker centre there'd be no one there to assist father. Father asked mother to help out a bit in the morning. She could come home earlier to make lunch for younger sister before she went to school. Father didn't want younger sister to get involved. She was too young, he said. Hok Leong had started helping out at the stall in primary five. Father cherished his daughters so elder sister didn't have to help out a lot as well. Mostly it was elder brother who went to give a hand. Nobody went against father's wishes. He didn't talk to his children a lot, just gave orders. All fathers seemed to be like that.

On the third day, Hok Leong looked for a chance to slip away from his buddies during the recess period so that he could approach the new Indonesian classmate. He wanted to talk to her before she raised the issue. He told her: "I don't have time this week but next week onwards we can begin the extra coaching. But it's only Mondays, Wednesdays, and Fridays. Is that all right with you?"

Still sitting all by herself, the new girl took a bite from the little snack that she had brought with her. Slowly she nodded her head.

Many years afterwards, this scene continued to haunt Hok Leong, to stick in his memory. It was the first time that he spoke with Chiu-yun.

4

Hok Leong didn't have many lasting memories of childhood. He didn't remember much about his school life, or about things that happened outside school. Life consisted of mainly two areas. One covered the hawker centre, the other covered his estate.

It was only in recent years that father managed to get a stall in the hawker centre. Before that he operated a mobile food cart, went everywhere to get customers, and often got "Saman" or fined for illegal hawking. "<u>Saman</u>" was the Malayanised word they used for such offences, derived from the English word "<u>Summon</u>."* At that time, Hok Leong was young and couldn't assist father at the food stall, he only heard about all this later. For a while, a man, an "uncle," came occasionally to look for father. Around half a year later, father started to operate a won ton noodle stall in the hawker centre. When he got older. Hok Leong learned that "uncle" was actually a government inspector charged with regulating street hawkers, what they called a "Teh Gu" in local Chinese. Father went to see this Teh Gu, gave him some "coffee money," which is to say a bribe, and asked the man to help him apply for a place in the hawker centre. Much later, Hok Leong felt that it was wrong to use serious words such as "bribe" or "corruption" to describe things from that era. At that time it was commonplace. Whether it was a big project or a small one, everyone had to give a little "coffee money" when they wanted to accomplish something. So Hok Leong didn't consider it a bribe. In fact he

---

* Underlined words and phrases in the text appear in English (or Malay) in the original and are not translated. Some of these words and phrases have been modified to conform to the rules of English grammar and usage. The original also contains snatches of English pop-song lyrics. For ease of reading, these are italicised but not underlined.

felt that this way of doing things carried a certain refinement and civility. It suggested a human touch.

The youngsters who went to the hawker centre to help their parents knew each other but never said hello. They maintained impassive, stony exteriors while observing what each other did. Hok Leong didn't like the other youngsters. Among them there was only mutual disdain or dislike. Even then two of the girls got his attention. At the coffee-drinks outlet two stalls away from them, there was a girl with healthy tanned skin and long silky hair that she kept pushing back over her shoulders when it slid to the front, which was often. The gesture was very pretty. She studied in a girls' school next to Hok Leong's but was unfortunately a year older than him. In his secret heart, Hok Leong called her Black Gold.

Another young girl helped out at a stall selling *chee cheong fun* or rice noodle roll. Hok Leong's parents occasionally chatted with the girl's mother who ran the stall, but he didn't talk to the girl. This girl had a lovely, tinkling laugh and was the same age as Hok Leong, but liked to act grown up. Sometimes she even put on make-up. But she used so many hues and tints that she looked a bit gross, like an <u>art palette</u> of some kind. Hok Leong also gave her a nickname: Colour Palette. Hok Leong's mother didn't like Colour Palette.

Both girls studied in English-medium schools. Hok Leong's English was super poor, so they couldn't really talk to each other. They could have used one of the Chinese dialects to communicate but that would have been strange, giving the impression that they were unschooled or illiterate. But the main thing was that they didn't get a chance to shoot the breeze.

Among their customers were a pair of university students who were dating. They often made Hok Leong feel like he'd done something wrong, that he was useless. Each time they came, they would ask: Been busy lately with schoolwork? How are things in school? A teacher in Hok Leong's school was a classmate of theirs at the university, so they often asked about his situation as well. Before going off they always gave the same parting advice to Hok Leong, telling him to be diligent, and saying that it was okay if he had to repeat a year. A year older, a year wiser, the schoolwork easier to understand: very quickly he would catch up with the others.

Hok Leong always kept his head down when they spoke to him. He appeared to be listening, and also looked like he wasn't. He always hoped that they would go away quickly, that they'd spare him the hassle so that he wouldn't get singled out by his parents. Even then he liked listening to them. School seemed easy when they talked about it. He even had the urge to rush home and complete his homework or prepare for lessons. But the urge never lasted long. It was a momentary thing, especially when he got home and his friends came looking for him—very quickly he forgot about it.

Hok Leong's friends were all from the same estate. At that time nobody came knocking on the door asking graciously, "Is Hok Leong in? Can he come out and play?" Nobody provoked parents like that. Of course, children liked to play; it was part of their make-up. But for many generations, it seemed, the words "play" and "wrongdoing" overlapped in the thinking of adults and couldn't be separated. The funny thing was, the neighbourhood kids always found ways to get around parents so that they could come out and fool around.

Hok Leong got along best with these kids. To get someone to come downstairs you had to do a "double-hand whistle." The "skill set" behind this whistle has not been passed down properly so it is now practically a lost art. To do the whistle, you form a half-circle with your palms and cup them together, one palm tightly grabbing the other. You align the two thumbs at the top and blow hard through the crack in the middle. If you practice hard enough you can even make it play a short tune.

The double-hand whistle was effective because parents didn't pay much attention to their kids. Whenever he heard the familiar tune, Hok Leong would go to the kitchen window to see who was downstairs and then try to find an excuse to slip out. Of course, his parents knew about it. On one occasion when he stepped out of the showers his mother even said to him: Hey, there's someone downstairs looking for you.

The friends who came most often to look for Hok Leong were Hung Lung or Red Dragon, Gao Sai or Dog Shit (yes, there really *is* someone with that name), Ah Mei or little sister, (but here referring to a guy *lah*, not a girl), Junior Brother, and Opium Addict. There weren't many places actually for them to play. They just gambolled about the place, looking for distraction. For example, they would stand by the roadside and wait for a car to appear. When it came near, say about ten plus metres away, they would dash across suddenly giving the driver a great shock, and forcing him to apply the emergency brakes. Or they would climb a large tree with one person shaking it from below to see who fell down first. Or after a big rain they would jump into the giant monsoon drains, try to avoid being flushed away by the flood water. When they discovered later that copper and tin foil pieces could be exchanged for cash, they also kept an eye out for those treasures when they played.

Fisticuffs was the way to settle things if somebody crossed another person, or if you didn't like the look of him. At that point they hadn't progressed yet to fighting with weapons.

Hok Leong recalled that one time in secondary two, he got into an altercation with a classmate during Physics. He couldn't remember the person's name or the precise reason for it. Eventually they both sprang up from their seats, the tables screeching as they got pushed back, and giving the teacher, who was writing something on the blackboard, a big shock. The teacher, who was near retirement, blinked owlishly at the two young bucks from behind thick bifocal glasses. He knew what was happening. Hok Leong and his opponent sat down resentfully. The teacher turned back to the board to continue writing. Before teacher completed the turn, Hok Leong and his opponent had already made an appointment: after class that day they would meet behind the assembly hall to "settle the matter."

Somehow Hok Leong made it through the rest of the lessons. When he got to the back of the hall, however, the other guy didn't show up so he left it at that. Hok Leong didn't know how "the back of the hall" became the designated place for students to settle disputes. Actually it was just a small five-foot-wide strip of land between the assembly hall and the perimeter wall of the school, the ground uneven, the grass cut irregularly unlike the athletics field, so that not many people went there. Because not many people went there it had gradually become the school "coliseum."

The school he attended had a decent academic reputation. A decade after he left, it even got selected for the "special" school programme. How did a place like that get a student like him? The day after the altercation, he remembered, his new Indonesian classmate saw him and immediately asked: "Why did you act like that yesterday?"

Hok Leong didn't have an answer for her. Why didn't she know that fighting was bound to happen when people got together? Why didn't she know that it was like doing homework and by mistake you write the wrong character or word? Bound to happen. Of course, he failed to remember that when his primary school friends organised a reunion one person would never appear, never get to appear. That person was beaten to death in a melee fight. His photo even appeared in the newspaper.

5

Hok Leong only realised when he started to help his Indonesian classmate that he didn't know how to proceed. How does one *do* revision? He wasn't a teacher. He didn't know how or what to teach. He asked the Indonesian classmate, what do you want to revise? She shook her head. Eventually, Hok Leong got her to read a passage from the textbook. If she didn't understand anything, he tried to explain it. When there was something that Hok Leong didn't know, he said, I'll go ask about it and get back to you. When he got home he'd thumb frantically through his elder sister's dictionary, searching for an answer.

The Chinese standard of the Indonesian classmate wasn't too bad. After five to six sessions they had covered all the material studied in class. Hok Leong said, "That's it. We only reached this bit."

The girl looked at him for a moment. Carefully, in a small voice, she said: "Can you continue to help me?"

Hok Leong was taken aback. He stared at her and completely forgot to say "No." To continue meant he had it in him to be a teacher. Could he really do that? Softly, she asked again: "You *can* help me, right?" She mistook him forgetting to say "No" for him actually saying "Yes!" He was too lazy to correct her mistake. After all, he figured, a bit of coaching never hurt anyone. Nobody got killed.

But if they wished to continue, the same problem came roaring back. How do you revise? What do you revise? Naturally, Hok Leong didn't have any new ideas. So they returned to the same tried and true method. She read a passage from the material studied in class, and if she didn't know anything he'd try to explain it. The funny thing was, she had even more questions now with the newly-covered material. When he asked her why, she said she didn't know why. Was the teacher worse than him? That didn't seem plausible. Anyway, fourteen-year-old Hok Leong felt that this coaching malarkey was a good thing. It didn't give him all that much confidence in the subject, but it was still something to be proud about.

When the results came out at the end of the year, the Indonesian girl surprisingly obtained better results in Chinese than him. She scored eighty-six in the exam, he eighty-two. "Sorry," she said. Hok Leong didn't know how to respond. Eighty-two was plenty enough for him. He'd never gotten such a score in the past. He got to benefit as well because he gave her some tuition. The point was that he never thought of comparing his results with hers. What concerned him more was that his pedagogy seemed to work: it produced a good student. For a long time this gave him a great amount of happiness.

Apart from Chinese, Hok Leong also profited greatly in two areas. He passed his English and Maths. Passing these two subjects was immeasurably more important than the Indonesian girl obtaining higher scores in Chinese than him. It was the first time he passed those subjects in secondary school.

Hok Leong helped coach the Indonesian girl, but in the end it became a matter of mutual aid. After they became more acquainted, the Indonesian girl often asked—before they started the Chinese revision—"How's your English?" Or: "Have you completed the Maths exercise given in class?"

Hok Leong only thought about these things when she raised them, usually shaking his head in response to her questions. On her part, she progressed from "let me help you with that" when they first got acquainted to the more severe "just because I don't ask about it doesn't mean that you should keep quiet!" after they became thoroughly familiar with one other. But still Hok Leong didn't like to bring it up. Especially when it came to Maths. After he learned the Chinese mnemonics for the subject—Jia-Jian-Cheng-Chu, He-Cha-Ji-Shang—he more or less understood what was happening and could follow the lessons. So in the end it wasn't clear who was helping who.

After the results came out, Hok Leong was put into the Technical stream. He had to switch to another school. The Indonesia girl was retained in the same school, where she would study in the elite Science stream. On the last day of school, the girl asked: "How will you help me with my Chinese if you get transferred to the new school?" Hok Leong didn't have an answer. She added: "How about your English?" Again, Hok Leong didn't know what to say. He never thought about things like that. All he knew was that he was put into the Technical stream because he did well in some aptitude test.

The Indonesian girl ran out of questions to ask. A large Mercedes Benz pulled slowly into the school driveway and headed towards them. She waved goodbye to him, got into the car, closed the door, and again waved eagerly at him. Hok Leong stared dumbly at the vehicle as it pulled away. He didn't know that he was supposed to wave back.

A gust of wind appeared after the vehicle exited the school compound, blowing the leaves on the ground hither and thither. Hok Leong felt a tightness in his heart. It felt odd. He realised finally that it was the last day of school.

6

Hok Leong felt dispirited the entire holidays. He couldn't find the energy to do anything. His mother said that he was like an old man, stuck in a rut. Hok Leong thought: going to a new school meant he would have to say goodbye to another bunch of classmates. Although he wasn't that close to them, they were at least a few that he got along with, fooled around with, failed tests with, and even fought with. In the future he would have to get to know another bunch of schoolmates, to choose from among them those he liked, although the choices were getting limited, and it seemed like the only thing he could do was to contact former classmates, except that after switching schools there were now less things to discuss, less common ground, and at any rate they were too lazy to contact one another. It was like when he moved from primary school to secondary school—friends and contacts falling in droves by the wayside.

Having to coach the Indonesian girl was a bit of a bore, but it was also the only time he actually did some schoolwork. After the holidays that would go as well.

During the school vacation he did meet someone from his class, someone he didn't know that well earlier, whose home was only two road-crossings away from his. The classmate asked Hok Leong to go to his house to play. After many years Hok Leong still remembered his name, Lim Tee Bo. There was another person who also went to Tee Bo's home to play, but Hok Leong forgot his name.

What the so-called "come around to play" amounted to was calling female classmates on the phone and having a little chit-chat. For Hok Leong, this meant that he had entered another era, the telecommunications era. Hok Leong didn't have a phone in his home. He had never heard of it, didn't know that the sound transmitted over the line would be like that.

The first time he heard a voice coming over the phone was the voice of the Indonesian girl. It seemed so real. What made it hard was that it felt like she was whispering into his ear. It felt closer than when they studied together in the library. For Hok Leong, it was also the first time a girl spoke so intimately to him. She spoke to him because Tee Bo, after getting through to the girl, refused to reveal his identity and passed the receiver to Hok Leong. The Indonesian girl continued in a voice grown sultry and provocative: "Oh…Who is it?"

Hok Leong took the receiver from Tee Bo, heard her query and immediately replied: "Hok Leong!"

Tee Bo raised his hand and slapped the back of Hok Leong's head.

"Ouch! Why did you do that!" Hok Leong cried.

"Where are you?" the girl asked.

"Tee Bo's house!" he answered.

Again, Tee Bo slapped his head. He grabbed the receiver from Hok Leong's hand.

So for his first telephone conversation, Hok Leong fielded two questions, uttering two short phrases in the process. Tee Bo continued to talk cheekily to the Indonesian girl. After a while he replaced the receiver without passing it to Hok Leong. Then he called a few more classmates. They only stopped when Tee Bo's sister came home from work and Hok Leong had to go home. He was curious how Tee Bo had managed to obtain so many of their female classmates' phone numbers. He felt grateful to Tee Bo for this, his first time using a phone, so he always remembered his name.

For the next few days after that, Hok Leong went regularly to Tee Bo's home. What he cared about was chit-chatting with the Indonesian girl. But she kept asking him about his new school, which Hok Leong had no clues about. So the talk became staccato. She'd ask him something, and he'd have to do it before he could give a satisfactory answer. For instance, she asked: "Where's the school?" Hok Leong had no choice but to go home and check.

Really, he didn't care two hoots about it. The next day when he told her the location she asked: "Have you been there?" "Er, no," he replied. When he got home that day he told his mother that he had to go check out the new school. After scouting it out, however, he was again unprepared when the Indonesian girl asked: "Have you bought the new school books yet?" So he had to check up about that too. Indeed it was quite a nuisance. But Hok Leong also liked the feeling that he was being looked after.

She probably needed someone to look after, Hok Leong reasoned to himself, for the next moment she was telling him: "Here's my home number. Call me this evening at seven thirty."

Repeating the number in his head, Hok Leong stealthily picked up the ball-point pen from the coffee table top, strode to the washroom, and wrote the number down on the inside of his hand. He told Tee Bo that he had a stomach ache. He had to go home early.

It took forever for seven thirty to arrive. Time stood still. At home Hok Leong took out his school textbooks and began to read. Chinese, English, Mathematics—they were all from secondary two. He hadn't bought the secondary three textbooks yet. Repeatedly, he ignored the double-palm whistle coming from downstairs, his estate friends calling him. When he could no longer stand the sight of the books he went to his mother: "Is dinner ready yet, mother? I'm hungry." After dinner, he again checked the clock: six thirty. Hok Leong laid on his bed, he didn't know what to do. His eyes grew heavy.

When next he opened his eyes, Hok Leong realised that he had dozed off. He jumped off the bed and again checked the clock: 7.35 p.m.! He gave a strange yelp and ran out of the house.

Hok Leong had prepared a stack of ten cent coins. He had transferred the Indonesian girl's telephone number from his hand to a slip of paper that he brought along with him. The public pay phone was in the street across from his apartment block, propped in a corner of an Indian convenience store located next to the staircase area of a row of HDB shops.*

When the call got through he glanced at the clock in the store: 7:39 p.m.!

"Hello!"

Hok Leong recognised the voice but forced himself to ask politely: "Is Chiu-yun at home?" This was the first time he used

---

* HDB—Housing Development Board. Singapore's public housing authority.

the Indonesian girl's name—Chiu-yun.

He remembered her reply, her laughter: "Your voice sounds so strange!" she said.

Hok Leong didn't say anything. After a while she said, "There's someone talking next to you." It was the Indian store owner chatting with one of his customers.

Hok Leong explained that he was calling from a pay phone inside a convenience store. Chiu-yun was surprised. She didn't know that Hok Leong's flat lacked the apparatus. Hok Leong didn't elaborate. His self-esteem was damaged. When Chiu-yun learned that Hok Leong's father operated a won ton noodle stall in the neighbourhood hawker centre, she wanted to go there to eat but he was discomforted. She was curious about everything that concerned him. For her, it was fresh and interesting. Hok Leong, not expecting that anything in his life could be attractive to her, tried his best to answer her questions. They kept talking, stopping only when the Indian store owner indicated that he wanted to close for the day. Hok Leong and Chiu-yun agreed that he would call again the next evening at seven thirty.

That night, Hok Leong kept tossing about in his bed, unable to fall sleep. He had the bottom bunk of a double-decker bed, slept in a "room" carefully fashioned from the clutter of a one-room HDB flat. Hok Leong ran over the details of his conversation with Chiu-yun. Everyone was asleep. His brother slept in the bunk above. Mother and younger sister slept on a wooden board on the floor right by his side. Elder sister was no longer a young girl. Mother let her sleep in the kitchen. Father slept in the small living room.

Chiu-yun probably had her own room and bed at home, Hok Leong thought. She found the details of his life interesting, unusual, *different*. Hok Leong was unimpressed by that kind of difference. What was so great about his house not having a telephone? In his corridor, none of the flats had a phone. His father being a food stall operator was also not something to shout about. What was different was that, in the hawker centre, every hawker was the father of a different person. What Chiu-yun found interesting and unusual, Hok Leong had about it a wealth of feelings that he couldn't enumerate.

7

When Hok Leong went to the hawker centre the next morning, he paid additional attention to the other stalls where the children came to assist their parents. They were really not that dissimilar from Hok Leong and Chiu-yun. Black Gold and Colour Palette in particular didn't seem different at all. Hok Leong also scrutinised the younger customers—those around his age—who came to patronise their stall. They didn't seem all that different from each other.

That afternoon, Hok Leong didn't go to Tee Bo's flat after helping out at the food stall. He went out with Red Dragon and his gang. Whenever the group went gadding about, Red Dragon was the one in charge. They were used to him being the leader.

Almost everyone in the group had failed his exams and had decided to stop school. Not counting Hok Leong, Ah Mei was the only one continuing his studies. The attention that Hok Leong paid to the young people in the morning had probably affected him, for now he found that, compared to those youngsters, this group whom he hung around with so much were actually quite different. Take Tee Bo for instance. Tee Bo liked to swear, but he did that only when he was angry. In comparison, Dog Shit and Junior Brother cursed all the time. They wanted people to know that this was how they talked. And, furthermore, they gave the impression that they were fighting whenever they opened their mouths. From the beginning, Hok Leong had not liked that. It was okay to fight, he reckoned, but there should be some method and rationale to it. Not crazy fighting like that. Another thing that pissed him off was their manner of walking. The way that Red Dragon and his posse walked made Hok Leong feel like he wanted to beat them up. Later on, Hok Leong also realised that while they occasionally borrowed money from him, they hardly ever of their own volition returned it. Like with Opium Addict, you had to practically push them to the verge of fisticuffs before they handed over the money.

When he called Chiu-yun that evening, she shared with him some details about her family. Her parents were both in Indonesia. Father was a businessman. Mother looked after her two younger brothers. Everybody was worried about her being on her own in Singapore. In about a year or two, her two brothers would probably join her as well. A friend of Chiu-yun's father helped to look after her while she was in the republic. As before, they chatted till the Indian store owner indicated that he wanted to close shop. Before she hung up, Chiu-yun, switching to English, said "<u>bye-bye</u>" to Hok Leong.

Hok Leong had concluded earlier that day—just that morning in fact—that there was really no difference between Chiu-yun, Black Gold, and Colour Palette. But now after chatting with Chiu-yun, he felt that she was different. How so? He couldn't put it into words. He reminded himself that, before hanging up the next day, he should say "<u>bye-bye</u>" to Chiu-yun.

On the way home, Hok Leong suddenly realised that a group of four to five guys were trailing after him. He quickly crossed the road. Immediately, they crossed the road after him. Realising that something was amiss, Hok Leong broke into a sprint, heading towards his apartment block. Behind him someone shouted "XXX your mother" in Hokkien dialect, followed by "Get him!" Hok Leong increased his speed. For the first time in his life he realised that being able to run fast brought certain specifiable benefits. The group behind him couldn't keep up. They started to flag and fell further behind. Only then did Hok Leong glance backwards. He couldn't make them out properly. Everything was indistinct. One person seemed to move with a pronounced limp. So weird, Hok Leong told himself. He hadn't offended anyone. Why would anyone want to beat him up?

8

Secondary three—the start of the school year. From the first step that he took into the classroom, Hok Leong didn't like the look of his classmates. The first time he stepped into the new school, he hadn't liked it as well.

Apart from Hok Leong, there was one other student from his alma mater, still wearing the old uniform, someone he hadn't met before. The guy came over to say hello. His name was Wong Ah Hor. In addition, two guys who knew Wong came over; they were from an institution located near their previous school. One was named Hong Ying-jun, the other Chang Tee Soon. Why did people have names like that? Ah Hor, Ying-jun, Tee Soon. Hok Leong wanted to laugh but controlled himself, nodding carefully as he made their acquaintance. During the recess period, they huddled together to shoot the breeze, worrying various topics like elderly people reminiscing about back in the days. Even so, it was better than sitting alone staring into space.

That evening at the appointed time, Hok Leong again gave Chiu-yun a call. Chiu-yun hoped that Hok Leong would come over to her house to help her with her Chinese when he didn't have extra-curricular activities in the afternoons. At first Hok Leong said okay. Then he said that he had to discuss the matter with his mother. Unlike their previous phone conversations, they ended earlier that evening. They had to get up early the next day for school. On the way home, Hok Leong clutched carefully in his hand a stout stick that he had prepared earlier. The stick had a nail protruding from one end, forming a mace of some kind. Luckily the group from the previous night did not appear again. If they did, his lousy one-nail club probably wasn't enough for self-protection, Hok Leong figured. He decided that he should find a new place to make his phone calls.

That evening, Hok Leong told his mother that teacher wanted them to stay in school after class to get some extra tuition. He couldn't help out at the food stall. Mother hesitated. She didn't know how to respond. They usually didn't get many customers in the afternoon, Hok Leong continued, father should be able to cope by himself. Furthermore, elder brother and sister were now in the morning session. They could also lend a hand at the stall. Mother didn't react to his words. He took that as *de facto* yes, she had given her permission.

Chiu-yun was overjoyed when she heard the news. She wanted Hok Leong to come over to her house the very next day. They agreed to meet at two o'clock in Katong Shopping Centre.

9

Chiu-yun had blossomed during the holidays.

From his seat on the stone steps of the Katong Shopping Centre forecourt, Hok Leong scrutinised Chiu-yun as she approached his location. The afternoon breeze caught her sleek black hair, blew it sensuously about her neck and shoulders. Without her school uniform, Chiu-yun looked taller, more mature. Hok Leong stood up to welcome her. He still wore the uniform of his former school, from secondary two, although it no longer fit him. Chiu-yun came close and reached out eagerly to shake his hands. Seeing his lack of response, she changed her greeting to a joke: "You're dark and thin. Gosh, what did you *do* during the holidays?"

Hok Leong was quick on the uptake. "Sorry, you've got the wrong person."

A vehicle drew to a stop next to the forecourt entryway. It was the one that Hok Leong had seen in school before the holidays. Chiu-yun went to it and opened the door for Hok Leong. Hok Leong took a step forward, then stepped back gallantly to let Chiu-yun go first. Chuckling graciously, Chiu-yun climbed into the car. Hok Leong felt that he had done something small but meaningful. He even spoke to the driver. "Thank you," he said.

Chiu-yun gave a little laugh. "You're not usually like this in school?"

Hok Leong knew that Chiu-yun enjoyed this other side of him. "This *is* the real me," he said.

"You've grown up!" Chiu-yun said.

No, he grew up a long time ago, he thought, and gave a silly little laugh.

10

Chiu-yun's house was located about ten minutes away from the shopping centre. The distance was walkable. After that first time going by car, Hok Leong and Chiu-yun always preferred to walk. Many years later, he preferred not to dwell on the scenery along that stretch of road, especially the section near Chiu-yun's house, so he avoided it religiously. His remembered a quiet street, the fierce sun, the shadows formed by huge trees on both sides of the road covering most of the road surface. He remembered vapour tendrils rising from the areas where the sun's rays struck the exposed tarmac, sometimes the light so bright he couldn't open his eyes. He remembered the hot wind, the leaves caught by the airstream, sighing like a broom in use, like something being swept away. He remembered long-drawn-out cicada cries that stopped suddenly—an iconic instance of a proverb he later learned in school to describe a sound that suddenly stops. Many years later he still hated going out after lunch, not only because he wished to avoid the tropical heat, but also to avoid scenes like that, scenes laced with memory, feeling, and passion.

The house looked ordinary from the outside. This was the impression that stayed with Hok Leong, his recall altered perhaps by the passage of time. A normal looking corner terrace house, but enough nevertheless to stretch the horizons of a young man, to open his eyes to the world.

What really opened Hok Leong's eyes was the interior of the house. He had never seen such magnificence. Compared with Hok Leong's one-room flat, "luxurious" was the right word to describe it. Everything from the ceiling to the floor caught his attention. And then there were the electrical appliances and accessories: it basically had the full range and lacked for nothing. Nowadays you could see such items in movies from the eighties, indeed they had become collectibles. The Hok Leong of that "period" saw something else too, another proverb meaning to gasp in amazement, to acclaim as a peak of excellence.

Shortly after he sat down on the settee, a maid bought over a glass of orange juice, a drink that you also didn't see that often during that period. Thank you, Hok Leong said softly. Chiu-yun sat next to him laughing gleefully, enjoying his stupefaction. Hok Leong ignored her. When did she become so vibrant and cheeky? he thought to himself.

Chiu-yun took out a Chinese textbook from her school bag and handed it to Hok Leong. Hok Leong browsed through it. He could cope with that. No worries. Chiu-yun gave him other textbooks but he only glanced at them. Apart from Chinese, he wasn't interested in the other subjects. Chiu-yun asked Hok Leong if she could see his textbooks as well. He hadn't bought any, he confessed. He only had the book list, which he retrieved from his bag and handed to her. Chiu-yun inspected the list and gave a cry: "How come everything is in English? The only thing in Chinese is the textbook 'Chinese language'!"

"Really?" Hok Leong took the list from her hand. He hadn't looked at it carefully yet.

Chiu-yun asked him about the new school. Hok Leong didn't know much about it so there was a limit to what he could share. He could only listen to her talk about *her* school and class. The guy whom Hok Leong almost came to blows with was still in Chiu-yun's class, she revealed. Tee Bo and the rest were in the same school but different class.

None of the teachers had assigned any homework that day, so Chiu-yun suggested that they sing some songs. She took out her guitar and asked Hok Leong to make a suggestion. Hok Leong shook his head. He only knew the songs taught in school during music lessons, or snatches of songs overheard coming from the neighbours. It wasn't something he paid attention to. In the end he could only say: "you decide." Chiu-yun didn't hesitate. With a practiced hand she began to tune her guitar, then she launched into an English song:

> *When I was young, I'd listened to the radio,*
> *Waiting for my favourite songs.*
> *When they played I'd sing along, it made me smile.*
> *Those were such happy times, and not so long ago.*
> *How I wondered where they'd gone.*
> *But they are back again, just like a long lost friend,*
> *All the songs I love so well…*

11

Hok Leong couldn't recall what time he went home that day. He couldn't remember what else he did with Chiu-yun, or what precisely happened after the maid fetched the glass of orange juice.

He only remembered that the first English song he heard was sung by Chiu-yun. It was "Yesterday Once More" by The Carpenters. Later he heard the original version sung by Karen Carpenter, but he always felt that Chiu-yun's "cover" version was pretty good.

Hok Leong's English was poor. He didn't use it much, didn't move in a circle where people listened to English pop songs. He didn't know that an English-language song could sound so catchy and melodious. He asked Chiu-yun if she could give him the lyrics for it. On the spot, she began to teach him the words to the song. Hok Leong had little musical talent so she helped him. They spent a warm, magical afternoon learning the ballad, singing it again and again.

The guitar was something that Chiu-yun taught herself to play. Before that she had studied the piano, which they moved on to after a while. Chiu-yun played the piano and wanted Hok Leong to sing accompaniment. But he wanted her to do both. He enjoyed watching her perform. Languorously, she sang song after song while Hok Leong watched, transfixed.

Hok Leong felt like a protagonist in a martial arts novel, like he had entered another dimension where everything was fresh, beautiful, and fine. Chiu-yun, the person who brought him into this world, also seemed other-worldly and ethereal. Compared to her, Black Gold, Colour Palette, and even Hok Leong's two sisters seemed entirely different.

Hok Leong would have liked to stay there forever but eventually he had to return home.

12

A loud shrill whistle pierced the night air. The whistle sounded again. On an evening when Chiu-yun wasn't free and Hok

Leong had stayed home, checking up in a dictionary the unfamiliar words from the lyrics to the <u>John Denver</u> hit song, <u>Take Me Home, Country Road</u>, Red Dragon came looking for him.

Hok Leong went downstairs bare bodied. Red Dragon said that a few days earlier Junior Brother was beaten up at the fresh-produce market. Hok Leong immediately thought of the gang that had chased him a while back. The five of them—Red Dragon, Dog Shit, Junior Brother, Opium Addict, and Ah Mei—wanted to take revenge. They wanted Hok Leong to come along. Hok Leong went upstairs to grab a T-shirt. When he returned, Red Dragon led them to a nearby clump of tall grass, stepped in and emerged with six wooden clubs, one for each of them. Together, they headed for the market.

The market was dark, quiet, almost deserted. The rows of shops next to it were also preparing to close for the night. Hok Leong had telephoned Chiu-yun from the Indian grocery shop located there, the one next to the staircase area.

They hid at the place where Junior Brother got hammered—the car park behind the shop apartments. They broke into two groups. Red Dragon, Junior Brother, and Ah Mei formed one group. The remaining three formed another group.

While they waited, Opium Addict gave Dog Shit and Hok Leong each a cigarette. They lit up and inhaled. Nobody said anything. Red Dragon and his group lit up as well. Like in the proverb where the guy guarded the proverbial tree stump waiting for rabbits to appear, they waited. When their cigarettes were almost finished, three guys appeared. Red Dragon raised himself a little, took the still burning stub out of his mouth and flicked it away. Here were the rabbits, his action said. Everyone killed their cigarettes as well. They waited expectantly for the next set of instructions.

Their rivals, who were themselves hunting for rabbits, neared the lorry behind which crouched Red Dragon and his party. Red Dragon stepped out suddenly. "XXX your mother," a guy in the rival group shouted out in Hokkien dialect. "This way!" he cried. Immediately they turned around.

Hok Leong recognised the familiar voice. It was the group that had chased him earlier. With Opium Addict and Dog Shit in tow he stepped out from behind his hiding place. Seeing themselves boxed in, the rival group turned to one side and ran. Hok Leong and his friends gave chase. The guy with a limp ran slower than his compatriots. Red Dragon reached him first, swung his club, and hit him in the back. "Arrrggghhh" he cried and continued to run. Red Dragon swung again, this time hitting him on the shoulders. After that Red Dragon stopped. He didn't give chase.

Just like that the fight ended. Hok Leong felt his chest heaving, his heart pumping furiously. He gasped for air. The wheezing that he experienced was worse than on the previous occasion when they had chased after him.

13

The uniform code for Hok Leong's new school was different from Chiu-yun's school, meaning to say, his alma mater. Hok Leong, now in secondary three, wore long pants when he went to school. The boys in his previous school—both secondary three and four—still wore shorts. Hok Leong was glad that he had switched to a new institution.

Hok Leong studied six subjects. Responding to Chiu-yun's entreaty, he had bought the textbooks for four of them: Chinese, English, Maths, and Physics. When they revised their schoolwork, Chiu-yun always insisted that he take out his textbooks first. First they covered Hok Leong's four subjects, then they went through Chiu-yun's four. Because the textbooks were different, they effectively revised twice for each subject. Hok Leong couldn't find words to describe his vexation. In his entire life this was probably the first time he worked as hard as this. There were no textbooks for the remaining two subjects, metal work and technical drawing. In any case, Chiu-yun didn't study those subjects and didn't know anything about them, which was just as well!

The vexation and frustration didn't last long, for Chiu-yun's mother had decided to hire a tuition teacher. On Mondays and Wednesdays, the tutor came to help Chiu-yun with English, Chinese, and Maths. When Hok Leong encountered difficulties with these subjects, including Chinese, they directed his queries to the teacher as well. Hok Leong couldn't understand why Chiu-yun needed such assistance. She was already streets ahead of him. Apart from Mondays and Wednesdays, Chiu-yun's Thursdays and Saturdays were set aside for extra-curricular activities, that is, for Chinese calligraphy and guitar. Her mother had requested that she take up the former, while the latter she did for herself. Tuesdays and Fridays were the only days where Hok Leong and Chiu-yun could meet up.

Chiu-yun's busy days were also "free" days for Hok Leong. Not having to revise his schoolwork, he could go off and play. Oddly enough, he didn't yearn so much for such freedom after he started studying with Chiu-yun.

Chiu-yun often felt that she was too busy. She wanted to stop the calligraphy lessons. "What should I do?" she asked Hok Leong.

A part of Hok Leong wanted her to continue. But greater still was his desire to see her end it. "Just stop it!" he said.

Of course, Chiu-yun didn't do that. She could handle the calligraphy. More than that she found time to revise *both* sets of schoolwork, his and hers, including the work that Hok Leong *didn't* do because he didn't go to her house on her busy days.

Chiu-yun was curious. Why didn't his teachers assign any homework, she asked. Hok Leong explained: "Teacher said we're grown up now. We decide for ourselves whether to hand in homework, whether to join extra-curricular activities." Hok Leong never bothered much about ECA. He didn't want to waste even more time in school. As an excuse he told Chiu-yun that he was busy at home.

What did he enjoy about school? she continued.

Metal work and technical drawing, he replied.

Chiu-yun frowned. She had taken such courses before with Hok Leong. He had secretly helped her to file down the metal pieces, to saw wood, and to complete the technical drawings. Female students tended not to like such subjects. They couldn't understand why the school made them suffer through them. Continuing her line of inquiry, Chiu-yun posed the more pertinent, more challenging question. "What do you want to do in the future?" she asked.

Hok Leong shook his head. He had never thought about the issue. He didn't know how to formulate a response.

"Then why do you study in a technical school?"

Again Hok Leong shook his head. "I did well in the aptitude tests!"

"So what do you want to do in the future?"

Hok Leong shrugged his shoulders.

That day, Hok Leong took Chiu-yun's question home with him. When he went to bed that night he was still clueless, he didn't have an answer.

14

His classmates didn't have answers as well.

Everybody said: "Are you crazy? Why think so much ahead? The future is a long time away. You don't know what will happen. If you think too much, you'll go crazy."

"Everybody" here referred to the three guys he met on the first day of school: Ah Hor, Ying-jun, Tee Soon. At first Hok Leong didn't like them. But after interacting with them for a while he realised that they were all right. Responding to the topic that Hok Leong raised, Ah Hor added: "Why do you need to study so much? Just finish secondary four. That's good enough. Why complete another two years of senior high? Those who take that option continue to study. We start work first and gain an additional two years of experience. Isn't that more or less the same?"

Hok Leong felt that Ah Hor's words made great sense.

The people whom Hok Leong hung around with all felt that "secondary-four-was-enough." Their teachers also treated them as grown-ups who should practice autonomy. So after the recess period, more than half of those on the class register often upped and "disappeared." Hok Leong also joined the exodus, but for metal work and technical drawing he stayed behind. He liked those subjects. There was no pressure, the teachers for those classes were friendly, they liked to chit chat, to shoot the breeze. Hok Leong often wondered why other teachers couldn't be like them.

"Disappearance" often meant going first to the library located near their school, but not to borrow books or to read. Instead it was to leave their bags at the check-in counter, stepping in making a big round and then leaving separately one by one. It was easier to go gadding about without their school bags.

Sometimes they went to the movies, where they might meet girls from neighbouring schools who were also skipping classes. They found ways to get to know one another. After that they sometimes went to the hawker centre together, or hung around in the public park or shopping centre. Once they even went to a photo studio and took some pictures. Everybody thought those meet-ups would continue, but one day when the appointed time came nobody wanted to go. Eventually Hok Leong and his friends didn't get to see the photographs that they took with the girls.

If you wanted to meet girls who were skipping classes, it was better to go watch some human interest movie or drama. Girls tended not to like martial arts films. But boys also didn't much like human interest movies.

During those halcyon days when happiness was ordinary, nobody thought about the question that Chiu-yun had raised. They bothered about where to play, where to find girls. The "secondary-four-was-enough" mind-set was indeed quite wonderful!

15

Soon Hok Leong had something else to be worried about.

A few times while studying at Chiu-yun home he saw her speaking on the phone. Finally one day he couldn't control himself. "Who is it?" he asked.

Chiu-yun didn't seem particularly concerned. "It's Tee Bo. He's great fun. He often calls me at home."

Hok Leong had almost forgotten the name. He didn't expect Tee Bo would still be in contact with Chiu-yun. Furthermore, his intentions seemed quite clear. "Isn't Tee Bo in the same school as you?" Hok Leong asked coldly. "You mean school's just finished and immediately you need to chat over the phone?"

Chiu-yun didn't catch the implication behind Hok Leong's remark. "He's in a different class," she said. "Anyway, he's a good friend of yours, right?"

Hok Leong wanted to say—No, he's not my friend. We just hung around a bit during that one holiday break. But feeling that those words might be too revealing, he took a different tack: "You sure have a lot to talk about!"

Chiu-yun gave a little laugh but didn't respond. Hok Leong didn't like the way she parried his thrust. Her laughter left him nonplussed. Unable to settle the matter, he had no choice but to let it rest.

He didn't expect her to add, as if a light bulb had lit up in her head: "If you think it's a bad idea, I won't talk to him." She seemed to want to figure out his feelings.

Of course, Hok Leong wanted her to end those conversations. But he continued to control himself. "It's up to you," he said in a cool, indifferent tone of voice.

16

Colour Palette had eloped with a guy.

Hok Leong overheard his parents talking about it. What happened to her seemed a great pity and Hok Leong had a lot of question marks about it. The impression he had of her shattered into many pieces.

Father wanted mother keep a good watch on the two young ladies at home, to make sure they didn't go bad. Mother changed the topic. She said they should consider moving to a bigger flat after Hok Leong's elder brother and sister finished secondary four and came out to work, when they had a bit more money. She said lots of sixteen to seventeen year old girls in the neighbourhood had eloped, or else they suddenly had big bellies—who knew what kind of unmentionable jobs they were doing? She said the neighbour living diagonally across from them, the taxi driver, had a wife who was over a decade younger than him. It turned out she was actually the "second wife," the mistress.

Father said jokingly that he should also go drive a taxi. Mother first gave him a big scolding. Then she said that the guy who sold vegetables in the fresh-produce market also had a second wife. Father and mother started to gossip. They mentioned a lot of names, like they were reading from a class register of some kind.

Hok Leong wondered how his mother knew so much about so many people. His immediate response was that he mustn't do anything to embarrass Chiu-yun. He mustn't make her a butt of ridicule and gossip.

17

Before the June holiday break several things happened all at once. First, Hok Leong's school work improved tremendously. This was an important "event." He scored above seventy in his Maths, Physics, and Chinese exams. He didn't do so well for English, which he had expected, and also for metal work and technical drawing, which he hadn't. He didn't mind that at all and was in fact quite happy. The most important thing was that, overall, he had improved.

Chiu-yun naturally did much better than him. She had higher marks even in Chinese, for which she was a little embarrassed. Hok Leong didn't see what there was to be awkward about. He never thought about being better than her in anything. Her lowest scoring subject was already higher than any of his. He knew that she represented something entirely different in his life. That was enough.

Chiu-yun had to return home to Indonesia for the holidays. She would only be back a week before school re-opened. Hok Leong felt despondent when he heard the news. He couldn't very well ask her not to go. The whole experience made him spoil for a fight.

After that two other things happened in quick succession. The first was that his classmates wanted to go <u>camping</u>. He agreed immediately when they asked him. Then Red Dragon came to see him. He said that the guy they jumped the other evening had contacted them via intermediaries saying that his group wanted to negotiate a truce of some kind. The guys in the rival group were from block thirty thereabouts. They agreed to meet at six in the evening in two days' time at the playground located between their domain, which was around the block ten area, and the rival group's domain.

Hok Leong couldn't refuse. He felt like he wanted to beat somebody up.

Red Dragon said that on the appointed day they would go to the playground at around three in the afternoon to hide some weapons in preparation for the face off. Hok Leong didn't respond directly. He said if there was time after school he would join him.

After that, Hok Leong and his classmates got busy "collecting" utensils and tableware from the school canteen so that they could use them for their planned camping trip. On the appointed day for the negotiations, Hok Leong's classmates wanted to leave during the recess break to go buy provisions for their trip, but he said he couldn't join them. He wanted to go home early so that he could help Red Dragon.

On the day in question, the boys followed the same "route" they always used when they skipped class, making their escape from a large sewer located near the back gate. The back gate was not much used and was usually locked. But because they didn't consult their astrology almanac that day, they weren't prepared when the principal suddenly showed up at the perimeter fence, unlocked the metal gate, and stepped through. In one shot he caught the whole lot—they were all lined up preparing to sneak out.

18

The principal raised the centimetre-thick rattan switch in his hand and brought it down hard on Hok Leong's backside. He hit him again, and then again. Each time, Hok Leong gasped and arched his body into a bow. He crooked his knees sideways so that he could clench his buttocks tight together. He grabbed his buttocks with both hands and his eyes started to tear.

The principal pointed to the three boys he had just

punished, indicating to Hok Leong that he should join them. He was still angry. The boys stood in a row staring at the principal, awaiting his next move. Hok Leong was so terrified he couldn't remember most of what the principal said earlier. He remembered him repeating, "You're supposed to be in class and you want to scamper away. What do you take school for?" The nagging went on forever, like something his mother might have said.

The form teacher came to fetch his charges. The principal told the teacher to give them half an hour after school to eat lunch, and then to return them to his office. In the future, they were to attend every class, hand in every assignment. He would check personally to make sure that they did as instructed.

19

1:30 p.m. Hok Leong found himself again standing at the same spot in the principal's office. He wondered what time he would get to leave school. If they didn't release him soon he would miss the appointed time for stowing the weapons.

The principal wasn't as angry as before, but he didn't speak to them, just made some phone calls and left the room. The boys stood in a row, not talking, just standing. The door to the staff room was located just outside the office. They couldn't really talk to one another.

There wasn't much in the office: a cabinet, a settee, a low table, a larger office table, a chair. On the table stood a stack of files. There was also a telephone, a potted plant, a porcelain cup, a stationery cup with several pens in it, and a sheaf of paper. The centimetre-thick cane used earlier to inflict pain laid on the sheaf of paper.

The walls were empty. Only the area behind the principal's chair had a picture. The picture had many words in it that Hok Leong couldn't understand. Above the picture was a clock. With nothing to do, they followed the clock, tracked the second-hand as it swept around the clock face. They listened to the footsteps of teachers entering and leaving the staff room, heard them cough, heard them shuffle paper. Not much talk went on inside the staff room.

The sounds outside the room grew faint, less distinct. The stipulated time for stowing the weapons came and went. By the time the principal came back it was already four o'clock.

He wasn't angry anymore. He sat down, took a sip of water from the cup, and set it down again. With a great show of concern, he asked each boy what job the boy's father did.

Ah Hor's father worked in a shipyard. Ying-jun's father drove a taxi. Tee Soon's father was a barber. After he heard this, the principal slowly puffed out his cheeks. He looked from one boy to the other. "Look, guys! These jobs are really tough. You mustn't disappoint your parents." He flashed them an unaccustomed smile: "Go home! Your parents are waiting for you!"

Many years later, Hok Leong still remembered the expression on the man's face, the way he excused their transgression, his encouragement and support, his high hopes for their future.

20

When Hok Leong got home it was already five o'clock. Immediately, he felt something wrong when he reached the foot of his apartment block. There was nobody downstairs. A hush had settled over the area, but it wasn't the kind of hush where everybody was too busy to come downstairs. It was the kind where a great dispute had happened. Everyone wished to avoid it.

When he reached home, Mother cautioned in a harsh tone of voice: "Make sure you stay home after dinner! Don't go running everywhere!"

Hok Leong went to look for his elder brother. "Red Dragon is dead," he said. "He was supposed to go for some negotiation talk but he tried to stow weapons at the meeting place before the appointed time. They beat him to death."

Hok Leong was dumbfounded. He couldn't say anything. His brother asked, "Did they come to look for you?"

Hok Leong shook his head. Brother continued, "Dog Shit was injured in the fight. The rest have been arrested. It's good that you're not involved."

Hok Leong slowly nodded his head. Would those who were under arrest reveal his name, he wondered. He was anxious, not about whether his name would pop up in a confession, but about his compatriots. He worried about their safety. The only one left now was Ah Mei. Ah Mei was still schooling. He wondered whether, like him, Ah Mei had been delayed in school. He wanted to go find Ah Mei but there was no way that he could leave the flat.

That night, Hok Leong mulled over the incident. He didn't know whether being punished by the principal had prevented him from being arrested, from being killed, whether it amounted to a fortunate thing or an unfortunate thing. He didn't want to forsake Opium Addict and the rest. But he also didn't want his parents or Chiu-yun to know about his involvement with them.

The next day on his way to school, Hok Leong took a detour by Dog Shit's flat. The house had a hush that indicated something immense had happened. Hok Leong went to look for Ah Mei, but he had already gone to school. "Don't come looking for him," Ah Mei's mother told Hok Leong.

Everyone's mother would probably issue such a warning, including his own, Hok Leong thought. He got jostled a lot that day in the packed bus going to school. He felt dispirited. It wasn't only Chiu-yun who would be absent during the coming holidays, his neighbourhood friends would be absent as well.

21

Chiu-yun had to leave on the first day of the holidays. The day before that she suggested that they go catch a movie. It would be the first time they watched one together. The title was *Love Forever* starring Brigitte Lin Ching-Hsia and Chin Han.

After watching the movie, Hok Leong saw that Chiu-yun's eyes were red and puffy. He laughed at her silliness. Chiu-yun stared levelly at him. "Weren't you touched by the movie?"

Of course, Hok Leong didn't feel anything.

They said their goodbyes outside the cinema. Chiu-yun looked meaningfully into his eyes, "Remember to do some revision. And please also do your holiday homework!" Saying that she turned and gracefully went off.

Hok Leong stared at her retreating back, her long hair catching the wind. He would miss her the entire holiday.

22

Hok Leong spent most of the holidays with Ah Hor and the guys. When he wasn't helping out at the hawker centre he was with them.

Colour Palette came back. Hok Leong saw her at her parent's stall, her movements wooden and stiff. She had no make-up, didn't open her mouth to speak, had lost all spirit and colour. Again Hok Leong thought about Chiu-yun. He mustn't ever put her in such a situation.

On the second day after Chiu-yun left, Hok Leong went camping with Ah Hor and the guys. People who went camping at Pulau Ubin usually boarded the ferry at Changi, but they chose to take a ferry from Punggol instead. The boatman even praised them for their insight. "You guys sure know your stuff," he said. They asked him to find them a place with not too many people. Sure enough, the boatman found them a deserted stretch of beach. They arranged with the man to fetch them in three days' time at around sunset.

The spot was beautiful. Under an expansive sky, a vast patch of forest and ivory-coloured sand greeted them, the azure water so clear that they could see the bottom, the tropical fish darting and playing. After they got off the boat, they could hear only the waves, nothing else. Without the waves, they could imagine a comforting, everlasting quietness. The most important thing was that they also found a well in the vicinity.

Where should they pitch the tent?

Discounting the beach and tangled forest full of deadwood—and who knows what dangerous animals—there didn't seem to be a place where they could put up a shelter! The boat was long gone. What could they do?

After searching around for a while they finally found a rocky area right by the forest and seafront. It looked like somebody had pitched a tent there in the past. There was no other choice.

All four had never pitched a tent in their lives. After much trial and error they eventually put up an odd-looking contraption. The stakes couldn't hold in the shallow soil, so they had to prop up the tentage with whatever they could find on hand. The tent flaps had to be tied willy-nilly to rocks that they arranged around the perimeter.

Tee Soon went to draw water. Suddenly they heard a great shout, then the sound of Tee Soon grumbling and cursing. Everybody came running. The only well in the area was a wreck. There was four maybe five inches of water in it. They spotted some ugly scale deposits. The liquid that they drew up had a layer of oil on the surface. They couldn't drink or use it.

Luckily they had brought some water with them. They decided to stay in the area. Tomorrow they would look for an alternative water source.

They had some instant noodles for lunch and then spent an entire afternoon swimming, playing, frolicking in the water. By evening they were exhausted. For over an hour they fought the gathering wind, trying to build a fire. The macaroni that they cooked over the diminutive flames refused to come to boil. Eventually they threw it away and had biscuits for dinner.

When night fell, they couldn't see the fingers on their outstretched hands. They huddled together in the tent but after a while found it boring. There was nothing to do, then somebody suggested they go for a walk, so off they went. Each of them had a personal "weapon"—a wooden club, a machete, a giant torchlight, a tape recorder—which they clutched carefully as they headed into the jungle. Along the way, Taiwanese singer Wan Sha-lang's valiant ditty "Unforgettable Dream" helped to dispel the tranquillity of the night, gave four fifteen-year-old boys a modicum of pretend courage.

The darkness was broken by soft light from the stars above, an oceanful of them. For some reason Hok Leong suddenly thought of Chiu-yun. He figured that the night sky she saw in Indonesia would probably be full of stars as well.

"There's somebody there!" Ah Hor cried suddenly.

They headed towards the single point of light in the forest. Indeed there was a house located amid the dense shrubbery. The inhabitants of the dwelling glared warily at them as they drew near.

Ah Hor waved politely as he went by. "<u>Hi</u>!" he said. The others followed suit, waving carefully at the people inside the house. Seeing that it was a group of students on a camping trip, the inhabitants inside waved politely as well. "<u>Hi</u>!" they said.

They drifted around pointlessly. Suddenly Ying-jun called out: "We're going around by torchlight, but these are all sand tracks and they're all the same. How do we get back?"

They aimed their torches at the network of laterite tracks around them. It was true. They all looked the same. At that point they got anxious, started to scold and curse. They tried to retrace their steps following what each considered to be the right path. But they got nowhere. The cursing got louder, fiercer.

What should they do?

Ah Hor suddenly spotted the moon. "The moon is in the east. West is over here!" he cried.

Within a minute they had walked out of the forest.

When they got back to the camp site no one felt like sleeping. They laid down on the rocks near their tent, chatting and reminiscing. The song now playing on the recorder was the elegant theme song from the movie, "The Heart Has a Million Knots." Hok Leong recalled the movie that he had watched with Chiu-yun, *Love Forever*. He thought about Chiu-yun's long, beautiful hair.

Ying-jun said: "The two meals we had today were awful. Tomorrow, I want to go to the quay side to buy breakfast. Who wants to go with me?"

"Me!" Hok Leong replied.

Ah Hor asked: "Is the quay far away?"

"How big do you think Ubin island is?" Ying-jun said. "We're in the west. Tomorrow we head east, we should be fine."

Later, they went back to the tent to sleep—not exactly sure when that happened. Hok Leong dozed for a while and then woke up. He wasn't used to sleeping in a tent. He heard a noise outside, like some animal moving around nearby. Carefully, he peeked out of the tent. Idiot! Arsehole! Tee Soon was outside engaging in hand to gland combat. Hok Leong turned around and went back to sleep.

After a period of time—not sure how long—they suddenly woke up to a shrieking, howling wind. They had never heard wind howl like that before, like somebody bawling and keening, so strong it almost blew the tent away. Worse, it started to pour. Torrents of water from sky and forest seemed to come gushing straight at them. It seemed that they had erected the tent on an area adjoining a slope. Some camper had dug a trench there in the past. Because they didn't study the terrain properly they had built their tent right over it. Eventually they had no choice but to hold up the tentage with one hand and tidy the items inside with the other. They stood around uncomfortably, waiting for the storm to end.

In a while the rain stopped. In dismay they surveyed the post-calamity scene. How do you start? Go somewhere else? How do you do that in the middle of the night? In the end they shifted the tent away from the ditch, mopped dry their exhausted bodies and went back to sleep. They'd decide what to do tomorrow.

23

Everyone woke up before sunrise. Nobody slept well. Someone said, "Hang on! We've got good beds at home. Why travel to such a God-forsaken place to sleep on rocks?" Hok Leong thought about his mother. It seemed like he hadn't told her about his camping trip. She didn't know that her son was away.

After washing up they faced the first item on the agenda - where should they move the tent? They searched around without success. There was only that one available spot. Eventually they decided to shift the tent a bit higher, to try as far as possible to avoid the gully. Hopefully the Gods would be kind, would protect them from inclement weather.

The plan was: Ah Hor and Tee Soon would stay behind and re-strike the tent; Hok Leong and Ying-jun would go buy breakfast and try to find a new well. Hok Leong and Ying-jun found themselves suitable walking sticks and set off immediately. They estimated that they would be back within an hour.

The dwelling that they encountered within the dense shrubbery the night before did have a well, they quickly discovered. An elderly man was drawing water from it when they arrived. Ying-jun spoke to the man in Malay, asking politely if they could haul water there as well. Yes, they could, the man said.

Hok Leong and Ying-jun were overjoyed. They both gave odd little screams and thanked the man profusely. They continued on their way.

The forest hadn't woke up yet. In all directions, the morning haze hung low to the ground. Bird chirrups and tweets filled the air. Occasionally they spotted rubber tappers moving in the undergrowth, going home it seemed, the lamps on their foreheads still yet to be switched off.

Suddenly Ying-jun turned to Hok Leong. "Do you masturbate?" he asked.

Hok Leong found the question a bit abrupt, but still he replied, "Yes, I do. How about you?"

Ying-jun replied, "Yes, of course!" He gave a sly laugh. "Yesterday I saw Tee Soon engaging in hand to gland combat."

Hok Leong said: "Me too. Looks like the whole world knows about it."

They both burst out laughing. After they walked a bit more, Yun Jing asked: "Do you have a girl friend?"

Hok Leong understood what Ying-jun meant. He thought about Chiu-yun and immediately felt that he had disrespected her. She wasn't the kind of girl the boys described when they used the word "girlfriend."

Hok Leong shook his head. "What about you?" he asked.

Ying-jun replied in a low voice: "I used to have one. Not anymore. Bloody troublesome."

"What do you mean?"

Again Ying-jun answered in a disturbed tone of voice, "She doesn't want to split up."

"Then why do *you* want to split up?"

"She's acts like a crazy woman. I can't take it," Ying-jun said. "She's Ah Song's cousin," he added.

Hok Leong nodded. He didn't say anything.

Ying-jun explained: "Ah Song and I were in the same class in secondary two. She's the same age as Ah Song. She was in the class next door and often spent time with us."

Ah Song was now in Hok Leong's class. He hung out with a different gang, about five-six strong, led by a guy called <u>Peter</u>. Hok Leong and his cohort didn't think much about <u>Peter</u> and his cohort. They kept a wary distance from each other. The only thing missing from the situation was a spark to light the blue touchpaper.

Hok Leong asked, "You're worried she will tell Ah Song?"

Ying-jun didn't reply.

Hok Leong said, "Actually <u>Peter</u> is quite calculating, he keeps a careful watch on the situation. Whenever anybody gets reprimanded by the teacher in class, he's able to dodge it."

"<u>Peter</u> lives close to you," Ying-jun said. "You're in block twelve, right? He's in block thirty-five. I hear people there are quite fierce."

"How do you know?"

"At the beginning of the year I was still talking to Ah Song. He told me about it."

Hok Leong didn't respond. He thought about Red Dragon. After Red Dragon's death, word got around that his brother didn't intend to let things rest. The two factions were still at loggerheads, kept apart only by the martial-law ambience that had settled over the precinct. Hok Leong's brother had told him many times not to hang around the block-thirty-plus territory.

Ying-jun changed the topic. "You know we've been walking a long time. Looks like we made a mistake. Ubin is bigger than we thought."

They continued walking without saying anything. Their surroundings got brighter as the sun rose. They didn't know when they would be able to get out of the woods.

Ying-jun said, "This direction should be correct."

Hok Leong didn't respond.

"Once we get out of the forest we should be there," Ying-jun added.

Again Hok Leong kept silent. He hoped that they would quickly get out of the woods.

They lost track of time. By now the forest was fully lit. They could see clearly in all directions, and clearly they saw that they were still in the forest. They fell tiredly to the ground. Their throats were parched. They didn't know what to do. Suddenly the sound of an explosion reached their ears. They jumped immediately to their feet. More explosions followed.

"They're blasting the hillside, I think," Ying-jun said.

Hok Leong nodded. Soon after that they saw a lorry lumbering by in the distance. They shouted excitedly and gave chase. The lorry disappeared. Finally they reached a gravel road. The only problem was the sun beating down on them.

Ying-jun had a suggestion, "Let's follow the road and jog the rest of the way to the jetty. If not we'll take forever to get back."

They began to run. The scenery around them started to run too, as it were. The could see the sky so blue above, the clouds so white, the woods so green, the hillsides so arresting red. The problem was the sun, which continued to scorch and blister. What time was it? Ten o'clock? Eleven? They weren't wearing their watches.

Finally another lorry appeared and drew near them. Ying-jun stuck out his thumb. The lorry driver stopped his vehicle, stuck out his head, and addressed them in Chinese Hokkien dialect, "Where are you going?"

"The jetty."

"I'm not going to the jetty," the driver uncle said. "But I can take you part of the way. You can walk the rest. It's only a little bit."

They expressed their gratitude and climbed on board. Around fifteen minutes later the driver uncle stopped at a turn in the road and pointed out the way to them. "You can walk the rest of it. It's only a little bit," he said. They thanked him again and got down.

The driver uncle's "only a little bit" turned out to be a thirty-minutes hike. Hok Leong and Ying-jun sat exhausted in a coffee shop at the jetty. They checked the clock on the wall. It was well past eleven. They had been on the road for over five hours.

They each ordered a coconut, which they drained in two gulps. Then they each ordered a bowl of noodles. After that, Ying-jun said, "that's lunch, that's not breakfast," and ordered two slices of bread and a cup of coffee. Hok Leong was better. He only wanted a bottle of coke.

After eating, Ying-jun asked, "So what now? Don't tell me you want to walk back?"

Hok Leong shook his head tiredly. He closed his eyes. They sat quietly, didn't talk. The lady boss of the coffee shop thought that they were dozing off and came over. "You can't sleep here, young man," she said.

Hok Leong opened his eyes. "Now what?" he said.

Ying-jun shrugged.

They didn't want to walk back. They also didn't know how to walk back. In the end, Hok Leong had a brilliant solution. He congratulated himself on his ingenuity, "Let's go back to Singapore and take the ferry again!"

The two of them took the ferry back to Singapore. From Changi they took a bus to Geylang. They changed bus at Geylang, heading for Hougang. From Hougang they took a bus to Punggol. The ferry operator in Punggol opened his eyes wide when he saw them. "We swam back from where you dropped us," Hok Leong and Ying-jun joked.

When they reached the camp site it was already past four in the afternoon. Ah Hor and Tee Soon had a great laugh at Hok Leong's and Ying-jun's expense. They rushed to grab the Roti

<u>Prata</u> that the two bought for them from Punggol jetty.

24

On the third day of their camping trip they didn't know what else to do. Early in the morning they decided to go swimming. They climbed on each other's shoulders and paired off to wrestle fight. They sank their heads in the water to see who could hold his breath the longest. Losers had to drink a mouthful of the brine. Suddenly they heard voices shouting their names. But the area was deserted, and there were no boats in sight. How could such "voices of warning" reach them from afar? The more they talked about it the more they frightened themselves. Were there water spirits coming after them? Finally they decided to return to the beach.

Sitting on the sand they again heard voices calling their names. Damn! There really were ghosts in the vicinity!

Hok Leong suddenly saw in the middle of the straits a small wooden structure. It looked like there were people there waving at them. He shouted: "The kelong across from us! There's somebody waving at us."

Everyone saw them now. They were classmates from school! Hok Leong and Co waved at them. They didn't mix much with this group of students. Too well-behaved was the consensus. Of course, their relationship with this lot was better than their relationship with <u>Peter</u>'s posse.

Ah Hor said, "Let's swim over. What do you think?"

"Let's go!" Tee Soon said.

"I might not have the energy to do it," Ying-jun said. "I'll go find a piece of wood."

The four of them searched for driftwood that they could use as flotation devices. They each found a large piece, tested it a little and set off. Although the waves were small, they still grew anxious as they took in the vast, featureless sea.

Under the risen sun, the water to the east was a wash of light. Occasionally the reflections blinded them. They understood now the Chinese proverb that they had learned in school, the one about "gleaming crystalline waves."

Ah Hor suddenly shouted out in pain: "Ouch! There's jellyfish in the water. It bit me."

Everyone started to laugh at Ah Hor. Then they got bitten as well by the jellyfish. In a mad rush they started to swim, to put distance between themselves and the creatures. But quickly they grew tired and began to struggle. They should have conserved their energy, they realized. At that moment the waves began to grow in size, became stronger, taller. Each giant wave seemed to pitch them further and further away.

Tee Soon realised something was wrong. "There's an oil tanker coming at us! There's an oil tanker!" he cried. "Quick! Everybody hold hands! Grab each other!"

Now they were really nervous. They tried to catch one another but with the chunky lumber in the way they couldn't do it. They couldn't ditch their surrogate floats. They were too tired. After several unsuccessful efforts they decided to grasp the driftwood with one hand and hook the other around the next person's neck. But each time they formed a circle, the waves pulled them apart. They formed a circle, then the dashing waves broke them up. Finally they all found a grip, four becoming one. They drifted in the water gasping for breath.

The waves grew increasingly savage. Slowly, a giant curtain began to screen out the light. Years later, Hok Leong remembered the fear brought on by the realization that one's judgement day had arrived. All the while the waves continued their onslaught. Every time someone got pried loose they tried in as short a time as possible to restore their formation. They clung on tightly to each other—yes, they were fighting for their lives.

The waves slowly returned to normal. Gradually, the

tanker left them behind. They rested for a while, drifting, then continued swimming towards the kelong. After climbing onto the structure they celebrated their safe arrival with great bellows of laughter. They played and fooled around with the other clique of students.

The owner of the kelong heard that someone had swum over from the opposite shore. He came over to warn them, speaking in Teochew dialect, "Aiyoh, young man. How can you do that? It's dangerous." He agreed to treat them to lunch. After that he would send them back by boat.

They had a lavish, sumptuous lunch. Everything was seafood—steamed seafood, fried seafood, even raw seafood. Just like that they managed to cadge a good meal.

When they got back to the campsite everyone was exhausted. No one had the energy to suggest something new. They sat around singing, dozing, or staring impassively into space. For no good reason Hok Leong again thought of Chiu-yun.

25

Shortly after he returned from the camping trip, Junior Brother and Opium Addict came to ask Hok Leong if he wanted to join their triad gang. They had just joined themselves. Hok Leong didn't know that you could be asked so baldly to join these kinds of organizations. He didn't know how to reply. If he rejected the offer, it would sound like he wasn't much of a brother. He didn't have the right spirit, the right loyalty. If he accepted, he wouldn't feel good. And here he thought about his father, his mother, and about Chiu-yun. In the end he gave an oblique answer, saying that he had to help his father at the stall, he didn't have time. The two understood what he meant, they didn't insist. Junior Brother said: "That's fine, Hok Leong. If anything happens in the future you can still come to look for us. We're still friends."

Hok Leong nodded. He felt bad that he wasn't much of a brother. After Red Dragon's death, they hadn't met up at all. Furthermore Hok Leong didn't take the initiative to find them, he didn't know why. Now that they had come looking for him, and Hok Leong had chosen not to join them, he felt that their connections were being severed. Their ties were unravelling.

26

After suffering through most of the holidays, Hok Leong finally had a chance in the last week of the vacation to hear Chiu-yun's voice. They spoke on the phone the whole night, Hok Leong hanging up only when the Indian convenience store owner had to close shop. Hok Leong and Chiu-yun agreed to meet up the next day.

They met in Lotus Flower Coffee Shop in <u>Katong Shopping Centre</u>. Chiu-yun had again gotten prettier. But she retained still her artless, charming demeanour. During the holidays she had travelled to Australia, and now she made Hok Leong a present of a key chain that she bought there. The chain had a picture insert. It showed an autumnal scene with light blue sky capped by soft cotton clouds. Many years later, Hok Leong realised that the scene had conveyed a young girl's exquisite, meticulous sensibility. An autumnal day with white clouds: the meaning of Chiu-yun's name in Chinese. She had, as it were, given herself to him.

The young Hok Leong didn't know such things. The young Hok Leong's attention was captured by the new, let's call it knowledge, presented by the setting. Perched on a semi-circle settee, it was his first time in a coffee shop, first time drinking a concoction called <u>Coke Float</u>, or Coca-Cola with ice cream. Chiu-yun had ordered it for him. Also, he learned that "going on vacation" meant travelling to a foreign country for a few days, enjoying the scenery. He knew nothing about that:

overseas travel, coming back, giving someone a little present, a little key chain. He himself didn't have a key because there was always someone at home who could open the door for him. He didn't have a room of his own, or even his own wardrobe or cabinet.

Chiu-yun saw that Hok Leong had gotten taller and darker. "Gosh! What did you do during the holidays?" she asked, although she already knew. Hok Leong said jokingly that he too went "overseas" to Pulau Ubin. He filled her in on the interesting details of the trip, but he didn't have a present. During the trip he had collected some beautiful sea shells but had forgotten to bring them home with him. Chiu-yun said the next time he went camping he must bring her along.

Really? Hok Leong didn't respond directly and Chiu-yun didn't wait expectantly for an answer. They didn't pay that much attention to the details of their conversation. They were back together again. That was the important thing. The month-plus vacation had given them many things to talk about, enough to last forever it seemed. From two in the afternoon they chatted till six. They had dinner, then they continued talking till the place closed for the night.

That evening, Hok Leong walked Chiu-yun home from the shopping centre. The moon loomed large in the sky, as though someone had pasted it there. It gave the impression of coolness. Like a couple of strangers they walked in total silence, but their hearts were filled with each other. Occasionally they glanced at each other and gave a little laugh, afraid that any loud sound would dispel the night-time tranquillity, and also the serenity in their hearts. When they reached Chiu-yun's house she opened the door, turned in the doorway and seemed to move her lips, uttering a silent <u>bye-bye</u>. She waved gently at him. Wrapped in a cloak of night-time lustre she entered the house.

27

The first thing that happened after school re-opened was that Ah Song came looking for Ying-jun. He said Ying-jun had deceived his cousin and wanted him to take responsibility. Ying-jun didn't feel that he did anything improper. Matters between a man and a woman were for them to decide. Outsiders shouldn't interfere. Ah Song said his cousin wanted Ying-jun to give a pubic account of his actions. Ying-jun replied, a break-up should be done with panache, with élan. What public account are you talking about? She replied that he deserved a beating. Ying-jun couldn't be bothered to talk to her, the nerve of that girl. He slammed the phone down and showed his open hands to Hok Leong and the boys. He gave up, his actions said.

As expected Ah Song went to <u>Peter</u> for help. Even then Ying-jun refused to meet up but Hok Leong suggested that they reconsider. If they didn't settle the matter, Ying-jun could find himself the target of an ambush. The other clique might set some trap or something. In the end they agreed to meet in the school canteen. With so many students coming and going, the place was the right spot for a dialogue. Nobody had to worry that things might get physical.

28

As things turned out, it was the form teacher rather than <u>Peter</u> who accosted the four of them, saying that he wanted to talk. They thought that they had done something wrong, but it was only the teacher offering some verbal encouragement, advising them to study hard.

The teachers now took attendance every lesson, and the principal also gave instructions to the school staff to keep a watch on those places where students might sneak out of school. Because of that some students decided there and then not to attend classes. Ah Hor was one of them. He had always felt that it was enough to complete secondary four. The other three guys also felt the same, but for propriety's sake they were prepared to go to school, to show face to the principal. Hok Leong was the worst. He had Chiu-yun keeping a watchful eye on him, but he couldn't tell the others about it.

Physical presence in a classroom didn't mean that you had to pay attention during lessons. So some students began bringing martial arts novels to school. They inserted these works in-between their open textbooks, which they erected strategically on the desk in front of them during classes. After a while, some of the girls began to copy the behaviour. However, they preferred romance novels by either Chiung Yao or Yan Qin. The teachers probably knew all this. As long as nobody got disturbed, however, they were fine with it.

Hok Leong had read most of the martial arts novels, so he began borrowing the romances of his female classmates to read. His first Chiung Yao novel was *Flying Rosy Clouds*, whose blend of fine writing and emotional investigation gave him a pleasant surprise. Gradually, he began to read more of her works.

29

Peter's group had agreed to talk things out in the canteen, so after class one day they all congregated in a corner of the facility.

There wasn't much to discuss. Everything kept going back to whether or not Ying-jun had deceived Ah Song's cousin. Eventually Hok Leong grew impatient and bluntly told Ah Song, "Look! This is meaningless. When guys and girls break up, everyone gets hurt. Stop this one-sided self-pity. Go ask your cousin, how exactly is she worse off or deprived? If Ying-jun can make amends let him do it. But don't talk it up like some big event that never ends. If things are over deal with it.

Don't be aggrieved. Who will dare to have a girlfriend if you get beaten up every time you break up?"

Ah Song was taken aback. He stood up angrily. Peter reached out and restrained him. He looked at Hok Leong. Hok Leong stared levelly back at him. Everyone in the two groups sized each other up. Hok Leong figured that Peter wouldn't do anything. If he resorted to violence, Hok Leong wouldn't reciprocate. He'd let the school deal with it.

After a long while, Peter said to Ah Song: "Go ask your cousin how exactly is she hurt or harmed by this. If there's nothing then just forget it." With that, the entire group left the canteen.

Now everyone could heave a sigh of relief. Ah Hor said that Hok Leong had exposed the heart of the matter. Peter had no choice but to back down. "Damn right! If every break up means that you get beaten up who will dare to have a girlfriend!"

Tee Soon said Hok Leong should be careful about Peter. He had lost face this time around. Another time he'd find a way to retrieve it. Hok Leong didn't know why he got so impatient. He had figured rightly that Peter was the kind of person to size things up, who was careful and calculating. As long as you occupied high ground and held the upper hand, he would back down. Indeed he was proved right.

Hok Leong's behaviour that day was in keeping with his personality. On a second occasion later in life he would act exactly like that.

But of course the young Hok Leong didn't know this. The young Hok Leong took to heart the warning delivered by Tee Soon. On the way home that day he stopped at a stationer's and bought two steel rulers. He figured Peter wouldn't act alone, a single ruler wouldn't be enough. He filed down one end of the ruler, made it sharp. The other end he wrapped in paper so that it functioned as a handle. Now he had a sword, two swords. Hok Leong didn't set out to make a sword. He just felt that it was odd to have both ends of the ruler level like that. It felt strange. When he travelled to school he could keep both rulers in the front compartment of his school bag, the part without a zip. He could easily whip them out if necessary. In school he would take them out of the bag and keep them close to his body.

30

The next day after school, Ah Hor and the guys had some matters to attend to. Chiu-yun had to stay in school for some extra-curricular activity. So Hok Leong had no choice but to go home alone. At the bus stop he spotted Peter and several schoolmates waiting for the bus. They turned to look at Hok Leong. Hok Leong didn't know if this was a coincidence or a planned manoeuvre. He slipped a hand into his schoolbag and gripped the handles of his two rulers. Peter and Hok Leong lived in the same precinct and took the same bus home. Hok Leong decided to board the first bus that came along, whatever it was. He would go somewhere familiar and change to another bus heading his way.

Peter and his cohort didn't board the bus that he took. Hok Leong heaved a sigh of relief. He decided in the future not to use that particular stop. If, unluckily, he found himself in the same bus as any of that lot he would look for the earliest opportunity to slip away.

Mother was in nagging mode when Hok Leong reached home. Her target was his elder sister: "The daughter of the family that sells rice noodle rolls got herself pregnant! She got rid of the baby. The next time you meet a guy please bring along your eyes! Don't be vain...."

Hok Leong went to the food centre. He went deliberately to the rice noodle roll stall. "Colour Palette" was there helping out. She didn't have any make up, didn't open her mouth, seemed to have lost all her spirit. Standing at his father's stall, Hok Leong spotted Black Gold who glowed with health and vigour and was the complete opposite of Colour Palette. Again Hok Leong linked the whole thing to Chiu-yun. He mustn't do anything to harm her, he told himself.

31

The movie adaptation of *Flying Rosy Clouds* was screening at an open-air cinema in Joo Chiat. Hok Leong wanted to see if there was any difference between the book and the film. He invited Chiu-yun to watch it with him. Chiu-yun's eyes were red-rimmed when she left the auditorium. After wiping off her tears, she said brightly, "Open-air cinemas are fun. We must come here often. Also, I'm going to find the piano score for the music in the movie. I want to play it for you."

Chiu-yun quickly found the score and lyrics of the titular song. She even checked the meaning of the difficult words that they didn't know. Qian Quan meant "inseparable." Chou Mou meant to be "sentimentally attached to somebody." Then she played the song for Hok Leong:

I ask the colourful clouds where they are flying to
I willingly follow them.
If miraculous fate allows us to be together, death brings no regret.
My tender feelings are as deep as the ocean
For yours you may ask the sky.
Swear that we accompany each other, be inseparable as the years go by.

How can I leave you? How can I discard you?
You're always in my heart, believe me.
I hope that our two hearts can be a haven, can be forever

attached.
Apart from you who else can be my partner?

As he listened to the song, Hok Leong felt his eyes starting to glisten. He didn't know if he was responding to Chiu-yun's singing, or to the lyrics penned by Chiung Yao.

32

When they met on weekdays at the Lotus Flower Coffee Shop, Hok Leong and Chiu-yun usually discussed only their schoolwork. So when weekend arrived and they couldn't find anything to do in the evening they would still meet there. It didn't feel monotonous or boring.

Hok Leong no longer liked <u>coke float</u>. He preferred <u>ice lemon tea</u>. Chiu-yun liked the <u>chendol</u> dessert served by the place. "It reminds me of Indonesia," she explained.

She took a book out of her bag as she slurped on her food. "I asked my Chinese language tuition teacher. He said Chiung Yao likes to cite classical verse. The title of *Flying Rosy Clouds* is taken from one such verse." She opened the work in her hand and began to read aloud from it:

Colourful autumn clouds easily scatter, easily disperse, even the swallows feel pity
Reunions and separations but no explanation, at times depressed, at times elated.
When wild goose returns, before frost comes, the slated meeting draws near,
But why not send a missive? Why still silent?
Oh better not think about the past, better lie and watch the setting sun.

She stopped, seemingly deep in thought, "That first line,

'autumn clouds easily scatter.' Is that it? Is that where the title comes from?"

"Oh, and another thing!" she added, taking out a slip of paper from between the pages of the book. She started reading from the paper. It was a poem by the Song dynasty lyricist Zhang Xian:

> *Twittering cuckoos announce again the end of spring.*
> *Saddened, I pick a flower for remembrance.*
> *Fine rain and harsh winds, green-hued plums at the season's end.*
> *In the grounds of Yongfeng garden, empty but for the catkins drifting like snow.*
> *Strike not a string of the Pi Pa, for it cannot such bitterness express.*
> *The heavens don't grow old, true love persists.*
> *My heart is like cobweb, doubled, in the middle are a million knots.*
> *The night is nearly over, the lamp burns down.*

"'Heart like cobweb, in the middle are a million knots.' That's where 'The Heart Has a Million Knots' comes from," Chiu-yun continued, referencing a song that Hok Leong knew, one that stemmed from another Chiung Yao novel of the same name.

There was only so much erudition that Hok Leong could bear. "You mean you actually went and found all that stuff!"

"Of course! Beautiful poetry is meant to be learnt by heart!" Chiu-yun replied.

After that she went through the difficult words of the poem with Hok Leong, clarifying them one by one. *Chan Zhou* was a bookish version of *You Chou*, meaning "to be worried." Another character *Rui* referred to *Hua Mu*, or "flora." The term *Ti Jue* referred to *Du Juan Niao*, the common cuckoo bird. *Yao*

Xian was a metonym for *Pi Pa*, the Chinese lute.

If Hok Leong could claim in the future a modicum of learning beyond the philistinism of his compatriots, he knew that it stemmed from this period of interaction with Chiu-yun. She subsequently gave him a copy of a much-loved Chinese classic, *Three Hundred Tang Dynasty Poems*. "Check it out when you have the time," she said. But Hok Leong never had free time on his hands. Even if he had, he figured, he wouldn't spend it reading *Three Hundred Tang Dynasty Poems*.

At that moment Hok Leong discovered that a few tables away from him was someone he preferred not to see. It was Peter. He sat chatting with a girl and hadn't noticed Hok Leong. Peter and him seemed to be entwined by fate, Hok Leong thought with dismay. He turned quickly to Chiu-yun and suggested that they go somewhere else after finishing their refreshments.

Chiu-yun didn't have any objections. After they left the shop, however, she realised that he didn't have another destination in mind.

"So why did we leave the place?" she asked.

Hok Leong had no choice but to say, "There's someone from my class in the coffee shop. I don't like him."

"Let's not come here in the future," he added.

Chiu-yun stared blankly at him.

He nodded his head earnestly at her.

33

After that encounter, Hok Leong and Chiu-yun changed their meeting spot to the lobby coffee shop of the nearby Sea View Hotel. It was quieter there, more elegant, more suitable for quiet conversation, and thus obviously better for doing homework. Chiu-yun should have brought them there from the beginning, they agreed.

Hok Leong didn't want Chiu-yun to know about the unfortunate things that had happened in school. Even more, he didn't want her to get entangled in them.

In school, Hok Leong's group tried their best to avoid Peter's group. Peter's group also tried to avoid Hok Leong's posse. They had a tacit understanding that both sides should avoid causing unnecessary trouble for each other. Nevertheless, there were times when they couldn't avoid contact.

This happened at the last metal-work class before the exams. Before class started Hok Leong went to the washroom, leaving his bag at the entrance. The entrance to the workshop where the class was held was still locked. Hok Leong's crew had yet to arrive. As he exited the toilet Hok Leong heard Peter cursing, "Damn, whose bag is this? Almost cause me to fall down." He saw Peter hold up the bag in his hands. He was about to throw it aside.

"Stop!" Hok Leong shouted. He rushed to retrieve his bag.

Peter saw Hok Leong. For a moment his face went blank and he stared dumbly at Hok Leong. Hok Leong also stopped. He fixed his attention on the bag, glad that it still contained his two ruler-swords.

Peter quickly recovered. He tossed the bag to the ground by his feet. "Come and get it!" he taunted.

Hok Leong hesitated. How could he retrieve his bag?

At that moment, a gravelly voice piped up: "Fighting is it?" It was the metal-work teacher. "Both of you come to my office," he said in a berating tone of voice.

Hok Leong picked up the bag. He handed it to Tee Soon, who had just arrived. "Look after it!" he said.

Inside the office, the metal-work teacher continued to rebuke Hok Leong and Peter: "You boys come to school but you don't study. You only know how to fight." He reached out and gave them a hard rap each on the back of their heads. They twisted their necks in pain. "What is this thing so important that you need to fight over it? You mean someone must die in order to resolve this issue? You want to fight? Okay, go ahead. Fight now!" Again he hit them hard on the back of their heads. "Or else you both fight me. Come on! Both at the same time. Come on!"

The teacher's reaction surprised Hok Leong. It also suggested that things were not so serious. The teacher continued sternly: "I don't keep tabs on students who are insolent. If I react to things like that it will just add to everyone's unhappiness, including the sense of grievance that students have against me." Seeing that Hok Leong and Peter remained silent, he continued: "I'm not afraid of you boys hating me. What I care about is that, if you fight, you'll become enemies filled with bitterness and hostility. You won't distinguish right from wrong, good from bad, and this thing will never end. Do you understand?"

At that moment <u>Peter</u> spoke up in an inveigling tone of voice, "Teacher, we weren't fighting. We were just quarrelling. Ask Hok Leong if you don't believe me."

Hok Leong nodded his head.

The teacher began to laugh. "What the hell. You're not women. What is there to quarrel about?" Again, he rapped them each on the back of their heads. "Okay, shake hands, both of you. Get the hell back to class!"

<u>Peter</u> held out his hand. Hok Leong gripped it and shook hard. Again he felt that he had a chance to size up <u>Peter</u>. He saw him clearly now.

34

It could easily have been worse. But just like that the metal-work teacher had helped to avert a potential disaster.

The exams over, the prospect of a long holiday again loomed ahead of him. Hok Leong didn't like school holidays now. Once the vacations came, Chiu-yun would return to Indonesia. It was just as well that his results weren't too bad. He passed every subject and even obtained an average general score of seventy-eight, which was much better than he expected. Hok Leong's friends also passed their exams; for their school, forty-five was considered a pass. Chiu-yun couldn't understand such a system. Her average general score was ninety-three, or twice the general score of Hok Leong's friends.

Hok Leong suddenly remembered that Chiu-yun didn't return to Indonesia for the year-end holidays when she was in secondary two. Chiu-yun explained that she had just arrived in Singapore then and needed to get used to the environment. Her parents came over to accompany her instead.

The night before an enforced separation is difficult for those involved but for that reason it is also special. They decided to go to the seaside. They sat back to back, Chiu-yun leaning on Hok Leong like he was a support or buttress of some kind. Hok Leong could feel her rhythmic breathing, her back rising gently up and down. He closed his eyes and listened to her inhale. He wished that they could continue to sit like this, be like this. With her back against him, Chiu-yun sang the theme song from the Taiwanese movie *Rhythm of the Waves*:

Mademoiselle, why do you wonder alone by the seashore?
Mademoiselle, aren't you afraid that the sea will start to thrash and roll?
Ah....it's not the waves, it is my beautiful clothes flapping in the wind.
Even if black mist fills the sky, I want to fly, to fly like the seagull.

After she finished singing the song, Chiu-yun stood up, took off her shoes and walked barefoot on the sand, treading on the forewash of the breaking waves. For the entire vacation they would be apart, they would only meet next year when the school reopened.

35

With Chiu-yun gone, Hok Leong's life suddenly lost its centre of gravity. Apart from helping at his father's noodle stall, he spent all his time with Ah Hor and the boys. They watched movies, had meals together, went swimming, chased girls, and window-shopped. They didn't go camping. Camping was too tough. In the future after they got conscripted there would be plenty of time for that. Instead they went <u>barbeque-ing</u> during the weekends, trying on each occasion to get some girls to join them. After two or three times however they also got sick of that, so watching movies became their main standby. Sometimes they even caught two or three movies a day. The vacation became meaningless and stifling.

Hok Leong's elder brother and sister completed their secondary schooling. Brother obtained an apprentice welder position. Elder sister wanted to continue her studies. In the meantime she worked as clerk in an office. Again Hok Leong became the only sibling giving a hand at the food stall, although he had plenty of autonomy. Because his results were good, mother let him be. If he needed to go somewhere, he would tell her that he needed to do something in school. Usually she released him.

Black Gold often appeared at her parent's stall during the holidays. When Hok Leong saw her he naturally thought of Chiu-yun. He wanted to understand Chiu-yun, to figure her out, but in truth he didn't know her at all. He didn't know what she thought, what she wanted, whereas she seemed to understand him perfectly, and even kept an eye out for him. For instance she had asked him earlier what he wanted to do in the future. But graduation was end of next year—how was he to know the answer? Black Gold probably didn't know what she wanted to do, right?

The most inauspicious thing that happened during the holidays was that Hok Leong spotted Peter at the food centre. He recalled the earlier occasion when he spotted Peter in the coffee shop. The man was like a ghoul; it seemed foreordained that he would shadow Hok Leong, torment him. Fortunately Peter didn't see him. They both lived near the hawker centre, so Hok Leong should have known that their paths would easily cross. Hok Leong prayed that Peter wouldn't find out about his father's food stall. Or else he could come anytime to create trouble. After spotting Peter, Hok Leong told his father that he had a stomach ache. He then hurried home.

Ah Mei came to the door shortly after he got back. Hok Leong was surprised to see him. Their clique of neighbourhood toughs had disbanded after Red Dragon's death. He had almost forgotten about Ah Mei.

Ah Mei told him that, when Red Dragon and the others went to hide weapons on that fateful day at around three o'clock, he had left school and was already home in his flat. He didn't want to join them.

Hok Leong didn't understand. "What do you mean?"

Ah Mei's face screwed up in pain: "I didn't want to fight."

Hok Leong kept silent.

Ah Mei added, "I don't want to be hacked to death just like that."

Hok Leong remained silent.

Ah Mei asked, "Do you think I'm gutless? I'm a coward"

Hok Leong shook his head. He didn't know whether shaking his head meant "gutless" or "not gutless."

Ah Mei said, "I didn't tell anyone. I just left."

Again Hok Leong didn't react.

After he closed the door, Hok Leong took out the two make-shift ruler-swords from his school bag. He stared dumbly at them for a while, then returned them to the bag. Straightaway he took them out again, and after a while again returned them to the bag. Eventually he took out one of the swords and ran downstairs. With all his might, he threw it into the dense shrubbery.

36

Hok Leong went to school. His best mates weren't there. He had come to buy textbooks for secondary four. Chiu-yun had directed him to do that.

The form teacher spotted Hok Leong in the compound and came over specially to talk to him. He said, "If you maintain your performance, there's a good chance that you can make it to senior high." He encouraged Hok Leong to keep it up, don't lose heart.

Hok Leong nodded his head.

Senior high. As he left the compound with the new books tucked under his arm, Hok Leong mulled over the two words. It was the first time that he thought about them.

37

Secondary four. The first day of school. Teacher and students were *exactly* the same. It was like the last day of school the previous year fast forwarded to the first day of school of the current year—there was nothing fresh or unusual about the scene. Somehow Hok Leong survived the lessons, enduring till the end of class. Ah Hor and the others wanted to go to the cinema. Hok Leong lied, said that he had to give a hand at his father's stall. He had arranged to meet Chiu-yun at the coffee shop in Sea View Hotel.

Chiu-yun wore a new hairstyle, a perm. She looked very sophisticated. "Do you like me with straight hair or permed hair?" she asked. Hok Leong answered simply, "I like both."

Chiu-yun wasn't happy. "Totally insincere!" She pointed at the faint fuzz over his upper lip. "Gosh! When did you become so old?"

Hok Leong replied: "Do you like it?" Chiu-yun nodded. "Not bad!" Hok Leong repeated her accusation, "Totally insincere!"

Chiu-yun had gone to England for the holidays and had even spent Christmas in London, a white Christmas. She had just returned the previous evening and was still suffering from jet lag, she needed to get more sleep. Hok Leong listened attentively but had nothing to contribute. England, London, Snow Flakes, Christmas, Time Difference—these were things beyond his ken. He could only ask, "So, which do you prefer? Australia or England?"

"England."

Chiu-yun took out a present and gave it to him, a <u>Teddy Bear</u>. Unwilling to part with the toy, she gave it a big squeeze. Hok Leong accepted the present but didn't know what to do with it.

"Hug it! Give it a hug!" Chiu-yun said.

Hok Leong reluctantly embraced the bear. He thought: A grown man squeezing a cuddly toy. How does that look like?

Chiu-yun asked, "Is it a happy feeling? Is it comfy?"

Hok Leong reluctantly nodded his head. What feeling was she talking about? He placed the soft toy on the coffee table.

Chiu-yun took it all in. She opened her purse and rummaged in it for a while. Hok Leong spotted her identity card lying propped up in the purse. He wanted to see how she looked like in her ID but inadvertently caught the printed date of birth—1959.

Chiu-yun held out a pound sterling banknote in her hand. "Here, take this as a memento. You don't look like the kind of person who likes playing with teddy bears."

Hok Leong didn't take the banknote. "No, no, that's not

true!" He picked up the toy and carefully patted it on the head. "Your date of birth is 1959?"

Chiu-yun pretended to be angry. "You peeped into my purse! Who gave you permission?"

Hok Leong didn't respond directly. "I was born in 1960," he said.

Chiu-yun stared blankly at him for a moment. "Oh?" she said in a soft voice.

38

Hok Leong came home and dropped the teddy bear onto his bed. Like the bear, he too flopped onto the mattress. Younger sister saw the soft toy and came over immediately to give it a squeeze. "Aiyoh! So cute!" she said.

"Put it down!" Hok Leong said harshly. "Don't touch it!" He couldn't understand why young girls liked such cuddly toys.

Younger sister dropped the teddy bear onto the bed. She too adopted a harsh tone of voice, "What rubbish! Boys playing with soft toys. Is it a present from your girlfriend?"

Hok Leong ignored his sister. What he cared about was that Chiu-yun was older than him by a year.

Would it bother Chiu-yun that he was younger than her by a year?

39

After the business between Ying-jun and his former girlfriend, they didn't hear him talk about the matter. Soon after the school re-opened, however, he found himself a new girlfriend, and even brought her to meet them. Everyone was impressed by Ying-jun. Tee Soon said Ying-jun couldn't get by if he didn't have a girl. He used a Hokkien dialect phrase to explain the situation, "If you can't get fish, prawn will do." Everyone joked that Tee Soon couldn't even get a small tiny shrimp. Tee Soon said that he wanted "expensive" fishes. He wouldn't settle for an ugly girl, nor would he accept someone older than him.

Ah Hor taunted him, "Are you looking for a girlfriend or a wife?"

"How can you get someone older than you?" Tee Soon replied. "Are you looking for a girlfriend or an elder sister? You tell me."

"That is what they call lack of motherly love," Ying-jun cried.

Everyone hooted at the idea.

40

It was a long time coming, but Hok Leong's family finally entered the modern era—the one represented by the telephone and the television. Furthermore the television was coloured, not black and white—a fourteen-inch colour TV.

Elder brother had suggested it. To contact friends you needed a phone. To get proper rest after work you need a telly, he figured. Father and mother weren't opposed to the idea. Having a phone meant Uncle and Grandma could easily contact them. And watching TV at night was really quite fun. They didn't have to spend too much money on those items as well. The important thing was that Hok Leong and his younger sister of their own volition completed their homework. Mother was fine if she knew that they weren't distracted by the contraption.

Apart from those two items, their house also lacked other electrical appliances including an electric rice cooker, a refrigerator, a fan, a transistor radio and so on.

Now that they had a television and a phone, the opportunities for discord between Hok Leong and his elder brother also increased. Busy with their own affairs, the two siblings didn't talk a lot with one another. For them, friends were more important than family. Their disputes in the past were due to elder brother wanting Hok Leong to give a hand, Hok Leong not wanting to and so on. But now that they had the two gadgets, the opportunity for friction also greatly increased. They sometimes wanted to watch different programmes being aired at the same time, or they both wanted to use the telephone. Even when mother stepped in and scolded them it didn't help. When she got angry she would say—get rid of them, sell the TV, cut the phone line—but Hok Leong knew his mother wouldn't do that. She herself loved to watch TV and to chin wag. It was just as well that Father didn't know about the disputes set off by the appliances. Otherwise both items would really disappear.

41

Hok Leong seldom spoke to Chiu-yun on the phone at home. Apart from not wanting his family to know about her, he also preferred to meet her in person. Even then, he hardened his heart one weekend and stayed away from her. He lied to her, said he had to celebrate Ah Hor's birthday, then went out and caught a movie with Ah Hor and the boys. He remembered what Tee Soon said about age difference and relationships and was struck by it. Hok Leong really couldn't accept that Chiu-yun was older than him by a year.

But as he sat in the auditorium watching the movie, his conscience spoke up. He wasn't a man. If he could lie to Chiu-yun who else would he not deceive? If he could lie to her now, what more in the future? Enveloped by soothing darkness, he wished that he could hear her voice.

After the movie ended, he found a public phone and dialled Chiu-yun's number. They agreed to meet the next day at the lobby coffee shop in Sea View Hotel.

Surprisingly, on the way home that evening, he bumped into Junior Brother. He was walking by the roadside when

Junior Brother suddenly flashed by on a motorbike and called out his name. Junior Brother didn't stop to chat. Swiftly, his visage vanished into the night.

Hok Leong stopped by the roadside, deep in thought. When was the last time they met, he wondered. For no good reason he sat down on the pavement. He didn't know why. He felt like sitting down, so he did it—and then he sat there thinking about Red Dragon.

42

Hok Leong and Chiu-yun sat in the lobby coffee shop, sipping the drinks that they had ordered. Hok Leong kept his eyes trained on Chiu-yun. She didn't seem to mind that she was a year older than him. When he deliberately brought up the topic, she said, "Oh forget it! You look much older than me anyway, like an old fart."

That was true. He did look older than his elder sister. When his two sisters got angry with him they called him "old fart." Now he happily played the role.

Chiu-yun didn't ask where he went the previous evening, or whether he had a good time. Hok Leong wanted to know how she spent the evening but was afraid that she would have questions of her own to pose to him. He didn't dare to ask.

In the end, the talk again turned to the topic of age difference. Hok Leong asked why she didn't join a secondary three class when she transferred to their school. Chiu-yun said she didn't know why. She was halfway through secondary three when she left Indonesia. The Singapore school wanted her to join a secondary two class. Her parents agreed. And that was that.

"Anyway, that's all to the good," Chiu-yun said. "If not I would be short of one Chinese teacher," she added, and gave a happy laugh.

43.

The "O" level exam results were announced.

Observing the visage of his seniors, Hok Leong noticed that the disappointed faces outnumbered the happy ones. Those with no-big-deal, indifferent faces seemed to outnumber the first two groups.

Hok Leong wondered what expression he would wear on his face the next year when he received his own results.

As expected elder brother didn't do well. But he didn't want to continue with his welding apprenticeship. These past few months he had been brushing off the slag and spatter "shite" created by the soldering work—he didn't like it.

The other option was to work in an <u>office</u>, to buy coffee for others and do odd jobs. But brother also hated that idea. He would rather work in the hawker centre. Father didn't express an opinion when he heard the decision. In his secret heart, Hok Leong was glad. In the future he wouldn't have to give a hand at the food stall.

Elder sister couldn't make it to senior high, but she could study commerce in one of the private schools. Father also didn't express an opinion about that. Turning to Hok Leong, who was watching TV, he asked, "What about you?"

"Anything's fine," Hok Leong said offhandedly. He hadn't given any thought to the matter.

Father said earnestly, "Don't say anything's fine. If you really want to study then do it properly. Being a hawker isn't fun, there's no future or prospect. If you study a bit more you can work in an office. You won't have to buy coffee for other people."

With his eyes fixed on the television screen, Hok Leong again gave a nonchalant reply. "Aw," he said non-committedly.

44

Hok Leong was helping out at the food centre when Black Gold came by with her boyfriend. Both of them wore school uniforms. His was different from hers. They simpered and giggled as they took their refreshments. The guy even helped to serve customers, delivering coffee to a number of tables.

Hok Leong felt that they were showing off. He didn't want to watch anymore and switched his attention to the shop selling rice noodle roll. Colour Palette was immersed in her work, retrieving dirty crockery from the tables. She seemed to have lost weight. She had lost her previous haughtiness and even seemed a bit pitiable or wretched.

Colour Palette raised her head and caught Hok Leong staring at her. Hok Leong pretended that nothing had happened and went away.

Hok Leong had no desire to follow in elder brother's footsteps, to shift *won ton* noodles in a hawker centre. He also didn't want to be an office boy, to buy coffee for other people. He didn't work hard in school and didn't know how to improve. He suspected that if studied the textbooks he bought he would improve. He saw Chiu-yun steadily getting better. He knew you could only be a "scholar" if you had the aptitude for it. Chiu-yun had it. He didn't. Furthermore Chiu-yun took tuition classes. She had a tutor to answer her queries, to clarify doubts. Hok Leong didn't want to rely on Chiu-yun for everything. He also didn't want to put on bookish airs when he hung around with his buddies in school.

He studied because he didn't want Chiu-yun to be disappointed in him.

45

Chiu-yun told Hok Leong excitedly that there was an ice-skating rink in Katong Garden. She asked him to go there with her. Hok Leong figured that she must have visited the place with her class mates. Hok Leong had heard about the facility. But among his friends no one had expressed interest in it, so he had yet to go there.

Chiu-yun was a good skater. She had picked it up in Indonesia. Hok Leong wore a long-sleeve T-shirt that he had just bought. He stood by the rink side, not daring to enter the arena. He rubbed his hands continuously and blew mist from his mouth.

Chiu-yun skated several times around the rink and then slid to a stop before him. "What's the point of coming if you don't step in?" she said, insisting that he do so. Hok Leong almost fell as he took the first few steps. He held her so tight that she almost fell. Chiu-yun didn't care. Holding tightly onto his hand she circled the place, going round and round, then she released him. By then Hok Leong had learned the basic moves and could skate by himself. Chiu-yun pretended to be angry, "I don't believe you picked it up so quickly! How am I going to bully you if you do that?"

Hok Leong stuck out his chest and struck a victory pose.

Chiu-yun kicked out at Hok Leong with her right leg. The icy water on the rink, caught by her skate, splashed over him. Chiu-yun turned and scooted away. Hok Leong chased after her but couldn't keep up. He crossed to the opposite side, waited for her to complete her round. Chiu-yun saw Hok Leong preparing an ambush. Skating as hard as she could she crashed into him. They almost toppled over. They clutched each other and laughed gaily. Chiu-yun continued to torment Hok Leong. In one swift move, she stamped the blade of her skate on the ice, bent down to pick up the shards released by the action and shoved them down Hok Leong's shirt front. Hok Leong gave a strange shout. Chiu-yun skated to safety. He made some ice shards of his own and chased after her.

Whether he caught up with her or not, today was their happiest ever moment together. Nothing could beat it.

46

Hok Leong only had time to savour the events of the day at night, as he laid on his bed at home.

He recollected in detail how it felt to hug Chiu-yun. More than once she had crashed into him and held him tight, so tight that he didn't know how to respond. He soon learned to play in the same way. There wasn't the feeling of a real embrace, real passion.

They held hands as they skated. She had such soft hands, he didn't want to release them. In the future, he would always remember the Chinese proverb describing the feeling, to cherish something so much you couldn't bear to part with it. And also the way her long hair brushed against his face, her heady scent and the giddiness it wrought in him.

But he couldn't specify what exactly he felt when he held Chiu-yun; he couldn't reach that feeling.

They were too busy playing. They didn't have the time, and he couldn't hold her too long. If he had to spell it out, he would have to say that it was like Chiu-yun hugging her teddy bear: happy and comfy.

Hok Leong took the soft toy that she had given him and held it close to his chest. Nothing. No feeling at all.

As they sipped refreshments at tea time, Chiu-yun said that her younger brother was a better skater than her. Together with their mother he would be coming to Singapore during the mid-year vacations. He was coming to study in the city as well, so she wouldn't have to return to Indonesia during the holidays.

Hok Leong wasn't particularly happy when he heard the news. Chiu-yun's mother and younger brother coming to the republic was the same as her going home to Indonesia. With her younger brother here, they might not have time to meet up so often.

47

The mid-year exams came and went. Hok Leong did extremely well. He even got into the school top-twenty name-list. Naturally, he was overjoyed, but in front of Ah Hor and the others he pretended that it was nothing. It didn't affect him.

Chiu-yun was happier than him it seemed. She asked him where he wanted to go for his senior high education. He hadn't thought about that, hadn't thought about the future. What's the use of thinking about it? If you don't have the capability it's a waste of time, a daydream. Actually, no. He *had* thought about the future when it came to the matter of winning the lottery. That was probably more realistic. If you buy a ticket you have the same chance as everyone else. But if you wanted to study and didn't have the aptitude for it, well, then you set yourself up, you suffer. He didn't believe that studying hard could affect aptitude and ability. Studying hard was an idea that people used to dispel the pain of disappointment: I studied hard for it, I did my part. His own conclusion was, take one step, see what's ahead –one step at a time.

Naturally, Chiu-yun didn't share his views. She didn't know that her level was different. Her don't-study-hard was already more than his full barrage onslaught, if somehow he could pour all of himself into his studies. In his mind there was only one thing: he didn't want to spend his time working in an <u>office</u>, buying coffee for other people.

Chiu-yun wanted to continue her studies in the same school, which also offered senior high education. She was worried that her scores wouldn't be enough, because the entry requirements were high. Hok Leong was surprised that someone like her had to worry about such matters.

The day before the vacations they went again to the skating rink. Chiu-yun was animated and buoyant. They held hands and flew around the perimeter. They played boisterously, and held each other tightly.

Hok Leong kept trying to recall the feeling, the sensation of holding Chiu-yun in his arms. But once he left the rink it floated away like he was suffering from a bout of amnesia.

48

Chiu-yun's mother and younger brother came to Singapore. Hok Leong and Chiu-yun couldn't meet up. For a whole week they spoke to each other only by phone, each conversation lasting less than ten minutes.

Hok Leong moped around the house. He wanted to watch television but it hadn't started yet. He had to wait till six in the evening when they played the national anthem and started the programming. Hok Leong laid on his bed. He called Ah Hor and the others on the phone but nobody was in.

Mother saw him moping around and asked him to give a hand with the water chestnuts. They used it in the fillings for the won ton dumplings. Hok Leong didn't fancy it. It was exasperating, these chores were usually not done by him. He hurriedly changed into his street clothes. As he closed the door, mother shouted after him: "You have O levels exams this year. Don't go running all over the place." Hok Leong felt that she was being unfair. She never gave the same kind of pressure to elder brother and sister.

After he left he didn't know where to go. The movies? The coffee shop in Sea View Hotel? In the end he decided to go to the skating rink. He had no choice but to return home because he needed his long-sleeve T-shirt. Mother thought that he had nowhere to go and asked him again to help her slice the water chestnuts. Hok Leong didn't say anything. He took his shirt and left the flat. With his mother's admonishment ringing in his ears, Hok Leong shut the door, trapping her reprimand indoors

The skating rink was full of people. It was the holidays after all. Hok Leong didn't know why he went there. Any place with air-conditioning would have been fine. It would have been the same. He should have gone to the movies, he thought. But that would have been odd as well. One person laughing at the funny parts, one person getting excited and anxious at the scary parts: a bit like someone not right in the head. Skating by himself also seemed ridiculous. But at least it was better than staying at home slicing water chestnuts.

Suddenly he noticed someone beckoning at him. It was Chiu-yun! Hok Leong felt a pang of joy that he couldn't describe. Next to her stood a guy about the same height as her. Her brother?

They stopped and came together. Hok Leong carefully hid his feelings. Chiu-yun made the introductions. "My younger brother, Jia Xin." She hesitated: "My school mate, Hok Leong." Jia Xin nodded at Hok Leong. Hok Leong had the feeling that her brother didn't like him.

"You're alone?" Chiu-yun asked.

Hok Leong nodded his head.

"Do you want to join us?"

Hok Leong tactfully declined the offer. "That's fine. Bye!" He waved at her and went off.

Chiu-yun was surprised but seemed to understand his conduct. She skated over to him, "I'll call you tonight."

Hok Leong again nodded his head. He took the opportunity to lean on the barrier by the rink side, watched as Chiu-yun skated pass him, her figure growing smaller as she retreated into the distance. For the first time he encountered the experience of sending her off, felt the sorrow that it engendered. It was colder than the ice on the floor.

49

Chiu-yun called Hok Leong on the phone. She said she was having dinner outside with her folks. She hadn't reached home yet. Hok Leong said that was fine. He replaced the receiver and laid down on his bunk bed. After that the telephone rang again a few times, but it wasn't for him. Later on he heard in a daze his brother saying that he was sleeping. By then Hok Leong was too tired to get up.

He saw Chiu-yun again three days later at the coffee shop in Sea View Hotel. Enveloped by the sickly golden light cast by the lamps, he didn't know where to begin.

Chiu-yun apologised. She described what she had been busy with the last two weeks and told him her plans for after the school reopened. "Jia Xin is new to Singapore. He hasn't made any friends yet. After my mom goes back, we'll have to keep him company. I hope you can come as usual to my house to revise with me. You can also help Jia Xin."

Hok Leong nodded his head.

50

The holidays were over. School re-opened, the last half-year of secondary four. For most of Hok Leong's school mates, it was like the holidays starting half a year earlier than scheduled. Everyone knew that the school preliminary exams weren't important. It was the O levels exam results that mattered. Whether or not you made it to senior high depended on the latter, not the former. Teachers no longer had any influence on students, disciplined slackened, the atmosphere went bad.

Lessons became something you could attend or not attend, it didn't matter. Many students knew they didn't have a chance of making it to senior high and had already given up. In this group, the guys waited for national service conscription, the girls waited to see whether they could get accepted into private schools.

The number of students who skipped school kept increasing. Most of those who came spent their time on the sports field or playing courts. Only the few who thought they had a chance to further their studies or who didn't want to give up or who feared being punished attended lessons. Hok Leong of course didn't attend class. He looked askance at those who did. What gave him pain was that, the teachers came a few times to the sports field to round up those who weren't in the classrooms, to force them to attend lessons. Although the personal attention was a kind of flattery, Hok Leong felt bitter about the whole thing. If you're no good then you rightfully belong to that group. Marking time in the classroom made no sense. One time the teachers got really angry and activated the principal to come catch recalcitrant students at the sports field, but word got out and they scattered like fraidy-cats before he arrived.

The principal even went class to class to give pep talks. But he couldn't guarantee that working hard meant you got your just rewards, right? What's the point of working hard and then not seeing results? Wasn't that a waste of time?

Hok Leong remembered that the ambiance was like that: a bunch of disheartened and demoralised students, wandering aimlessly without a purpose. They didn't know what course to follow, and, as an institution, the school also didn't know how to comfort them, how to find them a better path, how to perk them up and give them hope.

In his secret heart, Hok Leong knew that their book-learning days were numbered.

51

Chiu-yun's younger brother started his schooling in Singapore. Chiu-yun was especially busy, and complained that she was like a mother. Hok Leong only got to see her on the fourth day after the school reopened, turning up at her terrace house because she pressed him to make the effort.

Hok Leong spotted Chiu-yun's brother when he reached the house and greeted him amiably; but her brother only nodded vaguely and gave him a condescending glance, the kind of glance rich kids gave to those they considered beneath their notice. If he wasn't Chiu-yun's brother he would have walloped him, Hok Leong thought to himself. Furthermore, her brother was frequently intrusive as Chiu-yun and Hok Leong revised their schoolwork. Again and again he disrupted their conversation.

Hok Leong's initial impression of Chiu-yun's brother, obtained at the ice-rink, was now doubly confirmed. In the evening, when Chiu-yun suggested that they all have dinner together he said that his mother had already prepared the evening meal. As Chiu-yun saw him to the door, he said: "I won't come here again to revise my schoolwork."

Chiu-yun was taken aback but seemed to understand his predicament. She didn't respond to or query his judgement. Looking hurt and aggrieved, she said in a small voice: "I'll call you again at home." Hok Leong regretted the hasty decision that he made.

As he laid on his bed at night Hok Leong went over the details of the day. If he didn't go to Chiu-yun's home he would probably meet her only once a week. If she had to accompany her brother on Saturdays their opportunities for meeting up were even further reduced. The important thing was that he had let Chiu-yun down. Why were rich kids exactly like how they were portrayed on television? Why were they so irritating!

As sleep continued to elude him, Hok Leong got off his bed and went to the laundry drying area at the back of the kitchen, in what was also the only area of the house with some proper ventilation. More euphemistically you could call it a veranda. Hok Leong's father made his barbequed pork there and also smoked his cigarettes. In their home, father and mother divided the labour needed to keep the noodle stall going: father bought the ingredients for making roast pork; mother did the marinating; father roasted the meat; mother made won ton dumplings; father made the soup base. If elder brother wanted to take over the business, he would have to learn from both of them. Hok Leong had never thought about taking over any trade or business. He didn't want to be a hawker, to have his children slighted by school mates and friends.

He had asked his parents in the past the secret to making good barbeque meat—how was their recipe different from other people's concoction? But the answers were always obscure, like some arcane martial arts treatise that had to be carefully analysed and explicated. Mother said, the easiest mistake to make is that you forget to massage the meat. Huh? Massage for pigs? Yes. The more you massage, the softer the meat; the easier it is for the sauce and water to get absorbed. And you must have an adequate amount of water. If not you get defeated even before you fire up the barbeque. Mulling over her words, Hok Leong felt that she was articulating pugilist esoterica, nothing to do with cooking. Father on his part said, hey, you don't need any special kind of Kung Fu. Everything comes down to one thing: hard work. You put effort into turning the splits, into checking the strength of the fire. That's all there is. Did their answers sound perplexing? Did speaking and not speaking amount to the same thing—they might as well have stayed silent? Hok Leong often felt that they were joking with him, they were pulling his leg.

Mother was in the washroom next to the veranda. She

spotted Hok Leong leaning disconsolately against the window railing. "Why aren't you sleeping?" she asked.

Hok Leong answered flippantly, "I'm enjoying the moon-lit sky."

Mother got off her stool and came over to stand next to him. She peered at the sky. "But there's nothing," she said. Suddenly she realised the situation and struck Hok Leong on the shoulder. "Idiot! It's the first of the month! How can there be a moon!" She went back to her washing.

The night sky was a blank. No moon and no stars. Everything outside was still and quiet. Hok Leong thought about another evening similar to the current one, when he had gone to the seaside with Chiu-yun. He thought about the way they sat back to back, the way she sang *Rhythm of the Waves*.

All at once Hok Leong spotted a group of men downstairs, each holding in his hands a bludgeon of some kind. They quickly vanished into the maze of concrete formed by the flats.

Hok Leong wondered about Junior Brother and Opium Addict. "Could they be in that group?" he asked himself.

52

Marine Parade Library was better than he had expected. The air-con was strong and bracing. It was quiet. You couldn't talk or eat. An efficient place: in an hour or so he had finished all that he needed to complete. Hok Leong never went to libraries. At any rate he never went to such places to study, to borrow books, or to read. But now he started to like it. Although it felt pretentious, the challenge of communicating in undertones with assorted eye gestures and body language was quite fun.

The place was suggested by Chiu-yun. Poor Chiu-yun. After they finished their homework Hok Leong made a special effort to invite her for refreshments at the lobby coffee shop in Sea View Hotel. Chiu-yun was delighted. She didn't talk about her younger brother. She smiled gaily as Hok Leong shared with her his positive impressions of the library, which was now their designated spot for doing school work and for revision. After he finished, she asked, "If we can't come to the library would you still come to my house?"

Hok Leong didn't know how to answer her. "I haven't thought about it," he said. After a while, he added, "Should be, I guess. We need somewhere to"–he gave a big gulp–"do homework."

53

Whether it was to see Chiu-yun or to do school work, Hok Leong would have continued going to Chiu-yun's house, her younger brother wasn't actually an obstacle. What Hok Leong didn't say was that it was only because of Chiu-yun that he did any school work at all.

Chiu-yun naturally worried about Hok Leong's performance. They had only half a year left before the "O" levels exams. From who knows where she produced a stack of previous years' exam-papers which she prompted Hok Leong to complete. As he sat in the library working through the questions he felt like he had become a question-answering machine of some kind. It was terribly frustrating. Chiu-yun said, "The whole point is to turn you into a machine so that you answer correctly without thinking about it. That's what my tuition teacher said."

For Hok Leong, going to school now was more relaxing than studying in the library. He could re-read his martial arts novels. The teachers didn't do much, just focused on revising the material covered earlier, preparing for the exams. What was more fun was the principal coming occasionally to do spot checks. Hok Leong liked it when the principal did his rounds. For those few minutes it felt like a real school. It was a pity that the principal didn't do any teaching.

54

When everybody felt that it was a long way off and you wished it would come earlier so that nobody was prepared, everyone suffered the same fate, you wouldn't have to undergo the pain of anticipation like some death row inmate; but you also prayed it would never arrive so that you didn't have to face cruel, inhuman punishment—wrapped in that strange mind set the exams finally began.

A week before the exams, Chiu-yun's parents came to Singapore. A sense of foreboding swelled in Hok Leong but he brushed it aside, saying in an exaggerated tone of voice, "Wow, it's just an exam. And they're actually here!"

Chiu-yun responded provocatively, "Do you want to meet them? They're fine. They really are."

Hok Leong didn't answer yes or no.

Even then, he still met Chiu-yun's parents two days before the exams. After revising their studies at the library that day, Hok Leong walked Chiu-yun home. As they strode down the narrow avenue near her home, a Mercedes Benz quietly pulled up near them. Chiu-yun was taken aback but graciously introduced Hok Leong as she stepped into the vehicle. He was her school mate, she said.

Hok Leong courteously greeted Chiu-yun's parents: "Hello Uncle! Hello Auntie!" His eyes followed the retreating car as it headed towards Chiu-yun's driveway.

Hok Leong didn't get a chance to take a close look at Chiu-yun's parents. He didn't know what they thought of him.

55

The day before the exams. Remarkably, Chiu-yun didn't have any jitters. She even wanted Hok Leong to accompany her to Katong Shopping Centre. She had always wanted a pair of earrings but the school didn't allow such an accessory. After the exams, she figured, no one would care, so she would finally get to fulfil her desire.

They entered one of the jewellery shops. As they mulled over the rows of earrings on display, Hok Leong noticed that several of the jade pendants were engraved with one of the words in his name, "Fu," meaning "wealth" in Mandarin Chinese. It was also read as "Hok" in the Hokkien dialect. He looked for the other character in his name, "Liang" or "Leong" meaning "good" or "decent." There were none. People wanted wealth but not goodness it seemed.

Chiu-yun couldn't find a pair of earrings that suited her taste, so they went to Lotus Flower Coffee Shop for some refreshments. They hadn't been there for a long time. Looking around the eatery, Hok Leong remembered the first time they went there. It was just over a year ago. Everything had changed, but he couldn't put a finger on what precisely was different. He recalled Chiu-yun teaching him how to sing <u>Yesterday Once More</u>, her ordering a <u>Coke Float</u> for him, the way she sang *Rhythm of the Waves* by the sea shore, the two of them hugging-colliding at the ice-skating rink, her parents coming to Singapore, and then tomorrow the exams would begin.

"You're not anxious about tomorrow?" Hok Leong asked Chiu-yun.

"No. What's there to be anxious about? I've trained myself so that like a machine I can do the questions, no need to think. How about you?"

Hok Leong lacked confidence in himself. "I don't know. I have to see the questions first, then I'll know."

Chiu-yun gave him some encouragement. "You should be fine, don't worry. Let's not talk about that. Let's talk about something else."

Hok Leong suddenly asked, "did you parents say anything about me?" He had a bad feeling about the entire affair. Chiu-yun's parents arriving in the wake of her younger brother was a large obstacle, much larger than the brother.

Chiu-yun gave a laugh. "You mean you're such a big shot they have to comment on you?" she joked. "No, of course not." After a moment's consideration, she added, "Actually, my mom did say something. She asked me, is that the school friend who often studies together with you and helps you to revise your school work? I said, yes, that's him! After that, she didn't say anything."

Hok Leong thought to himself—No reaction at all? What kind of reaction was that?

Chiu-yun said, "Shall I find time after the exams to come to the food centre? To meet your parents, see how they look like?"

Hok Leong rolled his eyes and pretended to go into a faint.

56

The "O" levels exams finally arrived. Hok Leong's first paper was in the afternoon. As Chiu-yun had said, there was nothing to be anxious about. But it wasn't because he had trained himself to become a machine and operate like one. It was because anxiety accomplished nothing and he had already given up. Hok Leong called Ah Hor and the others. They also didn't seem to set much store by the exams. Surprisingly it was his elder brother who put weight on it, telling Hok Leong as he went off to work in the morning: "Remember my advice! Don't end up buying coffee for other people!"

Hok Leong didn't reply.

The afternoon paper was Chinese. Hok Leong knew he would pass the exam, it was only a question of how much. As he worked through the questions, Hok Leong realised that he knew the answers. He was almost like a machine, answering by rote. Ah Hor and the others left the exam hall early. Hok Leong checked his answers twice before handing in his answer script.

He didn't want to end up "buying coffee for other people."

In the evening, Hok Leong gave Chiu-yun a call. She had two papers that day, Chinese in the afternoon, Higher Maths in the morning. They discussed their respective answers for the Chinese paper: they were almost all the same. Now they felt confident about the subject. Before she replaced the receiver, Chiu-yun said "thank you" to Hok Leong.

Hok Leong didn't know how to express his gratitude. He could only reply, "I also thank you." They burst out laughing when he said that.

57

Hok Leong's examination period was longer than Chiu-yun's by two days. His additional subjects were Metal Work and Technical Drawing. After the ten-day ordeal, Hok Leong's last paper was Technical Drawing. After finishing the paper, he left his drawing template and T-square in school. He hurried to the coffee shop in Sea View Hotel to meet Chiu-yun.

Chiu-yun arrived at the shop before Hok Leong. She sat at a seat with stylish antiquarian table-top lighting, quietly reading a book. Her elegant posture and long gleaming tresses struck Hok Leong from a distance. He didn't feel like coming closer. He watched her, delighting in the experience until she noticed him and beckoned him over.

As he sat down, Hok Leong spotted a pair of small star-shaped earrings dangling from Chiu-yun's ears. They were about two centimetres long and were half-hidden by her hair. Hok Leong pointed wordlessly at the adornment.

"Is it beautiful?" Chiu-yun asked.

Hok Leong bent close to examine it. In a deliberately lowered tone of voice he said, "Not beautiful."

Chiu-yun frowned. She raised a hand and fingered one of the earrings. "Really?"

Hok Leong again bent close to the accessory. In a low voice, he said, "it's fake." He gave a hearty laugh.

The exams were over, and they had also graduated. For the moment at least, there was a pause in their formal education. The moment they had waited for so long had arrived. "Finally, it's over!" Hok Leong declared in a relieved tone of voice.

"You should be happy!" Chiu-yun said.

"I'm not that amazingly happy to be honest," Hok Leong answered truthfully.

"Me too," Chiu-yun said.

"Maybe we're getting old," Hok Leong said. "There just isn't that much to be happy about."

Chiu-yun agreed. "Yes, and next year we move on to senior high. Have you thought about where you want to enrol for further studies?"

Of all the things in the world, Hok Leong dreaded hearing that question the most. He shook his head, "Let's wait till the results come out, okay? I can only wait for the school to choose me, not the other way around."

Chiu-yun continued, "So what do you intend to do for the next few months?"

"My classmates all intend to find a job. My father said there's no need for that. Just help him out at the food stall."

"Isn't your elder brother helping out at the stall?"

"He's getting conscripted. He has to do national service," Hok Leong said. "What about you?"

Chiu-yun asked eagerly, "Does your father need an extra helping hand?"

"You mean you!" Hok Leong said. He leaned back away from Chiu-yun.

"Am I that awful?"

"Look, working in a food stall isn't as easy-going or as pleasurable as you think it is," Hok Leong said in a low voice. "The worst thing is that people look down on you."

"Really?" Chiu-yun didn't seem to believe his words.

Hok Leong thought for a moment. "I've faced it since I was young. Growing up it was there. Now it's still there."

"Even now?" Chiu-yun was taken aback.

"Some of my classmates still look down on me because of that, Hok Leong explained. "The one we saw the other time at Lotus Flower café. He's one of them."

"But why? Why are they like that?"

Hok Leong didn't reply. After a while he asked, "You still want to do it?"

Chiu-yun nodded. "Yes," she said in a small voice.

Of course, Hok Leong wouldn't let Chiu-yun work in a hawker centre. He even regretted telling her so much about his situation. Her life consisted of all the beautiful things in the world. Hok Leong's world had only one immeasurably lovely fairy tale. It was difficult to know the next step in that story, or where exactly it would go next.

58

Hok Leong went to the food centre to give a hand at his father's stall. He saw Black Gold wearing pretty clothes and make-up. Her father said that she had found a job. Hok Leong went to take a look at Colour Palette. She hadn't gone; she was still there. For some reason, Hok Leong wondered whether that meant that Colour Palette would *always* be working at the food centre. Would she *always* be there, selling her rice noodle rolls? Black Gold had managed to walk out. It didn't matter whether Colour Palette was vain or not when she left home earlier. She sought something they wanted. Who among the "second" generation kids like himself, Colour Palette, and Black Gold didn't want to leave that kind of life? To see no more the contempt of strangers. To work in an office instead of stir-frying or simmering. The problem was—not everyone achieved that dream. Some failed. Colour Palette for instance, and also his elder brother. Did anyone ever achieve this dream of escape? Who knows? He hadn't ask. Would Black Gold eventually fail as well?

Hok Leong didn't know whether he would get to escape that kind of life. His future didn't seem to be in his hands.

In the afternoon, Ah Hor called him on the phone and asked if he wanted to meet up. Hok Leong didn't agree because he had arranged to go ice-skating with Chiu-yun. Ah Hor and Hok Leong started to talk. Ah Hor said that the day earlier, he had gone for a job interview at an electronics factory in Bedok together with Ying-jun and Tee Soon. They would know the answer in the next one to two days. Hok Leong asked if the three of them intended to work permanently at the factory. The moment the words left his mouth, he felt it was the kind of question that Chiu-yun might ask. Ah Hor said they would work till they got the call up to serve in the military. The rest would have to wait till after they completed their national service. When Ah Hor asked him the same question, Hok Leong said that for the moment he would help his father at the noodle stall. Like them he had yet to figure out what to do after national service. Hok Leong felt that the future became a bit clearer because he spoke about it with Ah Hor. But tried as they did, they couldn't shake off the low, dull spirit that hung over their conversation. Eventually they agreed to meet up on Saturday; they would try to catch a midnight movie.

59

Ah Hor, Ying-jun and Tee Soon were hired by the same electronics factory but were put in different shifts and didn't get a chance to meet up at work. Their lives grew more settled. Hok Leong's schedule also became firmed up. In the morning he gave a hand at the won ton noodle stall. After lunch he went home. In the afternoon he went out with Chiu-yun. They shared meals, held conversations, caught movies, and went shopping. At night, he went out with his mates, where again they shared meals and conversations, caught movies, and went shopping. Actually they didn't shop all that much. Most of the time they shared meals and chit-chatted. Hok Leong felt that, for this period of his life, he needed to be with the guys more than he needed to be with Chiu-yun. The guys shared many complicated emotions that Chiu-yun couldn't really appreciate.

That Saturday, Hok Leong had dinner first with Chiu-yun. They went shopping. After he saw her off, he met up with Ying-jun and Tee Soon to catch a midnight screening of a Taiwanese movie, *Brilliant Days*. Ah Hor had to work the midnight shift and couldn't join them, even though he was the one who had suggested the outing.

After the screening, the trio left the theatre and walked slowly towards Elizabeth Walk, their heads filled with the scenes and music of the show. Everyone's mood was affected. Ying-jun, who had a greater sense of rhythm than his compatriots, hummed intermittently the two set-piece songs of the movie. Hok Leong desperately racked his brain recalling the words to the first song:

> *Do you remember our past and dreams?*
> *Those hope-filled days, that brilliant time?*
> *To pursue ideals, we walked through darkness and pain.*
> *We shed tears, we shared laughter.*
> *May you remember, forget never*
> *Our time together, those brilliant days that we had.*

The second song was terribly sad and also quite difficult to remember. Hok Leong only remembered parts of it:

When I am dead, my dearest,
Sing no sad songs for me;
Plant thou no roses at my head,
Nor shady cypress tree:
Be the green grass above me
With showers and dewdrops wet;
And if thou wilt, remember,
And if thou wilt, forget.
I shall not see the shadows, [...]
And dreaming through the twilight
That doth not rise nor set,
Haply I may remember,
And haply may forget.

Much later, Hok Leong learned that the first song was by the Taiwanese singer and songwriter Luo Dayou. The music for the second song was also composed by Luo, with the lyrics taken from Xu Zhimo's translation of the poem "When I am Dead, My Dearest," by the English poet Christina Georgina Rosetti.

That day, Hok Leong felt that the songs were moving, but didn't put much significance into it. Instead of the boys, he should have gone to see the movie with Chiu-yun, he thought. She could have helped him remember the tune and lyrics.

60

The next day, Chiu-yun phoned Hok Leong up early in the morning. She needed to see him immediately. Hok Leong glanced at the clock. Seven a.m. Chiu-yun wasn't the kind of person to play practical jokes. "What's wrong?" he asked. "What happened?"

"Can you come see me now?" Chiu-yun couldn't control herself. "My father wants me to fly to the UK next week!"

Hok Leong was surprised. "Whatever for?" he asked.

"To further my studies!"

Hok Leong didn't know what to say.

Chiu-yun whimpered, "My father wants me to go there to study. He said the term has already started…."

Hok Leong broke her off. "I'm coming now. Meet me at Sea View Hotel coffee shop."

Hok Leong changed into his street clothes, yelled "I'm going out" and quickly left the flat, not caring whether his mother had heard him or not.

At the foot of the block, he hailed a taxi and jumped into it. He had never placed much hope in the idea that he and Chiu-yun could be together. But he didn't think the problem would take shape suddenly in this manner. He went through the situation: he didn't have a solution, basically he didn't know what to do. The only thing that he could do was to get Chiu-yun's father to change his mind.

He was willing to give it a try.

61

Chiu-yun was there when he arrived. She had been crying. She went up to Hok Leong. She wanted to hold him close, but, discomforted by the setting, reached out instead to grab his hand.

It was tough going for Hok Leong. Seeing the desolation on Chiu-yun's features, he could only hug her gently and help her sit down. Hok Leong had a thousand and one questions circling in his head. Not knowing how to proceed, he started with probably the dumbest one: "You really have to go?"

Chiu-yun nodded.

"You've discussed this thoroughly with your father?"

Again she nodded.

"How about I speak to him?" he suggested.

She shook her head. "It's useless. He's already bought the air ticket." She started to cry again.

Hok Leong didn't know what to say. He patted her hand gently and tried to console her.

She grabbed his arm. "I don't want to go now!"

Hok Leong nodded sadly.

"I want to finish high school here!" She started to cry again.

Yes, if she could study here maybe he could join her somehow. As he watched her cry, his eyes also started to tear.

"Please don't cry!" he pleaded.

Chiu-yun tried hard to stop sniffing.

"If you really have to go, when will it be?"

"Next Friday. The midnight flight, I think."

"So only five days left?"

Chiu-yun nodded.

"Did you father say anything else?"

"He applied on my behalf. He said the term has already started."

"Why such a rush?"

"He said compared to other students, I'm already late by a year."

"But you can finish your pre-university here and then go, right? There's plenty of time!"

"He said since I have to go, I might as well go now." Chiu-yun started to cry again.

"That sounds like a businessman's mind-set," Hok Leong said softly.

Chiu-yun turned to Hok Leong, "Do you have a solution?"

"I'd like to discuss this with him," he said.

62

Hok Leong returned home extremely late that night. He racked his brains for a solution but couldn't find one. He wanted to talk things through with Chiu-yun's father, but she wouldn't let him.

At lunchtime, he had excused himself for a washroom break, during which time he had placed a call to Chiu-yun's home. He wanted to talk to her father.

The phone rang. A man answered the call. It was Chiu-yun's father. Hok Leong's heartbeat went up suddenly. He couldn't say a word and remained tongue-tied. Chiu-yun's father said "hello" a few times and replaced the receiver. Hok Leong heaved a sigh of relief when he got disconnected. He leaned against the wall, wondering why he had become so worm-like, so useless and unresponsive. He was the kind of guy who could, weapon-in-hand, charge into a melee fight with the likes of Red Dragon. When did he become such a coward?

Again, he placed a call to Chiu-yun's home. But the moment the phone started to ring he put it down. He knew that, if again Chiu-yun's father answered the phone, he would again stay speechless. He didn't know why.

When he returned from the washroom, he thought about asking Chiu-yun to leave her parents, but he knew she wouldn't agree. Even if she did, it accomplished nothing. He thought about Colour Palette. Colour Palette eventually had no choice but to return home after her elopement. If Chiu-yun did the same thing, he might well never get to see her again. Also, he didn't know how he could arrange things after Chiu-yun left home. How could he take care of her, shelter her? He knew he didn't have the resources or the ability. Chiu-yun would not even arrange a meeting between him and her father.

Sixteen years old. What can you do at sixteen? It seemed like there was nothing he could do. Deep in his heart Hok Leong wrestled with failure, with the understanding that he couldn't fight for what he wanted. He didn't know why he had become so useless and inactive, or, put in a better-sounding way, why he seemed so calm and unflustered. He should have gone to find Dog Shit and the others, or Ah Hor and the boys. With gang in tow he should have gone to see Chiu-yun's parents to negotiate the matter. Or else to trash their terrace house, to wreck it.

No. He knew he didn't want that. That kind of action accomplished nothing. Chiu-yun would eventually have to go anyway. Maybe this was what it felt like to be grown up, to face disappointments. Sixteen years old. Why was it that being grown-up meant you couldn't do anything?

After lunch, Chiu-yun and Hok Leong again went <u>shopping</u>, which was actually their euphemism for ambling around in a mall, doing nothing, enjoying each other's company. After dinner that evening, they went to the seaside. Chiu-yun broke into the opening bars of *Rhythm of the Waves*. In the middle of the song, she started to cry. Hok Leong didn't tell her to stop, didn't console her. He felt that he was useless, a worm. He had totally wasted his sixteen years on earth. He too began to cry, but he didn't let Chiu-yun see his tears.

Late that night, they finally said their goodbyes and went home. They agreed to meet again the next day.

63

They knew they couldn't do anything. Their time together had entered a countdown sequence. On the first day, they went to the ice-skating rink. No other place gave them such tranquillity, such freedom from scruples and worry. They held hands and skated around the rink, they hugged each other, laughed gaily—and tried their best to forget about Friday. More than anything, their silence about the issue showed that they were becoming resigned to the arrangements made by Chiu-yun's father.

And even if they weren't, really, what could they do?

When they got tired, they left the rink and went to a coffee shop in Orchard Road, the one opposite Mandarin hotel. It was located in a row of converted single-storey dwellings that catered specifically to tourists. The various shops, boutiques, carpet retailers, and hair salons there were all full of foreigners.

The first thing they heard when they entered the establishment was the live music and singing coming over the speakers. They found a table next to a window overlooking the busy thoroughfare. They savoured the ambience: the tropical trees lining the road, some pedestrians in a hurry, some chatting lazily with friends, the cool air in the room and soothing music. It felt like they had entered a movie set or scene.

They both ordered <u>ice lemon tea</u>. Chiu-yun broke the silence. "One of my classmates took me here. That's how I got to know the place."

For a while, Hok Leong fiddled with the artificial roses nestling in a vase on the table top. He wouldn't let it rest. "Did your father discuss the issue with you again?"

"I don't think he will raise it again. It was also like this when I first came to Singapore."

"Will you talk to him again about it?"

"It's no use," Chiu-yun said. Trying to lower the tension, she gave a sudden laugh. "I've thought about it. We can write to each other, chat on the phone. In half a year's time I can probably come back. It'll be like in the past when I had to go home for the holidays, everything will pass very quickly."

Hok Leong nodded. Was she beginning to accept the situation that she faced?

The <u>ice lemon tea</u> arrived. Chiu-yun took a sip. "Hold on for a while," she said.

She went to the side of the room where a singer on a raised dais was giving a live performance. She had just finished her set. Chiu-yun spoke to her for a while, then took over the guitar that she had been using. The songstress left the stage. Chiu-yun took her seat and began to tune the instrument. She leaned towards the microphone stand, "<u>I would like to sing a song to my best friend</u>!" she said. She started strumming the guitar. In a serene voice she began:

When I was young I listened to the radio,
Waiting for my favourite songs.
When they played I'd sing along, it made me smile....

The patrons in the establishment, spotting the changeover and seeing that it was an Oriental girl, broke into applause.

The applause rang out again after she finished the ballad—louder this time. Somebody whistled. Chiu-yun returned happily to her seat. Hok Leong eagerly clapped his hands. "You're just as good as the professional singer!" he said.

Chiu-yun said laughingly, "You should sing one too."

Hok Leong surprised her. "Okay, sure!" he said. He left his seat and made his way to the dais. The performer engaged by the establishment had yet to begin her new set. Hok Leong spoke to her for a while. Like Chiu-yun he took over the stage. Clutching the microphone in his hand he said nervously, "<u>I would like to sing a song to my best friend too</u>!" He sang acapella:

When I am dead, my dearest,
Sing no sad songs for me;
Plant thou no roses at my head,
Nor shady cypress tree:
Be the green grass above me
With showers and dewdrops wet;
And if thou wilt, remember,
And if thou wilt, forget....

Chiu-yun clapped her hands enthusiastically when Hok Leong finished his song and returned to their table. "How come I've never heard you sing?"

"I went with Ying-jun and the others to watch *Brilliant Days* last Saturday. We caught the midnight screening," Hok Leong explained. "The day after that I wanted to ask you to watch it with me. Then you told me the news about going to England. Ying-jun found the lyrics for the song."

"There's a movie theatre nearby. Let's go watch it now!"

"But we haven't finished our <u>ice lemon tea</u>!"

"Aiyoh! There's no time!"

64

When they stepped out of the movie theatre, Chiu-yun showed Hok Leong the piece of foolscap on which she had scribbled down some musical notation. She turned her red-rimmed eyes to him and laughed. "I love it! I took down the notes for the title song. Let's go home and get my guitar. Let's sing it at the seaside!"

Before Hok Leong could reply she had hailed a taxi. The taxi slowed to a stop before them.

Hok Leong got into the vehicle. He couldn't control himself, "You're crazy!"

Chiu-yun stared at Hok Leong, "Yes, I'm crazy!"

65

The next day they again met at the ice-skating rink. Hand in hand they skated around the perimeter. They embraced when they felt like it, they put their faces together, they skated like they were searching for the furthest reaches of the universe.

When they got tired they again returned to the coffee shop in Orchard Road. They took the same table next to the same brightly-lit window. The same plastic roses nestling in a vase greeted them. Chiu-yun wanted coffee. Hok Leong again ordered <u>ice lemon tea</u>. When the coffee arrived, Chiu-yun took a sip of the liquid and scrounged up her eyebrows in dismay. Hok Leong offered to exchange his drink with hers. Chiu-yun refused. She added more milk and sugar to the drink.

Hok Leong had a sly smile on his face, like he was waiting for an opportunity of some kind. Chiu-yun realised something was up. "What's the matter," she asked. "Is there something you want to say?"

Hok Leong put his hand into his pocket and retrieved a small gift box. "For you," he said.

Chiu-yun was surprised. She happily received her present and weighed it in her hand, tried to size it up.

"Open it and take a look!"

It was a jade pendant. It had the character "Hok" carved into it in gold, meaning good fortune, happiness, or luck. "I didn't know what to buy, thought about it for a few days, just bought it today," Hok Leong said. "I was looking for the character 'Leong,'" he added, "but I couldn't find it."

He noticed that Chiu-yun seemed a bit down-hearted. "You don't have to wear it if you don't like it! It's just that it has my name in it. It seems cool, so I bought it for you."

Chiu-yun replied. "I'm fine. Don't worry about it." She tapped the front of her chest, "It's a great present!" She looked meaningfully at Hok Leong. "I've got something for you too."

Hok Leong was surprised, "Such a coincidence?"

"Not a coincidence. It's two hearts beating as one." Chiu-yun took from her bag a gift box slightly larger than the one that Hok Leong had given her. "For you. I bought it this morning too."

Hok Leong opened the present. It was a branded Swiss watch. "Titoni! That's really expensive, Chiu-yun! How can you buy something like this!"

"It's okay. I don't know what to buy for a guy. Do you like it?"

"I—LOVE—IT!" Hok Leong replied, deliberately extending

the pronunciation, "but it's too expensive."

"No, don't say that," Chiu-yun said. She turned serious. "I asked my mom about the flight. It's so-called Friday, but actually only ten minutes pass midnight. On Thursday morning I have to go with my mom to say goodbye to the uncle who took care of me when I first got here. It's winter in the UK now. I have to buy some stuff for daily use on Thursday afternoon."

"So we can't even meet up on the last day?"

"I don't think so."

Hok Leong kept silent.

"We still have today and tomorrow. We can play to our heart's content. Common! Time to get on stage!"

66

The last day.

As in the past, Hok Leong waited for Chiu-yun at <u>Katong Shopping Centre</u>. He wore the wristwatch she gave him. The first time Hok Leong waited for her there was at the start of secondary three, right after school re-opened. Hok Leong sat on the stone steps that led to the forecourt, the afternoon breeze caught Chiu-yun's sleek black hair as she approached him, blew it sensuously about her neck and shoulders….

A vehicle appeared, drew near, and slid to a stop. It was Chiu-yun's car. Hok Leong checked the windows. Chiu-yun sat in front. A pair of sunglasses shielded her eyes. She waved at him.

Hok Leong saw immediately that she was wearing the jade pendant that he had given to her. He got into the car, "When did you learn how to drive?"

Chiu-yun started the ignition and drove off. "When I was in Indonesia. From young I liked to steal the keys and drive around secretly."

"Is it safe?" Hok Leong asked.

Chiu-yun pondered the question for a while. "Are you afraid of death?" she asked.

"No."

Chiu-yun increased her speed. It looked like she was thinking about the topic. But then she said evenly, "Me neither! If I die I don't have to go to the UK. So good. No worries." Again she increased her speed.

Hok Leong didn't say anything. He didn't tell her to slow down. He hadn't expected that—here, now, on their last day— she would get so agitated. He really didn't know her well.

"Where do you want to go?" he asked.

Chiu-yun gave a laugh. "I don't know. Anywhere where there's a road. When the roads runs out, we turn back, find another one, continue going." She looked at Hok Leong.

Hok Leong agreed. "Great plan! Let's go. Let's die together!"

Chiu-yun laughed uproariously. The pendant around her neck swung and caught the light.

67

Hok Leong and Chiu-yun didn't die that day.

They went "touring" around Singapore the whole day, although they had no idea where they went. When something attractive or scenic caught their attention they stopped the car, disembarked, took snapshots with a camera. When they got hungry they went looking for food. When they got tired they found a secluded spot to rest and recharge. They returned to the familiar environs of Katong only late in the evening. Along the way, Chiu-yun had a request, "I want to take a picture of your father's stall. I've never been there."

Hok Leong nodded.

When they reached the food centre it was already ten o'clock. Most of the stalls were closed. Hok Leong's father didn't operate at night—he had closed shop a long time ago. Chiu-yun's arrival at the centre caught the attention of the stall operators who had yet to close for the day—they got curious. When Hok Leong and Chiu-yun reached the stall, Hok Leong switched on the overhead lights so that Chiu-yun could take a picture. Chiu-yun passed the camera to Hok Leong, picked up some implements and made like she was cooking a pot of noodles. Hok Leong took her photo. The other operators probably didn't know that their work place was worth a snapshot, he reckoned.

When they returned to the car, Chiu-yun had a new request. "I want to take a picture of your home."

Again Hok Leong took on the role of a tour guide, explaining the layout of his estate and giving directions. They drove to the car park near Hok Leong's apartment block. Chiu-yun shut the engine and got off. 'Where do you stay?" she asked.

Hok Leong pointed to one of the units. The lights were still on. After taking a shot of Hok Leong's apartment, Chiu-yun approached one of the ground-floor units. The door to the flat was open. She made like she was passing by, went up to the doorway, peered in, and quickly surveyed the place.

"It's small, isn't it?" Hok Leong said when she returned.

Chiu-yun's response surprised him. "It's great. Everyone close to one another. Feels very much like home."

Hok Leong didn't know what to say. Chiu-yun didn't elaborate. They returned to the car and stood next to it.

Hok Leong didn't want to speak. To speak now meant he had to say goodbye. He looked at Chiu-yun, a gentle smile playing across his features.

Chiu-yun spoke first, lowering her head, "Thank you, Hok Leong!" She very seldom called his name, "I really don't know how to say goodbye to you."

Hok Leong didn't respond. He didn't want to engage in that kind of talk.

Chiu-yun glanced at Hok Leong's face and again lowered her head. "I think we both know what the other person wants to say." She took a deep breathe, kept her head down. Her voice grew faint. "Please don't come to see me off tomorrow," she said.

Raising her head, she added "I will write to you."

Hok Leong didn't dare to look at her. He couldn't. He kept his eyes fixed on the jade pendant dangling at her neck.

Chiu-yun lowered her head again. She moved close to Hok Leong and hugged him tightly.

"Goodbye!" Chiu-yun said suddenly. Without looking back she turned swiftly, opened the car door and stepped in.

As she turned, Hok Leong noticed her glistening eyes, her tears. Before he could react, she had started the engine and drove off.

He stood rooted to the spot, didn't know what to do, kept looking stupidly at his watch.

10.27 p.m., it said.

10.27 p.m. The moment time stopped.

They didn't know then that they would never meet again

2

EILEEN

1

<u>Eileen</u>'s appearance was preordained.

Everyone needed good mates during the two-and-a-half years of compulsory military service, when everything "green" meant wretchedness and misery. Everyone needed buddies who were going through the same ordeal. But more than that, they needed someone of the opposite sex who could be a soul mate, someone to whom they could pour their hearts out.

At nineteen, the road that many guys took was that switch from school to army barracks, to undergo what Hok Leong's mother called the alchemy of "becoming an adult." This was also the first time that Hok Leong experienced how complex adult society could be, how black became white, how people stabbed each other in the back, how they happily sat on fences and cleaved to those in power. In barracks, one got to learn about different kinds of inhumanity and nastiness. When weekend arrived, naturally, sharing a meal with buddies became de facto group therapy, a chance to bellyache, complain, get things off their chest. Ah Hor and the boys had completed their compulsory service quite a while back, which is to say that they had reached their <u>R.O.D.</u> or "run out date." What they now faced was the inequity that society routinely meted out. Hok Leong's concerns no longer resonated with them, so when the weekends came around a new set of friends—Hok Leong's army buddies—began to take their place.

Eileen was the sister of John who was in the same platoon as Hok Leong. She was a year younger than them.

One night, Hok Leong went with Alan, Lee, and Michael to Black Street to eat clay pot rice. They waited over half an hour but their orders did not arrive. As they were leaving, someone called out to them. Surprisingly, it was John. His mother ran a shop selling refreshments in Malay street, diametrically across the road from them. With John acting as go-between, their food quickly arrived. John excused himself and went back across the road.

After dinner, nobody felt like visiting lady boy Zhen Zhen or some make-belief sexpot Cherie Chung. Although they seldom hung out with John, they felt that they should get some refreshments at his mom's place. When they got to the shop, they found that it was doing a roaring business. But there was only John's mother making the drinks while John and his younger sister waited on customers.

Hok Leong and the guys just wanted to get some refreshments. But they didn't have concrete plans that evening, so they fell to helping out at the outlet, becoming, as it were, temp-job workers. Maybe they did so because John's sister was there, for they felt that she was really cool. She was easy-going and good-humoured. They swiftly became friends. Without rancour or misgiving the four boys extended a helping hand. Soon John's sister seemed closer to them than even John. Hok Leong, who had grown up in a food centre, was in his element. At one shot getting and remembering the orders of four, five customers, relaying the instructions, bringing the drinks over, at times even joining John's mother in the kitchen to make the drinks—all this came naturally to him.

When they finished it was almost ten o'clock. John's sister had vanished some time back. John's mother wanted to buy them supper to express her gratitude. After that John had a logical extension to the evening: he suggested that they go to a <u>disco</u>.

The <u>disco</u> was located next to the Singapore river. In the cavernous hall, the music pumping, youngsters got a chance to let off steam, to get close to their partners, to console each other, and to scream and yell. <u>John</u>'s sister was there with two friends in tow. It wasn't clear when she got there. Everyone crowded around and made their formal introductions. <u>John</u>'s sister was called <u>Eileen</u>. Her friends were <u>Lisa</u> and <u>Susan</u>. Because they now had a mixed crowd, the atmosphere improved, the talk grew vibrant and energetic. Soon they were matching up and pairing off, playing the game that youngsters perennially play in a group situation, one they never get tired of.

Dancing was something that Hok Leong learned *after* he joined the army. He was lousy at it. <u>Lisa</u> didn't even dance with him, just coolly waved hello. He knew that she was there to dance and wasn't uncomfortable that she blanked him out.

Between <u>Eileen</u> and <u>Susan</u>, Hok Leong still got on better with the former. It was just as well that <u>Eileen</u> didn't find him unappealing, for he ended up dancing a few times with her. Extending conversation threads that had started in the coffee shop, their talk was lively but intermittent, often broken up as they joined up for a while, and then morphed into a new group. Did she come every weekend to help her mother? Not possible! she replied, and suddenly Hok Leong was reminded of the long-haired girl who used to help out at the food centre, the one he dubbed Black Gold. For a long time Hok Leong had not gone to the centre. Was Black Gold still there?

After a longish break, <u>Eileen</u> asked, where did he learn how to <u>take orders</u> and all that waitering stuff? He was good at it. Hok Leong didn't want to reveal too much. From the army, he replied. Then somebody joined them and they turned to a different subject. <u>Eileen</u> went off to dance. Hok Leong looked for someone else to talk to.

After quite a while they found themselves again seated next to each other. They fell to talking about their current situation. <u>Eileen</u> worked as a <u>clerk</u> in a company and was thinking about taking up <u>book-keeping</u>. But her real love was fashion design. Probably she would move in that direction. Furthermore, she moonlit as a model during weekends. It so happened she didn't have any assignments recently, so she had gone to help her mom at the shop. She came across as a go-getter, someone who faced the future with panache and spirit. Hok Leong said evenly that he was waiting for his exam results. If he did well he would go to university. If not, he would join the labour force.

After that someone else joined them. Again they switched to a different conversation topic.

They left the disco after midnight. The results of the earlier matchmaking game-play could now be broadcast. Hok Leong and <u>Eileen</u> formed a pair, <u>John</u> was with <u>Susan</u>, <u>Lee</u> was with <u>Lisa</u>. Why was it three girls and five boys? Everyone pondered the question but didn't voice it. It didn't seem important. Maybe it really wasn't important. Everybody came to play, to have a good time. If two persons got on well, they were "together." "Together" meant this evening, a specified period of time, or perhaps something stretching into the future? Nobody gave it much thought. After all, they were only nineteen.

They left separately. <u>Lisa</u> and <u>Susan</u> lived near <u>John</u> and <u>Eileen</u>, so the four of them shared a taxi. The remaining guys went back in a different vehicle. Time seemed to circle back to the start of the evening—actually it was the previous day's evening—to the point just before they decided on having clay pot rice for dinner.

2

Hok Leong had no inkling that an <u>Eileen</u> would appear at that point in his life.

Many a times, he considered that his life came to a standstill shortly after the secondary four year-end exams, on that whatever Wednesday night, at exactly 10.27 p.m. He felt this way even though the subsequent two years of senior high education brought plenty of changes large and small. During that period he gave tuition to a primary school kid. One day he taught the kid the story about the quiescent insect pupa that turned into a butterfly. Although a bit arty-farty, he felt that the story described him well. He wasn't sure whether he was now a butterfly or a moth or a housefly. But 10.27 p.m. on that Wednesday night was definitely the moment of his moulting and sloughing, for now he was returning deliberately to fly back and forth over the empty pupal casing, mourning ceaselessly that transformation and loss.

On Chiu-yun's last full-day in Singapore, Hok Leong went to his father's noodle stall first thing in the morning to give him a hand. Even his father was surprised. Hok Leong tried his best not to call Chiu-yun on the phone. But eventually he couldn't control himself and placed the call. It seemed nobody was around. No one picked up the phone. After lunch, Hok Leong went home to take a nap. His mother asked why. He said he felt ill. Less than half an hour later, complaining that he couldn't sleep, Hok Leong wanted to go out again. His mother asked why was he doing that if he was ill? Hok Leong ignored her and then, changing his mind, told her he was going to see a doctor.

When he got downstairs, he didn't know what to do. He went to the bus stop and took the first bus that came without looking at the number. The bus meandered around and finally reached the seaside. Hok Leong didn't know why he was there. He got off the bus, found a phone and tried to reach Ah Hor and the others. They weren't contactable. Hok Leong took another bus heading towards Katong. He got off at the <u>Katong Shopping Centre</u> stop and sat for a while on the stone steps leading to the centre forecourt. It didn't feel right, he realised. He glanced at the wristwatch that Chiu-yun had given him, then went to a cinema and caught a movie. He fell asleep in the auditorium. He hadn't slept well the previous night. Or maybe he hadn't slept at all.

When he stepped out of the theatre it was getting dark. Again Hok Leong placed a call to Chiu-yun's house. As before no one came to the phone. Hok Leong decided to go home. When he stepped into the flat his mother asked why he came back so late. He ignored her and went to sleep. The moment his head touched the pillow he dozed off. When he got up it was past nine o'clock. Hok Leong asked his mother whether anyone had tried to reach him. She said no—no one. Did he want to take his dinner? He had already eaten, he said.

Chiu-yun probably wouldn't try to contact him, he thought despondently. He regretted listening to her. He didn't even know her flight number and details. He went to the balcony of his flat and stared into the night sky. The jets taking off from nearby Paya Lebar Airport all flew directly over his block. Each time a plane went by, he mouthed a silent goodbye. He wanted to say farewell, but he didn't know which plane was taking Chiu-yun away.

After noon the next day he received a call from Chiu-yun. She was calling from one of the London airports. The flight had taken twelve hours. The time there was six something in the morning. It was bitterly cold. Hok Leong didn't have much to say to Chiu-yun. Listening to her was enough. He was satisfied. They agreed to speak again the next day in the afternoon.

The next day, Chiu-yun again placed a long-distance call to Hok Leong. Again, Hok Leong tried not to talk too much. He wanted to hear her speak and laugh. After a long chat, when they finally got tired, Chiu-yun said she wouldn't call again. They should communicate by air mail and she'd write the first letter. She gave him her telephone number so that he could call her whenever he wanted.

A week later, Hok Leong received the first missive from Chui-yun, a three-page communique describing in detail all that was happening to her in London. The paper she used was pink in colour, each sheet had an imprint of an angel playfully shooting an arrow at an apple held in the mouth of a snake. Hok Leong felt agitated and happy at the same time. Specially for this he too went out and bought a printed letter pad. His was blue, with each sheet sporting an imprint of a butterfly foraging for honey under a blue sky. He wrote Chiu-yun a two-and-a-half page letter in reply, explaining in the process the figurative meaning that he attached to the butterfly.

After that, their weeks were dominated by the back and forth ferrying of angels and butterflies, a period that included the announcement of their secondary-four examination results. Although he didn't do well in English, Hok Leong's scores were good enough to get him into senior high. He left his institution and joined a new school with a reputation for academic rigour. Yes, he studied in a good school.

Soon after that his family moved to a new flat. They left behind a Lim-Yew-Hock era apartment block that was older than Hok Leong, a place that Chiu-yun had visited on her last day with him, and moved into a four-room flat in one of the new towns. Passing by his old residence one day, Hok Leong was shocked to find that they had demolished the block and levelled the ground. He felt straightaway that all of his past was buried, together with his memories, his early teen years now a blank sheet of paper. He also stopped going to the food centre. Although still doing his military service, elder brother was preparing to take over the reins of the food stall from father. Busy with his studies, Hok Leong no longer went there to give a hand. All this occurred in a short span of a little over a year. As a result, he often felt that his life had begun anew at seventeen. When he entered and left the new flat, he sometimes forgot who he was.

London-based Chiu-yun continued to send over her angel missives, telling him that she was studying accountancy, and she had to take English classes as well, to re-take the subject. When she checked her dictionary on snow-bound nights, she recalled the bright sunny days that she had experienced in Singapore. How she hoped that Hok Leong could be by her side, to accompany her and to make less onerous the dark wintery nights.

Spring arrived. Chiu-yun despatched the good news, describing the first darling buds of the season, the ambience as the days grew warmer. She was busy but happy. When the summer holidays started she said that she wouldn't be coming back. Her father wanted her to see England, to travel around a bit.

The news surprised him. He placed a call to Chiu-yun in London but no one answered the phone. Postcards from different parts of England started to appear in Hok Leong's mailbox. After the school re-opened, Chiu-yun was extremely busy with her studies. Her letters grew less frequent, their content more sparse and laconic. Hok Leong had a premonition, a sense of foreboding. Then she said that she wouldn't be coming back for the winter holidays as well. She wanted to travel to the continent with her school friends.

After long deliberation, Hok Leong decided that he would stop writing. He wouldn't call her as well. He felt that they were acting out a common enough episode from the play titled "standard occurrences of an overseas student's life." Like the year earlier when Chiu-yun's father wanted her to study in England, he didn't know what to do. All this while Hok Leong kept himself apart from his senior high classmates, lived only in the eco-sphere formed by angel and butterfly. What happened in class didn't concern him. He poured his energy into his studies and hung out with Ah Hor and the guys.

Postcards from different parts of Europe started to appear in Hok Leong's mailbox, but he received them without pleasure. Instead he went traveling with Ah Hor and the guys. They went to Genting Highlands and Cameron Highlands in Malaysia. Yes, he too went travelling.

A pile of cards stamped with the postmarks of different countries greeted Hok Leong when he returned from Malaysia. He gritted his teeth and controlled himself. He went out with Ah Hor and the guys. A new letter arrived from Chiu-yun. She must have returned from her travels. He appraised the thin, meagre envelop. He didn't open it because he didn't want to be hurt. Chiu-yun didn't call him. Then one day, he wasn't sure when, the angels stopped coming. By then the new school year had started. On the day that he realised what had happened, he didn't go to school. He went to the lobby coffee shop in Sea View hotel and spent half a day there. He sat there awash in pain, a pain that he had intuited the previous summer.

That the small nothing-doing chrysalis could actually turn into a butterfly was all down to Chiu-yun. Hok Leong didn't bear her any grudges, didn't blame her. In fact, the dominant emotion was one of gratitude. The butterfly knew that one day it would have to moult and leave the cocoon. It chose to leave earlier although the pain was great.

Hok Leong tried hard not to think about anything. In a year's time he would be entering the army. What Ah Hor and guys said rang true—everything had to wait till *after* he completed his military service.

3

Soon after the pre-university exams concluded, Hok Leong enrolled in the army.

He remembered well the feeling that came over him at

CMPB* as he boarded the three-tonner truck. He didn't know where they were headed, how his days would pan out. He had never been so unsure or uncertain. The dressing-down began the moment the new recruits boarded the truck. Along the way, Hok Leong kept glancing out of the vehicle, trying to work out where they were going. The journey took quite a while. As they deboarded the truck, the dressing-down continued. It seemed the new recruits could do nothing right. The ones delivering the reprimands seemed a bit crazed, as if they wanted everyone to be wrong all the time. Hok Leong wasn't afraid of the training, he could take it. But he hated the unequal status, the inequity, as well as the abuse that came with it.

Ah Hor and the guys came to see him off. Laughing uproariously, they ran their hands over his buzz cut, commented on how cute he looked without his hair. They had started their military service earlier and had already completed their stint. The other conscripts had girlfriends who came to see them off. Hok Leong was the only one without a partner. Someone even thought that he didn't like girls.

After they got to know each other well, the weekends became the focal point of their lives. Among the draftees was a Girl Supply Officer who could be trusted to pep up their outings. Together in a group they went to the disco, they smoked, drank, and danced. Everything that happened in camp, everything unfair and perverse was consigned to the dazzling lights and clamorous music. Occasionally they fought. Nothing could beat fisticuffs as a way to let off steam. Actually there was something. Some of the guys went whoring. But nothing could beat unfairness and unreasonableness as a way to instigate fights. But after fighting, they quickly made up and again went together in a group to the disco.

---

* CMPB—Central Manpower Base, the main despatch centre for enlistees.

The exam results were announced. Although his English scores were poor, Hok Leong's results were good enough to get him to university. Father and Mother were overjoyed. Mother even said: "If it gets you through university, we don't mind a few more years of flogging our won ton noodles." Hok Leong had always thought that he would get to savour this moment with Chiu-yun. He hadn't expected that, instead, it would be with his parents.

Father seldom went to the food centre nowadays. After completing his military service, elder brother had taken over the noodle business. Realising that he hadn't gone there for a long time, Hok Leong decided to visit the food centre to take a look. The stall rented by Black Gold's father was now a *zhuchao* outlet selling home-style Chinese dishes. Like Hok Leong's brother, Colour Palette had taken over her mother's business and now ran the place herself. He went to her stall and ordered a nonya dumpling, a piece of taro cake, and a rice-noodle roll. Colour Palette saw that it was him and gave him a smile. Hok Leong returned her smile. They were now "adults." She had grown up. There wasn't a lot of make-up on her face, so much so that she almost didn't fit her given nickname. Hok Leong felt that meeting an "old friend" like this was very satisfying, very meaningful. They hadn't seen each other for a long time. Meeting up again, everyone looked much better, more mature and worldly wise. Everyone had a story to tell, had experienced ups and downs, but still didn't know what the future held.

Hok Leong thought about his former companions. What had happened to Dog Shit, he wondered. His previous flat and the apartments around it had all been torn down. Only two blocks of one-room apartments housing elderly single folks were left standing. Dog Shit, Ah Mei, Opium Addict, Junior Brother—where could they have moved to? Growing up seemed to involve hanging out with a particular group of people, then the environment undergoing a drastic change, everybody splitting up, then hanging out with a *different* group of people. This was repeatedly performed and enacted.

4

The next instalment of the performance took place in military barracks. After three months of basic military training, a period of suffering came to an end. Although it was only three months, the hardships that they endured had forged something significant, something worth remembering.

Hok Leong was sent to an army engineer unit, an extremely gruelling posting. He discovered that, despite the overall emphasis on standardisation, he was different from other people. The colour of the name tag above his left uniform shirt-front pocket was different. Most of the others' were deep green in colour. Some had green mixed with a small strip of orange or red. But Hok Leong's name tag was uniformly orange in colour. Somehow everybody knew the meanings attached to the hues and called Hok Leong a <u>Chinese helicopter</u>. Later on Hok Leong found out what they meant. Deep green meant you spoke English as your main language. Orange was standard Mandarin Chinese. Red meant you spoke mainly Hokkien dialect, the hallmark of the so-called Hokkien squaddie. An extra colour strip meant you could speak a little of the language designated by that colour.

The draftees who enlisted around the same time as Hok Leong were mainly senior high school graduates. There weren't any Hokkien squaddies among them. A number of the conscripts were Chinese speakers. They made up a small minority. Hok Leong was one of them. He didn't know why everyone called him <u>Chinese helicopter</u>. Much later, one of the older orange-coded soldiers explained to Hok Leong the origin of the term. It seemed that, once upon a time, a graduate of a Chinese school had tried to pronounce the words <u>Chinese</u>

educated in English but got it all wrong. The words came out as Chinese helicopter, which henceforth became a term to designate Chinese-educated enlistees.

Hok Leong didn't like such banter or mockery. He had a sense of humour, he told himself. It was just that the story sounded apocryphal. The words "educated" and "helicopter" were too different. More importantly, Hok Leong had a poor command of English. He felt like the mockery was directed at him. Responding to jeers like this, he could only say, self-mockingly, "Yes, made in 1960."

A made-in-1960 helicopter, that is.

John and the rest didn't use the phrase Chinese helicopter when they spoke to him. John was fortunate. He was one of those who sported a small red strip on his name tag. He could speak Hokkien, but what came out was mainly swear words. Alan, Lee, and Michael all used deep green name tags. Alan was, in addition, a devout Christian. What surprised Hok Leong was that, among them all, he got on best with Alan. He reckoned that this had to with Alan's religious beliefs. He wasn't obsequious when he dealt with higher-ups. He wasn't overbearing when he dealt with his peers and those below him. He never sabo other people, meaning that he didn't try to pass the buck or give them trouble. And he never tekan others as well, tekan meaning to oppress or to bully. All in all, Hok Leong felt that Alan was a well-brought-up young person. Nevertheless, for someone like him to survive in the army wasn't easy. From the training that they had gone through, the others could appreciate his qualities and his toughness. They all respected him, Hok Leong included. Michael in contrast was an expert bull-shitter, well suited to a job in sales. Slowly they started to avoid him. They stopped asking him to join them on their weekend jaunts. Lee was a bit like his name, nondescript and unremarkable. It was easy for the others to forget him. Lee's strongest suit was that he didn't pressurise other people, didn't cause offense. <u>John</u> in turn was the kind to help you out when your clay pot rice order got overlooked in a side-street eatery—he would make a great grassroots leader. Hok Leong didn't know if he was impressionistic, or whether his new mates had particularly arresting personalities. But it seemed like his neighbourhood and secondary school friends had less clear-cut, discrete attributes, they seemed to make less of an impression on him. Furthermore, the two years of pre-university schooling was, for him, a period of convalescence. He didn't even get around to learning the names of all his classmates. He discovered that the tone and quality of the interactions with them was different from his dealings in the past with his neighbourhood and secondary school friends. He couldn't handle so much change, so he had kept himself apart and didn't let anyone in.

5

<u>John</u> joining their social circle helped to solve a problem that they faced—discounting for the moment the problem of <u>Michael</u>—which was where to go for meals on weekends. The week after their outing at the disco, they decided to visit Black Street again. They confirmed their decision in <u>camp</u>, then everyone went home first before joining up at the locale.

Like the previous week, <u>John</u> helped them to order chicken rice and then returned across the street. Again they went to help out at the drinks shop after finishing their dinner. <u>Lisa</u> and <u>Sharon</u> were there as well. Without anyone saying anything, everyone understood that they had formed a kind of unit; they would seek their diversions together.

Hok Leong noticed that <u>Eileen</u> was there. He tried to get her attention but she was busy. When she turned around he waved at her again. She gave a surprising response. "I actually saw you earlier," she said. "Hi!" she added. In reply, Hok Leong made like he was fainting.

With seven youngsters crowding around the place, the outlet became lively and vibrant. Nobody grumbled about having to work on a weekend. They shared a common objective which was more than just dancing in a disco.

The work at the shop had given them a chance to observe each other, to grow close. When they went to the disco their interaction was artless and relaxed. Nobody tried to change the pairings formed naturally, as it were, the previous week. And this also gave Hok Leong a chance to see <u>Alan</u> in a new light. Both at the drinks shop and at the disco, <u>Alan</u> didn't seem to mind being the odd one out among the paired-up youngsters. In response, everyone tried to include him, to ignore the proverbial three-is-a-crowd situation.

Hok Leong and <u>Eileen</u> appeared to be long-time friends, but were in fact doing a kind of try-out. Both tried hard to be amiable and congenial, to accommodate each other. Hok Leong liked that <u>Eileen</u> was generous and open-hearted. He liked her model looks and figure. In high-heels she was almost as tall as him. Modelling seemed like an ideal job for her, although Hok Leong didn't know what exactly it entailed. She should chase her dreams, he told her. When <u>Eileen</u> asked about *his* future plans, however, he was dumbfounded. "University" was his answer, making him sound like a goody two-shoe—how strange!

"What about <u>John</u>?" He tried to change the subject.

"Him! He only wants to do his music thing!" <u>Eileen</u> said in a disapproving tone of voice. "I told him if you continue like this, you'll starve to death."

Hok Leong didn't know what "doing his music thing" referred to. "I'm sure he'll be fine," he replied. He wanted to say that it was better than tending to customers in a coffee shop but decided to keep that opinion to himself.

"Guys don't seem to care about their future," <u>Eileen</u> suddenly said. Although talking ostensibly about her brother, it looked like she was directing her words at him, telling him that she didn't like his vague response.

Hok Leong tried to explain, "Guys have to take a longer road before they can think about their future. National service is like a debt that you have to pay. And then if you want a university degree, that's another four years of schooling. We can only approach things step by step like this, there's no choice. You can't predict what will happen in five, six years. Nobody knows what will happen."

Eileen seemed to agree with him but also looked frustrated. She seemed to understand the matter, but it also looked like she didn't want to give herself any trouble.

"Come! Let's Dance!" she said flamboyantly.

6

On the third weekend, they again spent the first "half" at the coffee shop, but for the second "half" John suddenly said that Susan and him wouldn't be coming to the disco. The rest didn't know what to do. Less one pair like this, Alan's odd-man-out situation seemed even more anomalous. Eventually, Hok Leong suggested that they go to the café restaurant at Shangri-La Hotel.

Less and less of them showed up in subsequent weeks. First it was Alan. The others were already an item. Why should he come along? Hok Leong felt sorry that he had been left out. It didn't seem honourable that good mates should split up because of dating, because of women. Everyone came out to shoot the breeze, to get some diversion, to have fun. Why was he cast out? Then Lee and Lisa also excused themselves. In a little over three months, the vibrant coffee shop set up had changed out of recognition. Now it was only Hok Leong coming over to give a hand. Hok Leong wondered what John's mother made of the situation.

Eileen sometimes asked him, "Why are you still coming over on weekends?"

"To see you, of course!" Hok Leong replied.

After the coffee shop closed for the night, they often went ambling hand in hand to the "seaside." Back then, the land reclaim work at Stamford Canal had just started. Nobody expected that in ten, twenty years' time the place would be so transformed. They also liked to stroll up and down Elizabeth walk, to watch the waves and listen to the breeze. When they got tired, they rested on the forecourt of Parliament House. They tilted their heads to stare at the sky. They pondered the star-lit firmament. The surf, sea breeze, stars—yes, these things come with love when you're nineteen.

Under a moonlit sky, Hok Leong kissed Eileen. That night they climbed over the fence surrounding the land reclaim site. Lying on the newly-made acreage, Hok Leong stroked Eileen's long straight hair. He heard his heart hammering crazily. He brought his face close to her's and sought her lips. Actually the details at this point are hazy. Naturally, the narrative needs to be recounted, but a lot is speculative and imagined. He knew there was moonlight. On the way home, he saw the moon. The crazy heartbeat was, for sure, a definite thing. He was so nervous that his hands shook. He felt blood coursing in his head. As to how exactly or precisely he kissed Eileen, he couldn't say. All he remembered was that, after everything, she rested her head on his shoulders. Circa 1979, on some piece of just-reclaimed land that was later to become Marina City, he held her in a deep embrace.

7

The weekend after that Hok Leong and Eileen didn't watch the moon together.

Normally, Hok Leong didn't go home when he left camp. Because he had to return before midnight, he usually went out with <u>John</u> and the boys. After <u>booking out</u>, they'd find some place for a meal and drink and then later on hurry back to camp. Occasionally he called home to ask if everything was fine. Usually there was nothing, so he was surprised when his brother said that Ah Hor was looking for him.

Ah Hor said that he would be leaving Singapore the following week. He was signing up to work on a vessel. Was Hok Leong free to meet up next week? To see him and the old gang? Hok Leong replied that he was free, after which he gave <u>Eileen</u> a call. Fortunately <u>Eileen</u> had a modelling gig that weekend. They agreed that Hok Leong would pick her up at the hotel after she finished her show.

When he met up with the guys, Ah Hor revealed that he had signed up to work as a laundry man on a cruise vessel. The ship would ply the Caribbean sea. Since he couldn't find a job that suited his taste in Singapore, he might as well do a bit of traveling while he was young, while he could handle it, he said. Tee Soon had asked Ah Hor to keep a watch out, to see if there were any vacancies on the vessel. He too wanted to go walkabout, to see the world. Ying-jun didn't fancy that kind of life. Ying-jun's brother had a friend working in Saudi Arabia. With the friend acting as intermediary, Ying-jun had applied to work there too. But he didn't know whether he would be selected. It seemed like everyone was planning to leave the country. Hok Leong felt despondent.

Ah Hor said that, among the four of them, Hok Leong's lot was the best. He had university waiting for him with open arms, or, rather, open doors. He wasn't forced out of the country like them. Hok Leong gave a short bitter laugh. He too wanted to travel while young, he said, to see and savour the world. Unfortunately the university wouldn't keep its doors open very long.

They had stepped out of the same secondary school only a few years back. It was a pity that things hadn't gone smoothly, that the future now seemed so fraught and uncertain. Hok Leong sat drinking with Ah Hor and the guys, finishing jug after jug of beer. He thought it was a normal get-together. But under the circumstances, he couldn't leave. He didn't want to leave. But now the appointment with Eileen loomed large in his mind and he began to get worried. When nine-thirty arrived he knew that he wouldn't be able to fetch Eileen at the hotel on time. He placed a call to the coffee shop. Eileen's mother answered the phone. If Eileen called home, Hok Leong said, tell her he couldn't fetch her at the hotel. She should go home first and he would join her later. Hok Leong hoped that Eileen would call home when he didn't show up at her show venue.

By the time he got back to the table, his sense of despondency had lifted, but a feeling of unease soon replaced it. His friends didn't notice the change. He hung on valiantly, determined to stick it out. By the time they said goodbye it was nearing midnight.

Hok Leong quickly took a taxi to the coffee shop. The shop was closed but the door wasn't locked. A solitary light was on. Hok Leong knocked gently on the metal door. Somebody came downstairs and opened it. It was Eileen. She was waiting for him. Hok Leong apologised for his tardiness. He tried to pull her into an embrace but she pushed him away.

She took a seat at a table. "My brother hasn't come home yet," she said evenly.

Hok Leong sat down next to her and tried to explain the situation. "These guys are my former classmates. One of them is leaving the country next week to work overseas. Another wants to do the same. The third just applied for a job in Saudi Arabia. I had to stay."

Eileen aimed a disparaging glance at Hok Leong. "How come your excuse sounds like the one my brother gives when he comes home late?"

Hok Leong explained further. "These guys have been my close friends since secondary school. We went <u>camping</u> once by the seaside. We went for a swim. We didn't notice that an oil tanker was bearing down on us. By the time we did, it was too late. The giant waves were already upon us. We could easily have died. The only thing that saved us was that we held on tightly to each other–."

<u>Eileen</u> interrupted Hok Leong. "Four guys hugging each other?"

"But of course! Who says you can't?" Hok Leong reached out again to embrace her.

"My mom is upstairs!" <u>Eileen</u> said hurriedly. Hok Leong didn't care.

"I have another modelling gig next weekend. Can you come to see me?"

Hok Leong nodded. He lowered his head to kiss <u>Eileen</u> but she avoided his lips.

"My mom hasn't slept yet!"

Hok Leong could not care less.

8

Hok Leong sat languidly on the settee, bored out of his mind. For over an hour he had acted the part. Occasionally, he had even smiled amiably at his companions.

After the runway performance, he had accompanied <u>Eileen</u> and her friends to a <u>disco</u>, he taking up the role of her "boyfriend" while she laughed and partied with her mates. The outing had allowed him to see another side of her, a tomboy aspect worlds apart from the impression she gave on the runway. If this side of her surprised him, the earlier <u>Eileen</u> had left him gobsmacked. She was an entirely different person, tall, sexy, but also wraithlike and insubstantial. He didn't know that she had such a range to her personality but was happy to accept the many-sidedness of his girlfriend.

Despite being surrounded by women, Hok Leong didn't like the situation he found himself in. He also didn't like the men who worked with the women. He didn't know precisely what they did, but he felt discomforted by their girliness as they interacted with the models. Still, Hok Leong didn't voice his thoughts. He had overheard someone saying earlier, "<u>Eileen</u>'s boyfriend is great. He's fine sitting quietly by himself."

Hok Leong laughed inwardly at the tribute. Since when did he become a stage prop for <u>Eileen</u> to put on display? She probably hadn't expected that, he thought, although he had heard one of the girls gossiping earlier to another model, talking about them. In a voice filled with nastiness, she had said, "<u>Show off</u>. I'm sure they won't last." The girl who said that hadn't come to the <u>disco</u> with them.

Hok Leong felt terrible when he heard the girl. "Won't last" was obviously directed at him, the implication being that, while <u>Eileen</u> thought she had found a good catch, he on his part was only playing with her. Hok Leong wanted <u>Eileen</u> to know that he wasn't "playing" with her. So he sat and waited patiently for over an hour, bored out of his mind.

But to put it that way was also an exaggeration, for instead of being bored witless he had actually spent the time thinking about Dog Shit and the others. Before leaving the flat that evening his brother had asked him if he had seen the papers. Dog Shit was dead—he had been beaten to death in a fight. In a state of shock Hok Leong went to check the newspapers. It only said that Dog Shit was involved in a staring incident. Apart from that there were no other details. Of his five close childhood companions, two were dead. Red Dragon, and now Dog Shit. Two others—Junior Brother and Opium Addict— had joined the triads, which meant that they could go anytime as well. Only Ah Mei hadn't gone down that road. He wondered how the three were doing. Were they all right? Hok Leong also thought about his close secondary school friends. Ah Hor had chosen a seafarer's life. He didn't know what awaited Tee Soon and Ying-jun. If they left the country as well, he would have only <u>Eileen</u> and his close friends in the army.

In all likelihood, he thought, <u>Eileen</u> wouldn't turn out to be a second Chiu-yun.

9

I started a joke, which started the whole world crying.
Oh! But I didn't see that the joke was on me...oh no...
And I started to cry, which started the whole world laughing.
Oh! If I'd only seen that the joke was on me....

The words nearly made him break into tears. After Chiu-yun left he had practically stopped listening to music. Nothing, no tune or ditty, left an impression on him or made him feel anything. He certainly didn't know that the <u>Bee Gees</u> had a song like this.

I started a joke. Instead of laughing the world began to cry. But more hilarious than that, or perhaps something worth bawling over, was that the joke was on me. What kind of logic was that? Yet each sentence carved a rut into Hok Leong's heart, each sentence made him think of the vagaries of his nineteen years' existence, of Chiu-yun's coming and going, of the postcard sent by Ah Hor—it all made him downcast and morose. Ah Hor's postcard had a postmark from the Caribbean Sea, with a toponym that Hok Leong didn't recognise. Ah Hor confessed that life on the vessel was tough. He worked over twelve hours a day. At night, he practically keeled over in a faint when he went to bed.

<u>John</u> said that Hok Leong sang well. Hok Leong replied facetiously, "<u>I started a joke</u>....

John and the others had started a band, probably what Eileen meant when she said that you could "starve to death" if you took it up seriously. Everyone liked pop music. It was a great chance to get everyone together. John arranged for them to meet on Sunday at a studio that you could rent at Peace Centre. After the two-hour jamming or, rather, mutual bombardment session they would return to camp. They had already done this a few times. This was the first time that Hok Leong joined them. Hok Leong couldn't play any instrument so he was put in charge of vocals.

They discussed the name that they wanted to give to the group. "Let's call it The Joke!" Hok Leong said immediately. John, Lee and Michael liked the name, it had a whiff of the avant-garde about it. With furrowed brows, Alan said, "that sounds weird," so they left it at that.

On the way back to camp, Alan said, "Maybe Joy is a better alternative?" It took them a while to figure out that Alan was talking about the band. They liked the name. It matched everyone's raison d'être, which was after all to spread merriment. Hok Leong didn't expect that, with a simple change of lettering, Alan could turn a meaningless jest into something pleasurable. He cracked a joke in response. "Looks like we'll have to convert and become true believers!"

Everyone laughed. John said to Alan, "You're only helpful when it comes to us. In camp, your magic doesn't work."

They started talking about a tattooed-all-over Hokkien soldier nicknamed "Three Stripes" in Alan's platoon, the moniker suggesting that he was an NCO rather than an ordinary squaddie.

Lee said, "Alan has authority above ground, officially, but Three Stripes has authority below ground, as they say."

Hok Leong's interest was piqued. "I'd like to meet this guy," he said coolly.

10

After lunch that day they went to <u>Alan</u>'s dormitory and hung around the area.

<u>Alan</u> sat at the table waiting for Three Stripes, who presently arrived. Hok Leong felt a stab of irritation when he saw the guy. He didn't like the large spider tattoo on his arm. It was too gaudy. As an indication of personal creed, it suggested wickedness, something that a bully might wear with pride. The way he ambled about the room also irritated Hok Leong. His walk conveyed contempt for everyone around him. Someone like that needed a good hiding; Hok Leong would happily volunteer his services.

Three Stripes sat down languorously in front of <u>Alan</u>, looking as though he owned the room. He addressed <u>Alan</u> in Chinese Hokkien dialect. "What's up <u>Sergeant</u>! Anything new?" His tone was exaggerated and supercilious.

<u>Alan</u> said in a sober tone of voice. "Somebody <u>complained</u> about you—said you tried to bully him." His speech was a hybrid of English, Mandarin and Hokkien.

Three Stripes replied immediately. "<u>Sergeant</u>! Food can be plentiful but words must be judicious. Why would I bully anyone? You got the wrong guy!"

<u>Alan</u> said calmly in English. "No. It's you."

"You've made a mistake <u>Sergeant</u>! Do you have any evidence!" Three Stripes parred and parried.

"Yes, there's a witness."

"Then get him out! Let's talk about it. It's just a misunderstanding!"

Hok Leong was afraid that <u>Alan</u> would ask the poor foot soldier involved to come and stand his ground. More than that, he was afraid that <u>Alan</u> would lose control of the situation. "I'm the witness," he said in English, and stepped forward.

For a moment, <u>Alan</u> and Three Stripes looked dazed. Hok

Leong strode to the table and took a seat. The three of them formed the apex points of a triangle. Hok Leong continued: "We won't arrange a confrontation between you two because we want to protect the other party. But we'll compare your version of events with the complainant's version of events."

Hok Leong gave <u>Alan</u> a glance and picked up a file that laid on the table. He opened the file and surveyed its contents. "Somebody complained that you tried to force him to eat raw chilly."

"No way!" Three Stripes cried. <u>Alan</u> didn't seem to understand the situation but quickly resumed a serious demeanour.

Hok Leong addressed Three Stripes in Hokkien. "Hey towkay boss! This is an army camp, not a coffee shop." He returned to the topic at hand. "You tried to make him eat chilly because he refused to switch his <u>duty</u> date with yours. It's as simple as that."

"No such thing!" Three Stripes shouted.

"No such thing?" Hok Leong said harshly. "Then why would anybody <u>complain</u> about you?"

Three Stripes started to get anxious. He gave a glance at <u>Alan</u>.

"Answer him," <u>Alan</u> said after a moment's hesitation.

Three Stripes had enough of the fraudulent accusation. He noticed the letter opener lying on the table and reached for it. Hok Leong was faster. He pushed Three Stripes' arm away and in the same move grabbed the fountain pen inside the pen holder on the counter-top. The two men reared up from the table, grappling and pushing. The table and several of the chairs toppled over, together with the waste paper basket. Hok Leong forced Three Stripes to the side of the room, up against the wall. Attracted by the commotion, <u>John</u>, <u>Lee</u>, and <u>Michael</u> all came over.

Hok Leong looked sideways, gestured to his friends that he

was okay. Adjusting the pen in his hand, he drew an "X" on Three Stripes' throat. He used his bodyweight to keep Three Stripes pinned to the wall. "Do you believe that if I push this pen in here I can make you stop breathing?" he said coldly.

Three Stripes stared at Hok Leong, his face full of hatred.

Hok Leong contemplated his next move. He took in the name tag on Three Stripes' uniform, pinned just above the front shirt pocket. "For God's sake, don't dishonour your name tag. My tag is also orange in colour," he said softly in Hokkien.

Three Stripes didn't respond. His tag was red with an orange border.

Convinced that Three Stripes would no longer resist, Hok Leong let him go.

John strode to the toppled-over table and picked up the letter opener lying next to it. "It's clear what happened," he declared. "You attacked Sergeant Chan. We have witnesses and we have the evidence."

Nobody said anything. They didn't have a script that described the next move. Alan had merely said that he had received another complaint about Three Stripes, that he had again bullied one of the privates. Everyone gathered round to watch the drama. They didn't expect that things would get this way.

Throughout the episode, Alan had maintained a grave demeanour. Eventually he said to Three Stripes, "Go apologise to the person you tried to intimidate."

Three Stripes turned and went away.

Everybody heaved a sigh of relief.

11.

"It's a necessary evil."

Late that evening, Alan asked Hok Leong to come out for a

beer. They started talking about the incident in the afternoon. <u>Alan</u> felt that the phrase accurately described the run-in with Three Stripes.

Hok Leong gave a wry smile and replied in Mandarin, "Use violence to control violence?"

"I don't believe in that," <u>Alan</u> said. "But more than that I don't believe that force can settle disputes. That way lies hate and more hate."

Hok Leong continued to smile gently. He took a sip from the can in his hand.

"But sometimes violence can solve a problem quickly and conveniently," <u>Alan</u> continued. "Especially in an institution like this."

Hok Leong thought that <u>Alan</u> was making a confession of some kind. He cracked a joke in response, "So you're grateful for my intervention?"

<u>Alan</u> didn't confirm or deny his words. He quietly drank his beer.

Oddly enough, Hok Leong now felt a stirring within himself. "Actually, I do regret it."

<u>Alan</u> gave him a look of incomprehension.

"I hope you don't think that I'm the type that likes to fight. It's just that this is not the first time I've brawled like this. I did use violence to solve problems in my younger days. I thought as I grew older that would stop."

"Did you consider that Three Stripes might take revenge on you?" <u>Alan</u> asked.

"Yes and no. But whether it's yes or no, I have to take responsibility for my actions." After a long silence he gave a sigh. "Character! You can't change character!" he lamented.

<u>Alan</u> didn't agree. "No, I read that as someone bravely doing the right thing. To tell the truth, in the heat of the moment I really didn't know what to do."

"Do you know why he left it at that?"

"Yeah, I was going to ask."

Hok Leong kept silent for a while. "I told him that, like him, I also have orange in my name tag."

<u>Alan</u> stared impassively at his drink. "I don't have a colour."

Hok Leong corrected him. "Yours is green. Deep green." He paused for a moment. "But recently your green hue has faded a bit."

"What happens if you mix green and orange?"

"I don't have any training in fine arts. But I think it's yellow. Orange is red plus yellow. Green is blue plus yellow, I think."

"So, in actuality, there's no orange, and there's no green as well?"

"Oh course there is! I'm orange. You're green."

"<u>Eileen</u> is also a greenie."

Hok Leong hesitated for a moment. He looked away and changed the subject. "<u>Anyway</u>, both your parents are lawyers. You're going to be a lawyer as well. If I get into trouble in the future, will you represent me—give me a good price?"

<u>Alan</u> didn't answer the question posed at him. "People change. I believe the next time we discuss this issue, things will be different. Maybe our character or our temperament will have changed drastically. We may even get nostalgic about the current situation. You never know."

Hok Leong continued to drink his beer. He mulled over what <u>Alan</u> had said.

12.

"You fought with someone in <u>camp</u>?"

The moment she saw Hok Leong, <u>Eileen</u> asked about the run-in with Three Stripes. Damn!

They had agreed to keep the matter to themselves. But <u>John</u> had still gone and told his sister.

Hok Leong remained noncommittal. "What if something

happens to you?" <u>Eileen</u> added. "Won't he be aggrieved about the incident? Sooner or later he'll come after you, right? Or maybe he'll come after me. Then what?"

Hok Leong didn't say anything. As he watched her runway performance later that evening a tinge of regret came over him. Why didn't he think about <u>Eileen</u>? Three Stripes could easily go after her. He hoped Three Stripes knew the underworld code, knew that a man of the world kept women out of it. Naturally he thought about Red Dragon and Dog Shit as well. Would he end up like them one day?

As usual, he joined <u>Eileen</u> and her co-workers when they went to the disco after the performance. As he watched them dance and chat, Hok Leong grew bored. It really wasn't his scene. As the group parted for the night, he asked Eileen, "Can we go out by ourselves the next time you have a performance? We don't join them?"

"I want to be a full-time <u>model</u>," <u>Eileen</u> said simply.

"In the future, can I come fetch you after you've finished dancing?" Hok Leong pleaded.

"It's entirely up to you!"

Hok Leong tried to placate her. "Shall we catch a movie tomorrow? I'll tell <u>John</u> and the boys I won't join them for the jamming session?"

"You should have stopped that music thing a long time ago."

"Shall we come out earlier for lunch and then catch a movie? I can look for them later at <u>Peace Centre</u>?"

<u>Eileen</u> had her own proposal. "How about we meet on normal weekdays as well—when you get a night's out? We don't have to wait till weekends, right? My brother goes out with <u>Susan</u> on weekdays. That way we don't have to rush so much on Saturday, and I can go in peace for my performance?"

Hok Leong liked the idea. Everyone got something out of it.

13

On Sunday Hok Leong went with <u>Eileen</u> to watch a movie. They even made out in the cinema.

Hok Leong was actually downcast before he met <u>Eileen</u>. In the morning Tee Soon had called to say that he was leaving on a vessel next week. He too had found a job on a ship. Could they meet up in the afternoon? Hok Leong said that he was busy but immediately felt crushed by the guilt that washed over him. Just because of a girl he was willing to forsake an old pal. He arranged to meet up with Tee Soon on Monday evening. Tee Soon's imminent departure meant that, among his close secondary school friends, only Ying-jun was left. If Ying-jun left as well his secondary school memories would all be carted away by them.

He knew why they wanted to leave the country. He would probably have left as well if he wasn't going to the university. The truth, dawning on them only after their secondary four graduation, was that they didn't amount to much. In a sea of people, as you walked and drifted around, it became clear that you didn't know where to go, what to aim for. Or, rather, everywhere was the same, the same difference. The idea that since you had to start from the bottom everywhere you went, therefore "secondary-four-was-enough" was too impractical, or was perhaps an error of judgement. It was actually only the minimum requirement, but nobody had told them that. In an area of low pressure and oppressive weather, the only choice was to strike out for sights unknown.

<u>Eileen</u> wasn't a movie person, but she liked to come out on Sunday. Hok Leong liked being with her. She always made him feel better and improved his spirits, like this Sunday for instance. They agreed that if he had the time to hook up on weekdays, he would phone her in her office.

That evening he went to <u>Peace Centre</u> and had dinner with

John and the boys. On the way back to camp, they started talking about Three Stripes. Alan said that he was the same, there wasn't much change in his behaviour.

Hok Leong exhaled nosily. The worse thing that could happen was no change in behaviour.

14

Hok Leong got up early. He went to check on the equipment that they needed for the next training period. As he ambled down the corridor, someone greeted him from behind, "Good morning Sergeant Chan!" It was Three Stripes. Before he could respond, Three Stripes added in Mandarin, "I'm going to change the colour of my tags to orange!"

By the time Hok Leong recovered, shouting "Good morning!" in reply, Three Stripes was already far way.

A sense of relief washed over him. The sunlight was suddenly mellow and gentle. The early sunrise in the camp was actually quite agreeable, he realised.

The night earlier he had met up with Ying-jun and Tee Soon for dinner. Ying-jun's application to work in the Middle East had been rejected. Not enough experience, someone said. Hok Leong was secretly thankful about that. Ying-jun wanted to find a job with good prospects but didn't know what sector he should join. The job at the factory was definitely a short-term thing, no point hanging around there. He asked Hok Leong what line of work he should pursue. Hok Leong couldn't imagine what would suit someone like Ying-jun. "How about becoming a gigolo!" he said in jest.

Tee Soon said, "Ah Hor and I don't have to think about this question for at least two years."

Hok Leong had some good advice. "The best thing is to do something you like. If not, then at least something with a high salary. If you prefer to think ahead, then maybe something that everyone needs."

"What about you?" Ying-jun asked. "What are you going to do after university?"

Hok Leong took a leaf from Tee Soon's book. "I don't have to think about that question for at least three years."

On the way back to camp, Hok Leong remembered that Ah Hor had sent him a postcard. He received it on Saturday and had forgotten about it. Ah Hor said he had visited a brothel. The girls in Puerto Rico had incredible figures, he said. Where was Puerto Rico? Hok Leong wondered. He was too lazy to check the atlas. Ah Hor said that, sometimes in the middle of the vast hazy ocean, he suddenly recalled their secondary-three camping trip, the one where they swam out to a kelong and nearly got smashed by an oil tanker, nearly bought-the-farm.

Hok Leong stepped out of his barracks room. The hill top behind which the sun rose every morning was shrouded in darkness. Standing in the corridor, he went through detail by detail what he could remember about the camping trip.

15

For some time after that, Hok Leong was extremely busy in the evenings. After the day's activities he had to shower, change into civvies, make himself presentable, rush off to see Eileen, and then after that he had hurry back to camp by midnight. Although he was rushed off his feet, Hok Leong believed that dating should be like this: sharing a meal, sharing a drink, finding somewhere quiet where they could walk, talk, and learn each other's take on the world, and also finding out, if they had contrary opinions, that they could still accept each other's point of view.

Hok Leong considered himself a lucky man.

Eileen had modelling gigs almost every weekend. She began to take it as a regular job. Hok Leong had no choice but to find his own distraction. Ying-jun wasn't the kind of person to leave an empty slot in his Saturday schedule. One day Hok Leong found himself at home on a weekend with no plans to go anywhere. Mother asked sister if he was fine. "Is your brother okay?" she asked.

Hok Leong pretended that he hadn't heard anything. You mean something must be wrong if you stay at home on a weekend? He also didn't want to help out at the food centre. So eventually he went to give a hand at the coffee shop run by Eileen's mother.

Senseless, right? Well, that's how it is! Senseless and boring!

Eileen's mother was naturally happy to see him. Hok Leong didn't understand the Hainanese dialect that she spoke. But the kindly old lady made him feel relaxed and welcome. After ten in the evening, business in the Bugis area started to slacken; it was the same for the drinks shop. After they closed for the night, Eileen's mother would order supper—usually a bowl of congee. Hok Leong also joined her for some congee. When Hok Leong gave a hand at the shop, Eileen tried to finish before midnight and rush home. When she got back, Eileen's mother knew enough to go upstairs, to leave the youngsters alone to themselves.

One night the midnight chime came and went. Eileen was still out. Her mother grew tired and decided to turn in for the night. Hok Leong closed the iron grill gate of the shop but didn't slot in the padlock. This made it easier for Eileen.

Hok Leong left one of the lights on so that Eileen would know he hadn't left yet. He laid down in one of the booth seats. The cushion was soft and comfy. After a while his eyes grew heavy. He dozed and feel asleep.

Sometime later, Hok Leong felt somebody touch his face, then kiss him full on the lips. He could smell perfume but didn't open his eyes. He held Eileen tight against him. She caressed the hair on his forehead. Kissing her gently, he shifted out of the seat and pulled her into the booth with him. She returned his kisses. Naturally he started from her hair, then explored her body. Eileen said urgently, "My mom is upstairs!" Hok Leong didn't let her finish the sentence. The spirit of youth burned fiercely in them as they explored the secrets and foundations of life.

16

Hok Leong kept having the feeling that things weren't real, weren't settled.

He remembered saying "I'm serious" to Eileen before he left the coffee shop. Eileen half-smiled at him but went off first without waiting for his taxi to arrive.

Hok Leong couldn't sleep that night. He tried to recall what happened that evening but everything was remote and hazy. He kept thinking about Eileen's half-smile, the way it mixed sweetness with uneasiness, and also a sense of loss. He told himself that he should let Eileen know about his feelings, that he wasn't playing around.

By the time he fell asleep it was near dawn. When he woke up he placed a call to Eileen, suggested that they have lunch together. The first few moments after they met up was terribly awkward. Eileen greeted him in an unnaturally loud tone of voice, asked him what he wanted to drink. Her actions unsettled Hok Leong, who also became unnatural. "How are you?" he actually asked, and praised her for her dressing. Between them there was a growing fissure, a breach; but thankfully everything soon returned to normal. Eileen quickly regained her poise and openness. She was still the old Eileen.

After lunch they went shopping. They drifted to a stop in front of a shop display window. Eileen drew close to Hok Leong. She leaned her chin against his shoulders. Hok Leong felt affectionate and warm, and also blessed by fortune. For a long time they stood before the display window, not moving.

17

Hok Leong's way of showing his "I'm serious" attitude was to bring Eileen home to meet his parents.

Eileen was shocked. She didn't want to go but these kinds of things couldn't be rejected. Fortunately, their timing was good. Hok Leong's elder brother and both his sisters were out. Eileen made up like she hadn't put on any make-up. She wore jeans, a lace-collar white T-shirt, and a pair of flat-heeled sandals. The only thing that stood out was the bit of lipstick that she wore, the whole ensemble making her look classy and delicate.

Hok Leong's father was generally fine if the girl wasn't exaggerated or showy. He didn't have any objections or observations, just said hello and left them alone. That left his mother, who also looked like she didn't know how to respond to the situation, although she still did better than Eileen.

Unable to speak Cantonese, Eileen intentionally used halting, half-past-six Mandarin to greet Hok Leong's mother. "Aunty, my name is Yu-jiao," she said.

Hok Leong didn't know that Eileen's Chinese name was Yu-jiao. He nearly laughed out loud. How could she have such a rustic, unstylish name? Unable to place the two together, he said hurriedly, "Her name is Eileen. Eileen is fine."

Eileen looked embarrassed. But Hok Leong's mother also didn't cover herself in glory. She didn't know how to pronounce the English name properly, just mumbled it a few times and left it at that.

The whole meet-up lasted maybe half an hour! Hok Leong used the excuse that they wanted to catch a movie to spirit Eileen away from the flat. Eileen could finally heave a sigh of relief. She gave a short, bitter laugh.

Hok Leong laughed gaily in response. "I didn't know your name was Yu-jiao."

Eileen swung a fist at his jaw.

18

Eileen felt that she had found the right boyfriend. Because she found the right guy, her luck had also arrived. For now she had assignments on Saturday evenings and Sunday afternoons. She told Hok Leong a few times that she wanted to resign from her company and become a full-time model. Hok Leong advised her to wait it out. The two-day performance-fee didn't amount to a regular pay check.

Hok Leong felt that he couldn't keep going to the coffee shop run by Eileen's mother. By coincidence he spotted an interview with an English-language teacher in the newspapers and decided to sign up for the classes run by the man. His Saturdays were free after all. The guy's name was Fu. He hailed from Beijing and had studied overseas in England. On the journey home after his studies, his vessel had stopped in Singapore. Finding the place congenial, he stayed on, and had remained single all this while.

Fu, who was retired, was vibrant and humorous. Hok Leong liked his classes and went every weekend. There were around ten plus students in total, most of them already working, most of them women. Hok Leong was the only national serviceman. After attending a few lessons, some of his seniors invited him to join them for refreshments after class, but Hok Leong always politely turned them down. He had to meet Eileen at the drinks shop. The other students were older than him; they probably wouldn't share the same interests, he thought. After receiving a few invitations, however, Hok Leong felt obliged to join them. But then the occasion turned out to be nothing more than a whinging session, with everyone bleating about their personal issues. Hok Leong was unimpressed. He attended a few of the sessions and then stopped going.

Unlike the students, their teacher, Mr Fu, was interesting and provocative. One day after class, Hok Leong stayed behind to ask him a question, after which Mr Fu invited him out for tea. The question that he asked wasn't really a question. "How can I improve my English proficiency?" he had asked. After they took their seats and ordered their drinks, Mr Fu replied, "Make it a part of your life." He added after a while, "Do you have a chance to practice your English in camp?"

Hok Leong nodded.

"You must persevere. No matter how poor you are, just don't give up."

Hok Leong continued to nod his head.

"To be honest," Mr Fu continued, "you won't get very good in English if you study only once a week."

"So we shouldn't come to class?"

Mr Fu explained: "Although we teach grammar and pronunciation, the impact is limited. The most important thing is that we create a learning environment. If everyone shares the language-learning problem that he or she has during class discussion, then you don't need to repeat the same mistakes. My role is limited. I only help to create a learning environment."

"So do I still need to attend classes?" Hok Leong asked.

Mr Fu answered without hesitation: "Actually, you can learn English everywhere you go. You can check the dictionary and learn new words. You can read the signs in shops and stalls. You can read the signs by the roadside. You can learn lyrics from songs, or read the newspapers. The most important thing is that you make use of the immediate environment."

Hok Leong mulled over the advice given to him. Was the army camp and <u>Eileen</u> good enough? Was he getting enough practice? After all he was free on Saturday. The lessons were interesting and the teacher was effective.

"Talking with you like this is better," Hok Leong finally said.

Mr Fu gave a big laugh. "Your way is the best," he agreed.

<u>Eileen</u> was busy on Sunday. Hok Leong found himself again turning to the boys in Joy, the band that they had set up. During the jamming session, they practiced a song by the Bee Gees. It seemed they had a liking for the band. The words in one of the quirky, fast-changing songs caught his attention:

Life going nowhere. Somebody help me.
Somebody help me, yeah.
Life going nowhere. Somebody help me, yeah.
I'm staying alive.

The song had hit a nerve, Hok Leong realised. His life was directionless, he needed a hand. Right now, he was merely staying alive. He should record the song for Ah Hor and Tee Soon, he thought. The postcards he received from them—some from the Caribbean, some from the Mediterranean Sea—were initially filled with complaints and laments. But after a passage of time even that had stopped. Now they just sent him a few simple words scribbled on the back of postcards showing the scenery of the place that they had fetched up in, telling their former classmate where they were at, how they were doing.

Life going nowhere, somebody help me!

19

With <u>Eileen</u> busy on the weekends, <u>Alan</u> and John got the impression that they had separated. Sometimes Hok Leong didn't feel like attending the Saturday classes with Mr Fu. On one of those occasions, he gave <u>Alan</u> a call and asked if he was free to come out. After all being with <u>Alan</u> meant he could practice his English: it was also a kind of language class!

<u>Alan</u> was curious about the situation between Hok Leong and <u>Eileen</u> but didn't want to intrude. He asked carefully, "Is <u>Eileen</u> busy?"

Hok Leong replied in an easy-going tone of voice, "Yes! She has a performance."

<u>Alan</u> heaved a sigh of relief. "I thought you guys had broken up."

Hok Leong was nonplussed. "Thank you for your well-wishes!" he joked.

The next time, it was John who raised the matter.

Hok Leong arrived early at the coffee shop in Malay street and bumped into John, who hadn't left yet.

"<u>Eileen</u>'s not here," John said.

"I know," Hok Leong replied.

"Are you guys alright?" John asked, his voice filled with concern.

Hok Leong laughed. "<u>Eileen</u> says if I hang out with you guys I won't be alright!"

"Why?"

"Anyone involved in this band business sooner or later starves to death."

John was not impressed. His voice took on a tone of rebuke. "Not bothering to accompany the boyfriend on Saturday and Sunday, she's the one who will get into trouble," he said. Realising that he had said the wrong thing, he added, "Help yourself to the coffee and refreshments okay? I've got to go!"

Hok Leong was surprised. Why did John admonish his younger sister? He wasn't put out by the idea that <u>Eileen</u> had to perform on Saturday or Sunday. But the fact that someone was sending her home started to make him feel uncomfortable. After ten in the evening, the streets outside the coffee shop usually got extremely quiet The traffic would dwindle, so too the people passing by. Hok Leong realised that, whenever he heard a car exhaust roar and a vehicle pull away, he would soon hear high-heels click-clacking down the corridor, and then Eileen would open the door and come in. Nobody could fail to be intrigued by the situation. Eventually Hok Leong went outside to take a look. The person driving the car was a guy. Eileen saw Hok Leong and said evenly, "He's my boss! He's a great guy. He always insists on driving me home."

Hok Leong replied, half-in-jest, "There are only two great guys in the world. One is your father, the other is your brother. Your father is no longer around, so there's only one good person in the world."

Eileen gave a laugh. "Huh? My brother? Forget it! There's only one good guy in the world—and that's you!"

Hok Leong was happy to receive the praise; their talk moved away from the earlier subject.

"Are you hungry?" Eileen asked. "Shall I make you some toast?"

Hok Leong felt that he was being too small-minded about the whole thing. Because the roar of the car-exhaust still reverberated in his head, however, he wanted to remind Eileen about the need for caution.

But then she had some good news to share.

"I'm going to appear in an advertisement," she said.

"What kind of advertisement?" Hok Leong asked.

"Lingerie."

Hok Leong didn't say anything. A quick frown pulled his brows together as he studied Eileen's face.

"You think it's too much?"

Hok Leong kept quiet.

"This is a wonderful opportunity! I'm finally going to be a model!"

Hok Leong could only stare at her.

"Don't worry! There's nothing perverted about it. If there is, I won't do it."

"If you think it's okay, then it's fine."

But Hok Leong couldn't help thinking about it. Was it him being too conservative? Or was it her being too liberal? He remembered what <u>Alan</u> had once told him, that <u>Eileen</u> was also a greenie. He wondered, "Was love affected by such colour coding?" <u>Eileen</u> liked going to discos. She liked to lose herself in a large crowd with pounding music and lights. He on the other hand liked to patronise coffee shops, to sip tea and chit-chat. In order to chase her dreams she was willing to hang around first with that group of people before she hung out with her boyfriend. Maybe <u>Eileen</u> was just free and open? She wasn't the type to waste time over trivialities? He on his part was petty and narrow-minded. Her boss sending her home for instance. While she didn't think much of it, he suspected that the guy harboured ill intentions.

In the end Hok Leong decided that he would trust <u>Eileen</u>.

20

Hok Leong didn't bring up the matter of the advertisement that <u>Eileen</u> intended to shoot. They went back to their usual activities. After hours on Saturday they had the entire coffee shop lounge to themselves. They huddled together at one of the booths, idling the time away, chit-chatting about heavy stuff and trivia matters. At other times they made out, slaked the youthful thirst that engulfed their bodies.

Everything was real and beautiful. Or at the least they were better off than the people around them. Ah Hor and Tee Soon did their arduous laundry work on vessels plying the seven seas. They often complained about their lot. Ying-jun broke up with his girlfriend. Asked why they had broken up, he said that he didn't know why. John and Lee had lots of complaints about their girlfriends. Among them, only Hok Leong could say that he was okay, "not too bad."

The "not too bad" period lasted till <u>Eileen</u> told him that she would be lunching with the son of the guy who owned the undergarment factory that had commissioned her advert. Hok Leong said in response, "Aren't you finished with the ad?"

Eileen didn't think much about it. "That's the thing. He wants to celebrate the completion of the shooting. My boss is also coming along."

In an agitated tone of voice Hok Leong said, "You've finished working on the ad. What's there to celebrate?"

"It's tough saying no to people like that," Eileen continued. "He knows I'm in accounts. He wants me to go work for him. I'll get a huge pay rise."

Hok Leong started to get upset. "Madame! Do you know what he intends to do?"

Eileen asked innocently, "What? Do what?"

Hok Leong raised his voice. "He wants to chase you, to seduce you!"

As if nothing was the matter, Eileen continued evenly, "There's no point doing that. I already have a boyfriend!" She couldn't help giggling as she said that.

Hok Leong was stumped. "And you still intend to go?"

"I'm going there because there's a new job!"

This was the first time that Hok Leong couldn't get through to Eileen. He couldn't tell if she was being naïve, or if she was deliberately setting out to annoy him. Clear as day she was walking into a trap, but she still acted nonchalant and indifferent.

"The job is a scam, Madame! The seduction is the real thing, you're playing with fire!" he said harshly.

Eileen only grew serious when he said that.

For Hok Leong, it was in for a penny, in for a pound. "And your boss! He's also not a good guy."

Eileen didn't agree with that assessment. "You don't have to worry about him," she said. "He has a wife. He has kids."

"These middle-aged guys with wife and kids are the most

dangerous ones around. They have worldly experience to draw on. It's young girls like you who get cheated, and you don't even know that!"

<u>Eileen</u> started to get upset. "Stop making it out like I'm a fool."

Hok Leong wouldn't let it go. "You're being naïve!"

<u>Eileen</u> grew irate. "Naïve? What about you? Can you be more mature? You actually get jealous about something as small as this? Didn't you use to say that it's important to chase dreams? To have a career?"

She had hit the nub of the matter—something that guys were sensitive about. "Yes, I'm immature," Hok Leong replied angrily. "I'm jealous. I've always known that your dream is to hang around with guys like that."

There was no reason to trash her dreams and aspirations. Eileen was cut to the quick. "I've *always* hung out with guys like that, Hok Leong. If you don't like it you don't have to come along."

"That's the thing! I don't like that environment. So I stopped joining you for your outings. Have you ever seen a guy wait for a girl in a coffee shop till eleven, twelve o'clock at night? Can't you change even a little bit—do it for me?"

<u>Eileen</u> started to cry. "What about you? Can't you change a little—do it for me?"

"I've already changed a lot of things about myself. Haven't you noticed?"

<u>Eileen</u> hardened her heart. "If you find it so tough-going, then maybe we should split up!"

Hok Leong was taken aback. "Okay, let's split up then," he said.

With that he headed for the door and left the shop.

21

Hok Leong was shell-shocked. He never expected that he would quarrel with <u>Eileen</u>, never mind break up. But just like that— he didn't know how it happened—they had fought, quarrelled, and brokened up. He couldn't believe it. He only wanted what was good for her. Fighting and splitting up wasn't his intention at all. As an item he and <u>Eileen</u> didn't have a problem. He couldn't understand why they fought. He only wanted to tell her not to be so trusting and gullible. <u>Eileen</u> should know that he accepted everything about her. He just couldn't accept the men who hung around her.

After that Saturday fight, he didn't give her a call. He didn't know what to say. What he wanted to say was already said. He didn't want to apologise. He hadn't done anything wrong, didn't see why he should say that he was wrong.

The following Saturday he again went to the coffee shop to give a hand, although he reached there later than usual. He wanted to see <u>Eileen</u>, not necessarily to say anything, or for anyone to apologise. He wanted to move on from what had happened the previous Saturday. In the future there were plenty of Saturdays for them to enjoy.

After closing the shop that evening, <u>Eileen</u>'s mother as usual invited him to share some congee with her, after which she went upstairs. As usual, Hok Leong kept one of the lights on. He made himself a cup of coffee and took a seat in one of the high-backed booths. He was thinking about their relationship, about their time together. Or perhaps he was mulling over what to say to <u>Eileen</u> when he saw her. Or perhaps he was thinking about nothing at all.

After a passage of time, he again heard the familiar vehicle exhaust roar. His immediate response was to stand up, leave the place, and head off in another direction before <u>Eileen</u> came back. When he reached Victoria street he spotted a passing taxi. Without thinking too much, he hailed it. The taxi slid to a stop. He got in and went off.

He didn't see Eileen following him, didn't realise that she had almost reached his location.

22

Hok Leong didn't realise that, just like that, he would break up with Eileen. He had told her before that he was "serious."

He felt disappointed; he didn't want to contact her. Why was Eileen still accepting a lift home from her boss?

Now Hok Leong needed to amend his schedule. Either he got used to spending time by himself, or he needed to find some new company. Even then he was waiting for himself to change, to accept Eileen as she was, including the men who turned up one by one by her side. He had confidence in himself.

His new footloose situation—the fact that he had split up with his girlfriend—was soon noticed by his mates. John couldn't say anything because Eileen was his sister. But Alan called and asked him out for a drink. After drinking for a while, some home truths began to surface.

Alan turned to Hok Leong, "Do you think Eileen suits you?"

The way he phrased it was perfectly clear. "Eileen *doesn't* suit you" was what he meant to say.

But Hok Leong didn't take it like that. The question surprised him.

"What do you think?" he asked.

"Let's pursue our colour analogy thing," Alan replied. It looked like he had given the whole thing some thought. "Eileen is a green name-tag person with some added-in red. You're an orange person with some red. So the part that overlaps for you two is the red bit. Eileen still has her green portion, and you still have your orange portion." He stopped and looked squarely at Hok Leong.

"Damn your colour analogy thing!" Hok Leong scolded Alan. "Mister! How old are you? Did you give a false age when you reported for military service?"

Alan chuckled. "Within me lives an old man," he confessed.

Hok Leong upbraided him again. "No wonder you can't find a girlfriend. I'm sure you'll end up with an old woman."

Alan smiled, "Thank you for your well-wishes."

"What about the two of us. You and me?" Hok Leong asked.

"I'm not interested in you, Mister."

Hok Leong put on a show of anger, "I'm talking about the colour theory, idiot. You're green. I'm orange. How come we're at a bar having a drink together?"

Alan turned serious. "I found out later that I too have an orange portion. My orange portion stems from the fact that I am still a Chinese person."

"So we interact because we have orange in common?"

Alan nodded. "Yes, I believe that's true." Returning to the earlier topic, he added, "You and Eileen should have more than just the orange portion in common. Go check it out. You should have other overlapping colours. No one is just one colour. We all have different colours."

Hok Leong gave up on him. "Alan Tan," he joked. "How come you can get everything so clear and concise from just looking at the colour?"

Alan gave a big laugh. "You taught me how to do this. You're my *sifu*!"

23

Hok Leong gave the matter some thought. What else did he and Eileen have in common? While he was doing that, John told him that she had switched jobs. She was probably working at the said undergarment factory, Hok Leong thought. She really did it. He was glad that he didn't contact Eileen. If he did, they would probably have fought again over the issue.

Three months later, Hok Leong heard from John that Eileen had quit her job. She was now a full time model. Hok Leong felt that he was right the first time around. The son of the factory owner wasn't an honourable person. Or maybe she made the switch with his full approval? Anyway whatever the situation or outcome, she was now a full time model. That was her dream. She had her own road to travel; she must follow her own nose.

After that he had no news about Eileen. Together with his army mates, he reached R.O.D., his run-out-date marking the end of his military conscription. After that he went out a few times with Alan and John and then, just like that, that two-and-a-half-year life was suddenly over. It wasn't just his army mates who grew distant and unfamiliar. His feelings for Eileen had also cooled. Hok Leong was astonished at the turn of events. He believed in Alan's "colour theory" and had thought that they would eventually patch up.

Alan and him were the only ones moving on to the university. Same as Hok Leong's secondary school friends, the others now stood poised over a key turning point in their lives. Sure enough, Alan was studying law. Hok Leong read Mechanical Engineering. Although they were in the same university, they didn't meet up. Military service over, everyone entering a new phase of life with new challenges, losing contact with army mates—all of that wasn't surprising. After all their "colours" were different.

What he remembered of that intense two-and-a-half-years sojourn was principally Eileen. Tied in with that was Joy, and a snatch of song that went like this:

And I started to cry, which started the whole world laughing.
Oh if I'd only seen, that the joke was on me....

3

HSIAO-YUAN

1

A twenty-three-year-old girl with the given name Hsiao-yuan, meaning small wish. The name was jejune and a bit odd. But odder still was that, in combination with her surname, Xu, her full name meant "to make a small wish." Her parents were really too cool!

She was a <u>clerk</u> in the <u>office</u> of the factory that he worked at, with responsibility for taking and confirming orders. Hok Leong was a <u>technical officer</u> in the facility, a Japanese company that made printed wire boards. It was a small company with lots of young people. Hok Leong often hung out with the clerks from the office; they often had lunch together.

Hsiao-yuan's bearing and manner of speaking was different from her colleagues; but she liked to hang out with them. After they got to know one another well, Hok Leong asked, "Why do you work in a place like this? You don't belong here."

"So where do I belong?" Hsiao-yuan asked.

"A school, a cultural organization, a government body of some kind. Any place that isn't a factory."

Hsiao-yuan gave a small laugh. "You don't belong here too."

Hok Leong thought for a while. "I came through the <u>mechanical</u> engineering route. If I don't come here, I have no place to go."

"I worked in several places after I graduated from senior

high," Hsiao-yuan replied. "They didn't work out. If I don't come here, I have no place to go as well."

"Why didn't you study in the university?"

Hsiao-yuan again answered honestly, "I couldn't get in."

Hok Leong responded in kind. "Well, I did get in, but then I had to leave."

"Why?" she asked with great concern.

"My English is lousy."

Hsiao-yuan laughed gently, "Me too."

2

Hok Leong was surprised that he failed his English language test. Actually he didn't fare well in his other subjects too. He had spent the entire year in university lagging behind the others, chasing up on his schoolwork. When the results were announced, the realisation that he would have to repeat a year made him re-visit a topic that he had mulled over frequently in secondary school: whether he was the kind of person who could go far in his studies.

The obvious answer was that he *wasn't* that kind of person.

He didn't want to repeat a year. Apart from the financial pressure on his family, he also believed that he would do alright if he entered the workforce. The assumption was perhaps akin to the "secondary four is enough" nostrum that he had followed and later rejected. But he also knew that, if he worked hard, he would be fine.

The problem was—how would he convey the decision to his parents? He remembered well the seldom-seen joy on their features when the A-level results were announced and he told them that he was going to the university. "If you get to do this, we don't mind spending a few more years selling won ton noodles," mother had even said.

How could he tell them now that he was quitting?

He tried the direct approach. "I'm going to stop school!" he told his father.

Father was smoking a cigarette. He stopped short suddenly with his mouth hanging half-open.

Hok Leong studied his features. His father had grown old, he realised. Hok Leong tried to comfort him, "Let younger sister study in the university. She's better than me."

Father recovered his senses. He understood that his son had grown up, that he wouldn't take the path lying before him unless there was a good reason. "As long as it's your own decision, we're fine with it. If it's your decision, we're okay. Don't worry about your mother, I will tell her about it," he said. He was worried that Hok Leong's mother would grumble and complain.

Mother was concerned when she found out. "You're not going to study anymore?" she asked.

Hok Leong nodded. So that was that. She didn't raise the matter again.

Unconcerned about the salary stipulated in the advertisements that he saw, Hok Leong threw himself into the task of looking for a job. He searched for companies with a non-Anglo background. He didn't want a situation where he had to leave after a year because his English was poor. So he ended up working for a Japanese company.

During the interview, the manager asked, "You completed secondary four some time ago. What did you do in the interim?"

"I did A-levels. Then I joined the army."

The manager continued suspiciously, "But you wrote secondary four in the highest education column on the application form. And you only submitted your O-level results."

"Your advert said O-levels qualifications was enough."

A man sitting next to the manager piped up for the first time. In simple English, he said, "I am Akita Hiroichi, if you have been selected by us, can you bring your 'A' level certificate?"

"Sure!" Hok Leong replied.

Akita Hiroichi was the boss. Hok Leong later learned that, read in the Chinese manner, his name was *Hengtian Guangyi*. Everyone called him Akita san.

Akita san continued, "Is $550 a month enough for you?"

"If you perform well we will raise your salary," the manager added.

The figure given was rather low. "Okay!" Hok Leong said.

"When can you start?" the manager asked.

"Anytime."

"Tomorrow?" Akita san asked.

Hok Leong nodded. He had a feeling that Akita, the Japanese boss, would be easier to handle than the local manager.

His presentiment turned out to be correct.

That was three years ago.

3

Hok Leong realised one day that he had forgotten when exactly Hsiao-yuan joined the company. "I came a year after you!" she reminded him.

Anyway, they were always busy then. Many colleagues came and went during that period, nobody had time to keep tabs on those around them. Seen from today's perspective, it was the era of turbo-charged growth—the period during the mid-1980s when Singapore underwent what became known as "rapid development."

During that era of "rapid development," Hok Leong had to work over-time almost every day. Twelve hour shifts became commonplace, and oftentimes he had to work even longer, from eight in the morning till ten at night. He went back only to sleep. Apart from that he did nothing else. Mother complained one day, "During national service you said you had to stay in camp, at university you said you were busy and couldn't come back, and now you're so busy you only come home to sleep at night. What kind of job are you doing?"

Hok Leong knew that he hadn't spent much time at home during the last six to seven years. There was nobody around actually. Elder brother had married some time back and had moved out. He seldom saw his sisters. Elder sister worked as a nurse and had to do shift work. Younger sister worked in a bank. What she did he had only the vaguest knowledge. It was tough for his parents. After elder brother took over the noodle stall they had both retired, but only to find that their home had become an empty nest.

Hok Leong didn't know how to respond to his mother's entreaty. He was already 23. Soon he'd be 25, then 30. He had to work hard *now* and build a successful career. He had already failed in romance; at university he had failed in his studies. He was letting everyone down.

A year after he joined the printed wire board company, Hok Leong obtained a big raise, from $500 a month to $750. The reason given was that the company had done well, his excellent performance was part of that. Hok Leong knew the raise meant merely that he was now at the same level as the others, but he was satisfied.

A year after that he was promoted to <u>technical officer</u>. His performance was the best among the <u>technicians</u>.

During that period, even the <u>office girls</u> had to do over-time. Hsiao-yuan wasn't too pleased about that. What raised her hackles was that the manager wanted them to give themselves Christian names. Compared to Chinese names, Christian names were easier to remember. The manager was the one who had interviewed Hok Leong when he joined the company. His name was <u>Steven</u>. For Hok Leong, <u>Steven</u>'s actions brought to mind the <u>Alan</u> that he knew during his national service days.

They were both "deep-green-name-tag" types. But while <u>Alan</u> was willing to mingle with other colours and hues, <u>Steven</u> wanted *everyone* to have a little "green" in them, so that it was easier to communicate.

The problem was—how do you find "green" colour types in an industrial factory setting?

Hok Leong was already the "greenest" among the personnel at the factory!

When it came time to choose a Christian name, a group of <u>office girls</u> playfully came up to Hok Leong to ask for his new moniker. Hok Leong couldn't care less about such things, but they insisted that he give them a name. The manager had given specific instructions, they said. Hok Leong, who was reading the papers, suddenly spotted an article about the kung fu movie star Jackie Chan. He turned to the girls, "<u>Jackie, I am Jackie Chan</u>!" he said, brandishing a fist.

The assembled <u>clerks</u> looked at him with furrowed brows. "Why not? My surname is also Chan!" Hok Leong insisted in a dignified, confident tone of voice.

From then on, Hok Leong became <u>Jackie Chan</u>. He didn't think much about it. After all the staff in the company continued to call him Hok Leong. His <u>Jackie</u> name only came into use a few years later.

After that kerfuffle, Hok Leong asked Hsiao-yuan. "So, what's your <u>Christian name</u>?"

"<u>Jennifer</u>," Hsiao-yuan said, "they chose it for me."

Hok Leong stared at her. Tried as he did he couldn't see how the name suited Hsiao-yuan. He couldn't place the two together.

4

That period of incessant overtime suited Hok Leong's state of mind. He didn't have a girlfriend, didn't have distractions, didn't have time to think licentious or tawdry thoughts. The company was good to him. Everyone was too busy to indulge in trifles. Everybody was happy. Their overtime pay was actually higher than their regular salaries.

Because he had to take a <u>taxi</u> home every day, Hok Leong decided that he might as well buy a car. He bought a small second-hand one, around eight years old, which also made him the go-to guy for a lift home after work. As it turned out, the last person to be dropped-off before his home was Hsiao-yuan. For one thing, she lived in <u>Katong</u>, he <u>Tampines</u>: the drop-off was convenient and he didn't have to make a detour. For another thing, the other <u>office girls</u>, playing the game that young people are wont to play, wanted to pair them up. It was akin to his national service days, like the way they had managed their trips to the <u>disco</u>.

Hok Leong paid no heed to these games. He was already twenty-five. Of course he wanted a girlfriend. But he knew that he had no accomplishments to speak of, and Hsiao-yuan herself didn't seem to come from a hoi polloi background. He remembered well the "colour theory" that <u>Alan</u> had expounded, the idea that partners should be well-matched in terms of background and status. He didn't harbour any illusions about his suitability for Hsiao-yuan. Furthermore, he wanted to "focus on his career," as they say. Ever modest, he didn't think that the phrase properly applied to him, but still he wanted to give it a try, whatever the consequences.

For a period of time, Hok Leong sent Hsiao-yuan home almost every day, but they didn't talk about serious things in the car. Furthermore, he didn't really know *where* she stayed. The destination was supposedly <u>Katong</u>, but it turned out to be in <u>Siglap</u>. Luckily they didn't have to pass by <u>Katong Shopping Centre</u>, his old haunt. Hsiao-yuan usually got off in front of <u>St. Patrick School</u>. It seemed she didn't want to be sent directly to her doorstep, which was fine with Hok Leong. He was worried that she would get into some bother if her family members saw him dropping her off. She was probably thinking the same thing herself, he reckoned.

Hok Leong had never thought about dating someone like Hsiao-yuan. She was good looking, with fine features, fair skin, and delicate manners. She was beautiful and graceful. The problem was that her upbringing caused her to mute some of these attributes. What got through, obvious to everyone who saw Hsiao-yuan, was her poise and bearing. That was the reason why Hok Leong said that she wasn't suitable for a job in a factory. Her other qualities only appeared when she hung out talking rubbish or gossiping with the lunch-time crowd and temporarily put aside that upbringing.

The lifts that Hok Leong gave Hsiao-yuan were prosaic affairs, but the other office girls were intrusive about it. In a voice filled with care, they kept asking Hok Leong how he was doing with Hsiao-yuan. This caused her great embarrassment and she refused to take any more lifts from him. Hok Leong was fine with that. He found it hard going when he rode in the car with her. He had to constantly rack his brains to come up with trivial, not-too-serious things to talk about—it wasn't easy.

Even then, the trivial things they spoke about could also lead to unforeseen consequences. One time after work, Hok Leong asked Hsiao-yuan if she wanted a lift home. She had yet to call a taxi so she agreed. They hadn't ridden together for some time, so in the car they really didn't know what to say to each other.

Hsiao-yuan returned to an old topic of conversation. "You mentioned that your English is poor. Have you thought about signing up for language classes?"

"Yes! I used to take tuition classes when I was in the military."

"You need to find a good teacher," Hsiao-yuan reminded him.

"I did! The papers actually published an interview with the

guy." Hok Leong wanted to show that he was earnest about the matter.

Hsiao-yuan grew curious. "Where did they hold the classes?"

"Chinese chamber of commerce."

Her voice grew an octave higher, "The teacher's surname. Was it Fu?"

This time it was Hok Leong's turn to be intrigued. "How come you know that?"

"I took classes there as well."

"That's strange," Hok Leong said, "how come I never saw you around the place?"

After exchanging details, they realised they had missed each other by a whisker—their classes had been back to back.

Hsiao-yuan asked, "So why did you decide to stop?"

"Teacher said you only need to be in an English-speaking environment to learn the language, it doesn't have to be at his place. My entire camp was English-speaking."

Hsiao-yuan didn't believe him. "Liar!" she said. "Do you know what's my relationship to the guy?" she added.

Hok Leong had no idea. He hoped he wasn't her father.

Hsiao-yuan told him solemnly, "He's a friend of my father."

Hok Leong was glad that he wasn't her dad. "The world is too small," he said.

Hsiao-yuan asked suddenly, "Do you want to see him?"

Hok Leong had always felt that his former teacher was an interesting person. "Sure!" he replied.

Hsiao-yuan now seemed to have some reservations about the arrangement. But having made the invitation, she had no choice but to press ahead.

"Shall we go after work on Friday?"

In the end, it was this trivial, not-too-serious topic of conversation that changed the direction of their lives.

5

Mr Fu also lived in the <u>Siglap</u> area, right behind the <u>Killiney</u> coffee shop that had opened in recent years, at a spot where there used to be a movie theatre. After work on Friday, Hok Leong and Hsiao-yuan drove to the locale and had dinner at a Western food restaurant run by a Hainanese family. Hsiao-yuan knew the proprietor and attendants well. They knew her preferences; she didn't have to place an order. The boss even stepped out of the kitchen to say hello. The familiar environs allowed a different, more laid-back Hsiao-yuan to emerge. Hok Leong enjoyed the change.

Hok Leong was conscious that he had to behave like a guest. Hsiao-yuan explained that the eatery was, so to speak, her family restaurant. The proprietor had seen her grow up, had seen her elder brother grow up. Hok Leong mulled over the revelation. First, she had a brother. Second, she had, from young, taken meals regularly at a restaurant. He was right. She hailed from a privileged background. He could have guessed from the locale actually. The Siglap-East Coast vicinity was a posh, middle-class kind of place.

Hok Leong shared some details about his family, namely that his parents, elder sister, and elder brother all didn't take Western food. In his home, only Hok Leong and his younger sister enjoyed such fare. Indirectly, he revealed his family background.

Looking back on the experience, he realised that he couldn't remember how the food had tasted. In those days, he wouldn't have known how to appraise the cuisine anyway. He remembered that he asked for ketchup and chilli sauce. Hsiao-yuan told him that they didn't provide such condiments. At that point he didn't know that he had made a *faux pas*, had lost face. When he understood later that he had blundered, the incident continued to cause him pain.

After dinner Hok Leong wanted to pay for the meal but discovered that Hsiao-yuan had already paid for it. She had also ordered take-away. "It's for uncle Fu," she said.

Hok Leong was embarrassed; he wasn't used to a woman paying for his food. It grew worse when the proprietor said that Hsiao-yuan rarely brought guests over for a meal; it was a privilege. Hok Leong didn't like the boss being such a blabbermouth.

Before going to uncle Fu's house, they stopped by a convenience store. Hsiao-yuan bought some bread, butter, and jam. It felt like she was bringing him to *her* place, Hok Leong thought.

Instead of *uncle* Fu, Hok Leong preferred to use the Chinese term for teacher, *laoshi*, to address Mr Fu. Fu *laoshi* lived in an old-style single-storey terrace house. Although a bit old, the house was uncluttered and clean. Hsiao-yuan had the key to the iron-gate. Hearing the sound of the gate, Fu *laoshi* shouted from inside the abode, "Is that you Hsiao-yuan?" He switched on the lights and opened the door. Hok Leong's presence surprised him.

"Hello Fu *laoshi*," Hok Leong said.

"Hello uncle Fu," Hsiao-yuan added, "I've brought over a visitor."

For a while Fu *laoshi* looked at Hok Leong. "I know you but I can't remember the name. You took one of my classes."

"His name is Chan Hok Leong," Hsiao-yuan said, "He's my colleague. We found out recently that we took back to back classes with you. We just missed out getting to know each other."

Taking the food that she had bought, Hsiao-yuan headed for the kitchen. She seemed to consider the place her own home. As Fu *laoshi* catered to his guest, Hsiao-yuan tried without success to switch on the kitchen lights. Fu *laoshi* eventually noticed the problem. "It stopped working a few days ago. It's spoilt."

Hsiao-yuan put the food pack down and aimed her chin at Hok Leong, "No problem. We have a specialist in our midst."

"No, no, he's a guest," Fu *laoshi* hurriedly said.

"No problem, no problem," said Hok Leong. He went to the kitchen and examined the lights. "The blub is blown, I think. I'll get a replacement."

Against Fu *laoshi*'s protests, he headed for the door, saying several times that it wasn't a problem. Hsiao-yuan gave Hok Leong a quick wink and raised her thumb in approval.

Hok Leong returned to the convenience store that they had visited earlier. In a while he was back. He screwed in the new bulb. Immediately the lights went on.

Fu *laoshi* thanked Hok Leong profusely for his help. He addressed Hsiao-yuan. "See! Isn't it better to study science and technology? What's the use of all that humanities scholarship?"

Fu *laoshi* wanted to pay Hok Leong for the new light bulb but he refused the compensation. He felt odd that, although a guest, he was also helping with the household chores; his status was changing. Seeing that Fu *laoshi* had yet to take his dinner, Hok Leong urged him to eat. "Yes, I eat now. I eat now," he replied.

Hsiao-yuan brought over a pot of tea that she had brewed. The three of them sat at the table, chatting amiably. Observing how Fu *laoshi* ate, Hok Leong later realized that it all came down to how you wielded your knife and fork, and also the attitude that you took. He had ordered the same dish earlier, but Fu *laoshi*'s manner of eating was different. His simple meal of pork chops seemed immeasurably more enjoyable than the one that Hok Leong had just partaken. Put simply, it came down to elegance or stylishness. Such terms hadn't come into fashion yet during that era, so it was a revelation to learn that slowing down was important. The way you drank tea for instance. If you sip slowly and take your time, new subtle flavours will actually appear!

"Is there a problem?" Hsiao-yuan asked? She was observing him carefully.

"Nothing, no problem," Hok Leong said. Embarrassed, he knew that the response "no problem" was unlikely to satisfy Hsiao-yuan. "The tea has a light, fragrant flavour. It stays in the mouth a long time," he added.

Fu *laoshi* agreed. "Excellent! A connoisseur in our midst! Yes, this is a new brand, I just bought it," he said approvingly.

Hsiao-yuan made a joke. "Of course! I forgot that we have an old British hand in our midst! An expert!"

Fu *laoshi* laughed happily. "Who? Who's this old British hand that you're talking about?" He looked left and right and made like he was searching for someone.

Everyone laughed.

They continued to chit-chat and drink tea. Most of the time it was Hsiao-yuan and Fu *laoshi* doing the talking.

When they left it was already ten o'clock. As they got into the car, Hsiao-yuan asked Hok Leong, "Where did you learn that?"

"I saw my father changing the lights in the flat," Hok Leong said.

"You never did such things in the past?"

"At home, it's always my dad changing the lightbulbs."

Hsiao-yuan wanted to pay Hok Leong for the new fixture but again he refused. "You've already bought me dinner," he said.

They started talking about Fu *laoshi*. Hsiao-yuan's home was barely a minute away from his residence. She didn't get off immediately when they reached her home. "Uncle Fu saw us grow up, me and my elder brother. He's very close to my family. You could even say that that he spoils me."

Hok Leong stopped the car by the side of the road. "He never got married," she continued. "He wanted to make me his god-daughter but father said I should make the decision myself when I'm grown up. I don't really want to be fettered by these old-style relationships, but in a way, yes, I'm closer to him than even my father. I see him almost every week."

After that little confession, Hsiao-yuan looked evenly at Hok Leong. Hok Leong returned her gaze. Without meaning to do so he had entered another person's story. He could only sit and listen attentively while she talked.

Hsiao-yuan gave a laugh. "Okay! I've got to go. Thank you! Bye!"

She waved and left the car.

6

Hsiao-yuan didn't invite Hok Leong to join her the following week. Hok Leong didn't bring it up. After all, as ordinary friends they didn't have to meet up every week. Moreover, the twelve-hours-plus shifts that Hok Leong clocked in didn't leave him with much time for anything. He only remembered that Fu *laoshi* had a certain panache and elegance that he wished could be adapted for the work place. Elegance there probably meant an unhurried pace and careful attention to detail, but that was impossible to achieve in real life! Once Hok Leong got busy such things tended to fly out of the window.

About a month after the initial visit, Hsiao-yuan brought it up again. "Uncle Fu wants to see you. Do you have time?" she asked Hok Leong.

Hok Leong agreed. This time they met for dinner at a peranakan restaurant near Fu *laoshi*'s home. Again the proprietor came out of the kitchen to greet them. He even joined them at their table, ladled rice and soup for them, and served them from the dishes that they had ordered. Fu *laoshi* spoke to the man in English. At one point they fell to talking about English literature and classical music. Hok Leong and Hsiao-yuan didn't know enough about these subjects to join in.

Occasionally their elders made a joke or discussed the origin of the dishes on the table so that the young people wouldn't feel left out.

After dinner, they sent Fu *laoshi* home. Along the way he turned to Hok Leong, "I'm bored at home, so I told Hsiao-yuan to tell you that I would love it if you could visit me when you have the time. You can come every week. She said it's up to you." He patted Hok Leong on his shoulders. "Do visit me when you're free. I can't do much but I can offer my hospitality. I hope the jokes we made just now were alright with you?"

Hok Leong smiled and nodded his head.

They met again two to three times after that. Each time it was Fu *laoshi* treating them to a meal. Hok Leong gave the matter some thought. He told Hsiao-yuan one evening as he was sending her home that he didn't want to be a freeloader. "The tap at the kitchen sink is leaking. How about next week we pack some food there, and after dinner I fix it for him?"

Hsiao-yuan was overjoyed but answered cautiously, "Okay, sure. There's no such thing as a free dinner huh?"

The following Friday they bought some food first and then drove over to Fu *laoshi*'s home. It was dark when they got there. They decided to do the repair work the next day. Fu *laoshi* didn't agree initially, but after a while he decided that it wouldn't do to leave a tap leaking in the kitchen. He accepted the offer of help.

They tucked into the food that Hok Leong and Hsiao-yuan had bought. After dinner Hsiao-yuan again made some tea. Hok Leong was intrigued by the music coming from the old-style turntable. He examined the LP cover that Fu *laoshi* passed over to him. "Butterfly Lovers Violin Concerto," it said.

"This version is not bad. But the one by Yu Lina is still the best," Fu *laoshi* said.

Hsiao-yuan bought over the tea that she had brewed. She said flippantly, "Wow! Our Mr Chan has plenty of diversions.

He knows his tea and he knows his music!"

She deliberately asked a tough question to test him out, "My father always says that he and uncle Fu are die-hard carry-overs from the republican China period. They still try to preserve the legacy of the May Fourth movement. Does our Mr Chan know what this May Fourth legacy consists of?"

Hok Leong looked nonplussed at Fu *laoshi*. He was out of his ken—it wasn't fair.

Fu *laoshi* gave a small laugh. "Gosh! Just listen to her talk," he said, trying to change the subject.

Hok Leong felt that he needed to answer Hsiao-yuan's question. The answer should be something erudite and scholarly. "Something to do with black ink?" he ventured, using the metaphor that referenced such things.

Hsiao-yuan glanced at uncle Fu, who laughed but didn't say anything. Their expressions told Hok Leong that he was incorrect.

Fu *laoshi* again tried to smooth things over between Hok Leong and Hsiao-yuan, "Yes, something with lots of black ink," he joked.

Hok Leong replied forcefully, "That's definitely something that I don't have." He reminded himself that this was precisely where a great gulf existed between him and Hsiao-yuan.

"No problem," Hsiao-yuan said, "You have an excellent teacher, someone who is both a May Fourth votary and an <u>old British</u> hand."

"Aiyoh, don't listen to her rubbish talk!" Fu *laoshi* gave a laugh. He gestured at the pot of tea on the table, "There's some freshly brewed inky stuff here. Who wants to have some?"

Everyone laughed. Hok Leong's jollity was a bit forced.

Fu *laoshi* took a sip from the cup in front of him. "Don't worry about such things, Hok Leong. I have some books and records here that you can check out. If something strikes your fancy you can bring it home. If you like it, you don't have to return it."

Hok Leong smiled. He said mildly, "maybe it's better that I drink more black ink first."

7

The next day Hok Leong came over to fix the tap in the kitchen. The problem actually stemmed from wear and tear on the rubber hose attached to the pipe. He only needed to change the hose. Again, Hok Leong went to the convenience store located near the main road and bought a new fixture. After he returned, he needed only ten minutes to get everything fixed. Fu *laoshi* thanked and praised him profusely, making Hok Leong feel awkward about the matter.

The other water fixtures in the house were probably worn-down as well, Hok Leong thought. Sure enough, the one in the back garden was also leaking. Hok Leong suggested that they check all the water points in the house and change their rubber hosing if necessary. Fu *laoshi* refused to consider the matter. "Let's have lunch first," he insisted. Lunch was actually still some way off. But Hok Leong didn't know how he could turn down the invitation.

Fu *laoshi* decided to make some Northern-style pot-stickers. He "invited" Hok Leong to check out the books and manuscripts in his study while he got everything ready. Again, Hok Leong felt terribly awkward and kept returning to the kitchen to ask if he could lend a hand. Every time he did this, Fu *laoshi* "invited" him, so to speak, back to the study. When the pot-stickers were ready it was already lunchtime. Hok Leong had never tried the dish before. It was similar to the won ton dumplings that his family sold at their food stall but he couldn't get used to the taste. He wanted that very day to bring over some piping hot dumplings from his home so that Fu *laoshi* could try them out.

After lunch, Hok Leong repeated his offer to fix the faucet

hoses in the house. Fu *laoshi* was full of apology for the trouble that he was causing. He shouldn't take advantage of younger folks, he kept saying. Hok Leong didn't know how to respond. He went all over the house checking the water points and fixtures. Six of them needed changing.

After changing the hoses, there was still some time yet till dinner. But again Fu *laoshi* said that Hok Leong should have another meal with him. The money that Hok Leong helped him to save on his utilities bill was enough to pay for several dinners, he insisted. Hok Leong wasn't hungry. Thanks to the pot-stickers, his stomach was filled with flour and meat.

This time they went to a seafood restaurant. Naturally, the proprietor of the establishment also knew Fu *laoshi*. Hok Leong wondered how many of the restauranteurs in the neighbourhood knew Fu *laoshi* and appreciated his patronage. As with lunch, it took a while before they finished preparing and cooking the food. By the time, the dishes were served it was near dinnertime. Hok Leong realised that Fu *laoshi* had an unerring sense of timing. Everything that he did was easy and unhurried.

Hok Leong liked the chilli crab that they ordered. Fu *laoshi* said seriously, "Hsiao-yuan also likes this dish. If you get the chance, you should invite her to come to this restaurant."

Hok Leong knew what Fu *laoshi* wanted to say. "We're good colleagues. That's about it," he said.

Fu *laoshi* gave a laugh. "You don't have to emphasise the colleagues bit. I can see that. I can also see that you're not bad. Of course, that's got nothing to do with the fact that you helped me with some repairs."

Hok Leong couldn't say anything. He was never comfortable when praise came his way.

Fu *laoshi* continued, "I'm going to sound like a broken-down record, I'm sorry. I've known Hsiao-yuan since she was a kid, I saw her grow up. She's also not bad." He thought for a while and gave another laugh. "I heard that you've known each other for quite a while but you're not together. I'm even more anxious than you about that!"

Before Hok Leong could respond, Fu *laoshi* cut him off, "I know you want to say that you're not suitable for each other. Is that correct?"

Hok Leong nodded.

"Believe me, son, you make a good pair. In fact you're extremely well-suited."

Hok Leong was surprised at his choice of words, that he had put it as plainly as that.

Fu *laoshi* again gave a laugh. "Since I'm playing match-maker now, I'll go full tilt, okay? In for a penny, in for a pound, as they say. Hsiao-yuan has a bit of the little madame about her, I know that. When she feels like it, she's attentive, when she doesn't feel like it, she's distant. Yes, she is a bit spoilt. After all there's only her and her elder brother at home. And she can be snobbish at times. Like the other day when she brought up that May Fourth legacy thing. Who cares about that?" He added vigorously, "What's the use of finding a boyfriend who knows these things? What, in reality, are these passed-down customs and habits. Basically things that we can't cast off!"

He gave a glance at Hok Leong. "Look at you, clean as a whistle. No cultural baggage to speak of. Isn't that better than Hsiao-yuan? Because of her background she's poisoned by this cultural legacy business."

"Anyway," he continued after a pause. "I've already spoken to her about it. These external things aside, the important thing is that she has a good character."

Hok Leong understood that Fu *laoshi* didn't want him to keep in his heart the unpleasantness from the previous day. He didn't react strongly, just smiled and sipped his tea.

Seeing that Hok Leong didn't speak up, Fu *laoshi* thought that he was considering the matter. He continued to supplement his reasoning, "I say you guys are suitable for each other because you can make up for each other's shortcomings and deficiencies. You have a technical background, you can help pull us humanities types out of our imaginary universe and back to reality. You can use your particular way to instruct and edify. She knows how to take advice. It's just a matter of time."

Hok Leong felt that his prospects had improved, but still he kept silent and quietly sipped his tea. Fu *laoshi* added, "You also have good self-cultivation and an eye for detail. Like the other day when you figured out immediately the attributes of the tea and music. That's not easy. I didn't have such insights when I was your age."

He pointed at the chilli crab on the dining table, "This dish for instance. Tell me—what's the most important thing when it comes to eating chilli crab?"

Hok Leong thought that Fu *laoshi* was making a joke. He uttered the first thing that came to his mind.

"Crab," he said.

Fu *laoshi* was stunned. He started to chuckle. He guffawed. He laughed so hard that he started to choke. Hok Leong quickly poured him some tea. Fu *laoshi* took a drink from the glass and calmed himself down, "I always thought that the most important thing was the chilli. With just one word you pulled me out of my delusion. The most important thing is the crab! Aiyah, how could I be so muddle-headed! See! A new pugilist king appears under the heavens. Little brother, I humbly stand aside for you!"

Hok Leong didn't know if Fu *laoshi* was serious or if he was kidding. He had answered glibly the question about the seafood dish and got praised for it. What a great guy! But Hok Leong was also surprised at Fu *laoshi*'s gift of the gab, at the way he called him little brother. Were these maybe the more superficial aspects of that May Fourth legacy that they kept talking about?

Fu *laoshi* continued happily, "See what happened? I thought I'd give you a simple question to answer, but I didn't even know how wrong I was. See how your intuitive answer easily toppled my so-called experience? That's why I say, don't worry that Hsiao-yuan is ahead of you in certain matters. Those things have nothing to do with life. Whether you know them or not is not important. You're quick and observant, eager to learn, and you're not afraid to blaze a new trial. Very quickly it will become her following you rather than the other way around.

That was what he had been worried about, Hok Leong realised. For him, that was the nub of the issue.

Seeing that Hok Leong didn't react in an obvious manner, Fu *laoshi* tried a new tack. "So, how about it? Has my advertising campaign affected you yet?"

Hok Leong could only smile.

"Don't worry," Fu *laoshi* said. "I'm in too much of a hurry. The customer should first consider the matter."

After he dropped Fu *laoshi* off at his home, Hok Leong mulled over three things that Fu *laoshi* had said:

—Believe me, son, you make a good pair. In fact you're extremely well-suited.

—You can use your particular way to instruct and edify. She knows how to take advice.

—Don't worry that Hsiao-yuan is ahead of you in certain matters. Those things have nothing to do with life. Whether you know them or not is not important. You're quick and observant, eager to learn, and you're not afraid to blaze a new trail. Very quickly it will become her following you rather than the other way around.

8

Hok Leong went out and bought a copy of the *Butterfly Lovers Violin Concerto*, the one by Yu Lina. He also went to the library and borrowed a copy of the folktale commemorated by the music.

He remembered suddenly how Chiu-yun had taught him the lyrics to <u>Yesterday Once More</u>, how he went to see the movie *Brilliant Days* with his classmates, how he had liked the title song for that movie, and how he had sung "<u>I Started a Joke</u>" with his band while doing his military service. At every stage of his life, someone new had taught him to enjoy a different kind of music, bringing him as a result into a different world. Each song had captured faithfully his state of mind.

Hok Leong believed that his life shouldn't be too dissimilar from that of Ah Hor and the boys. So after he dropped out of university, he was happy to move on to a factory job. He was serene about the situation, was prepared to spend his entire life working as a <u>technician</u>. Much like Chiu-yun, however, the appearance of Hsiao-yuan and Fu *laoshi* had ushered him into a different world.

Hsiao-yuan wasn't Chiu-yun. He and Hsiao-yuan were both in their twenties. They had their own experiences and ideals, their own choices to make. Both pondered the question of what attributes they shared, and also what they didn't share.

9

During this period, labour had the upper hand. Employees chose their bosses, *not* the other way round. The companies in the sector were all expanding crazily, with many workers jumping from one outfit to another for small increases in pay. Hok Leong's company had to bus in its workers from Johore and then fetch them back at the end of their shifts. There was even an incentive payment if you introduced new workers to the company.

The <u>technicians</u> and <u>technical officers</u> in Hok Leong's company were also prone to job-hopping. To reduce such losses,

Hok Leong was promoted to <u>assistant engineer</u>, becoming the first person in his company to attain that honour. The increase in salary aside, the new post was an attempt to use "job title" as a way to reduce staff turnover. Hok Leong's previous <u>technical officer</u> designation had also served the same function.

<u>Akita san</u> told Hok Leong that he should give <u>Steven</u> a hand by taking on some admin duties. <u>Steven</u> was manager; he was also an <u>engineer</u>. Together with the other Japanese <u>engineers</u>, he helped to steer the development of the company.

Hok Leong was transferred to the main office. The <u>office girls</u> there insisted that he celebrate the occasion by giving them a treat. Hsiao-yuan also wanted a treat and arranged to meet with Hok Leong and uncle Fu on Friday evening. But later on uncle Fu spoiled the occasion, telling them that he needed to visit a friend. He asked them to call on him instead after dinner. Much later they learned that he had engineered the rebuff so that Hok Leong and Hsiao-yuan could spend some time together.

Unaware of such manoeuvrings, Hsiao-yuan suggested that they have something simple at the East Coast food centre. They could invite uncle Fu out for a meal on another day.

At the food centre, they ordered barbeque fish, rojak, and satay, which they washed down with some fresh coconut juice.

At one point, Hsiao-yuan turned to Hok Leong and asked, "So what are your plans for the future?"

Hok Leong hated these kinds of questions. In the past he never had an answer when Chiu-yun or <u>Eileen</u> grilled him about such things. And now it was again the same line of questioning.

He could only say, "I just got promoted. Don't even know what I have to do yet. I was thinking that I should just give it some time!"

Hsiao-yuan pressed on, "Have you thought about how long you want to do this, or whether you want to change to another line of work?"

Hok Leong knew that his response would only disappoint her. He answered carefully, "After working three years and still not seeing any kind of future I did think about changing to something else. But I really didn't know what I wanted to do. I knew I would probably end up with another <u>engineering</u> or technical position unless I switched to <u>sales</u>, like those guys who sell parts and accessories to us. It's tough coming out to work on your own."

Hsiao-yuan didn't express any strong emotions. She said evenly, "I don't think I will stay here for long."

Hok Leong was surprised by her frankness. He responded in kind, repeating his initial impression of her, "I've always felt that you're not suitable for a place like this."

"Things are good for you here. You've made some progress, so you don't think about leaving," Hsiao-yuan said. "But it's different for me. The <u>overtime</u> is certainly attractive but I can't be a <u>clerk</u> my whole life right?"

"But there *is* a way ahead," Hok Leong reminded her. "Several of the lady <u>managers</u> also started out as <u>clerks</u>, right?"

"Common, in every line of work or trade, a master will appear," he added, using the proverb that conveyed the idea. Figuratively it meant that, with enough diligence, one could produce outstanding achievements in any task.

Hsiao-yuan feigned annoyance, "The only new master here is you."

Hok Leong was happy to take some <u>credit</u> for his hard work.

After dinner they went to Fu *laoshi*'s home. Hsiao-yuan went around the house testing the faucets that Hok Leong had mended.

"Okay, you don't have to worry about losing your job," Hsiao-yuan said. "You can do this as well." Turning to Fu *laoshi*, she added, "What about me? Is there anything I can contribute or assist with?"

Fu *laoshi* thought for a moment. "Come visit me frequently! Bring him along!"

Hsiao-yuan heard the implication behind those words. "He now has special emeritus status because of his services to the state," she said. "He can come anytime he wants!"

10

Hok Leong finally found out what Akita san meant when he said that he should "do a bit of admin and give Steven a hand." What it meant was him doing odd-jobs for the two of them.

For instance, he was tasked to field phone calls that they would rather not handle. In the past the secretaries used to handle such calls. Now it was Hok Leong's turn, or rather it was Jackie's or Jackie Chan's turn. Basically his superiors had concocted a number of duties and shoved them in his direction.

Steven wanted him to seek out business opportunities from the telephone calls that came their way. But wasn't that the job of the sales department? Even the people in sales were stumped by the idea. Hok Leong didn't care. He did as he was told. But the callers who contacted them usually wanted to make money from *their* company. How could there be business opportunities there? Steven didn't let that bother him. On one occasion he turned to Hok Leong and asked, "How is your business?" Fortunately, Hok Leong had made a note of the phone calls and queries that he fielded. He made copies of his records, gave them to Steven, and briefly explained the situation. Steven nodded his head approvingly.

Of the calls that came Hok Leong's way, only one stood out. A new company, a local set up, wanted to enter a joint venture with Hok Leong's outfit. Was this what he had been waiting for? Had opportunity knocked at last?

Apparently, they wanted to jointly manufacture certain component parts used by Hok Leong's company. Akita san asked Hok Leong to talk to them. Hok Leong had no experience in these matters and was wary about the situation. He reminded himself not to make any assumptions.

As it turned out, Hok Leong met up with three individuals who were only slightly older than him. There were inexperienced and exacting. It quickly became clear that they wanted free access to the technology honed by Hok Leong's company. This was no joint venture.

Akita san could be considered a kind-hearted person. He let Hok Leong participate in four of such meetings before he pulled the plug on them. He told Hok Leong, "There's no Father Christmas in the business world. But it doesn't matter if there's a joint venture or not. After all, we both operate in the same sector. It's okay to make friends with them. The important thing is that we don't make enemies."

The other party didn't think like that. They concluded that Hok Leong's outfit was an enemy, so naturally the vaunted business "opportunity" didn't amount to anything. Nonetheless, Hok Leong remembered Akita san's words and held on to the wisdom that they contained.

To "do a bit of admin" also meant that Hok Leong had to draft letters and reports—this was the part that gave him the greatest headache. Hok Leong's first report involved a piece of machinery that had broken down. He wrote a one-and-a-half A4 size length report—a dense mesh of fine-detailed diagrams and words—and was worried that he hadn't written enough. After Steven corrected the report, only a quarter of the text remained, together with two simple diagrams. The rest got deleted. Even worse, the remaining text was criss-crossed with red ink. Hok Leong acknowledged that his English was poor. But to be corrected like that was close to humiliation.

The worse part was that Steven said Hok Leong "didn't know whose side he was on" when he wrote the report. "Machines break down every day," he explained. "The important thing is not how it got spoilt, but that we followed the correct instructions when we used it.

In plain words, <u>Steven</u> was saying, the crux of the matter had to do with *who* paid for the insurance and repair fees.

"You write down what really happened," he continued. "And you put in so many details. But the more you put in the more it's our fault, not theirs. How are we going to do business if you do that?"

Hok Leong's first impulse when he got back to the general office was that he should return to being a <u>technical officer</u>. He didn't know how to write these kinds of reports. By coincidence Hsiao-yuan also came into the office at that moment. Hok Leong tossed the report to her. She grabbed it and quickly perused the contents.

"This is too much!" she cried.

Hok Leong took the opportunity to let off some steam. "This kind of work cannot be done!" he said.

Hsiao-yuan's gave a surprising reply. "Don't you think that he's trying to show off his authority? To put you down? Ignore him!"

Hok Leong said reluctantly, "So should I correct it for him?"

"Of course you should!" Hsiao-yuan said. "If the first <u>assistant engineer</u> gets shot down after being promoted to the main office, who's going to take up that position? In the future he'll become even more bossy."

Hok Leong suddenly remembered Fu *laoshi*'s approach to things, the way he did everything with grace and refinement. He decided to take a leaf out of his book.

"Okay, alright! I'll do my best then," he said in a changed tone of voice.

"So, what do you want with me?" he added.

Hsiao-yuan made a show of being annoyed. She pointed to the document in her hand, "I need your signature, <u>Mr. Jackie Chan</u>!"

Hok Leong apologised for holding her up. After signing the document he asked after Fu *laoshi*. "I haven't treated him to a meal yet. How about this Friday? Are you free?"

"The real question is whether *you're* free. I go there every Friday," Hsiao-yuan said.

11

When Friday came around, Hok Leong passed to Hsiao-yuan another report that he had drafted and which <u>Steven</u> had corrected. Like the earlier one, his "essay assignment" was awash in a sea of red ink.

"Oh my gosh!" Hsiao-yuan cried when she saw the document. "Isn't the teacher a bit too strict with you?"

Hok Leong said dispiritedly, "He said I have <u>Ching chong English</u>. It's poor."

"Do you need me to type it out for you?"

Hok Leong felt aggrieved. "No, it'll give me a chance to learn how to type," he said.

The restaurant they went to was located in Katong and served *peranakan* food. As usual, the proprietor knew Fu *laoshi* and was on good terms with him. By the time they reached the eatery Fu *laoshi* was already there. This time around Hok Leong paid great attention to the food that they served.

The pièce de résistance was the fermented red tofu stew. The ingredients included braised pork belly meat, pig rind and intestines, chicken wings, fried and dry tofu, squid, and Chinese spinach. Together with that they also ordered *ikan selar* fried in chili sauce, Nonya-style mixed curry vegetables, and five-spice meat rolls. There was so much food that they couldn't finish it. Hok Leong especially loved the tofu stew base and didn't touch much of the other ingredients or dishes, just scooped the sauce into his rice.

For dessert they had <u>chendol</u>, barley, and black glutinous rice to choose from. Hsiao-yuan suggested that they each order a different dessert and try out each other's dish. She also ordered some to bring back to her mother and father.

When Hsiao-yuan went to place a call to her parents, Fu *laoshi* asked Hok Leong, "Did Hsiao-yuan tell you that she wants to leave the company?"

Hok Leong was surprised but didn't show it. "No," he said evenly, maintaining his smile. "Maybe in a few days she'll tell me."

When Hsiao-yuan returned, they asked her what she wanted to order for her folks. They started talking about the food. Hok Leong observed her carefully. She didn't look like she wanted to leave her job.

After they dropped Fu *laoshi* off, Hok Leong asked her, "Are you going to leave the company?" His words sounded harsh.

Hsiao-yuan was taken aback, "Uncle Fu told you about it?"

Hok Leong nodded.

"I was thinking the day after tomorrow when I hand in the resignation letter I would tell you about it. I need to give one week's notice!"

Hok Leong kept silent. They reached the tarmac abutting the front of St Patrick's School. He brought the car to a stop.

Hsiao-yuan explained, "I don't want to spend my whole life working as a clerk. I never intended to stay long." Hok Leong listened attentively but didn't respond.

"I actually went to university, but I left because I didn't want to continue my studies," Hsiao-yuan continued. "I enrolled in a Chinese studies programme but basically it operated in an English-speaking environment. After I left I taught for a while in a school. My father, mother, brother, and sister-in-law—they're all teachers. Later I discovered that the school environment was also not what I had expected. I didn't want to be like my family members so I went in a totally different direction. I joined an electronics factory thinking that to go somewhere radically different was also not bad. But it's also not a place where you can stay long."

She paused and gave a laugh. "Look at you! You've just been made <u>assistant engineer</u> and you're given such a hard time. I'm just a <u>clerk</u>. When will I be like you—some kind of <u>assistant</u> whatever with a bit of status? And even if I get that position, I wouldn't want to be harassed like you. Like you, I would also want to transfer out again. In the end if you have to leave you might as well take the plunge when a new opportunity comes along."

Hok Leong nodded but continued to stay silent.

Hsiao-yuan gave a sudden laugh, "I've discovered that every time I say something you just keep quiet and let me talk on and on and spill everything out. I'm exhausted! Can we have a proper back and forth conversation please?"

Hok Leong said lightly, "My mother taught me not to interrupt others when they talk. This is me showing respect for you! Okay, I'll ask a question. What's this new company that you're joining? What does it do?"

Hsiao-yuan said breezily, "It's an advertising company. I'm the Chinese-language copy writer."

"That's wonderful! Such a great job, you should have left long ago. How did you hear about it?"

"It came from Uncle Fu. He did some translation work for them. As part of its expansion programme, the company wanted to establish a new Chinese-language department. They were looking for a full-time Chinese-language writer. Uncle Fu recommended me for it."

That's why Fu *laoshi* knew about the job, Hok Leong thought. "Is the company okay? Is it a good place to work in?"

Hsiao-yuan shrugged her shoulders. "The boss is a Westerner. I've never worked with Westerners. I don't know how it'll turn out."

Hok Leong thought for a moment. "You'll be fine."

Hsiao-yuan pointed to a small side road across the street from the school. "Please turn in there. The first turning point that you come to, that's my place."

12

Hsiao-yuan tendered her resignation on Monday. She would work there till Friday. The other <u>office girls</u> wished her well. "On a personal level we can't bear to see you go. But at the practical level we hope you leave as soon as possible!" they cried.

Some of the <u>clerks</u> teased Hok Leong, "See! We told you she's a catch but you don't take action. Now she's going to leave!" They made the whole thing sound like Hsiao-yuan had found a good match, and that they were extending their blessings to her. Their words and demeanour greatly annoyed Hok Leong.

Hsiao-yuan was popular in the company. She received numerous invitations from colleagues wanting to treat her to a meal, so the whole week she was busy saying goodbye. It was just as well that Hok Leong was busy. For almost the entire week he didn't get to see her. When Friday came around, he thought, "No matter what happens I have to treat her to a farewell meal. If lunch isn't possible, it'll have to be dinner."

He didn't expect that Hsiao-yuan would come looking for him. They shook hands formally and bid each other good luck. "Shall we have lunch together?" Hok Leong asked.

"Sorry, I have an appointment."

Hok Leong was disappointed. "You mean you're still saying your goodbyes?"

Hsiao-yuan gave a laugh. "It's already the last one."

"How about dinner?" she continued. "My treat. After dinner we go to see uncle Fu?"

"You're the one leaving. It should be *my* treat," Hok Leong said earnestly.

"You drive me home almost every day. I have my own private school bus taking me back. Really, it should be me repaying the favour."

"It doesn't matter who treats who," Hok Leong said. "Where's your new <u>office</u>?"

"Around <u>Cecil Street</u>, near Tanjong Pagar hawker centre."

"That's also on my going-home route," Hok Leong jokingly said. "Maybe you can treat me to more dinners if you continue to take my bus?"

Her reply surprised him. "Okay, sure! If you don't mind the hassle?"

They agreed to meet at six o'clock. Hok Leong felt less agitated after they spoke. His heart was more at ease. After she left he sat down loss in thought, his mind in a whirl, unable or unwilling to focus on his work. Oh dear! Could it be that he wanted her for a girlfriend? His actions seemed to say yes. Was he looking for trouble? He reckoned that Hsiao-yuan wasn't suitable for him. They came from different worlds. Hsiao-yuan's attitude and response was the important thing. She didn't seem to mind the attention he gave her. She seemed to accept it, to make him feel that it wasn't as impossible as he thought it was.

He climbed out of his reverie. No, he didn't want to waste anyone's time, his own, and also hers. He didn't want to do anything that he might later regret. But…but the exhortation that he got from Fu *laoshi*—that seemed to suggest that things weren't so hopeless?

Aiyoh! Let's do dinner first! The rest can come later!

13

The had dinner at a Hokkien restaurant located near Hsiao-yuan's new <u>office</u>. Hsiao-yuan said he should get familiar with the area so that it would be easier for him when he came to fetch her after work. Hok Leong didn't know whether he should take that as a joke.

Hsiao-yuan had already placed a reservation. When they arrived at the restaurant she exchanged greetings with the proprietor. As before, she was a regular customer of the eatery. "My father comes here occasionally," Hsiao-yuan explained, "His taste buds haven't left the old country. They are still in Fukien province."

For dinner they had fish maw soup, prawn fritters, dried tofu, fried noodles, and stewed nappa cabbage. Hok Leong enjoyed the meal immensely. He quite liked Hokkien cuisine and was glad that he and Hsiao-yuan had that point in common. But straightaway he found the idea odd. Him—adding up the things they had in common! What was he doing?

At one point he asked Hsiao-yuan for the phone number of her new company. Hsiao-yuan wrote the number on a slip of paper and passed it to him. Hok Leong glanced at the slip and gave a laugh. "Oh, Jennifer! Nice to meet you," he said.

Hsiao-yuan didn't take it lying down. "Nice to meet you too, Mr Jackie Chan."

"What's the name of your foreign boss?"

"Martin!"

Hok Leong asked in a concerned tone of voice, "Can you guys get along?"

"Can you and Akita san get along?" Hsiao-yuan shot back.

Hok Leong chortled. "You know you've spent the entire week performing your farewell concert tour!"

"Well, I'm popular in the office!" Hsiao-yuan replied merrily.

Why did he find that an arrogant thing to say? Hok Leong wondered.

"You're not bad yourself!" she added. "The girls in the office all like you."

Hok Leong was glad she said that but didn't know how to respond. He could only laugh.

Hsiao-yuan turned serious. "The fact that the girls like you.

That means you've got a good working environment. That business with <u>Steven</u>—just take it as a chance to improve your English without having to pay school fees. In the past you had to pay uncle Fu for his lessons right?"

Hok Leong acted like he had made a great discovery. "I know why you're popular! You know how to envisage a path for other people, to put together a plan and speak up for them. That's really important. I can never talk like that."

Hsiao-yuan suddenly stuck out her arm, "Quick, quick, grab my hand!"

Hok Leong grabbed it. "What's wrong?"

Hsiao-yuan laughed, "You give me so much praise it feels like I'm flying away. I'm so light!"

"Bye-bye!" Hok Leong said. He released her palm.

His actions surprised Hsiao-yuan. She gave a laugh. "That's strange. Why would uncle Fu like someone like you?"

"Your English is actually better than mine," Hok Leong said, changing the subject, "Why did you decide to take lessons from Fu *laoshi*?"

"Uncle Fu said I should improve my level of English," Hsiao-yuan said. She added earnestly, "He said your English is not bad as well!"

Hok Leong was pleased. "Well, okay, since he said that let's finish here quickly and go to his place."

Although Hok Leong made that remark, he actually didn't feel like leaving early. He wanted to spend more time with Hsiao-yuan. But even taking their time with the food, they shouldn't finish later than eight o'clock, right? At one point Hok Leong took the opportunity when he went to the washroom to pay the bill. When Hsiao-yuan discovered that he had stolen a march on her, she said that their next meal must definitely be on her. Hok Leong felt that she meant what she said—this was the real her.

By the time they reached Fu *laoshi*'s home it was almost nine o'clock. They apologised for their tardiness, saying in tandem that Hok Leong was held back by his work. They performed well together, and this also gave Hok Leong a warm, homely feeling. He made a silent apology to Fu *laoshi*. Sorry teacher!

By the time they reached Hsiao-yuan's place it was already ten o'clock. They glanced at each other and laughed. "<u>Bye</u>!" they said together.

Hok Leong stoked up his courage. "Shall I fetch you after work on Monday?"

Hsiao-yuan hadn't expected that. She leaned back into the car, one hand holding the open door. "Okay, sure!" she said merrily. "Looks like I'll have to fork out money to treat somebody again!"

"Yes, that's what you pay nowadays for school bus transport," Hok Leong said solemnly.

"I finish work at five-thirty. By the time I finish it should be around six?"

Six was early for Hok Leong. Hsiao-yuan realised that immediately. "Oh, yes. You finish at six o'clock. How about you give me a call before you get off work?"

Hok Leong agreed happily and drove off.

In a while he reached the highway. He thought: why didn't he like Hsiao-yuan from the beginning? Was it because of her status? Her class or family background? Her background gave people pressure. But after knowing her, it became less important, was no longer an impediment. Hok Leong liked that she was a classy lady, but he also worried about the difference in status. He knew himself. Growing up in a hawker centre, undergoing all those changes over the years, at the most he was still a <u>technician</u>. It wasn't a matter of putting yourself down, of lacking self-respect or being unduly humble. You can't fool people about class, about where you come from. The fact that he didn't like Hsiao-yuan at the beginning. It wasn't that he didn't like her—it was him trying to avoid a problem.

As he drove past the yellow-orange halos cast by the street lamps, he felt that he knew what was coming: an abyss, a great unknown. He couldn't stop himself jumping into it. Worse still, Hsiao-yuan was also about to take the leap. He didn't want to let her down.

His words and ideas sounded familiar. It seemed he had deliberated them in the past. Yes, he had, with <u>Eileen</u>. He had told himself before that he didn't want history to be repeated. Of course, the most important thing now was how he chose to handle the matter.

When he got back, he realised that elder sister was home. It was rare for them to meet up like this. They led such busy lives. "<u>Mi-C</u>, how are you, he said," using the local form of address for a nurse.

His sister didn't take it lying down. "I'm fine! Is there anything that <u>Mi-C</u> can do for you, Mr <u>Engineer</u>?"

"You're cursing me! You hope I fall ill!" Hok Leong laughed. "Have you seen younger sister?"

"No, I haven't. I think she's still working."

"Wah! She's even worse than me."

Elder sister replied jauntily in Cantonese dialect, "It's tough making a living, young fellow!" She switched back to Mandarin, "When we all meet up at home on the same day. That's probably the day that one of us wins the lottery."

Hok Leong didn't respond. He went into his room, ending a conversation that had yet to be concluded. That was how it was with family. You didn't have to worry about niceties.

14

On Monday, Hok Leong found himself clock-watching and inattentive, waiting forever it seemed for the workday to end so that he could fetch Hsiao-yuan. He felt like he was short-changing the company.

At one point <u>Akita san</u> asked Hok Leong to step into his office. Hok Leong thought that his inattentiveness had been spotted. He crept nervously into the office. When he realised that <u>Akita san</u> was concerned about something else, he gave a sigh of relief.

<u>Akita san</u> had seen Hok Leong greeting customers while dressed in a simple T-shirt. He wanted Hok Leong to wear a long-sleeved shirt, and, better still, a tie. "It's the polite thing to do," he reminded Hok Leong.

Hok Leong heard advice rather than a reprimand. He nodded vigorously.

"You should also prepare a jacket to go with your outfit. You may need it sometime."

Hok Leong continued to nod his head. In his secret heart, he told himself that it was better to be a <u>technician</u>.

Hok Leong left the office at six, telling himself that he would be back again the next day anyway. It didn't feel good, him "leaving early." Although it was the designated time to clock off, the fact that everyone was still busy made him feel awful, especially since <u>Akita san</u> had just that day summoned him into his office. Although <u>Akita san</u> spoke about Hok Leong's attire, it was possible that he was hinting at something else, that he had spotted him wool-gathering and dreaming.

Hok Leong phoned Hsiao-yuan only after he reached the bottom of her <u>office</u> block. She said she needed another twenty minutes. He had some free time, so he made his way to the nearby Tanjong Pagar food centre to get some refreshments. As he neared one of the coffee stalls he spotted someone familiar. His first reaction gave him a shock, that being to turn around and leave. After a while he turned back and approached the stall from a different direction, hoping that he had seen the wrong person. Tanned skin, uneven flat-top badly needing a trim, faded blue T-shirt, dark-green shorts. He was right. It was Junior Brother. His attention trained on the coffee that he was brewing, Junior Brother had not seen Hok Leong.

Hok Leong no longer felt like having a drink. He crossed the road absent-mindedly and wandered down one street after another. He recalled decade-old events, remembered how he used to gad about with Red Dragon, Dog Shit, Ah Mei, Junior Brother, and Opium Addict.

Thinking of the way he had just reacted, Hok Leong felt a pang of guilt. He couldn't forgive himself, but he also didn't feel like going back to greet Junior Brother. Why shouldn't he say hello? What was wrong with that? In the past they used to fool around together, and had even risked life and limb together. Now he avoided the man. Hok Leong examined the explanation he gave to himself: he had an appointment with Hsiao-yuan. But—how much time did it take to greet a man? In the end, Hok Leong confessed, since he no longer wished to hang out with him, there was no point going over to say hello. He might as well stay away.

Why didn't he wish to hang out with Junior Brother?

Hok Leong abruptly broke his train of thought and returned to Hsiao-yuan's office block. She was waiting for him. They went to a nearby Western food restaurant, found a table and sat down. They were all set to celebrate her first day of work.

Hsiao-yuan hadn't taken much trouble with her outfit that day, but Hok Leong felt that she was quite fetching." You look good," he said.

Hsiao-yuan gave a small laugh.

"How's the new company?" Hok Leong asked.

"It's a simple set up," she replied. "Under the boss there's an <u>account manager</u>, two English-language <u>copy writers</u>, and one Chinese-language <u>copy writer</u>, that being me. There's also quite a number of artists, and then the secretary of the boss. The most important thing is that none of them speak Chinese."

"So what did you do today?"

"Translation."

"What kind of translation?"

"Red wine! I had no idea what I wrote!"

"Huh? So how did you do it?"

Hsiao-yuan lowered her voice. "My dad is at home today. I asked him to check the encyclopaedia for me. I'm going to bring the entire set to the <u>office</u>."

"Is that allowed?"

"I have no choice! For instance, this thing about new-world wine versus old-world wine. How could I possibly know something like that?"

Hok Leong felt that something was amiss. "If you know nothing about things like that, how did you do your work?"

Hsiao-yuan again lowered her voice. "I read the previous translation! For all I know, it might have been done by uncle Fu."

"It looks like we're doing the same thing," Hok Leong said. "I write reports in English. You translate stuff from English to Chinese!"

Hsiao-yuan gave a laugh. "So, tell me. Did anyone miss me at work today?"

"I'm afraid you're not that popular, my dear," Hok Leong replied in an affected tone of voice. He grew serious, "<u>Akita san</u> asked to see me today. He wants me to wear shirt and tie when I meet customers. He also wants me to prepare a jacket in case I need it. The problem is I don't have a western suit. Sometimes, I feel like I should just stick to being an ordinary <u>technician</u>."

Hsiao-yuan thought differently. "I think it's better to accept the change, to take things as they are—in the present day. Focus on what you need to do. Do it well. Don't dwell on the past? You can always tailor a suit for yourself, you know, or even buy one off the rack. Looking your best when you meet customers—isn't that the polite thing to do?"

What she said made sense. He could accept that. "So I

basically follow your example? Like the way you dressed up today? Simple yet elegant?"

Hsiao-yuan laughed out loud. "I've worn this before at the factory, Hok Leong! It's not a new outfit!"

"Really?"

Hsiao-yuan was kind to him, "When you're in the same company there's no time to observe what the other party is wearing, isn't it?" She gave Hok Leong a once over. "Your outfit looks good too. Makes you look young and forceful."

"In the future, you'll be seeing a long-sleeved-shirt-wearing, tie-knotting <u>executive</u>."

"That's just sooner or later, isn't it? The fact that <u>Akita san</u> wants you to prepare a jacket, that means you've got a chance. I don't see him telling you that when you're a <u>technician</u>."

Hok Leong nodded. He was still thinking about the incident at the food centre, wondering if he should share it with Hsiao-yuan. In the end, he opened up, "I spotted someone just now at the hawker centre. When we were younger we used to hang out together in the same group. We fooled around a lot. Some of it was pretty dangerous." He paused for a while, "Once we got into a fight with another group. I was held up in school and couldn't join them. They went ahead without me and one of our group members was killed. This all happened when I was in secondary three."

Hsiao-yuan kept silent. She was shocked at the revelation.

"After that, another of our group members was also killed in a fight. The guy that I saw just now, he actually asked me then if I wanted to join a secret society."

Why did he reveal so much of that sordid past? Hok Leong immediately regretted his words. "I hope I didn't scare you?" he asked.

Hsiao-yuan shook her head. "No, it's fine. It sounds like the plot of a movie."

He had been too indirect, too oblique, Hok Leong thought.

He should say the words in his heart. "You know, I've always felt that this is the barrier between you and me. My background is very different from yours."

"Barrier? Is there one? But I think your experience is better than mine. I've only been a goody two shoes quietly growing up in a bubble," Hsiao-yuan said. She gave a laugh,

"Anyway, I'm still wondering how you look like in a western suit." Hok Leong didn't know how to respond. He too gave a laugh.

15

Hok Leong took a while to accomplish the task that <u>Akita san</u> gave to him, that being to wear a long-sleeved shirt and a tie. He did it in two instalments so that he could get used to the change, and also because he didn't want to surprise his colleagues. What surprised him was that nobody batted an eyelid when he turned up for work in an office shirt. He made a self-deprecating joke about the situation. "See! Nobody bothers to look at me," he told Hsiao-yuan, laughing gaily. About a week after his sartorial modification, somebody finally noticed the upgrade. One of his female colleagues remarked, "Looks like you're wearing long-sleeved shirts nowadays to work?" Hok Leong was prepared, "I bought a few of them at a sale, all half-priced!"

About a month after that Hok Leong added a tie to his get-up. One of his colleagues noticed the change immediately, gesturing from far away at the new item of clothing. "I have to meet some customers afterwards," Hok Leong explained. <u>Akita san</u> liked it. "<u>Smart</u>!" he told Hok Leong. After a week nobody bothered anymore to single him out. But now Hok Leong couldn't get used to the constriction around his neck. He kept pulling at his collar; he took the tie off when he went to fetch Hsiao-yuan. Many years later he finally understood what the change of outfit represented, what it symbolised.

After Hsiao-yuan left, the company quickly found a replacement. The newbie, <u>Lina</u>, was young, beautiful, and stylish, one of the clerks said. As before, the <u>office girls</u> started to play their match-making game, hoping to pair her off. The one who got the most marks was Hok Leong; but this time the tie-adorned him expressed his disapproval. "Look guys! Stop fooling around," he said.

The <u>office</u> cabal thought that Hok Leong wanted to spare Lina any embarrassment, but actually he was thinking about himself. Although their situation was still up in the air, he didn't want to spoil his chances with Hsiao-yuan. <u>Lina</u> was too young, he thought, surprised that he felt that way. At 28, this was the first time he deemed somebody too young. She wasn't all that pretty. And besides, he didn't believe that someone "young, beautiful and stylish" didn't have a boyfriend. Of course, he didn't tell Hsiao-yuan about <u>Lina</u>.

Hsiao-yuan didn't have to work on weekends. She had a five-day work week, rare in those days. Hok Leong tried his best to fetch her home at least three to four time a week. Saturday nights were, however, off-limits for them. He had asked her out before but she said that Saturday nights were reserved for her folks. It was her <u>family day</u>.

Hok Leong had never heard of such a thing. His family didn't have <u>family days</u>. They never thought that it was important to set aside one day a week to share food and chit-chat. If they ever had something like that it was probably on lunar New Year's eve, when they got together for the customary reunion dinner.

Hok Leong finally understood the nature of the barrier between him and Hsiao-yuan—this <u>family day</u> thing. Starting from there, like two slanting lines growing ever distant, their differences became appreciable. This included the way they talked, their mannerisms and body language, the way they handled matters and treated people. And even their basic views about the world.

Would the slanting lines ever switch direction, turn back, and connect or intersect? One of the parties involved was trying very hard. But Hok Leong couldn't be sure about the outcome.

Hok Leong wasn't pushy about the Saturday issue, but now Hsiao-yuan herself began to complain. "Why must <u>family day</u> take place on a Saturday night?" she asked.

Apart from the Saturday hindrance, they also had to set aside their spare time on Friday for Fu *laoshi*. That left Sunday, but the ambience then was different. On Sunday morning even the <u>shopping centres</u> were closed. In the afternoon you tended to see families with kids rather than courting couples; in the evening people stayed at home because they had to work the next day.

16

As he was free on Saturday nights, Hok Leong sometimes went out with Ah Hor and the guys. At dinner they prattled freely, but after that, the talk ceased and they went their separate ways. Nobody suggested that they catch a movie, go window <u>shopping</u>, or go yau-cair-hor as the Cantonese say, meaning to cruise around in a car. Their lives no longer overlapped that much.

A decade on from their school-going days, they had all experienced ups and downs in life and now made different requirements of it. Without common topics or experiences, their camaraderie was slowly ebbing away.

Things had not gone well for Ah Hor and Tee Soon after they returned from their seafaring adventures. Together with several friends that he made shipboard, Ah Hor had started a laundry business. But after only half a year he had been cheated out of his share. Unable to find a job elsewhere he had returned to working in a factory. Tee Soon said that he was doing odd jobs. They understood that he was doing something shady or dishonest and didn't press the issue. Ying-jun had taken over his father's taxi business. He said the taxi would soon be sold to a big company. He would end up being a hired employee.

The three of them didn't have girlfriends. Occasionally they visited a cathouse, but they never asked Hok Leong to join them. For some time now, not sure when exactly it happened, they had stopped asking him to join their outings. Hok Leong understood the situation. This was the distance or barrier between them. He didn't think about returning to the past—that was impossible. The day that he spotted Junior Brother at the food centre, he had probably done the right thing when he didn't step up to say hello. He had spared them the embarrassment of meeting and then discovering that they had little in common, nothing to share. There was a rhythm to these things. For some reason at a certain time people got together from all directions of the compass. They grew distant for some reason or no reason, because nothing happened or because too much happened, intentionally or unintentionally, in a particular way or in no particular way— after that even if you wanted to restore the past you couldn't do it. His friends from childhood, from his secondary school days, and even the different ways of handling things at work— all these shapeshifted with the passage of time, had a way of becoming passé or becoming history. Hsiao-yuan had said it well: "Maybe it's better to accept the change, to take things as they are—in the present day. Focus on what you need to do. Do it well. Don't dwell on the past?"

Hok Leong sometimes got lazy about contacting Ah Hor and the guys. Having nowhere to go, he sometimes went home early. On one occasion, Mother was shocked when she saw him. "What's the matter? Are you ill?" she asked.

From who knows where his mother had gotten the idea that if he wasn't out and about that meant he was ill. Since young she had fixated on it. Hok Leong stared at her: "Can you focus on something good for a change, mother? When I'm not around you say I never come back. Do you really want me at home?"

His mother gave a small laugh but didn't reply. It was only later—many years later—that Hok Leong understood why, when he could appreciate the conflicting emotions entangled in the matter.

Since she was around, Hok Leong took the opportunity to ask about his sisters. His mother wasn't sure how they were doing. Everyone was so busy. For the next few Saturdays Hok Leong deliberately returned home early hoping to catch someone. One week he lucked out: elder sister wasn't out on a Saturday and was actually at home.

Each time Hok Leong saw her he would ask, "<u>Mi-C</u>, how are you?" It was like the opening lines of a play or sitcom.

That week, his elder sister, who was watching television, answered in a bad-tempered tone of voice, "Lousy! Terrible!"

"What's wrong? Are your patients behaving badly?"

"Lousy English," she answered dispiritedly.

Speaking from inside her room, younger sister explained, "Her boss promoted one of her colleagues, the one who had an English-medium education. He didn't promote her." Hok Leong was surprised that younger sister was home as well.

"But elder sister's English is quite <u>okay</u>!"

"No matter how good you are, those educated in Chinese-medium schools will never have <u>okay</u> English lah!" elder sister said.

"The <u>seniors</u> at my place say the same thing," younger sister said. She stepped out of her room wearing street clothes, looking like she was planning to go out. "Chinese school students like us are finished lah! With our lousy English, we'll never get anywhere!"

Elder sister added, "No matter how good your English is, you'll never get promoted." The prejudice she encountered had made her angry.

"You work in a Japanese company, of course you don't know about things like this!" younger sister said.

"In every department, the head is bound to be someone who received an English-medium education," elder sister explained. "Those who received a Chinese-medium education will at most be number two."

"So how? What can you do?" Hok Leong asked.

"What else can you do?" elder sister said. "Don't you remember what mother's friend said? She said fathers should be prepared to send their children back to China."

"Who wants to go to China? Not me," younger sister said.

Hok Leong asked again, "So what can you do?" He went to the kitchen and poured himself a glass of water.

No one answered him. When he returned to the living room, younger sister had already left the flat. Elder sister had returned to her room.

17

Although Saturdays were off-limits, there was one particular Saturday when Hok Leong got to spend time with Hsiao-yuan.

A clerk in the factory office got married and invited them both to the wedding banquet. This would be their first time attending a banquet together. Hok Leong, who had never been hung up about dressing, found himself worrying about what he should wear. It felt like he was the star of the show. After pondering the matter for a few days he was no closer to a solution, so he asked Hsiao-yuan for help. Their "after work" appointment went from being a dinner date at a restaurant to a <u>shopping centre</u> trip to buy clothes.

It went well. Soaking in the ambience, they strolled leisurely through the mall, enjoying the cornucopia on offer. They had something to do rather than just <u>window shop</u>. As they went through various options, they got to understand each other's taste and likings. For the first time ever, Hok Leong felt that <u>shopping</u> wasn't a waste of time. It could help nurture their relationship. He also got to practice the easy-going deportment epitomised by Fu *laoshi*.

Hsiao-yuan probably didn't know all that much about what guys liked to wear, or what was in fashion. She strode a few times round the men's wear section and returned with two options: a long-sleeved T shirt and a long-sleeve shirt with a round collar. "It's better to wear something casual, something that doesn't look too officey," she said.

Hok Leong bought both outfits. "I'll probably need them later," he said.

Hsiao-yuan patted her chest, said off-handedly, "It's probably better if you build up the chest area. It'll make the shirt stand out and look impressive."

From Hok Leong's perspective it was obvious that she was making a request, a claim of some kind. That wasn't a problem. After all he had done his national service, had served in the army. How tough could it be after what he had gone through? The only problem was time. Where would he find the time to work out? In the end, he felt, it would probably have to be on a Saturday.

At the appointed time that Saturday, Hok Leong and Hsiao-yuan attended the wedding reception. It was a good occasion to publicise their relationship, to say that they were an item. Used to seeing them together, however, their friends didn't make much of it. Or rather, it was their dressing that caught the attention. Hsiao-yuan looked splendid in a black dress, the attire bringing out her sophistication and refined sensuality.

Everybody commended her on her looks.

With Hsiao-yuan in the spotlight, Hok Leong decided that he would get seated first. Lina arrived soon after them. She was dressed prettily as well and had a younger girl's beauty and grace. <u>Lina</u> also greeted everybody, but because she wasn't as familiar with the other office girls as Hsiao-yuan, she had less to talk about. She took a seat next to Hok Leong and started to chat with him. After a while, Hok Leong felt someone take the seat on his opposite side as well. He wondered whether he should tell the person that the place was reserved for Hsiao-yuan. He glanced at her. She was still busy nattering away. Not wanting to attract additional questioning, Hok Leong began to chit-chat with the new arrival but didn't ask him to vacate his seat. After a while, Hsiao-yuan, looking for a seat, discovered that the places next to Hok Leong were already taken. Hok Leong shrugged his shoulders and gave her a dejected smile. Hsiao-yuan wasn't able to ask anyone to change seats with her. She had no choice but to take the seat directly across from Hok Leong.

For Hok Leong, the banquet was excruciating and painful. <u>Lina</u> was, by nature, open-hearted and friendly. She spent much of the evening interacting happily with Hok Leong, who couldn't very well ignore her. Hsiao-yuan struck an "I didn't see anything" pose. Occasionally she smiled coldly at him, making him feel like he had done something wrong. She practically laughed out loud when <u>Lina</u> served him some food as he chattered with a neighbour. When Hok Leong, doing the courteous, expected thing, served food for those ranged around the table, she deliberately refused his kindness. "Thank you, I don't eat that," she said, refusing to soften.

After the banquet, Hok Leong tried to nip things in the bud. He said aloud, "Okay, as usual, I'll send Miss Hsiao-yuan home in my car!"

Inside the car on the way home, Hsiao-yuan said in a

sarcastic tone of voice, "Partnered with a beautiful girl. A happy night for you, Mr Chan?"

"Yes, a beautiful girl now by my side. Of course, I'm happy," Hok Leong joked.

Hsiao-yuan wouldn't let it go. "And serving food for you too! When did such a beautiful girl join the company? How come somebody doesn't dare to let me know?"

To prevent any misunderstanding, Hok Leong decided that he had better make things clear. He slowed the vehicle down and pulled into the car park of a public garden located next to the highway.

"What's the matter?" Hsiao-yuan asked.

"Nothing's the matter. Just want to talk!"

"That's too late, mister!"

"Don't you want to know about <u>Lina</u>?"

"See! It's all coming out!" Hsiao-yuan thought he had something to confess.

Hok Leong said carefully, "What I want to tell you is that I know nothing about her situation."

"I don't believe you!"

Hok Leong thought for a while. He took a deep breath and lowered his voice, "Whether or not you believe me, the truth is that I'm only interested in what you do. I only care about you." After that he looked Hsiao-yuan squarely in the face.

Hsiao-yuan had not expected that. She stared quietly at Hok Leong, waited for him to continue. Finding that he had nothing to add, and not knowing what to do, she dropped her gaze and made to turn away. Hok Leong suddenly grabbed her by the shoulders, pulled her close and kissed her. Caught unprepared, Hsiao-yuan laid in his arms for a moment, then gently pushed him away, turned her head, and looked out of the window. "When did you get interested in my situation?" she asked quietly.

Hok Leong didn't reply. His heart was hammering like

crazy. He had stopped at the car park because he wanted to explain things to Hsiao-yuan. He didn't know where he found the courage to do what he did.

Like Hsiao-yuan, he turned in the direction of her gaze and stared silently out of the window.

18

On Sunday, they met early and caught a movie, a morning screening. Hok Leong couldn't remember what he watched. They sat in the darkness holding hands, Hsiao-yuan leaning slightly against him. Due to the events of the previous night, or perhaps that very morning, they kept laughing gently at each other but didn't speak. In this manner they wrote a sequel to their relationship.

Hok Leong felt that a page had turned in his life.

They spent the whole day together, saying goodbye only after dinner. After leaving the movie theatre they had lunch, after which Hsiao-yuan suggested that they go buy a western suit for Hok Leong.

They made their way to the store. As he tried on the lounge suits on offer, Hok Leong couldn't get used to the image in the mirror. Hsiao-yuan also found it strange. The store assistant thought that they were fooling around because they kept laughing. In the end, Hsiao-yuan suggested that he buy something simple.

"The one with no feature is probably the best design feature. It never gets outdated, you can wear it anytime," she said.

After buying the suit, they still had plenty of time to kill. They went to a nearby music store where Hsiao-yuan bought two audio tapes—yes, this was the era when cassette tapes still ruled the roost. One of them was "20/20" by George Benson. One of the songs in the album was "Never gonna change my love for you." The other tape that Hsiao-yuan bought was Luo

Dayou's "Home."

The Luo Dayou purchase brought to mind the movie "Brilliant Days." For a moment, Hok Leong thought about Chiu-yun; his heart twisted with pain.

"Do you like the two singers?" Hsiao-yuan asked.

Hok Leong kept it simple. "I only know Luo Dayou," he said.

Hsiao-yuan was surprised.

Hok Leong explained, "I heard a song by him in a movie that I watched during my secondary school days. Couldn't escape it, I guess."

Hsiao-yuan patted his shoulders to express her admiration. "Wah! Still waters run deep!"

Hok Leong spread his arms wide.

They went to a McDonald's restaurant and found seats for themselves. Hsiao-yuan retrieved a <u>Walkman</u> from her bag. They ordered a <u>Coke</u> each, shared out an earphone, and sat listening to the title track of Luo's album:

Loving you gently, Loving you gently, my baby, my baby.
Think of you gently, missing you gently, these tears of mine, these tears of mine.
Who can give me warmer sunshine than you?
Who can give me sweeter dreams?
Who forgives me in the end? And comforts my pain-filled heart?
My family, my birthplace, the beautiful time of my childhood past.
That was the place I escaped from, and also the direction luring my tearful visage.

Hok Leong suddenly asked, "How old is Luo Dayou?"

"He's older than us, I think. At least thirty? Why do you ask?"

"Let's find a day when we both have time—I want to show you the place where I used to live."

19

After dropping Hsiao-yuan off that day, Hok Leong drove to his old home.

Most of the old apartment blocks had been torn down. Only two were retained to provide accommodation for elderly residents who were single. Hok Leong sat in his car gazing at the new flats towering around him. They seemed to engulf his vehicle. Luo Dayou was still crooning away on the cassette player. Hsiao-yuan had said that they should leave the tape in the car. Hok Leong didn't know why he suddenly wanted to see his old stomping ground. Probably had to do with Luo Dayou's music, he figured: "That was the place I escaped from!"

Hok Leong didn't feel that he had escaped from anything. Whenever he heard the phrase urban redevelopment, he felt that *he* was part of what got redeveloped. The bulk of his life had in fact been rebuilt. It was no longer assessable, no longer "brilliant."

Luo Dayou was again singing from the cassette player, "Haply I may remember. And haply may forget."

20

Exercising his authority, Steven now decided to pass two different accounts to Hok Leong to handle: one was a supplier, another, an old customer. It was a kind of test, an indication of the high regard in which he was held.

When he contacted the two parties, Hok Leong quickly realised what "high regard" meant. They were similar in nature: anxious and fearful, unwilling to take responsibility for any slip up. Hok Leong suspected that Steven had passed them to him because they were "orange" name-tag types. The funny thing was that both parties refused to communicate with Hok Leong in Chinese. They preferred to use what Steven called <u>Ching chong English</u>.

Start with the customer. After he had spoken with him for a while, Hok Leong could not control himself. "Hey buddy, are you from a Chinese-medium school background?" he asked.

"<u>No</u>!" the customer roared back.

Because it was a customer, Hok Leong was careful not to leave a negative impression. Hoping to lighten the mood, Hok Leong tried to make a joke about his manager. The most difficult thing that <u>Steven</u> had to do was signing his name on a document, Hok Leong said facetiously. He didn't expect that the customer would make the following retort: "<u>That's what you said, I did not say anything</u>."

Hok Leong had walked into it, had invited the rebuff. He quickly finished the conversation and replaced the receiver. In future, he should just stick to the script, he told himself.

A few days later, the guy called back. His tone was entirely different as he was looking to get some information. He had received some outlandish news—basically that <u>Steven</u> was leaving. "Was that true?" he asked Hok Leong, whose joke had probably caused the rumour to circulate. Hok Leong could only reply courteously that he hadn't heard of such a thing. He didn't expect that the guy would fly into a rage, reacting as if he had been humiliated. Hok Leong was a coward, he said. He didn't dare tell the truth. Hok Leong nearly laughed out loud. He wanted to repeat the man's words, "<u>That's what you said, I did not say anything</u>."

In the case of the supplier, the reaction was different. When Hok Leong asked whether he came from a Chinese school background, he didn't deny it but also didn't confirm it. He didn't answer the question. The conversation stayed suspended in mid-air. This was a tactic that Hok Leong could never learn. There was another tactic that he could never learn, which was how to answer unwelcome questions with a great laugh, glossing as such over the matter.

Hok Leong called the supplier because he sent the wrong parts to them. But as though his life depended on it, the guy refused to admit the error. "You made a mistake. We have a record," he insisted. The problem was that Hok Leong had only recently been put in charge of the account. He couldn't have made a mistake. The guy was blathering. Not wishing to shoulder responsibility, Hok Leong now started to argue with the man. But no matter what Hok Leong said, he repeated the same tune, "Someone at your end made a mistake. We have records."

From "you made a mistake" to "somebody at your end made a mistake": claims made without foundation; and shirking one's responsibility. Hok Leong no longer wished to contest the matter. He wanted to move pass the question of blame, which was to say that, tacitly, he was admitting to the error. Could his company return the parts consignment, he finally asked.

"This comes from you! You must send me a <u>memo</u>," the supplier pointedly said.

In the end, Hok Leong grew tired, meaning that he had lost. He agreed to the whole thing. He wondered when he could change the supplier. He also thanked <u>Steven</u> for showing him such "high regard."

When he complained to Hsiao-yuan about the kerfuffle, she imitated <u>Steven</u>'s tone of voice:

"<u>Jackie</u>! This is a test for you," she said.

By then Hsiao-yuan had worked in the advertising company for over half a year and was also facing workplace challenges. She complained that instead of being a <u>copy writer</u>, she was actually doing translation, nothing different from what uncle Fu used to do for them. She believed that Chinese- and English-speaking customers had different habits and outlooks. Rather than translate English adverts into Chinese, adverts aimed at Chinese-speakers should cater specifically for them. This latter option was bound to work more efficiently than the former. But from her bosses to her customers, nobody accepted the idea. Her Western boss wanted her to translate straight from the English copy. Her customers—those from the West as well as those that she called local westerners—also tended to fetishize the English copy.

Hok Leong recounted to Hsiao-yuan the name-tag system used in the army to denote speech community. He laughed and called himself a <u>Chinese helicopter, a made-in-1960 Chinese helicopter</u>.

21

The <u>made-in-1960 Chinese helicopter</u> now experienced a bit of good fortune.

One day, the outfit that he encountered in the past—the one that wanted to set up a joint venture with Hok Leong's company —contacted him by phone. Hok Leong had forgotten about them. It took him five minutes to figure out who they were, after which he couldn't make out what they wanted. It didn't seem like they were hoping to revive the old plan. So why did they contact him? After a long, interminable exchange, they had no choice but to spell it out, "We hope you can join our company and give us a hand."

They probably regretted the call, Hok Leong thought. He was so stupid they had to spell things out for him. Hok Leong's first reaction wasn't that feeling of stupidity, that came later. Recalling the incident to Hsiao-yuan, Hok Leong said his first reaction was to repeat what they had said: "You…want… me…to…join…your…company…to…give…you…a   hand?" After that his heart started to beat like crazy, as if he had done something wrong. Afraid that his colleagues might overhear him, Hok Leong quickly lowered his voice. In the end, the person on the line had to tell him to speak up.

He couldn't remember what exactly they discussed. He was extremely nervous. His only wish was that he wouldn't say anything wrong, that his words fitted the occasion.

"So did you agree?" Hsiao-yuan asked, going to the heart of the matter.

Actually, Hsiao-yuan knew the answer to her question. If Hok Leong had said yes, he wouldn't have told the story like that. From what she knew of his personality, she could make a good guess.

The reason that Hok Leong gave her was, "I don't like this poaching business." Other reasons came to mind later, including:

—If you use high salary to entice someone, you can also fire him or her at the drop of a hat.

—He didn't know how the outfit was doing. For all he knew, they might close down half a year after he joined them.

—<u>Akita san</u> treated him well.

Hsiao-yuan made an educated guess: "Since they can't get you, they'll probably ask someone else in the company."

22

Hok Leong's antics produced a cherished in-joke between them, what they later called a genuine classic.

Firstly, Hsiao-yuan's conjecture came true. After failing to recruit Hok Leong, the party that tried to hire him managed to entice one of the <u>technical officers</u> to join them.

Soon after that <u>Akita san</u> asked to see Hok Leong. Hok Leong didn't know whether he had heard something about it.

<u>Akita san</u> went straight to the point, "You've performed well. Do you have any interest in admin work?"

Hok Leong shook his head.

"How about if we make you <u>assistant manager</u>?"

Hok Leong spoke from his heart, "I still prefer the technical part of the job."

<u>Akita san</u> thought for a while. "How about if we make you <u>engineer</u>?"

"Can I say, no?" Hok Leong asked, "I know my own level."

<u>Akita san</u> suddenly mumbled something under his breathe. He stood up and gave Hok Leong a bow.

Hok Leong quickly rose and bowed twice to show his respect.

"When do you feel you can reach the level of an <u>engineer</u>?" <u>Akita san</u> continued.

"When everyone feels that I've reached that level."

<u>Akita san</u> browsed through the personnel file in his hands. "Twenty-eight year old! Very good!" he said.

Hsiao-yuan gave a big laugh when Hok Leong recounted the incident to her. "Only a Japanese guy will appreciate someone as stupid and as impulsive as you," she said. "You're not normally like this. Why did you act this way?"

It wasn't just her. Hok Leong's impulsiveness had surprised even himself. "I was nervous! A person's real personality comes out when you're nervous. And I get to show the level I'm at—my real level!"

He added: "Do you think I'm suited to be an <u>assistant manager</u> or <u>engineer</u>? I don't want everyone saying I'm not good enough after getting promoted, after which I get returned to my previous level, or, worse, I get fired. That's what I was thinking at that moment."

"Never mind," Hsiao-yuan said in a sardonic tone of voice, "everything's fine if the Japanese guy likes you."

Afraid that she might hurt his feelings, she added, "and also me."

Somehow word got out and went around. Only the two of them knew about it, so <u>Akita san</u> must have done it, although how he did it they couldn't be sure. No matter how it got out, the whole affair came down to one word—stupid—so stupid in fact that for years after that nobody came to knock on Hok Leong's door.

23

Another Saturday came around again.

Hok Leong went to the food centre to look for his elder brother. He hadn't seen him or his sister-in-law for a long time. Sister-in-law was pregnant. Nobody at home had said anything about it.

Hok Leong prepared a bag of boiled dumplings with extra fillings. These were packed separately from the soup. He also packed a bowl of noodles, to which he added some condiments.

Sister-in-law turned to him, "Is that for your girlfriend?"

Hok Leong made like it was a great mystery.

"When will you bring her home? Your elder sister also has a partner. Good things come in pairs."

Hok Leong looked at his elder brother.

"Don't look at me," his brother said, "I also got the news from her."

"The food is for my teacher. He's ill," Hok Leong said.

Fu *laoshi* had a bad cold. Hok Leong had told him the previous evening that he would bring over some noodles and boiled dumplings from his family stall so that he could try them out. Fu *laoshi* didn't want to impose on Hok Leong and kept insisting that he was alright. Before going to the food centre, Hok Leong had phoned him to confirm that he hadn't prepared dinner yet.

Fu *laoshi* tucked into the noodles and dumplings. Wonderful, really wonderful, he said, relishing the treat.

After a while, he felt that something was amiss, "Where's Hsiao-yuan? Why isn't she here yet?"

Hok Leong laughed. "Saturday is her <u>family day</u>."

Fu *laoshi* looked shock. "You mean you spend Saturdays by

yourself?"

Hok Leong nodded.

"What the hell kind of <u>family day</u> is this?" Fu *laoshi* said, getting upset. "Why must it be held on a Saturday evening? Why not Sunday? Or some other day?"

Hok Leong stared quietly at Fu *laoshi*.

Fu *laoshi* was still upset. "I'm going to talk to old Xu about this. That's her father. What epoch are we in? Still need to hog the children after they've grown up? I'm going to talk to him about it."

"The food's getting cold, *laoshi*," Hok Leong said mildly. "Please eat up."

24

Hok Leong went to Fu *laoshi*'s home again the following Saturday. Fu *laoshi* had told him to come visit him that week as well. Hok Leong got there early and was surprised to see several glasses of lime juice sitting on the coffee table.

Fu *laoshi* didn't prepare any food, which suggested that they were going out for dinner.

Fu *laoshi* knew that he was surprised by the drinks on the table but didn't say anything. After a while, Hsiao-yuan arrived. Behind her was a couple who were slightly younger than Fu *laoshi*, probably Hsiao-yuan's parents.

Hok Leong grew nervous.

Hsiao-yuan's was surprised to see Hok Leong. She quickly turned around. Her parents were also surprised that Fu *laoshi* had a guest.

Fu *laoshi* cheerfully made the introductions. "My student, Chan Hok Leong" he said. "Hsiao-yuan's parents," he added, nodding to Hok Leong.

Hok Leong gave a slight bow. "*Bo Fu, Bo Mu*. How are you?" he said courteously.

But in that era, actually, nobody used *"Bo Fu"* or *"Bo Mu"* to address their elders, the terms meaning roughly and respectively, "Uncle" and "Auntie." Depending on ancestral background, they used dialects—Hokkien, Teochew, Cantonese, and so on.

"Ah Jiek, Ah Jhim, How are you?" were the words that Hok Leong used. He could see Hsiao-yuan stealing a laugh on him.

"We're fine! Hope you're well!" Hsiao-yuan's parents answered politely.

Fu *laoshi* spoke up, "Okay! We've met. There's nothing to talk about at the first meeting, so how about we do it like this? Hok Leong, Hsiao-yuan, you guys can go off by yourselves. We oldies have our own things to talk about. You won't be interested in them."

Hsiao-yuan looked at her father.

"This is uncle Fu's home. Let's abide by his wishes."

Hsiao-yuan bid goodbye to everyone. Hok Leong followed her lead.

Fu *laoshi* made a joke before they went off. "The same rule applies, okay? Girls must get home before ten o'clock. If not, then don't bother to come back!" After that, surmising that something was wrong, he added laughingly, "Okay, don't go home, but you can come over here."

25

That was the first time that Hok Leong met Hsiao-yuan's parents. He always remembered it. It was also the reason why Hsiao-yuan's <u>family day</u> got shifted away from Saturday. On this matter, Hok Leong always felt grateful to Fu *laoshi* for his intervention.

That evening, Hok Leong sent Hsiao-yuan home before ten o'clock. They were both on edge, unsure how the little drama directed by Fu *laoshi* would turn out. They didn't have the mood to stay out late.

Hsiao-yuan's parents didn't say anything when she got home. It felt like nothing had happened. When she relayed that to Hok Leong on Sunday, they became even more worried. After three days, Hsiao-yuan's mother finally told her what had transpired. She told Hsiao-yuan "everything."

"Everything?"

Yes, everything. Hsiao-yuan recounted what her mother meant by "everything":

After Hok Leong and Hsiao-yuan left uncle Fu's home on Saturday, he had explained the situation. That young man is Hsiao-yuan's boyfriend, he said. He's twenty-eight years old, works as an assistant engineer in an electronics factory. He has great prospects ahead of him, and not just in his career. He's flexible and pragmatic.

I like him, uncle Fu continued, so you're not allowed to oppose the match. You can only say, yes. There's no room for discussion.

Hsiao-yuan's father said, Brother Ting—Hsiao-yuan explained that uncle Fu's full name was Fu Ting—how long have you known him?

Not sure, uncle Fu replied. Two, three years? I'm already a senior citizen, why are you questioning my judgement? What's the matter? You don't trust me?

Of course not, Hsiao-yuan's father replied. We've always felt that elder brother Ting has an eye for talent, like Bo Le from the Spring and Autumn period. But can I and Xiao Hua check him out first? Xiao Hua is my mother, Hsiao-yuan explained.

That's your problem, uncle Fu said, not mine. My precondition is that you don't scare him off. You mustn't arrange anything too formal. And furthermore you need to do something about your <u>family day</u> get-together. What era are we in? How old is she? Why are you still hanging on to such outmoded practices? You better be careful that your child doesn't miss the boat when it comes to marriage. Or else it'll be too late for regrets.

Feeling that something was amiss, Hsiao-yuan's mother asked uncle Fu: Brother Fu, she said, we've become enemies.

Uncle Fu gave a great laugh.

I'm fine with that, he insisted, then he tried to comfort his friends. Lao Xu, Xiao Hua. We've known each other for over thirty years. You still don't accept my good intentions? I've always treated Hsiao-yuan as if she's my own daughter. If she ends up in a bad marriage, I'll be even more heart broken than you.

Hsiao-yuan continued the story: "So my Mother asked me whether that young man will create heartache for uncle Fu. I said, how should I know? For all you know, maybe I'll be the one to cause him heartache. Why don't you ask him?"

Hok Leong didn't want to say anything too serious or heavy. "Tell your mother there's nothing to worry about!" he said.

Hsiao-yuan made like she couldn't take it anymore, she had enough.

"Go tell her yourself!" she said in a huff.

26

Hsiao-yuan had two pieces of news that she wished to share with Hok Leong: one good, one bad. He got to decide which went first.

Hok Leong naturally chose the positive one.

The good news was that one of Hsiao-yuan's advertisements had won a prize.

It was extremely simple:

Laws of vehicular motion:
Speed = Protection + safety distance
"Jie Xing" vehicles = Protection + Speed.

Jie Xing meant quick travel in Chinese, so the advert was using a pun to good effect.

"You mean something like this can win a prize?" Hok Leong asked.

"What do you think, Mr Jackie Chan?" she said, raising her voice.

The important part was what transpired *before* she got the award. After the English copy for the advert was accepted, the Chinese copy kept being sent back. The customer rejected "luxurious" and "respectable," which were terms taken from the English copy and translated directly into Chinese. In the end, Hsiao-yuan grew exasperated. Following her own nose she wrote a completely new copy for the Chinese ad campaign and sent it over. To her surprise it had been accepted.

For Hsiao-yuan, who had just joined the sector, this development was an important first step; it had led to her winning an award. So, of course, she had to treat Hok Leong to a meal.

And the bad news?

Hsiao-yuan's father wanted to arrange an *informal* meeting with Hok Leong.

This was definitely *bad news*. It "just happened" that Hsiao-yuan's elder brother Xu Ke and sister-in-law flew in from Hong Kong and were also present. So in an ill at ease but putatively "at ease" manner Hok Leong spent an *informal* evening at Hsiao-yuan's home, acting the part of a dutiful boyfriend.

Xu Ke was older than Hok Leong by a year; Hok Leong quite enjoyed his company. His name meant allowed or permitted in Chinese, so his presence denoted so to speak that things were permitted. Like the pun on Hsiao-yuan's name, which meant "to make a small wish," Hsiao-yuan's parents had outdone themselves with their son—they were coolness personified.

Nevertheless, Hok Leong had a feeling that the "little wish" he shared with Hsiao-yun would not be so easily "permitted."

Hsiao-yuan later told him that the happiest part of the evening for her was seeing the much improved condition of her sister-in-law. Xu Ke had gone to Hong Kong to study for two years and had initially left his wife, who was a teacher, in Singapore. Due to work pressure, however, she had experienced a bout of mental illness and had left her job to join him there.

Hok Leong was surprised. "Isn't she an experienced teacher?" he asked. "She's done it for quite a while, right?"

Hsiao-yuan explained. "The textbooks they used used to be in Chinese. Last year everything was changed to English."

"Oh-My-God!" Hok Leong cried.

Contrastingly, Hok Leong enjoyed some good fortune at his workplace. A few months after he rejected the job offer made by the set-up that had contacted him, he received an unusual phone call. It wasn't the guy who tried to poach him but rather the technical officer who had jumped ship. The chap said Hok Leong was lucky he didn't join the new company because it was facing financial difficulties. Could Hok Leong approach Akita san on his behalf? Could he have his old job back?

Hok Leong recalled the "classic joke" that had emanated from his encounter with Akita san. Once was enough to last a lifetime, he thought.

Naturally, the difficult customer who had contacted him earlier also wanted to ferret some information about the new company. He probably knew that Hok Leong wouldn't divulge anything, but he still wanted to ask. By now, Hok Leong had learnt an important skill from the supplier guy he encountered earlier, namely how to give a great laugh while passing over unwelcome questions. These two were no longer causing problems for Hok Leong. After passing their two accounts to Hok Leong, Steven had given him other accounts to handle. What was previously a small problem had been transformed— now there was none at all. On the day that Hok Leong received the phone call from the customer contact, he had to wear a lounge suit at his workplace. Some colleagues from the head office in Japan were visiting their factory. They were there for a meeting and Hok Leong was tasked to welcome them. Although the job was simple, the feeling was complex. Hok Leong recalled the aspiration that he had during his secondary school days, his wish that he wouldn't be an errand boy, that he wouldn't have to make coffee for those employed in an <u>office</u>.

27

With Fu *laoshi* working as a catalyst and guide, the next instalment in the story should have been, "and they lived happily ever after." Even if it didn't pan out that way, it should have been something close to that.

But, no, they didn't achieve the "lived happily after" bit.

Again, it started from an unexpected phone call. It was already past eight o'clock. Hok Leong was getting ready to leave the office. When the phone rang, it was either someone had called the wrong number, or else it couldn't be anything good.

It was Hsiao-yuan on the line. She was calling from her company. "Hok Leong, I'm sorry. I going to have to leave you," she said half-jokingly.

Hok Leong was shocked. He forced himself to reply, "Look lady. Don't give me a heart attack. It's not April Fool's day!"

Hsiao-yuan grew serious. "Our company wants to set up an office in Taiwan. Martin wants me to go give a hand. I've been thinking about it the entire evening. I wanted to figure out a plan before calling you. Then I realised I should just call you straightaway and get your help on this."

"Oh!" Hok Leong kept silent for a while. His head was a blank. "What do you want? Don't think about anyone else including me. What do *you* want?"

Hsiao-yuan said indistinctly. "I've always felt that the sky here lies too close to the ground. It's stifling, you can't breathe. Don't talk about standing straight and stretching your limbs. You don't even get much of a chance to raise your head."

She added in a firmer tone of voice, "You know what I'm talking about."

"Yes, I do," Hok Leong said. He took a deep breathe. "You know what? Go, I say! Since we're young, let's take a chance. Do what you want to do. If you don't succeed all it means is that you had to take a detour to reach your destination."

Hsiao-yuan was touched. "Thank you!" she said. "Give me two years please? If it doesn't work out I'll come back. I want to leave this place and get some air. I know what I'm getting into."

She explained further, "Martin actually wanted me to go for three years. I asked for one year. In the end we agreed on two years."

"Yes, do go! I know what you want to do."

Hsiao-yuan suddenly broke into a sob. "Thank you, Hok Leong!"

"If it's me I would want to go too."

"Really?" Hsiao-yuan said, controlling herself. "What I said flippantly to mom, maybe I'll be the one to cause him pain, I never thought it would actually come true."

"Don't say that. There's no such thing as who caused who pain. I'm also happy for you." He changed the subject. "Have you thought about how you're going to tell your mom and dad?"

Hsiao-yuan again started to cry. "No, I was more concerned about you."

Although Hok Leong was pleased with her response, he felt a great sense of loss and was close to panic. He lost control and started to blather. "How about I tell your mom and dad?" he said, "I'll be a little tell-tale."

"Don't you dare!" Hsiao-yuan said. She stopped crying and gave a small laugh.

After a few minutes they ended their conversation. Hok Leong replaced the receiver. He stretched his limbs and sank deep into his armchair. He laid there without moving, as if he was paralysed. His premonition had come true. He and Hsiao-yuan wouldn't have an easy time of it. As he went through the whole thing, his mind drifted to Chiu-yun. It was the same with her. He hadn't been able to keep her from leaving. And then she had "floated" away.

Even so he supported Hsiao-yuan. He knew what she was going through.

28

Hsiao-yuan's parents didn't express any approval or disapproval. Her mother asked, "Is your boyfriend okay with this?"

She nodded her head.

"Think carefully about it," her father cautioned her.

Hok Leong and Hsiao-yuan went to see Fu *laoshi*. He took it almost like a joke. "It's heredity! It's heredity!" he said mysteriously. "How old is mademoiselle?" he asked Hsiao-yuan.

"Twenty-five."

"Twenty-five? I left for England when I was sixteen to further my studies. You're already far above the average age of the foreign students cohort."

Fu *laoshi* and Hsiao-yuan looked at each other. His implication was clear.

"Do your parents oppose the plan?" he asked.

Hsiao-yuan shook her head, telling him that there hadn't been any reaction.

"Do they approve of it?"

Again Hsiao-yuan shook her head. No reaction from them.

"That means they're against it," Fu *laoshi* said. "Give them some time. They'll come around." He turned to Hok Leong.

"How about you? You should be fine with her plans, right?"

Hok Leong nodded.

"You're not afraid she'll have a change of heart?"

Hok Leong gave a silly laugh.

"You're cursing me, Uncle Fu! Stop it!" Hsiao-yuan complained.

"Why don't you get married before you leave the country?" Uncle Fu suddenly said.

Hok Leong and Hsiao-yuan looked at each other. The idea hadn't crossed their mind.

29

"I don't want to shackle you with marriage. If we're going to drift apart, it can happen here without anyone going overseas. It's not that I don't want to marry you, don't get me wrong. I just don't want to do it under such circumstances," Hok Leong said.

"You should understand what I mean," he continued.

Hsiao-yuan nodded.

They had left Fu *laoshi*'s place and gone to a fast food restaurant to discuss the suggestion made by him.

"I also don't want to make it too complicated," Hsiao-yuan said. "It's just an overseas work assignment! Why must we bring in the topic of marriage?"

"As long as we understand each other that's fine," Hok Leong said.

30

Fu *laoshi* went to Hsiao-yuan's home to speak to her parents. Hsiao-yuan related what happened:

When they saw Uncle Fu, father said, look, Hsiao-yuan, your lobbyist has arrived!

It's heredity! Uncle Fu said to my mother, Xiao Hua. Then he said to my father, going overseas nowadays is no big deal. Take it that she's going overseas to study. Things are different now. It's not like how it was in the past.

My father didn't agree. He said, brother Ting, study and work are different things. Yes, we live in a different era. But she's a girl…. Ai! Brother Ting! You spoil her too much. You're actually speaking up for her!

Uncle Fu didn't feel that that was such a horrible a thing to do. But, brother, he shot back, that's what it means to have a daughter. She's meant to be spoilt. And, you know, she's already twenty-five. There's no reason to keep her by your side! Isn't it better that she learns how to do the laundry, how to cook? If you don't give her a chance, how will she cope after marriage? She'll be fine. As parents you don't have to worry too much.

Uncle Fu had dinner in their home. After he left, she went to speak to her mother. "Mom! Uncle Fu says I've inherited some things from you. When I was young I used to wonder whether I'm actually your birth daughter. What's happening now proves that I am!"

Her mother was forced into a corner. "Okay, if you must go, then go!" she said softly.

Hsiao-yuan suddenly felt awful because she had caused heartache for her mother.

Listening to it all, Hok Leong thought that, among them all, her mother was the one who most didn't want her to leave the country.

31

Two weeks later, Hsiao-yuan left for Taiwan.

Hok Leong gradually lost the feeling that he would soon be losing Hsiao-yuan. Or perhaps it was him coming to terms with reality. He had experienced the feeling before—the last time it was Chiu-yun going to England to study.

It turned out that Hsiao-yuan took it differently. At times she grew anxious and panicky, "Let's just cancel the whole thing," she said. Or else she would say, "After I'm gone, will you look for Lina?"

"Can you show more confidence in me, Madam?" Hok Leong replied.

The shadow cast by Chiu-yun continued to bedevil Hok Leong. He even compared Hsiao-yuan's departure to him and Chiu-yun drifting apart. If fate treated him that way again, he would have no choice but to accept it. Because of that he also sometimes couldn't control himself. "You're concerned about me? I'm more worried about you," Hok Leong said, returning the compliment.

He didn't expect that, feeling fragile and sensitive, she would burst into tears, "You don't want me to go? Is that it?"

Hok Leong decided not to raise it up again.

During the two weeks hiatus, Hsiao-yuan did something that he didn't expect. Without him raising the matter, she suggested that he bring her to see his parents. Hok Leong imagined how the meeting would go. He gave a laugh. He knew how painful departure was, why she had suggested the meeting.

Again it was an *informal* event. There was no special arrangement, nothing that "just happened" to happen. Only Hok Leong's parents were there. He didn't tell them he was bringing someone home. Because of the sweltering heat, Hok Leong's father was even bare-bodied when Hsiao-yuan arrived. He wasn't wearing a shirt.

Hok Leong's mother knew that he wouldn't bring any girl home unless she was special. The one he brought back last time didn't become daughter-in-law. This time around, she liked the girl too, although they couldn't communicate properly. Again, she used a mixture of Cantonese and Mandarin. Hsiao-yuan couldn't understand what she was saying. It got better when

Hok Leong's mother mixed Hokkien into her lingo. Hsiao-yuan could speak Hokkien with her. But then Hok Leong's mother switched to a mixture of Hokkien and Cantonese and again Hsiao-yuan got lost. She turned to Hok Leong for help but he didn't feel up to it. "I don't understand my mother's Hokkien too," he said.

This meeting was more truly *informal* than the one that Hok Leong had experienced. They were in and out in fifteen minutes. After all, a quick meeting was enough. They could rely on intuition to decide whether they liked the person or not.

The day before the flight, they regained something of their natural composure. They arranged to meet the next day at the airport. Again, Hok Leong thought about the past, about Chiu-yun.

The people who ought to turn up at the airport were all there. Because Martin was there as well, the situation became quite formal. Hsiao-yuan hugged them one by one, saying goodbye. Hok Leong was last.

"I'll miss you!" she whispered into his ear.

Hok Leong held Hsiao-yuan and patted her softly on the back. He could feel her warm tears on his shoulders.

32

That evening, Hsiao-yuan placed a phone call to Hok Leong's office. In those pre-Internet days, that was their manner of keeping in contact. Every evening at seven, Hsiao-yuan gave Hok Leong a call.

Martin had some Caucasian friends in Taipei who were helping him. Hsiao-yuan on her part depended on the Taiwanese friends of Martin's friends. They took around a month to settle their individual lodgings, and also the location of the branch office. The office was located near the main train station. Martin lived in the Tianmu area, Hsiao-yuan found a place near the National University of Taiwan. Her landlords were a retired couple whose children were living in the United States. Surrounded by students at her place of residence, Hsiao-yuan found herself regaining a sense of purpose and spirit. It felt like she was returning to her student days.

Hok Leong again had to live a girlfriend-less way of life. As before, he visited Fu *laoshi* every Friday evening. On Fridays, Hsiao-yuan placed a phone call to uncle Fu's home instead of Hok Leong's office.

Because he didn't contact Ah Hor and the guys much, he also didn't go out much with them. Suddenly Hok Leong realised that he no longer had any friends. He had always depended on them for companionship. Now he didn't have any, didn't need any. He felt despondent. This was a new period in his life, one given over entirely to work.

Finally—and certainly, it was about time—Hok Leong thought about his family. His family had never been number one. He didn't know why. In the past, the number one position went to his neighbourhood buddies, then his classmates, then Chiu-yun, then Ah Hor and the guys, <u>John</u> and the guys, <u>Eileen</u>, his job, and now Hsiao-yuan. Even when he didn't have friends, or he couldn't hook up with friends old and new, he never thought about his family.

The latest news from his family was that sister-in-law had given birth. Hok Leong had become an uncle; elder sister wasn't sure when she would tie the knot with her partner; younger sister now had a boyfriend.

33

After a two month plus sojourn in Taiwan, Hsiao-yuan came home. Time seemed to fly, but also crept along slowly. She was only back for a week. Everyone said that she had lost weight but looked great. Hok Leong applied for leave so that he could spend some time with her, but they didn't have much time together. Even the conversations that they had were episodic and piecemeal. Hok Leong remembered asking her at one point, "What's the biggest achievement or result of your two month sojourn?"

"The billboards by the side of the road, the five-story-high banner adverts in the malls—all of them use great big Chinese script," Hsiao-yuan said.

Hok Leong didn't understand.

"This arrangement changes the landscape. It changes the face of the city, its entire appeal and impact," she said.

Hok Leong forgot how he responded. He remembered Fu *laoshi* saying that Hsiao-yuan had taken to the place "like a fish to water."

Yes, that was true. Hsiao-yuan had a contentment and exuberance that he had never seen before in Singapore. She had made the right choice. But tried as he did Hok Leong couldn't find it in himself to be happy. He thought about Chiu-yun and Eileen. They both had dreams and ideals. In the end they had chosen to leave him.

Like them, Hsiao-yuan had dreams and ideals. The difference was that he didn't know when she would leave. Hok Leong could feel it coming but couldn't do anything about it. He could only wait for it to happen. He couldn't change or rescue the situation. He was useless. He had always been like this.

Hsiao-yuan set aside two-hours of her home furlough to meet Hok Leong's parents. She brought little gifts for everybody—for his parents, his elder brother and sister-in-law, his baby nephew, his elder sister and younger sister. The only person to miss out was Hok Leong. "Yours is a bit special," she said. "I'll give it to you on another day."

On the evening before she left, they had dinner at Hsiao-yuan's home. After that they drove to East Coast park and found a place to park. Hsiao-yuan retrieved a small box from her bag. "For you," she said.

Hok Leong gave her a kiss and accepted the gift.

She wanted him to open it. Inside the box was a Chinese seal chop. Hok Leong stared hard at the engraving carved into the stone base but couldn't make out the words.

Hsiao-yuan seemed a bit deflated. It says "zhiwozhe," she explained—the person who knows me.

"Oh!"

"There's an additional engraving on the side," she said.

Hok Leong read the line: "The person who knows me understands my sadness, the person who doesn't know me wonders what I seek."

"It's a line from the Book of Songs," Hsiao-yuan said, referring to the oldest surviving collection of Chinese poetry.

Hok Leong said jokingly, "My heart also sorrows."

"What ails thee, Sir?" Hsiao-yuan asked.

"What I seek, Zhiwoze Hsiao-yuan."

Hsiao-yuan hugged him tight and didn't let go.

34

After Hsiao-yuan left, Hok Leong visited Fu *laoshi*'s home on *Saturdays* as well as Fridays. He made an additional commitment, jogging at East Coast park, where he also did some basic calisthenics. Hsiao-yuan had mentioned before that he should build himself up a bit. Jogging was crazy boring, so Hok Leong sometimes found excuses not to do it. In comparison, however, shopping alone or watching a movie by oneself was even worse. He considered learning Japanese, since, after all, he worked for a Japanese company. But because he knew himself he felt he would probably give up half-way, like the way he had given up on his English tuition. So the programme on Saturday was: jogging in the evening, after which he went home to take a shower, then to Fu *laoshi*'s place.

The problem was, he and Fu *laoshi* were running out of things to talk about. That was fine, Fu *laoshi* could take the lead with whatever topic or issue that he wanted to raise. After some time, he began to share with Hok Leong some of his life experience.

It turned out that Fu *laoshi*'s surname wasn't Fu. His original name was Pu-ting, "Aisin-Gioro Pu-ting," he said.

Hok Leong didn't understand.

"Have you heard of Pu-yi?"

He shook his head.

"The last emperor?"

He nodded.

"He's my distant distant cousin."

Fu *laoshi* wasn't Han Chinese? How come Hok Leong couldn't see that? Fu *laoshi* explained: "After the Manchu people moved into the central plains, they changed their habits and took up Han lifeways. There aren't any differences to speak of nowadays."

Fu *laoshi* began his History lesson. Taking his clan ancestor Khan Nurhaci as the first generation, Fu *laoshi*'s generation, that is, those who used "Pu" as part of their personal names, was actually the eleventh. The nine generations in-between had produced the following sovereigns: Hong Taiji, Shunji, Kangxi, Yongzheng, Qianlong, Jiaqing, Daoguang, Xianfeng, Tongzhi, Guangxu, and finally Xuantong.

Hok Leong knew less than half of the names.

Fu *laoshi* said that, after the reign of Qianlong emperor, the Qing dynasty began its great decline. Several of the subsequent emperors were not proper full-blood relations. Tongzhi emperor, whose personal name was Zaichun, died when he was nineteen. He didn't have sons and didn't have brothers. The worst thing was that his mother was the empress dowager Cixi.

Hok Leong had heard of that name.

Cixi decided that the next monarch after Tongzhi would be his younger cousin (on both the male and female sides), three-year old Zaitian, who later used the reign name Guangxu. Guangxu's father was Yixuan, the seventh brother of Xianfeng emperor. His mother was Cixi's younger sister, Wanzhen. That was why he was Tongzhi's cousin on both the male and female side.

Guangxu died at thirty-seven. Again, he didn't have any male offspring. Cixi chose Pu-yi, the not-yet-three-year-old son of Guangxu's fifth brother, Zaifeng, to be the next sovereign. The Qing dynasty collapsed during Pu-yi's reign. So Fu *laoshi* was actually born during the republican period which followed the dynasty's demise.

Fu *laoshi* and Pu-yi were very distantly related. They had in common their great-grandfather Daoguang emperor, whose full name was Aisin-Giora Minning. Daoguang had nine sons, five of whom were stillbirths or died young. Xianfeng emperor, whose given name was Yizhu, was fourth in the line of nine. Fu *laoshi*'s grandfather was one of those who died young. Their connections with the imperial household having diminished with time, Fu *laoshi*'s family was already semi-destitute when he was born. So the end of the Qing dynasty didn't bring him any loss.

Fu *laoshi* went to England to study because nobody took care of him. "We were poor," he explained. "There were many of us. No one took care of us or bothered about what we did. I was working as an errand boy for an Englishman. He fell ill and wanted to return home. He asked me whether I wanted to go. I didn't have anything to do. The country was in a mess, so I followed him to England. That old Englishman actually wanted to give me a leg up in life. He said I should study. He said agriculture was the bedrock of everything, never mind the so-called industrial revolution, so I studied agriculture. After graduating, I felt that nobody in the East was interested in agriculture, so I studied English. As long as somebody wished to study English, I would have the means to make for living."

After the Englishman died, Fu *laoshi* said he wanted to return to China. When the ship docked in Singapore, he heard that China was in great turmoil, greater than when he left. There were many Chinese people in Singapore, so he decided to stay for a while. The mayhem in China didn't let up, so he never thought about going back.

Hok Leong asked, "And somewhere in the middle you decided to change your name?"

Fu *laoshi* gave a laugh. "That's the thing! I don't have to tell people that I'm of Manchu origin and then have to repeat the long convoluted history that you just heard."

"How was it?" he added. "It's all very confusing and messy, isn't it?"

Hok Leong realised he now had something else to do on Saturday—he could go to the library to read up on Qing history. In truth, he hadn't understood a lot of what Fu *laoshi* told him. "It's fine, it's quite okay," he insisted.

Fu *laoshi* explained further that, for the name change, he had switched over the two left-side radicals of his original Chinese moniker Pu-ting. The radical" for "man" went from the logograph Ting to Pu, replacing the radical for "water," and giving Fu. The radical for "water" went from Pu to Ting and changed the meaning of the word, although it was still pronounced Ting.

Hok Leong wanted to ask whether there was such a thing as Ting with a water radical.

Without him asking, Fu *laoshi* explained, "Quite coincidentally, the character Ting with water radical means a body of water, and also means level ground or plain lying next to water. Singapore is basically a piece of ground with a shoreline!"

35

Hsiao-yuan didn't know about Fu *laoshi*'s background and travails. Her first reaction when she heard was, "How pitiful! From noble birth to an uncertain, wandering existence in faraway Nanyang." Nanyang or the South Seas was the general Chinese term for Southeast Asia.

Hok Leong made fun of her. "How pitiful! Due to work commitments a Singapore girl has to go to Taiwan!"

Hsiao-yuan muttered to herself for a moment. "That may well not happen," she said indistinctly. She seemed to want to continue but then controlled herself. After a while she switched to talking about her experience in Taipei.

This became their agreed formula. They treated each other like a journal or diary, telling the partner what had transpired that day. Much of it was like a soap opera, continuing a storyline paused or freeze-framed the day earlier. The details included news that Hok Leong's elder sister had married. Hsiao-yuan actually phoned his home from Taipei to extend her well-wishes. Hok Leong didn't know whether such actions amounted to love. At the least his life was enriched by her thoughtfulness.

For the next few Saturdays, Hok Leong didn't go jogging. Conducting his own History lesson, he went instead to the public library to read up on Qing history, and to borrow books about it. When he first borrowed the books his interest level was high. But after reading for a while at home his attention began to waver. He couldn't absorb the information. He repeated what he used to say in school, namely that he wasn't a scholar, he didn't have the right stuff. But whenever he felt that way he would force himself to continue. He didn't know what he was trying to prove.

After sharing his personal story, Fu *laoshi* began to share what he knew about Hsiao-yuan's parents. Hsiao-yuan liked to say that her parents were trying to "preserve" the legacy of the May Fourth movement because they had both graduated from Xiamen University in China. May Fourth luminaries such as Lu Xun, Lin Yutang, and Gu Jiegang had taught there. Hsiao-yuan's parents had attended all their classes—so they always felt that they had a responsibility to pass on the teachings imparted to them.

Xiamen university was set up by the Nanyang entrepreneur Tan Kah Kee. Tan's willingness to sacrifice familial wealth for the sake of education inspired many youngsters. To repay Tan's high-mindedness, Hsiao-yuan's parents decided to come to Singapore, to do something for the island. They also wanted to escape the suffocating control of their families, for Hsiao-yuan's grandfather on her mother's side had opposed their relationship.

Starting from Xiamen, Hsiao-yuan's parents travelled to Chaozhou, Guangzhou, and Nanning, the capital of Guangxi, and then southwards through Vietnam, Laos, Thailand, and Malaysia to reach Singapore.

When Hok Leong recounted what he had heard to Hsiao-yuan, she said "Oh my gosh! That's like basically the Long March! No wonder uncle Fu says I've inherited some kind of travel bug from them."

Hok Leong found it hard to imagine what they had gone through. When he got home he took a look at the atlas. From point to point on the map, the distance was over four thousand kilometres. The actual distance was definitely much longer. Hok Leong wondered whether he could match their feat. At first he said no, then he thought, maybe he could. If the occasion was right, he would.

Fu *laoshi* also shared with Hok Leong his first reaction to the news that Hsiao-yuan was going overseas. "When I first heard it, I thought, you know, it's heredity. She's following in her parents' footsteps. Xu Ke went to Hong Kong, and now Hsiao-yuan is in Taiwan. I thought to myself—what great aspiration drives this family? What summon or call have they received from the great beyond?"

On the topic of her family's "wanderlust," Hsiao-yuan at first brushed it off. "It's all a coincidence, I guess? Of course, uncle Fu can also say that it's something arranged in the world of spirits." After saying that she got worried. "Can you tell uncle Fu not to put it that way? So scary! Who's summoning us or beckoning to us? What aspiration are you talking about?"

Shortly after Hsiao-yuan's parents reached Singapore, the second world war started. Even before they could settle down they had to flee. They travelled to Indonesia and hid there till the Japanese surrendered. While they were there they got to know some fellow evacuees who were also teachers. After the war, they swiftly obtained jobs in the education sector; not just in any school, but in those run by the Hokkien clan association. Hsiao-yuan's mother eventually became a principal in a primary school. Her father taught in a secondary school.

Hsiao-yuan asked, "How did uncle Fu and my parents do it? What is it about that generation that gave them such determination, such powers of endurance?"

Hok Leong recalled something that Fu *laoshi* had said. "They weren't the only ones who needed that kind of hardiness. You're talking about the contemporary history of China," he said.

From Qing dynasty events to the contemporary history of China, Hok Leong knew that his future Saturdays would be busy, would be filled with "rich" and "substantial" reading activities.

36

Next it was time for Hok Leong to share his personal story, one connected no doubt with contemporary Chinese history!

Hok Leong said that his parents came to Singapore from

Malaysia. His father told him that grandfather had travelled from China to Malaysia. After making his money he had bought a small rubber holding in Johore. He figured that having a rubber farm meant you could put food on the table, his children wouldn't have to starve. Hok Leong's father didn't want to spend his life carving furrows into rubber trees for the latex, so he came to Singapore to look for a job. He tried his hand at everything, did everything. Finally he learned how to make won ton noodles from someone he knew, and later on began operating his own food cart. Then he went home and married mother. Both his parents were illiterate. The bowls of won ton noodles that they sold had paid for the upbringing of their children, had raised Hok Leong and his siblings. Now the bowls had been handed over to his elder brother.

After Fu *laoshi* heard this, he muttered to himself for a quite a while. "Struggle and effort! Struggle and effort!" he finally said, "Right there is the history of Nanyang!"

37.

When Hsiao-yuan heard the details above, Hok Leong was already in Taipei. With the passage of time, Hok Leong could no longer remember the Taipei of old, when it didn't have an underground. He remembered that it was around five-something in the afternoon when he stepped out of the airport, but already the sky was dark. Hsiao-yuan wore a pair of long boots, black silk stockings, and black cotton long T-shirt. Draped over her shoulders was an elegant, jujube-coloured shawl.

If Hsiao-yuan hadn't tapped him on the shoulders, he wouldn't have recognised his girlfriend. When he turned around, his first thought was that she had found the wrong person. Then he recognised who it was, and hugged her tightly.

Even so, the first words out of his mouth were, "Is it really that cold?"

"Just like to look gorgeous," Hsiao-yuan said, returning his hug.

"Really gorgeous," Hok Leong agreed, "and different from the Hsiao-yuan that I know."

Hsiao-yuan released Hok Leong. She gave him a once-over, taking in his short-sleeved T-shirt and jeans.

"In a few days you'll understand," she said.

A few days later Hok Leong caught a cold. He walked around in a daze, and so didn't have much of an impression of the city. He only remembered that the virtues stressed in the textbooks used in moral-and-ethics classes, qualities like devotion and filial piety, benevolence and honour, were all being used as road names in Taipei. It was scary—walking around the whole day being reminded about what one ought to do. The city also provided a primer to the cities and provinces of China, to its geography. You saw names such as Sichuan, Chungking, Nanjing, Wuchang, E-mei, Chengdu, and Kunming. Many young people probably couldn't understand why the ruling regime wished to give education lessons while they strode the streets of the city, why it remembered to do that.

Chiang Kai-shek memorial hall was one of the places that Hok Leong visited. The impression that stayed with him was the two large auditoriums that formed part of the complex, both resplendent specimens of old-style Chinese architecture, a stunning sight for a Nanyang lad like him. He also visited section two, Chongqing South road, where the refined, lettered ambience of the book stores so delighted him that he couldn't bear to leave the place. Influenced by the setting and spirit he bought several books that he later never read. What was worse was that, whenever he visited the area in the future, he promptly did the same thing.

Everywhere he went in the complex, he saw slogans such as "Protect state secrets and ward off spies! Everyone is responsible!" and "Beware! Enemy spies are by your side!" The numerous stone or bronze statues of Chiang Kai-shek all seemed to say the same thing: your leader stands with you.

Hsiao-yuan took Hok Leong on special trips to a number of places: to Ximending to eat duck tongue, to Café Astoria for afternoon tea, to some obscure side-street eatery to try beef noodle garnished with plentiful amounts of salted vegetables, and even to Shimen reservoir in Taoyuan to try its famous fish-served-in-three-ways delicacy.

A calligraphy-painting in a corner of the restaurant at Shimen reservoir caught Hok Leong's attention:

Why be filled with apprehension when life is merely a spark made by a flint, when it is as minuscule as the area circumscribed by the antennas of a snail?

Hok Leong didn't know whose poem it was, but something about the verse struck him to the quick. It promised to light the way forward, to act as a touchstone for the lad from Nanyang. As a keepsake, Hok Leong asked Hsiao-yuan to take a snapshot of himself standing next to the painting.

Many years later when they had already entered the age of the Internet, Hok Leong suddenly remembered the picture taken at the restaurant. He found the snapshot and typed the line of verse into <u>Google</u> search. He discovered that the words were from the poem, "On wine," by the Tang dynasty poet Bai Juyi. The line immediately after the quote went:

Since life is like that, one ought to be happy; whether one is rich or poor, the person who doesn't laugh is foolish.

When Hsiao-yuan's landlord learned that her boyfriend was coming to visit, he insisted on providing an extra room free of charge, so that they didn't have to spend a large sum of money paying for a hotel room.

When the landlord and landlady stepped out of the

apartment, Hok Leong quickly pulled Hsiao-yuan onto the bed. He kissed her passionately, caressed her body and fondled her. He cried at the top of his voice, "Next time I'm not staying here! I want to stay in a hotel!" Hsiao-yuan laughed so much the tears streamed down her face. In future visits Hok Leong always stayed at the same place.

Hok Leong also met two of Hsiao-yuan's colleagues. One was the account manager Ya Huan, whose name was easily mispronounced to mean "servant girl," which had then become a kind of nickname. She was in her early thirties. Hsiao-yuan called her Elder-sister Huan. The second colleague was the artistic director Hsiao-tsao, who wore a small pony-tail and a goatee. Hsiao-yuan called him Elder-brother Tsao. They were both older than Hok Leong, so he followed Hsiao-yuan's practice, addressing them as Sister Huan and Brother Tsao.

Hok Leong introduced himself as "Jackie" when they met. But for Hsiao-yuan's colleagues, he was basically "Jennifer's boyfriend." Hok Leong mulled over the situation. He probably needed to get used to that, to being known as "Jennifer's boyfriend."

When Hsiao-yuan's colleagues learned that Hok Leong worked in the electronics sector, they both said the same thing: "In our line of work, women are worked like men. Men are worked like slaves. Even so, it doesn't matter if you choose the wrong sector. The more important thing is that you choose the right boyfriend. The future belongs to electronics."

Although he spent some time with Hsiao-yuan's colleagues, Hok Leong didn't get much of a chance to say anything edgewise. Whether it was general knowledge or current affairs, work or family, politics or life, they both had well-thought-through views and opinions. Their ideas were detailed, precise, and confidently expressed. They readily shared and debated their viewpoints. Many things that Hok Leong had only considered or done in a particular way, they approached and did from a different way, or from a number of ways.

Hok Leong stayed for a week and had a great time. But his heart kept sinking. He knew the more he enjoyed himself, the higher the probability that Hsiao-yuan would leave him. The former was an "index" for the latter. If even he could enjoy himself, what more Hsiao-yuan? How could she leave after a year's sojourn?

He knew why Hsiao-yuan liked Taipei. But most of the time there he was fighting a cold.

38

After Hok Leong, it was the turn of Hsiao-yuan's parents and uncle Fu to visit Taiwan. Hsiao-yuan related how it went. The three elders were both unfamiliar and familiar with the place. Her parents practically knew more about Taiwan than her. Moreover their knowledge of and elegant use of Hokkien dialect gave her a shock.

They visited the National Palace Museum. Observing the treasures on display, uncle Fu kept shaking his head. He only broke into speech when he spotted the slogan: "Beware! Enemy spies are by your side!" He gave a laugh and berated the regime, "Old Chiang has gone crazy. He puts his nightmares on a wall so that he can get some psychological relief!"

Hsiao-yuan decided that she wouldn't bring them to visit the Chiang Kai-shek memorial hall.

After completing their visit, the three of them, together with Hsiao-yuan, flew to Hong Kong to see her brother, Xu Ke, and sister-in-law. They feasted and relaxed for three days in Hong Kong, then the six of them languidly and stylishly took a flight to Xiamen on the mainland.

Hsiao-yuan's parents didn't visit their old home. They didn't organise anything in advance, just visited Xiamen University, strolled around a little, and left. Hsiao-yuan said that although this was a dream trip for them, all manner of mixed feelings kept welling up in their hearts. For long moments they were quiet and subdued. Struck by some scenery or sight, they often stopped short and stared at it before recovering their composure, becoming again the tourists that they were. Many a times her father looked like he would burst into speech but controlled himself. "We're tourists," he insisted. "We're just tourists."

For Hsiao-yuan, his words brought to mind some lines from "Mistake," a poem by the Taiwanese writer Zheng Chouyu:

My clattering hooves are a beautiful mistake.
I am not a homecoming person but a passing traveller.

She didn't know whether her parents could ever be "homecoming" returnees; where was the place that fit such a description?

Hok Leong later provided a sequel of sorts to the trip. After Fu *laoshi* returned to Singapore, he asked him if he ever thought about returning to Beijing.

Fu *laoshi* shook his head: "My parents are gone. My brothers are not close, may already be gone. What's there to see? I'm an old foggy, a leftover from the previous previous dynasty! The forest flowers have shed their springtime red. How quickly they depart! Anyway the cold seasonal rains and winds will soon be upon us. There's nothing to see anymore."

Hok Leong guessed that Fu *laoshi* was citing some poet or writer, but he didn't have a clue who it was. When he recounted the conversation to Hsiao-yuan, she explained that he had referenced a poem by the Southern Tang dynasty poet Li Yu.

Titled, "The Joy of Meeting," the poem went like this:

The forest flowers have shed their springtime red; so short their span, so quick the departure.

*Why could they not resist the diurnal winds, the cold,
seasonal rains?*
*Strewn on the ground, mixed with tears, like the rouge that
anoint the faces of maidens.*
When will we meet again?
*As the waters flow unceasingly eastward, such is the burden
of life.*

Hok Leong wanted very much to ask Hsiao-yuan what she
felt about the poem but he didn't. The lament had stirred him
a little, had moved him, but he didn't know how to put his
sentiments into words. He didn't think carefully about it.

39

To live meaningfully, one should have expectations, something
to look forward to. For instance, waiting for Hsiao-yuan
to come visit him once every two months. Waiting for her
became a part of Hok Leong's life.

Other developments came their way and helped to enrich
the serial drama that was their lives, including the cliché bit
where a guy chanced upon an ex-girlfriend while fetching
the current one. Hok Leong was at the airport when he heard
someone call him. It was Eileen. He was terribly surprised.
But, really, what was there to be surprised about, Singapore
being the size that it is?

Eileen was her usual high-spirited self. She held out her
hand, didn't hide her happiness.

"Gosh! I haven't seen you in a long time!" she said.

It was a long time. Eileen had grown up; she looked
beautiful, prettier than he remembered. Hok Leong couldn't
think of what to say. "How is John?" he asked stiffly.

She gave a laugh. "I haven't seen him in a while too, although
we're both in Hong Kong." She added, explaining, "I'm still

modelling. I'm based in Hong Kong now. Every few months I'll come back for a while."

"Oh, okay!" Hok Leong didn't want to know too much about her affairs. "How's your mother?" he finally said. Immediately he felt that that was an odd thing to ask. It was laughable.

"My mom has retired. I heard that they're going to tear down the coffee shop," Eileen said. "Are you married yet?" she asked.

"No, not yet."

"Me, neither." She stole a glance at her wristwatch. "Here's my name card. Let's get in touch when I come back?"

Hok Leong gave her his name card. Eileen looked at it, then waved goodbye as she strode to the nearby departure gates. After entering the gates she turned round and continued waving. Hok Leong waved back at her. It felt like he had come to send her off. Everything seemed so natural. It was a scene that onlookers might envy.

Hok Leong realised that he was standing in the departure lounge. Why was he there? Oh, yes, to get a drink of water.

After buying a drink, he returned to the arrival hall. He found a seat, sat down, and waited for Hsiao-yuan's flight to arrive.

Hsiao-yuan was dressed in winter clothes. She hugged him tightly when she came out of the gates. He returned her hug, but couldn't shrug off the "disturbance" that Eileen had wrought in him. It felt farcical, him sending off his former girlfriend, then welcoming his current one.

Hsiao-yuan was lively and exuberant. She didn't notice his distracted mood.

"I want to eat chilli crab, satay, mee rebus, chendol, and also the *won ton* noodles that your brother makes," she cried.

Hok Leong had to laugh. "Be careful you don't get fat, young lady!"

"I don't care!" Hsiao-yuan said. "I'm already salivating!"

40

Hsiao-yuan of course wouldn't allow herself to get fat. She did everything in careful, measured ways, including looking after her diet. As Fu *laoshi* put it, she had "grown up." Unlike the old Hsiao-yuan, she was assured, confident, and firm in her manner. "You can see it in her eyes," Fu *laoshi* said.

Without being all that aware of the change, Hsiao-yuan was now used to making decisions for herself. What to eat for instance—a routine matter, but also potentially a great bother and hassle. In the past she usually pushed the decision-making to her elders. But now she was happy to take the lead, while others seconded her choices.

But wasn't that normal? If you don't make such decisions, eating itself becomes a problem, right? Besides, there were plenty of things that she wanted to eat.

Seeing Hsiao-yuan all "grown up"—the happiest person should have been Fu *laoshi*; but Hok Leong noticed that he didn't seem particularly overjoyed. He realised as well that she didn't have many plans this time around. She went to the <u>office</u> every day and threw herself into her work. "Once you get on-board you can't get off," she complained. "Aiyoh! Sister Huan is right! This job isn't fit for human beings!"

Hok Leong had actually applied for leave, but because Hsiao-yuan was so busy he cancelled it and returned to work as well. Almost straightaway he received a phone call from <u>Eileen</u>. She had called a few times but nobody answered the phone. No, there wasn't anything special. Just wanted to say <u>hello</u>, she said.

Hok Leong didn't expect her to call. He responded carefully, spoke prudently. <u>Eileen</u> said that in a few days' time when she returned to Singapore she would contact him. They should meet up for coffee.

On the eve of her departure for Taiwan, Hsiao-yuan gave

Hok Leong a gift. It was a tie.

"Its function is to tie you to me," she joked.

41

<u>Eileen</u> was her usual charming, debonair self, although she looked a bit lost at times. Hok Leong didn't know how those two contradictory traits could exist in the same person. Even so, he liked the combination. It reminded him of his younger, innocent days, when he was serving his military service.

What he was doing didn't make sense. He had just seen off his girlfriend, and now he was meeting his former partner. <u>Eileen</u> recounted what she went through after they broke up. Actually, she just spoke about her modelling career, didn't reveal anything about her personal life. Hok Leong also shared with her what he did after completing his national service stint, but skipping over the part that involved Hsiao-yuan. He had always kept in mind what he said once to <u>Eileen</u>, namely that he was "<u>serious</u>."

It felt like a new beginning for them. Hok Leong hoped that the feeling was an erroneous one. He also hoped that the presentiment he got from meeting Hsiao-yuan, namely that she was leaving him, was erroneous. The truth was that Hsiao-yuan had her own dreams to pursue. He knew that about her. He understood that.

Hok Leong felt that he wasn't much of a go-getter, he didn't have any prospects. The girls who knew him, those with ambition and drive, sooner or later all left him. On his part, he didn't know what he really wanted, what to strive for. His experience was that, the objectives he strove for had always come from someone else. From the time he started schooling to now, it didn't come from him. What he himself "wanted" was a basic starting criteria for anyone plotting a path through life. But he didn't even have that.

Eileen in contrast saw something she wanted, something that agreed with her go-getting and seeking. Now that they were grown up, she wanted them to give each other a chance, a fresh start. Because ten years had passed, however, an unfamiliar feeling continued to linger between them, sustained by the mutual reservations that they had. They couldn't bridge the gap.

In the end, Eileen said, "I told my mom about you. She hopes you can come see her when you have time. We can go see her together."

Hok Leong replied carefully, "I'll go say hello when I have the time."

All right they said to one another. Let's keep in contact, they said.

42

True to her word, Eileen placed a long distance call to Hok Leong from Hong Kong, that being her way of "keeping in contact." Although Hok Leong was busy he told her that he was okay. After chatting with her for a while they ran out of subjects, so they switched to talking about old acquaintances and friends.

Among the persons they discussed, the one that most piqued Hok Leong's interest was Alan. Eileen had bumped into him once at Hong Kong airport. He was waiting for a transfer flight to mainland China.

"Alan went there to do volunteer work," Eileen said, "some remote, far-flung place or something. He told me the place and the name of his organisation but after hearing it I forgot about it."

Hok Leong was surprised. Alan was slated to be a big time lawyer. Why do volunteer work?

"He didn't want to be a lawyer?" he asked.

"I asked him that," <u>Eileen</u> said. "He gave a laugh. He said he didn't want to help rich people. He wanted to help people who were poor."

That answer didn't surprise Hok Leong. As he had anticipated, <u>Alan</u> had turned out differently, he didn't join the herd. Hok Leong remembered that he had once chastised a "Hokkien" soldier while serving in the army. After that <u>Alan</u> treated him to a beer and they discussed the incident. <u>Alan</u> told him, "People change. I believe the next time we discuss this issue, things will be different. Maybe our character or our temperament will have changed drastically. We may even get nostalgic about the current situation."

Hok Leong missed those days, that period of life. He hoped that he could meet up one day with <u>Alan</u>, see how far they had grown and changed.

<u>Eileen</u> said Hok Leong was still the same. Actually, she hadn't changed that much herself. Even so, the society around them kept changing. Eileen should know that. Those decade ago versions of themselves, they weren't like that anymore.

43

Two or three days later Eileen again called Hok Leong on the phone. He initially wanted to reject the call, but then realised that he was being small-minded and horrid. Ironically, Hsiao-yuan called a few times but each time it was the same message, either "Hey! I can't talk today. I'm going out now," or "I'm still out. I'm calling from outside," before she hung up on him.

What this portended Hok Leong could well imagine. He didn't want to think about it.

Then it was Hok Leong's turn to make the trip to Taipei to see Hsiao-yuan. The day before he left, <u>Eileen</u> phoned him. He didn't tell her about the trip.

Hsiao-yuan was extremely busy. On most evenings, she

only got home after midnight. Although tired she radiated energy and vigour. She could pull all-nighters if necessary. On his part, Hok Leong only increased the burdens that she had to shoulder. She had to consider his needs and requirements all the time. Most of the time, she had dinner with her colleagues, Sister Huan and Brother Tsao, with Hok Leong joining them. Several of the meals took place after midnight, with Hok Leong practically half-asleep as he bit into his food. Hok Leong actually liked hanging out with them. He was content to be a kind of sponge, absorbing what they said. The only problem was that he still couldn't get used to his new identity, his status as "Jennifer's boyfriend."

Roaming the streets of Taipei by himself, Hok Leong could see what Singapore was losing, had lost. It wasn't just the street-food culture that the latter had banished. It was also a sense of humanity and thoughtfulness. In the future, whenever he thought about the city, Hok Leong recalled those traits with great fondness. Taipei was also losing some of those qualities, but not as quickly as his birthplace.

After he returned from Taipei, Hok Leong received a phone call from Eileen. He excused himself by saying that he had been traveling recently. That's why he didn't receive her call. He wondered whether he should place a call to her the next time around. It wasn't right that a girl had to keep making these calls.

44

After work that day, Hok Leong went to meet Fu *laoshi*. Fu *laoshi* said, "After you came back yesterday, the little generalissimo passed away."

For a moment, Hok Leong couldn't figure out what he meant. Fu *laoshi* had to use "plain" language to communicate. "Taiwan president Chiang Ching-kuo passed away yesterday, the day you came back," he said.

Because of that Hok Leong always remembered that Chiang Ching-kuo passed away in 1988.

"So," Fu *laoshi* continued after a while, "do you like Taiwan?"

Hok Leong nodded.

"What do you like about it?"

"It's very <u>Chinese</u> for one thing! Actually, parts of it is also quite Japanese, or, er, quite Republican era."

Fu *laoshi* gave a small laugh. "So you know about the Republican era as well?"

"I have an imagined notion of it," Hok Leong had to confess.

Fu *laoshi* didn't reply immediately. He took a sip of tea and fell silent again. "I like Taiwan too," he said after a long pause. "It wasn't easy. The old generalissimo, that's Chiang Kai-shek, had to withdraw from the mainland in such a hurry. And now, forty years later, look at the level of development that father and son have achieved."

Hok Leong kept silent. He knew Fu *laoshi* had more that he wanted to share.

Fu *laoshi* gave a sigh. "I like the place. But even so it doesn't have a place in my heart, I must say. It's like when I had to leave England. It was only after I came to Singapore that I realised I didn't have a home to return to."

He began to deliver his history lesson. "Do you know what slogan the Chinese United League used when they were plotting to overthrow the Qing dynasty?"

Hok Leong shook his head.

"Expel the Tartar barbarians! Revive China! Establish a republic! Distribute land equally among the people!"

Fu *laoshi* shook his head and gave a sardonic laugh. "You want political power, that's perfectly alright. But why humiliate other people in the process?" he said, referring to the derogatory way in which the slogan portrayed Manchu people.

"After he obtained political power, Sun Yat-sen started to use a new slogan," Fu *laoshi* continued. "The republic of the five ethnies, he called it, which meant peaceful co-development between the five major ethnic groups of China, namely Han, Manchu, Mongolian, Hui, and Tibetan. But, you know, the Manchus were actually the first to use that slogan. Their version was, the five-*ethnie* Commonwealth. The problem is, if you don't have political power, who will join you to form a commonwealth? And in the same way, I must say, I don't really want to join hands with those who won political power. I'm not interested in collectivism. I'm poor and backward. Who wants to join hands with me? Nobody!"

Fu *laoshi* suddenly realised that Hok Leong wasn't following properly; he was out of the picture.

"Okay, I'll stop. I won't bore you with this." He added after a while. "You're not like Hsiao-yuan. She likes this stuff."

"I did that deliberately," Hok Leong gave a laugh.

Fu *laoshi* nodded approvingly.

Hok Leong continued, "I don't like to get too engrossed in something, to keep mulling over it. When you get like that it's easy to miss the big picture."

Fu *laoshi* gave a big laugh. "Spoken like a true engineer! A science person! Aiyoh, this reminds me of the crab problem I posed to you earlier. What's the most important thing in a chilli crab dish? Me and Hsiao-yuan indulge too much in this. You can't see clearly when you do that."

He paused for a moment. "Have you noticed any other areas, I mean, areas where we're overly indulgent?"

Hok Leong laughed. "I'm overly indulgent about you two. I can't see clearly where you're concerned."

Fu *laoshi* chortled happily.

45

Ying-jun got married. Among the four of them, he was the first to get hitched. He had met his wife while working at the electronics factory in Bedok. She was from Malaysia.

The three of them—Hok Leong, Ah Hor, and Tee Soon—attended the wedding dinner as singletons, without partners in tow. From their school days till now, Ying-jun was the one who had the most girlfriends, who switched girlfriends most often. As a result, he was also the first to tie the knot.

Hok Leong asked at the banquet, "Why did he get hitched so quickly? Why not change a few more girlfriends?"

Ah Hor said softly, "The bride has a bun in the oven."

"No wonder!" Hok Leong said in a chastising tone of voice. "So that means minus one person the next time you visit the hen house?"

"Stop insulting us!" Tee Soon said. "As of yesterday, I can declare officially that we've all seen the light and have turned over a new leaf."

Everyone laughed uproariously at the revelation.

Tee Soon was still doing his "odd jobs," Hok Leong learned. It was touch and go whether he would get into serious trouble. After so many years, Ah Hor was still working at the Bedok factory. Because they both worked in the electronics sector they had more to share and discuss.

Amid the merriment and banter, Hok Leong felt strongly that this was *his* level. He belonged here. Fu *laoshi*'s level was too high for him. But he also discovered that the distance between Ying-jun and Co. and himself had grown large, was growing larger. He was alone. He didn't have any company.

46

"Mr Chan Hok Leong. Are you willing to take Xu Hsiao-yuan as your lawfully wedded wife?"

It was over ten in the evening. The television was still on. Hsiao-yuan had called him suddenly and half-jokingly said those words.

Hok Leong didn't know how to respond. She couldn't be calling him up at this hour to play a joke, right? They had just spoken by phone around two hours back, when he was still in the <u>office</u>. If there was something important surely she would have raised it then?

Hok Leong went into his bedroom to continue the conversation. He picked up the handset on the separate line in his room. Hsiao-yuan continued half-jokingly, "Hok Leong! I'm officially proposing to you. Are you willing to marry me?"

Hok Leong didn't reply. He glanced at the photo frame on his table. The frame bore a picture of him and Hsiao-yuan, taken at Taroko gorge in eastern Taiwan.

"What's wrong? What's happened?" he asked.

Hsiao-yuan suddenly gave a sob, "Uncle Fu just called."

What did he say? Hok Leong wondered.

"He said I mustn't get so busy with work that I forget about you."

Sure enough, Fu *laoshi* had observed that something was awry. "No, you haven't neglected me," Hok Leong had to say. "How can that be?"

"He said the water lily in full bloom mustn't forget the roots that give it nourishment."

"Aiyoh! He's taking things too seriously," Hok Leong said. "Since when did you neglect me?"

"Uncle Fu described our situation. I basically agree with him. I admit that I'm a flower that seeks the sky and air. Like the water lily I need to rise out of the water to get sunlight and dewdrops, and even to get accosted by insects. But all that requires the stem and stalk and the roots beneath the water surface..."

She paused for a moment, and then continued in an agitated

tone of voice, "Do you know that it's because of you that I have the courage to do this? I can do this because every evening I get to talk to you on the phone. If I've neglected you please tell me. I'll come back tomorrow."

The situation was worse than Hok Leong had imagined. He had to speak prudently, "Hsiao-yuan, I know that your life in Taiwan isn't easy. People want you to choose between your dreams and me. From the very beginning, I've expressed my support for what you're doing. I know why you want to go out. In fact, you're not just doing this for yourself. You're also doing it for me. You're fulfilling the dreams that I don't dare to chase. I don't dare to chase them because I don't have dreams, I don't have the prerequisites. From my younger days till now I've known that. You know that I don't match up to you in many areas. The only thing I can do is to support you."

Hsiao-yuan didn't reply immediately, signalling that she accepted what he was saying. But after a while she retorted, "But that's not the case at all! Uncle Fu says that you're stronger than me in many areas."

"He's trying to provoke you. He's too concerned about you and me pairing up for the long run."

Hok Leong paused for a moment.

"To be honest, I don't recognise these so-called strengths and attributes," he continued. "Fu *laoshi* has mentioned them before. But I don't see anything special. I don't know why he doesn't criticise me properly, and at the same time let me know the meaning of existence. For instance, this connection between flowers and roots. I really don't know that I'm so important at all. I grew up without supervision. Nobody has ever told me why I'm here, what use do I have. It was only after meeting Fu *laoshi* that I realised a measure of my self-worth. Of course, I also wish that I'm as important as you say I am. But because I have self-awareness I don't accept that so readily."

Hsiao-yuan had a different take on the matter. "I've always

accepted what uncle Fu said. And actually many things in my life have turned out as he anticipated. He's always given me guidance at different stages in my life, including when I joined the electronics factory, and also now working for this advertising company. I listen to him more than I listen to my parents. When he reminded me about you I got anxious straightaway. I really don't want to neglect you because of work."

"Don't worry about that!" As usual when things got heavy, Hok Leong worked doubly hard to lift their spirits. "Don't think too much, Miss Little-Flower-Girl-Xu," he said.

His witticism had an invigorating effect. Hsiao-yuan seemed to come around again. She cracked a joke in response, "So, are we still getting married, Mr Chan-Hok-Roots-and-Stem?"

Hok Leong hadn't thought about that. He didn't know how to respond.

Hsiao-yuan didn't wait for his reply, "I'm really pathetic. I actually propose to you?"

Hok Leong still didn't know what to say. "You think too much, Miss Little-Flower-Girl-Xu!" he repeated. "Please go to sleep! Good night!"

47

Hok Leong couldn't sleep. Fu *laoshi* was correct. But it wasn't clear whether his prognosis referred to Hsiao-yuan or to Hok Leong. Whoever it was, he had spotted something awry. It was just as well that he did so, for his intervention allowed Hok Leong and Hsiao-yuan to declare their feelings, to restore their mutual trust and connection.

After that Hsiao-yuan's little joke took centre stage. When were they going to get married? They didn't know when. Perhaps it was from that evening onwards that they prepared mentally for the event.

As it turned out, <u>Eileen</u> called Hok Leong the next day in the office. She had just returned from Hong Kong. She wanted to meet up with him. Hok Leong was glad that they hadn't started anything yet. He told her that he "wasn't free," he couldn't "meet up." She should know what that meant.

Again, Hok Leong felt that he had turned his back on her.

48

After that they were assaulted by some terrible developments. Hsiao-yuan's father and Fu *laoshi* both fell ill. Hsiao-yuan's father had to undergo a bypass operation to treat a cardiovascular blockage. Fu *laoshi* suffered a light stroke.

Hsiao-yuan rushed home. For half a year she couldn't go anywhere. Luckily the two men weren't despondent, were actually approaching things with rare good spirit. Fu *laoshi* said, "From the time I left China everything else has been a bonus. I'm almost eighty. I've lived long enough. The happiest thing for me is that I've stolen 'half' a daughter from old man Xu. And from there I've obtained 'half' a son-in-law as well. I'm even more ruthless than my old ancestor Nurhaci!"

He turned to Hok Leong, "Strange! I'm of Manchu stock. How come I got a stroke? I thought Manchus were supposed to die on the great steppes. Why am I lying in a bed!"

"You're more like a Han person nowadays. You've turned Han. Isn't that what you said?" Hok Leong replied. "And you're also Westernised. You're <u>Mister Old British</u>!"

Although they kept up their spirits, old age was clearly taking a toll. Fu *laoshi*'s deterioration was startling. Walking became tough for him. He started talking to himself. Occasionally he mumbled something in a language that none of them recognised. Hok Leong believed it was Manchu.

Hok Leong's mother was the first to link things together, which is to say the two elder folks falling ill and the two young ones maybe needing to tie the knot. "It'll bring good luck and good fortune. It'll change the atmosphere in the household," she said.

Hok Leong told Hsiao-yuan what his mother had said. On his part, he was concerned that Fu *laoshi*'s mental situation might get worse. If so, he wouldn't be able to enjoy their wedding, to share their joy. Hsiao-yuan agreed.

Hok Leong remembered the date. He was twenty-nine when he got married, she, twenty-six.

Before getting hitched they had to get a place of their own. They bought a second-hand, four-room flat in the Marine Parade area. It was close to Hsiao-yuan's parents and also to Fu *laoshi*'s home, thus allowing them to meet everyone's needs.

The wedding was a small event. They didn't have many family members and friends to invite. On this matter, they had a point in common. Both sets of parents had come to Singapore when they were young. Their relatives were located overseas. Hok Leong's parents insisted that they wanted to save money. Despite entreaties, they refused to invite their relatives from Johore. Hsiao-yuan's parents had long ago lost contact with their relatives in China. Their guests at the wedding were basically Fu *laoshi* and some of their former teacher colleagues.

Hok Leong invited Akita san and Steven to the wedding, together with several office girls who knew Hsiao-yuan well. Akita san actually didn't know that Hsiao-yuan used to work for him. He joked that he had made a mistake, had lost talent as a result. His way of making up for his "mistake" was to suggest that they take their honeymoon in Hokkaido. He would help arrange the itinerary. From him they also received a lucky red packet, namely a promotion to full engineer for Hok Leong. Akita san explained that "a promotion comes with a raise. When a man gets married, expenditures are sure to increase."

As for Ah Hor and the guys, Hok Leong only contacted them by phone. He said he was getting married and didn't plan on inviting anyone. On another occasion, he would arrange for them to meet up for a celebration of some kind. Hsiao-yuan's guests included her Caucasian boss Martin. Sister Huan and Brother Tsao also flew in from Taiwan to attend the banquet.

On the day of the wedding, Hsiao-yuan's father arranged for uncle Fu to sit next to him on the right during the traditional tea ceremony. Hsiao-yuan's mother sat on the left.

"Wonderful! A bonus!" uncle Fu exclaimed happily. He held Hsiao-yuan's hand and addressed her fervently, "My daughter, you're more beautiful than an angel."

After the simple ceremony, uncle Fu said softly to her, "Hsiao-yuan! You have great pride and you're always eager to be number one. You know that about yourself. So when it comes to household matters all the big decisions should be made by you. Leave the small decisions to Hok Leong. But, remember, what constitutes a big decision or a small decision, Hok Leong should be the one to make the distinction."

Hsiao-yuan couldn't control herself and started to cry.

49

The day after the wedding, Hok Leong and Hsiao-yuan flew to Tokyo. During the flight, Hsiao-yuan said laughingly, "I never thought we'd get married under such circumstances. I kept wondering when you'd pop the question to me. I thought, if the situation isn't right, I might say no, but that might mean that I'd destroy my own chances of happiness. I never thought we'd get married without you proposing to me. In fact I was the one who proposed to you earlier."

Hok Leong replied happily, "I've taken advantage of other people's difficulties!"

Hsiao-yuan didn't agree. "No, I think Father and uncle Fu made our marriage a foreordained event. I gratefully follow the path hewn by fate."

"Me too. Without Fu *laoshi* we wouldn't be together."

Hsiao-yuan gave a sigh. "I've been thinking that I shouldn't return to Taiwan."

Hok Leong stared levelly at her.

"Father and uncle Fu have deteriorated quite a bit because of their illness. And Mother is worn out looking after them. She's getting old too. Furthermore…" she looked carefully at Hok Leong, "I'm sure no man wants his wife to be constantly away from him."

"I'm fine actually," Hok Leong replied. "With modern jet transport I can easily reach you in less than a day. Are you sure about this? Wasn't it supposed to be a two-year stint?"

Hsiao-yuan replied mildly, "I've completed most of it anyway. Anyway the main benefit of an overseas posting is the boost to your vision and spirit. You don't lose those things easily. If you really need to go somewhere, as you say, it can be done in a day. The more worrying thing is that if you stay in this country too long, life becomes tedious. You start to cower behind ramparts. You want to rouse yourself but lack the strength or the know-how to do so. Like a frog in a boiling pot of water, you die a slow death."

"It doesn't have to be so bad, you know. People who are sensitive and daring will always see further than most," Hok Leong said. He patted Hsiao-yuan softly on the shoulder. "I'm sorry. Three men in tandem have destroyed your dreams."

"You're wrong!" Hsiao-yuan replied spiritedly, "It's because of these three men that I have my dreams."

4

JENNIFER

1

<u>Jennifer</u> was the name that Hsiao-yuan's colleagues picked for her when she worked in the electronics factory. After she joined the advertising firm she continued to use the name, which became the one that most people knew her by. That switch was a watershed moment in her life.

2

After the honeymoon, they discovered that the watershed moment didn't only encompass their marriage. It also comprised the loss of a cherished teacher and advisor. When they got back from Hokkaido they discovered that uncle Fu had passed away. Hsiao-yuan was devastated. She blamed her parents for not telling her earlier. But her mother pleaded with her, "Uncle Fu arranged it that way. He chose to leave when you were away. He didn't want you to be too heart broken."

Two days after Hok Leong and Hsiao-yuan left for Japan, uncle Fu had suffered another stroke, a serious one. When Hsiao-yuan's father reached him it was already too late. They managed to get him to the hospital but he never recovered. In those pre-handphone days, finding someone in an isolated, snow-bound corner of Hokkaido wasn't easy. Furthermore, Hsiao-yuan's parents didn't want to disrupt their trip.

The most difficult part of it for Hsiao-yuan was that uncle Fu left everything to her. His lawyer even came to confirm the bequest. Hsiao-yuan didn't care about any of that. Every Friday she and Hok Leong continued to visit his home, making belief he was still with them.

3

Hsiao-yuan was with child.

Immersed in their grief, Hok Leong and Hsiao-yuan weren't especially elated by the news. Hok Leong wouldn't let Hsiao-yuan come with him when he visited uncle Fu's home. He encouraged her to visit her parents, to meet up with friends, or even to visit Taiwan to get a change of scenery.

Hsiao-yuan wanted to work. But her appetite was bad; she vomited so much that she had to stop work, take leave, and stay at home. Her parents suggested that she come stay with them for a while but she refused. They had to visit her instead.

Hsiao-yuan complained, "By the time it comes to me, the human race has had zillions of offsprings. Why is there no evolution? Why does it have to hurt so much?" When the bulge began to show she cried, "I'm a pre-historic creature. I'm a Neanderthal."

Apart from looking after Hsiao-yuan, Hok Leong went each Friday to uncle Fu's home. To stave off despondency he kept himself busy cleaning the place or putting things in order. It wasn't easy, for after all his personal transformation and relationship with Hsiao-yuan had all been made possible by the man.

Fu *laoshi* had a subtantial collection of paintings and antiques. Hok Leong knew little about these things. His father-in-law sometimes came to lend a hand or to pay homage to a dear friend. When he saw the paintings, he said, "those pictures are probably worth more than this house."

The paintings were from the Qing dynasty and Republican period. There was also some canvases by local artists, mainly presents from Fu *laoshi*'s friends. Hok Leong's father-in-law didn't know much about ceramics, but he figured that the various items in the house—bowls, dishes and the like—were also from the Qing dynasty period.

After he cleaned the house and put things in order, Hok Leong was worried that some of the paintings might become mouldy without anyone noticing the deterioration. He took several of the paintings out of storage and hung them up in one of the rooms. He rotated these works. When his father-in-law saw the pieces he suggested that they turn the dwelling into a gallery of some kind. Hok Leong jumped at the idea for it gave him something to do. He first whitewashed the walls and got someone to install an electronic security system. He installed new air-cons and lights. Hsiao-yuan's father sent the paintings to be mounted. Prompted by a sudden impulse, he wrote the characters "Pu-ting Gallery" on a banner and hung it at the front door.

When Hsiao-yuan's physical condition improved she was invited to "tour" the gallery. Seeing the place changed beyond recognition, she couldn't control herself and started to cry.

In the future, the gallery became the go-to recreational space for Hok Leong. Apart from enjoying the artworks and antiques on display, he listened to the records that Fu *laoshi* had accumulated, and also read the books he left behind.

As far as Hok Leong was concerned, he had enough riches to last him the rest of his life.

4

Hok Leong's daughter was born in 1990. She looked like her mother, which was precisely what he wanted. He didn't want the next generation to be like him, to encounter the dangers that beset him when he was young. To pay homage to uncle Fu, Hsiao-yuan wanted her daughter's name to reflect his. Hok Leong asked his father-in-law how to do this. The old man raised his head slightly, cocked it in an easterly direction, and then in a westerly direction.

"Let's call her Chen Ting then!" He reeled off an idiom that chimed with her name, a phrase denoting a girl who was slender and elegant.

Hok Leong was struck by his erudition, that he could cock his head and just like that cite an adage or idiom.

When his daughter reached a full month in age, Hok Leong invited Ah Hor and the guys to join his family for a meal. It was customary to celebrate such occasions; he also wanted his old classmates to meet his wife and daughter. On the evening in question, Ting Ting kept bawling at the restaurant. They couldn't talk with the baby making a racket. Eventually Hsiao-yuan suggested that Hok Leong send them home first, after which he could re-join his friends.

Hsiao-yuan was still awake when Hok Leong returned home after the event. She told him, "When you sent us home just now I was terrified that you might not return, that you might not want us anymore."

Hok Leong pulled her into an embrace and held her tight. It was only many years later that they understood what had happened, that Hsiao-yuan's talk was a symptom of the post-natal depression that assailed and tormented her.

5

Ting Ting's arrival meant that the individuals in three different households became extremely busy. Apart from Hok Leong and Hsiao-yuan, their parents were also roped in. Occasionally Hsiao-yuan had to fly to Taiwan, which meant that the child had to stay with her grandparents.

Hsiao-yuan didn't want her parents to get overly tired. They were supposed to be enjoying their retirement. It's okay, her mother said. This way they could minimise the chances of conflict between Hsiao-yuan and her mother-in-law. "It's better that you have that distance, like a guest or a visitor. It's better for everyone," she said.

Hsiao-yuan also considered the feelings of Hok Leong's mother. "It's not right that I always run to my parents with my daughter!" she said. So she hired an "<u>aunty</u>" to help her at home.

"You worry too much," Hok Leong told her.

"I have no choice," Hsiao-yuan said, "all daughters-in-law are put into this position. You exist in a narrow crevice. You're always caught between two sides."

Hok Leong didn't understand, "You tried your best. If you offend someone so be it!"

"The problem is, they treat us so well. We really should be thankful!" Hsiao-yuan knew that Hok Leong wouldn't understand her difficulty. "You don't get it. The lives of daughters and daughters-in-law are different from that of sons and sons-in-law."

Hok Leong didn't know when Hsiao-yuan became so matronly or aunty in her outlook. Where was the haughty young girl that he used to know?

In the end, it was Hok Leong's mother who showed great perspicacity on the matter. Knowing that she hadn't received any formal education, she didn't suggest that she help look after her granddaughter. She wasn't pushy. She already had three grandchildren before Ting Ting: Hok Leong's elder brother had two sons, his elder sister had a daughter. Although none of them were cared for by Hok Leong's mother, she was already extremely busy. It was just that Hsiao-yuan was passionate about her role and duties. Every now and then she took Ting Ting to see Hok Leong's mother. And so those concerns had arisen.

As it turned out, this navigating between-two-sides ruckus was to come in handy, for Hsiao-yuan later drew on the experience for an advert that she wrote. The advert was used to sell infant formula. It even won her a prize:

Mothers and daughters squabbling over how to bring up the next generation
"Caring mother brand"—The formula that unites the generations.

While Hsiao-yuan helped to unite the generations, Hok Leong exemplified what she said about sons having a "different" kind of life. On one occasion when Hsiao-yuan was busy with work, Hok Leong took his daughter to see his mother, although in truth it was to let his mother look after her. After playing with Ting Ting for a while, he let her take the child downstairs.

Less than an hour later, Ting Ting and grandma returned home. Ting Ting was plastered all over with fine sand from the playground. Hok Leong wasn't pleased with that.

"Why did you let her play in the sandbox?" he asked.

"Isn't it fine, as long as the child likes it? What's the matter?"

His mother always had to have her own way of doing things, Hok Leong thought. She never listened to other people.

"What do you mean as long as the child likes it? Adults have to supervise, right?" His voice grew harsh.

His mother noted Hok Leong's annoyance but still tried to accommodate her son. "There are other kids playing there," she said mildly.

Why couldn't she admit it when she lost an argument? Hok Leong grew increasingly irritated.

"I don't believe other kids play like this. You didn't look after her properly. That's what happened."

Hurt by Hok Leong's accusation and callousness, his mother's attitude hardened as well, "I didn't look after her properly! This is exactly how we brought you up!"

His mother was like that. She liked to argue and debate. "It's because I have a mother like you that I grow up to become like this!" Hok Leong cried.

His mother grew livid. "You guys aren't fine, what's that got to do with me? Your father is so poor. The fact that we managed to bring you up is already a joke!"

Hok Leong wanted to continue. But from the corner of his eye he suddenly noticed Hsiao-yuan standing at the window grill, peering in, her eyes filled with tears. He didn't know how long she had been standing there.

She shook her head at Hok Leong, telling him to stop, telling him she couldn't believe what she was hearing.

Hsiao-yuan entered the flat. She slipped past Hok Leong as if he wasn't there and stopped in front of his mother. "I'm sorry, Mom. Please don't be angry. I'm sorry." She picked up her daughter. "I'm sorry, Mom, I'm going now" she said again. Then she turned and went off.

Hok Leong's mother didn't know what to do. "I'm fine, Hsiao-yuan," she half-called out.

"I'm okay. Don't worry about it."

Hsiao-yuan turned her head. "I know, Mom! <u>Bye-bye</u>!"

Hok Leong called out, "We're going now." He hurried after Hsiao-yuan.

Nobody said a word in the car going back. When they reached the foot of their apartment block, Hok Leong said softly, "You guys go home first. I'm going to drive around a bit and then come back."

Hok Leong drove aimlessly, heading nowhere. In the end he found himself slowing to a stop in a parking lot near his old home. Blaring from the music player was the title track, "Home," from an album by Luo Dayou. It was the first album

Hok Leong and Hsiao-yuan bought together. Originally they had it on cassette tape, now it was a CD:

> *Loving you gently, Loving you gently, my baby, my baby.*
> *Think of you gently, missing you gently, these tears of mine,*
> *these tears of mine.*
> *Who can give me warmer sunshine than you?*
> *Who can give me sweeter dreams?*
> *Who forgives me in the end? And comforts my pain-filled*
> *heart?*

Hok Leong got out of the car and sat on a bench at a nearby patch of grass. He stared at the new flats built over his old stomping ground, studied carefully the doorways and windows of the different households. He thought about his experience growing up, went over the relationship between himself and his family, between his family and himself. He thought about his relationship with his father, his mother, his elder brother, and his two sisters. In the end, he thought about the relationship between Hsiao-yuan and her parents.

A taxi pulled into the car park. A lady stepped out holding a young child. It was Hsiao-yuan and Ting Ting. Hok Leong was surprised. He stepped forward and took Ting Ting in his arms. She had been cleaned up, had taken a bath.

"Papa grew up here," he told his daughter.

She seemed to understand what he said. Or maybe not. She struggled in his arms, wanting to be let down. Hok Leong lowered her to the ground. Immediately, she ran off to a corner of the grass verge.

Hok Leong turned to Hsiao-yuan. "You saw the difference between you and me. That's my upbringing, my background," he said.

Hsiao-yuan didn't respond.

"That's the main difference between the two of us," Hok

Leong continued. "I thought I tried hard, but still…".

Hsiao-yuan remained silent.

"Please give me more time!" Hok Leong pleaded.

6

Hok Leong's company decided to open a factory in Shanghai. It had been talking about this for some time. After the 1989 Tiananmen incident, China had opened the Shanghai Pudong area for external investment. Many Japanese businessmen seized the opportunity. <u>Akita san</u> was one of them.

Hok Leong was one of those selected to help with the project. "<u>Jackie</u>!" <u>Akita san</u> said. "Among the people in the company, your Chinese is the best."

Hok Leong didn't agree immediately to the posting. Ting Ting was less than two years old at the time. He didn't know how to broach the subject with Hsiao-yuan.

<u>Akita san</u> had considered this detail. "Why don't you take your wife and daughter along!"

"Go by yourself! It's a rare chance!" Hsiao-yuan told Hok Leong when he brought it up. Her response surprised him. "It's like when I had to work in Taiwan. You can come back every one to two months or so."

She was right. If everything went pear-shaped, he could just come back. It wouldn't involve so many people.

So Hok Leong began a kind of semi-nomadic existence, flying back monthly to see his family. The nondescript urban environment that he encountered in Shanghai gave him a shock. Oftentimes, he couldn't work out where he was, especially when the roads were named after places. This included the roads named after the treaty ports that had been opened up for trade together with Shanghai, namely Guangzhou, Xiamen, Fuzhou, and Ningbo. But there were also roads named after Hankou, Nanjing, Chongqing, and

Sichuan. When he shared this observation with Hsiao-yuan, she said, "At the end of the day, the quality of a place doesn't come from the built-environment, it comes from its people."

After travelling back and forth for a while, Hok Leong felt that real life in Shanghai took place not in the numerous gleaming high-rises, but in the old lanes and residences known as Lilong lying behind, as it were, the skyscrapers. Real life also took place in the low-level shop houses that you found everywhere. Lilong life wasn't accessible to non-residents, but in the shop houses you saw all kinds of people interacting, packed helter-skelter with garments flapping on wash lines that seemed to stick right out of the narrow streets. For Hok Leong, this was the real face of the city: the shops were open all hours of the day; the children of shop owners going out or coming home from school; family members and neighbours moving in and out, gossiping or paying visits to one another. Then the customers inserting themselves into their lives, hearing the music they heard, watching the programmes they followed on television, or waiting for them to finish a meal or a drink....Compared to all this, the actual commercial transactions didn't seem all that important.

On one occasion, Hok Leong was strolling down Nanjing East Road when he noticed the televisions in one of the electronics retailers broadcasting a speech by a leading political personage. Among the sea of people traipsing down the street, no one stopped to watch the broadcast. In terms of brightness and colour, the television images couldn't compete with the neon ads on display. Hok Leong didn't stop as well. He was looking for something to placate his growling stomach.

He later told Hsiao-yuan, "There're no *isms* here. There's only consumption."

7

The factory that Hok Leong's company built in Shanghai was owned by <u>Akita san</u>'s family. His family had factories all over the place. The one in Shanghai was managed by executive staff from Singapore and Japan. <u>Akita san</u> and one of his uncles were in charge. In terms of family hierarchy, <u>Akita san</u> wasn't the most senior person there. So the pressure on the Singapore contingent wasn't too bad.

Hok Leong felt that he was there to study. Everything involved in setting up the facility, from not having a factory to having one, from dealing with the government to dealing with workers, all that was a great learning journey. Hok Leong's main role was to handle cultural liaison matters, the technology aspects were all handled by colleagues from Japan. What he didn't expect, what he considered the greatest bonus, was that he grew closer to <u>Steven</u> and <u>Akita san</u>. Sometimes he even went out with <u>Steven</u> for a drink.

What! Having a drink with <u>Steven</u>?

Yes, his relationship with <u>Steven</u> had improved, was no longer tense and aggravating. Because they had a common goal, because they had a chance to show goodwill and to communicate, the feeling developed that there wasn't all that much to be irritated or fearful about. Or at least, that was what Hok Leong told Hsiao-yuan.

Hsiao-yuan didn't agree with him. Now that Hok Leong was an <u>executive</u>, he was no longer the enemy, she said. He could be a friend. Hok Leong said that wasn't fair, she had preconceived notions about <u>Steven</u>. Official interaction and personal relationships were different things and should be separated, he said.

Although she was herself an executive, Hsiao-yuan reminded Hok Leong not to forget the road that he had travelled.

"Don't worry," Hok Leong intoned in a voice filled with conviction, "I will always be a <u>technician</u> at heart."

8

Getting a chance to share a tipple was great, for when they let their guard down they could talk about everything under the sun. One time Hok Leong was drinking with <u>Steven</u> in one of the Lilongs when <u>Steven</u> laughingly said, "Hey! I see you more than I see my family."

"Zhao-Mu-Xiang-Chu." Hok Leong deliberately replied in Chinese, using an expression that meant they were in contact from morning to dusk.

<u>Steven</u> made a gesture to show that he didn't understand. "<u>Now, you are the fish in the water</u>," he said.

Like-fish-in-water? <u>Steven</u> had cited an English saying that had a literal Chinese equivalent. Hok Leong gave a big laugh. It seemed that <u>Steven</u> had understood his earlier erudite expression.

"Actually, <u>no, I am the</u> Jia-Yang-Gui-Zi <u>in China</u>," Hok Leong continued, mixing English and Chinese into the same sentence.

"<u>What</u>?"

"<u>Fake Ang Mo ghost in China</u>," Hok Leong said, translating the Chinese portion of the phrase. Ang Mo or red hair was a Southern Chinese dialect term for Westerners.

<u>Steven</u> had not heard that expression before. He furrowed his brows.

Hok Leong explained. "In this place, we're no different from each other. We're both <u>bananas</u>," he said, meaning those who were yellow on the outside but white inside.

"Why so?"

"My middling command of the language doesn't mean anything here. You can't just know a bit of the language.

You need to know the subjects covered in <u>Chinese Studies</u> programmes, things like politics, culture, geography, history, and so on. Someone like my father-in-law is much better placed than me."

<u>Steven</u> laughed. "It's just as well that I'm ignorant then. Never mind, <u>you are still my teacher</u>, there's no need to bring in your father-in-law."

"You're also my teacher!" Hok Leong replied.

They reminisced about the time when <u>Steven</u> had to correct Hok Leong's written English in several of the reports that he filed. The recollection brought a great deal of merriment.

"My Malay is actually much better than my English. That's my real mother-tongue," <u>Steven</u> said happily.

Hok Leong was surprised, "So we are both using our second language to communicate!"

"What's your most fluent language then? The one you're most <u>comfortable</u> with?" <u>Steven</u> asked. The subject had piqued his interest.

Hok Leong thought for a while. "The one that mixes together the languages used by Chinese people, I guess. And also including bits of English and Malay lah!"

"How about when you were young?" <u>Steven</u> asked.

"I spoke Cantonese. I'm Cantonese. It was only later that I learned Hokkien from my neighbours and classmates."

"So you spoke Cantonese at home and Hokkien outside the house?"

"Correct! I began learning Mandarin when I started school, but with classmates I still used Hokkien dialect."

"When did you start learning English?"

"In primary school. But I wasn't serious about it."

"Actually we're quite similar," <u>Steven</u> said. "I speak Malay at home and Chinese dialects outside the house. I started learning English when I went to school. We had Mandarin lessons as well but I was also never serious about it."

"And now we work in a Japanese company."

<u>Steven</u> shrugged his shoulders.

Hok Leong looked around the <u>pub</u>. He really couldn't work out where he was.

9

Life was full of pressure. Sometimes it came in the form of advice given "for your own sake." For married couples, pressure usually stemmed from the recommendation that one should have a child while young.

Oddly enough, the pressure didn't abate even *after* you had a child.

First it was Hsiao-yuan's mother making the entreaty. "Ting Ting is already three years old. You should have another one. It's easier to bring up two children."

Hsiao-yuan probably didn't respond encouragingly to her appeal, for later on Hsiao-yuan's parents also repeated the advice while talking to Hok Leong. When he told Hsiao-yuan about it, she said, "I've heard that many times from my mom. Bringing up Ting Ting is already so tough, why should we have another child?"

After that, they didn't think much about the issue, until one day, Hsiao-yuan brought it up again.

"Your elder sister just said to me what my mother suggested earlier," she said.

"Huh? What did she say? Is she still working as a nurse?"

"She's no longer at the hospital. She joined a private clinic. She says "<u>aunty</u>" nurses like her are in great demand. They can take the hard work and they're also effectively English-Chinese bilingual."

"She used to complain that graduates of Chinese schools are slated to have a miserable time."

"Well, as they say, things change with the passage of time."

"What about that other matter? What did she say?"

"I thought you didn't want to hear about it," Hsiao-yuan replied. "She said it's easier to have two kids when they're closer in age. The alternative is that you struggle to bring up a <u>baby</u> and rest a few years, but by the time you have another one, you've forgotten how to do it. And you're older as well. That makes it very tiring. She said kids who are closer in age get along better as well."

The views of paternal aunt apparently outweighed the views of the older generation; they were willing to listen to the former.

"Didn't you say that bringing up Ting Ting is already a struggle?"

"Your sister said that if you bring up two children who are close in age, the burden goes up by at the most thirty per cent," Hsiao-yuan replied. After a pause she added, "She also said that you're already thirty-three."

Hok Leong was extremely irritated with his elder sister. Why did she have to be such a pest? Okay, she had two kids of her own. But why must others follow her example? Why couldn't she badger younger sister if she wanted to be nosy? Younger sister was married but didn't have a child.

Hok Leong had never planned for anything in his life. The one time he altered the pattern was to have a child, and it was partly because he was no longer a spring chicken. He hated plans and schemes.

Xuan Xuan's arrival stemmed from the instigation of her paternal aunt. Hok Leong preferred the way in which Ting Ting entered their lives. It wasn't fair to Xuan Xuan, that discrepancy, since they were later wont to observe that bringing up a first child was a matter of devotion and care. You read books and made sure to do the right thing, whereas bringing up a second child was a more offhand, blasé experience. You did it, so to speak, like you were feeding a pig. Because of that

Hok Leong cherished Xuan Xuan even more.

Xuan Xuan's name arose from the fact that she cried too much. Her maternal grandfather said that children must be happy, must display their beauty, not be a cry-baby. Again he uttered some erudite language to frame his observation, playing in the process on the homophony between the word, Xuan, which denoted a beautiful flower, and another character, also pronounced Xuan, meaning to clamour and make a racket.

So the second child was named Chen Xuan, meaning literally to display or lay out one's beauty (rather than cause a racket). Again, Hok Leong was in awe of his father-in-law's erudition and learning.

The year that she arrived, Hok Leong was thirty-four, Hsiao-yuan thirty-one.

10

Ensconced in Shanghai, Hok Leong and <u>Steven</u> were like brothers-in-arms fighting the good fight. Japanese staff apart, they held the highest appointments, so when <u>Steven</u> wished to take a holiday, he felt that he needed to tell Hok Leong about it.

"So where're you going?" Hok Leong asked.

"Malacca."

Hok Leong thought that he had misheard.

"Malacca," <u>Steven</u> repeated. "I like the place," he explained, "the language, the food, the social interaction, everything makes you feel <u>comfortable</u>. I lived there for a while when I was young. I've always liked it.

"I thought you'd prefer Australia or the US."

<u>Steven</u> took a seat near Hok Leong's desk. Looking like he was conducting a survey of some kind, he asked, "So what kind of places do you like? I mean, as a travel destination, or for a short-stay vacation."

"Taiwan, Japan, Hong Kong, all these are okay." Hok Leong checked to see how <u>Steven</u> reacted.

"For me, it's Malaysia, England, and Australia," <u>Steven</u> replied evenly.

Hok Leong laughed. "From the looks of things, we can't go travelling together."

"So where do you feel most <u>comfortable</u>?" <u>Steven</u> asked, continuing his survey. "I mean, as a place to stay."

"Funny, I've not thought about that," Hok Leong mulled over the question. "If I really have to say, I'd choose Singapore."

His reply came as a shock to <u>Steven</u>. "I thought you'd say Shanghai."

Hok Leong knew why he gave that response. "I grew up in Singapore," he explained. "I'm used to the place. Language is not an issue for me in Shanghai, of course, but in terms of culture, social system and day to day living there are huge differences between the two cities. After coming to China I realised I'm a <u>fake Ang Mo ghost</u>."

<u>Steven</u> laughed. As though he were consoling Hok Leong, he said, "Singapore needs people like you."

Hok Leong didn't know whether he meant that as praise or as censure. "How about you?" he asked.

"Malacca," <u>Steven</u> replied immediately.

"I thought you'd say Singapore." Now it was Hok Leong's turn to be surprised.

"But why?"

"The language environment!" Hok Leong said, referring to the fact that English was the dominant tongue in the republic.

<u>Steven</u> laughed bitterly but didn't respond.

11

All of a sudden, it seemed that everybody had fetched up in Shanghai, including Hok Leong's childhood friend Junior

Brother. Everyone could come to Shanghai, of course, but what was Junior Brother doing here?

The current Junior Brother, sorry, Mr Lim Chai Huat, was an honoured denizen of an out-of-the-way town in the greater Shanghai metropolitan area. His crammed name card identified him as "director" of a host of companies. "I'm the youngster who in Chinese mythology brings great fortune," Mr Lim Chai Huat said, alluding to the words Chai Huat in his name, which meant to get wealthy. "My companies do good deeds!"

"Director Lim," Hok Leong addressed him by that title.

"I think it's best that you call me Junior Brother, Mr President Chan!"

Indeed, the encounter had begun with Hok Leong hearing someone outside his office insisting that he wanted to meet "President" Chan.

"I've known him for a long time. There's no need for appointment lah," Hok Leong heard.

The voice was familiar, Hok Leong thought. He didn't know who in Shanghai could have "known him a long time" and was surprised when he spotted Junior Brother. He stepped forward to shake his hand, but Junior Brother, not hiding his delight, reached out and hugged him.

Hok Leong returned the hug. *When did you start to perform like this?* Hok Leong wondered.

Not wishing to disturb his colleagues, Hok Leong put on his jacket and took Junior Brother to a nearby coffee shop to get a drink. Junior Brother was wearing a full-length coat that flapped noisily in the strong wind. Hok Leong recalled the last time he saw Junior Brother: his dark, tanned complexion, the flat-top that badly needed a trim, his faded blue T-shirt and dark-green shorts, quietly brewing coffee in a drinks stall in a food centre. That was almost a decade ago, he calculated. And now the current Lim Chai Huat was outfitted with a branded

T-shirt and branded overcoat, together with brand-new black-coloured slacks

"I ran away," Junior Brother explained when he took his seat at the coffee shop. "The police were after me. I stole thirty-thousand dollars from my old lady and ran away. From Malaysia I went to Thailand, then to Vietnam. I entered China from Vietnam. I made my way up from Guangdong province. Many people cheated me along the way. But what can you do?"

"Anyone who makes his fortune here has an amazing story to tell, I'm sure."

"I decided to turn over a new leaf. When I reached my little town, I decided I would no longer run or hide. I told them I was an investor. I asked them what business I could enter. I came at the right time, I think. This was just after the Tiananmen incident. Nobody was here, only a few Taiwanese businessmen making household furniture. So I joined in. I started from the most simple, most crude kind of furniture. I followed what others did, I read magazines to improve my designs, I hired young people to help me. And now I've even been to Italy and Northern Europe."

Junior Brother took a sip of his drink. When he spoke again he seemed to be summing up the experience that he had garnered over the years. "Of course, they also helped me. Chinese people believe in honour and righteousness, they cherish emotional ties. If you stand by them when they go through hard times, they will remember your sacrifice. A society like this suits me, suits my character."

He squinted at the table in front of him. "This is made in Shenzhen. It's an imitation of a piece made by a Belgium designer. The material is okay but the workmanship is awful."

Sensing that he had said too much, he changed the focus.

"How about you?" he asked Hok Leong.

Hok Leong laughed. "My journey isn't as spectacular as yours, I'm afraid. All this while I've been working at the same

Japanese company. My boss wanted to come to Shanghai, so I came long as well."

He asked, "Shanghai is a big place. How did you find me?"

"Impressive huh?" Junior Brother said. "I saw a story in the newspaper about the launch of your company. They had a picture with you in it. I just asked around a bit and got the info."

"Impressive," Hok Leong said.

Junior Brother grew serious, "We're still good brothers. That's how I feel. What you feel doesn't matter. You can come look for me anytime in Shanghai."

Hok Leong remembered how Junior Brother and Opium Addict had come to look for him after they joined a secret society. They had asked him to join as well but he didn't agree.

On that occasion, Junior Brother had said: "That's fine, Hok Leong. If anything happens in the future you can still come to look for us. We're still friends."

Now Hok Leong gave a laugh. "Damn you! You hope I get into trouble!" he scolded.

Junior Brother guffawed, "Of course, if nothing happens you can still come to look for me."

12

One of the Shanghai universities wanted Hok Leong to come and give a lecture. The invite stemmed from a remote connection with an engineer of a company that had a joint project with Hok Leong's company. Apparently a former teacher of the engineer was looking for someone to talk about basic features of the electronics industry. Hok Leong's name had popped up.

"But I don't have any university qualifications," Hok Leong told his engineer contact.

"The honourable Mao Zedong was himself a librarian," his

counterpart replied. "What they want is someone with actual front-line experience of the industry."

Hok Leong didn't reply immediately. He asked Steven if it was fine. Steven joked that he wanted to register for the talk so that he could learn something from it. He encouraged Hok Leong, "Look at the new engineers we hire. Are any of them better than you?"

Hok Leong shrugged. "If I really take up the invitation, you'll have to help me correct the lecture script."

Steven suddenly said something in Malay, "Tiga orang, satu guru saya."

"Ah!" Hok Leong translated the phrase in his head, "When three persons walk together, one is bound to be my teacher." It was a famous saying from the Confucius analects. The usage seemed odd. Was Steven saying that he was one of the three?

"You are my only teacher," he responded respectfully.

Hok Leong subsequently turned to Akita san for advice. Akita san didn't object to the idea. "Keep an eye out for outstanding students," he said.

Everyone was fine with the idea. But Hok Leong was worried that he didn't have a strong enough theoretical background. He didn't want to repeat something taken from a textbook.

When Hsiao-yuan heard about it, she suggested that he change the topic to something like, "A Survey of the Singapore Electronics Industry in the 1980s." Hok Leong agreed. He knew enough about the subject to speak confidently about it. His counterpart was fine with the switch, so Hok Leong started preparing for his lecture.

His daughters wanted to come along when they discovered that papa was going to be a teacher for a day.

"Why?" he asked.

"Papa won't scold us," they replied.

As if in a dream, Hok Leong stood at the podium on the appointed day and gave his lecture. He kept thinking about how, when he was studying, the teacher had appointed him one day to help Chiu-yun with her Chinese. He had fought before in class, had read popular novels, had even skipped school.

He couldn't be sure if the students paid any attention to his talk.

13

Hsiao-yuan complained that the Chinese-language writers hired by her company had poor language skills. Hok Leong's immediate response was, "Look, you're not their Chinese teacher. Please don't take up that role."

Hsiao-yuan was surprised. "So what should I do?"

"Tell them they're poor. Let them make the changes themselves."

"It's not the <u>idea</u> that's poor. It's the language."

Hok Leong shrugged his shoulders. "<u>Yes, Steven</u>," he said.

Hsiao-yuan spurned the comparison. "No way I'm going to be like <u>Steven</u>. The problem now is that we can't find anyone to do the job. That's the key problem in my sector."

"Get somebody from overseas! That's what the electronics sector does best!"

"We're thinking about it!"

Hsiao-yuan's company had won quite a few awards for its Chinese-language advertisements. These were primarily the result of Hsiao-yuan's labour and effort. Hsiao-yuan often observed, "The company can't get by without <u>Jennifer</u>. That means that both company *and* <u>Jennifer</u> have a problem."

Hok Leong often advised her to pass on work to the younger staff members.

"But I've been doing that all this while! I started as a writer. As long as they have a minimum standard, I'll push the job out to them. But sometimes customers will phone me to complain.

Jennifer, have you seen the quality of the work? That's what they say."

Around half a year after that, Ting Ting, who was in nursery school, and her younger sister Xuan Xuan both joined their mother in Taiwan.

The plan had been in the works for a long time. Ting Ting had yet to start primary school, so they wanted to take the opportunity to send her and Xuan Xuan to Taiwan to learn Chinese. The original objective was as simple as that. But because Hsiao-yuan's company continued to face difficulty hiring Chinese-language writers, that only increased Hsiao-yuan's desire to move there. In the end, it was settled that Hsiao-yuan would indeed move to Taipei. All the Chinese-language ad work from Singapore would be handled out of the Taiwan office. Of course, Hok Leong also benefited from the change. As Hsiao-yuan put it, his journey home had been "reduced by half." Shanghai to Taipei was a much shorter trip compared to the Shanghai-Singapore route.

That consideration didn't matter much to Hok Leong. For him, flying to Singapore or to Taipei was the same. Wherever his family was located, that was home. Nowadays, he believed, space and time were no longer a concern. What mattered was what you wanted. Hok Leong knew what Hsiao-yuan wanted. By then she had been back in Singapore for five years. It was time for a change. You used day-to-day living space to barter for another kind of space, one that allowed contemplation and reflection. The only difference was that this time around they had two young daughters in tow.

Hsiao-yuan didn't agree with him. "No, it's not like that. In fact my mother will be there."

Hok Leong was surprised. When he showed his concern, Hsiao-yuan laughed. "Don't worry," she said. "She's my mother, not my enemy. Moms and daughters will eventually be together. Like me and my daughters. Four women keeping a watchful eye on each other. It'll be fine."

A month later, Hsiao-yuan's father also joined them in Taipei. He needed people by his side because of his heart problems. His arrival seemed to increase the pressure on Hsiao-yuan, but she didn't think so, "My parents are not <u>babies</u>. Don't worry, father and husband are basically on the same page."

After shifting to Taiwan, the two older folks could easily visit their son, daughter-in-law, and grandson in Hong Kong. Xu Ke had decided to stay on in Hong Kong after getting his academic qualifications. Like them, he was a teacher.

14

Hok Leong couldn't remember many details about his trips to Taiwan in 1994. He only remembered that there were many typhoons that year. At the end of the year, Chen Shui-bian was elected mayor of Taipei. Hok Leong was fortunate to witness the changes that had taken place since his first visit in 1987.

This time they chose to stay in the Beitou area although the rapid transit station there had yet to be built. They thought that transport would be a hassle, but the location also brought its own benefits. Hsiao-yuan could easily reach the Northern coastal roads, or she could explore the hilly forested regions outside the city. Along the way they got to enjoy the excellent local seafood and fresh produce such as fruits and vegetables. Adults and children were happy. Hok Leong didn't know how Hsiao-yuan got used to driving on the right side of the road. He had to look left whenever he crossed the street, but he couldn't even get used to that. He often caught a cold. He confessed to Hsiao-yuan, "<u>I am the outsider</u>."

<u>Outsider</u> derived great pleasure from the fact that Taipei now had the new-fangled Eslite book store. That bookstores could be outfitted in a trendy, fashionable manner gave him

a great shock. He continued to visit the old bookstores in Chongqing South road after they grew less popular, reviving therein his memories of 1987, and also enjoying the genteel, lettered ambience of a bygone era.

Hok Leong now had a different status. From "Jennifer's boyfriend" he was promoted to "Jennifer's husband." Sister Huan and Brother Tsao were still single. Hok Leong could converse with them more than he did in the past, but avoided talking about politics. Sister Huan and Brother Tsao wanted to take Ting Ting and Xuan Xuan as their god-daughters, but Hsiao-yuan had the same attitude as her parents. They could make the decisions themselves when they grew up, she felt.

Ting Ting attended an after-school programme near their place of residence. Her maternal grandparents were in charge of bringing her there. Hok Leong realised that Ting Ting already spoke Chinese with a Taiwanese accent. She emphasised interjections such as "oh" or "ye," elongating their sounds when she added them to expressions such as "really" or "so cute." It sounded strange, but coming from the mouth of a young girl, the effect was also quite lovely.

Xuan Xuan was also cared for by her maternal grandparents. Whenever they walked around the neighbourhood, they were surrounded by other grandparents. Hok Leong discovered that the older folks had taken to the place "like a fish to water." The elegant Hokkien that they spoke almost made him swoon. They liked to visit the nearby spas and bathhouses. They invited Hok Leong to come along, but he didn't fancy the intimacy or exposure that it implied. "Let's go separately by ourselves when we have the time!" he told Hsiao-yuan.

Hsiao-yuan was in great spirits despite her heavy work and family commitments. Commenting on her vigour and strength, Brother Tsao said, "Sister Huan and Jennifer are both iron ladies, but Jennifer doesn't look like one."

Hok Leong believed that Hsiao-yuan had made the right

decision in coming to Taiwan.

Responding to Brother Tsao's comments, Sister Huan said, "I'm not an iron lady. I'm an unfortunate lady who has no one to rely on. I can only rely on myself. Jennifer isn't some kind of iron lady as well. She's always placed Jackie as the centre of her world."

"No, not really," Hok Leong immediately replied. "I always follow her wishes!"

"That's because she's intelligent," Sister Huan replied. "Before you open your mouth, she's already done what she wanted to do."

Hsiao-yuan recalled what uncle Fu said at their wedding. "In our home, I'm in charge of the big decisions, he's in charge of the small ones. But whether something is big or small is decided by him."

Don't get upset Jennifer," Sister Huan continued her train of thought. "If Jackie hadn't agreed to your posting at the beginning, would you have come to Taiwan? Basically you don't have to worry about your family. You know that whatever happens, Jackie is in a safe place waiting for you. It's just like when we take a vacation. Why are we not worried about becoming unemployed? Because we know that when we get back the job is still there waiting for us. So it's safe to say that you've leaned on your husband in order to attain your current achievements. It's different for me. If I fly, I fly. If I don't, I die. There's nobody to cushion the fall or to rescue me. And now that you have two daughters, they also help to put into perspective the scale of your achievements."

Hsiao-yuan was nonplussed. "So, what should I do?" she asked.

Sister Huan chuckled. "You don't have to do anything. Because your life is good, I envy you!"

15

After a few months in Taiwan, Hok Leong's father-in-law visited his son, Xu Ke, in Hong Kong. Subsequently Xu Ke and his family came to visit them in Taiwan as well. As she was wont to do with guests, Hsiao-yuan took her brother and his family to the Yangmingshan national park. The going was difficult because they were four adults and three kids squeezed into a car. Halfway through, Hok Leong and Xu Ke got squeezed out of the vehicle.

Merrily they went to <u>Starbucks</u> to get a drink and to chit-chat.

The two men got along well. It wasn't just that they were related by marriage. The first topic that came up was whether anyone had considered returning to Singapore.

"I can't go back," Xu Ke confessed. "I'm used to Hong Kong. The environment, the language, the public discourse. There's also the question whether the people I worked with still want me."

"Aren't these people that you know well?"

"It's because we're familiar with each other. That's why I can't go back."

"How about the 1997 handover?"

"That's just an abstract term at the moment. In the future, I don't know," Xu Ke said.

He gave a laugh, "The coming handover has created a lot of left-behind people." He used the Chinese term for those who still identified with an earlier dynasty after power had changed hands, and who were left floundering as a result. "If you don't count the settler colonies, Singapore is probably a favoured destination for these British left-behind folks right? I mean, if you're talking about the former parts of the empire?"

Hok Leong hadn't thought about such matters. He didn't know how to respond.

Xu Ke continued, "In actual fact Singapore has many left-behinders. All kinds of them. Even more than Hong Kong."

Again Hok Leong didn't know how to respond. "How's your wife?" he asked, changing the subject.

"She's good. She uses Chinese to teach Mathematics now. She's gotten over the mental problems that she had."

"And your son?"

"He studies in an international school," Xu Ke answered. "How about you guys?" he asked. "Are you going to stay long term in Taiwan?"

Hok Leong thought for a moment, "Let's just give them a happy childhood first! Think about the rest later!"

16

The second time Hok Leong met up with Junior Brother was in a nightclub in the Shanghai bund area. Junior Brother brought along his wife, showing that he was serious about hooking up again with Hok Leong. She was local, was young, not yet thirty. She seemed like a typical small town girl but was sharp and astute.

Junior Brother told his wife to address Hok Leong as "Big Brother."

"Everything that involves Big Brother is also a concern of mine!" he added.

Hok Leong was older than Junior Brother by only a few months. This kind of bigging up talk, as though they were in a movie of some kind, made him uneasy. Once was enough for him.

Because Junior Brother's wife was there, they didn't talk a lot about the past. A week later, Hok Leong, returning the kindness, invited Junior Brother out for a drink.

Junior Brother asked immediately when they met up, "What up? Has something happened?"

"Yes it has!"

"What? Junior Brother grew serious.

Hok Leong gave a laugh. "You're going to treat me to some coffee."

"You!" Junior Brother was taken aback. He looked like he wanted to utter a vulgarity but then thought the better of it.

"So, do you spend time with Singaporeans in Shanghai?" Hok Leong asked.

"You, lah!" Junior Brother said. He shook his head, "Actually no! We always end up talking about the past. It's not easy for me."

Hok Leong didn't know how he should respond.

"Well, let's talk about the past then. Anyway, I've not had any news from anyone."

"I saw an article in the newspapers while I was doing my military service. It said Dog Shit was beaten to death in a fight. You know about that?"

Junior Brother remained silent.

"After you and Opium Addict came to see me that other time, Ah Mei also came to look for me. He said when Red Dragon went for the negotiations he was actually at home. But he didn't want to join in. He said he didn't want to be hacked to death just like that. He asked me whether I thought he was a useless coward, that he had no balls."

"You said he had no balls?"

"No, I didn't say anything."

Junior Brother sighed. "You guys were right. Opium Addict and I were only together for a short while. We loss contact."

"Can you still go back to Singapore?"

Junior Brother shook his head.

"Have you met your parents?"

"My dad is gone. Before he left I met him in Johor Bahru. I met several of my relatives there."

"Does your wife know about this?"

"I didn't say. She should know that my past is a bit murky," Junior Brother said.

"She didn't ask?"

"Over here, they're not that concerned about things like that."

"If anyone asks, including your wife, just say your family used to run a drinks stall," Hok Leong suggested. "Your father died. He left you a sum of money and you came to China. That's the old you."

"Or you can give that framework a little more details if you like," Hok Leong added.

"After my mother leaves, I'll have no one to answer to," Junior Brother said softly.

17

Slowly, the two girls grew up. Sometimes they complained about their mother. Ting Ting liked to say, "Mommy is always so fierce to us!"

"Tiger mother!" Xuan Xuan would chip in.

It seemed their happiest moments were when mother was absent.

Hok Leong thought that the children were being terribly rude. They let their mother down. Hsiao-yuan gave a bitter laugh. "That's how it's like between mothers and daughters," she said.

Hsiao-yuan was strict with the girls. Many a times they phoned Hok Leong in Shanghai when a decision needed to be made. Hok Leong thought that the questions they asked were trivial, so he agreed to everything. Later he discovered that these were things that Hsiao-yuan had disallowed, so they turned to him for help. Later he learned a new trick. Whenever they phoned, he would ask, "What did mama say?" or "Does mama have a suggestion about this?"

Hsiao-yuan wasn't concerned about them phoning him up. "It doesn't matter whether it's yes or no. The important thing is that they call their father, they appreciate his role in the family."

Hsiao-yuan also arranged for them to visit Singapore twice a year, mainly to see the girls' grandparents. They brought a ton of presents with them every time they went home, with gifts for everyone from grandparents to nephews. At first Hok Leong wasn't keen on the idea. But when he recalled the time he fought with his mother, Hsiao-yuan standing at the window watching them with tears running down her cheek, he agreed to everything.

18

Hsiao-yuan's company now wanted to set up a subsidiary in Shanghai. They were late to the game, but better late than never. The good thing about being late was that you didn't have to pay so much school fees. Your set up costs were higher of course.

It wasn't a deliberate thing. It started with some project or two that required them going to Shanghai, and finding a team of people that they could work with. Once that got confirmed setting up shop in the city became a matter of course. As they say wherever the water flows a canal is formed. Hsiao-yuan, Sister Huan and Brother Tsao were all shareholders of the new subsidiary, although Martin continued to be boss with their support. This was because nobody wanted to head the outfit. As a Westerner in a Chinese society, Martin got to enjoy white privilege, so they benefited from that as well. But of course they also acknowledged his exemplary marketing expertise.

Their Shanghai partner was a young man from the Northeast region. His name was Wu Liao. Yes, Wu Liao. His name was even cooler than Hsiao-yuan's small wish. Wu explained that the character Liao in his moniker was the Liao from Liaoning province. In full, his name had the connotation of "no limits or boundaries." But nobody caught that attribution, hearing instead the commonplace homophonous term, *Wu Liao*, meaning senseless or boring.

Because of that, no one wanted to address Wu Liao by his formal name. They felt that it was impolite. Brother Tsao as such altered Wu Liao to Wu Di, Di being younger brother. But because that appellation was a Taiwanese Hokkien cultural practice rather than a mainland one, the pronunciation of Di also got changed, following the rules of Chinese prosody, to another "Di" with a different tone meaning to enlighten. That "Wu Di" in turn took on the mantle of *another* homophonous phrase meaning "unrivalled or without equal," which is to say a paragon. Henceforth Wu Di was deeply grateful that Brother Tsao had given him a "second shot" in life by changing his name. *Wu Liao* was no longer boring or senseless. He was now an unrivalled paragon.

Because Uncle Fu was from the Northeast region, Hsiao-yuan asked Wu Di whether he was of Han background. This was after they had become familiar with each other. Wu replied that he was Han. His ancestors were officials who had been exiled to the border regions. His family members didn't have the physical features of the minority races.

Wu Di and the other younger staff members of the company gave everyone an understanding of how the new generation operated. He was hard working, intelligent, modest, and passionate. He increased the level of respect for his cohort. Brother Tsao observed that the can-do spirit exemplified by Wu Di was actually part of the new zeitgeist. When you internalised that zeitgeist it became part of your personality as well. It was a pity that such vigour had diminished in his country of birth, Hok Leong thought, for seeing it imbued in Wu Di had given him hope for the new generation.

The interesting thing was that the younger staff members were all non-locals. Whether they came from Shanghai, Singapore, or the US, they seemed to share the same traits.

In Shanghai, Brother Tsao was no longer "Brother." Here they called him "Tsao Ye" meaning Master or Uncle Tsao. In terms of age, seniority, and industry experience, the term of address suited him. Sister Huan was still Sister Huan. Nobody was foolish enough to upgrade her to Auntie Huan. Jennifer continued using her Western name. Not wanting to pander to hackneyed customs she preferred it like that. Nevertheless, the younger staff members felt that they should find a term of respect for her. Sister Jennifer was a mouthful, so they changed that to Sister Jen, and finally to Sister J, sister here meaning elder sister. Those youngsters had a way with words. Hsiao-yuan was happy with the change, accepting as well that she was getting old—she couldn't imagine that one day she would have a moniker endorsing her seniority. Martin's social status codification was the most interesting. The youngsters used the term "Ma Lao," Ma being a shortened version of Martin. Lao could be translated as "old" but designated something like venerable or esteemed. Nevertheless, Martin protested. "I'm not that old, right?" he complained. When she mulled over the incident, Hsiao-yuan felt that, from the use of names, nicknames, and manner of address, you could see the difference in culture.

19

Since husband and wife were based in Shanghai, family matters could be handled in a straightforward manner. The ideal solution was for everyone to move there, including Hsiao-yuan's parents. When Ting Ting entered primary school they could move back to Singapore.

Hsiao-yuan didn't see it that way. Why not stay put rather

than make a move? Ting Ting was starting school next year. If they moved to Shanghai they would have to relocate before they even got used to the place. The girls and her parents couldn't handle such a change.

So, for the immediate future, Hok Leong and Hsiao-yuan took turns flying to their Taipei home, taking care of family. Of course it was a bit odd. One evening years later, they found themselves again in Shanghai, not an easy matter to arrange. It was the start of summer. They leaned against the railings at a spot along the Huangpu river, surveying the different buildings and the construction sites along the two banks, the array of lights reflecting and refracting the cosmopolitan nature of the place. The spot—part of the Shanghai bund—was windswept and cool. Hsiao-yuan said to Hok Leong, "Shanghai is the forerunner of many great cities. It survived half a century of conflagration and now it's been reborn. It's a pity that I'm too old to take part in any of this. I don't have much time, emotion or energy left in me."

Whether you called it the Customs House or the Shanghai Custom Tower, whether you used the 1927 name or the post-1949 name, the clock tower at Number 13 The Bund rang at its designated hour, stately and drawn-out, drowning out the sounds of vehicles, the sounds made by men, its clang reverberating across time, and moving ever eastward with the flow of the river.

20

In 1997, the Taipei mass rapid transit system reached Tamsui. Ting Ting and Xuan Xuan didn't get a chance to try the extension. Ting Ting returned to Singapore and enrolled in a primary school. Both sisters didn't want to go back. Hsiao-yuan's parents also missed Taipei, and pined sometimes for the life they left behind.

The children got older. Husband and wife knew that they wouldn't always need their parents. That time would pass soon enough, so they tried to stay in Singapore as much as possible, which meant that they also spent a lot of time in airplanes.

They liked to bring the children to Pu-ting Gallery when they were in Singapore. The girls didn't know the history of the building. They played electronic games there or gambolled about in the garden. Hsiao-yuan tended to ignore them when they visited the gallery. It evoked too many emotions in her. Sometimes she would say to Hok Leong, "Look! Ting Ting has already entered primary school, so much time has passed."

Hok Leong gave a dry laugh, "You dye your hair nowadays too."

Hsiao-yuan let out a puff of air. "Just look at them! What have I done all these years? Apart from having two children, I've done nothing. I've frittered away my time."

"What else do you want to do?"

Hsiao-yuan shrugged her shoulders. "What about you?" she asked.

"I'm lazy by nature, I always fritter away my time." Hok Leong laughed, "My biggest dream in secondary school was that I wouldn't have to buy coffee for those working in an <u>office</u>. I wouldn't have to be an office boy."

"You had such a dramatic childhood. I'm only younger than you by three years. Why do I feel that you lived in a totally different era? Surely, you haven't wasted your time!"

"You haven't wasted your time as well," Hok Leong said. "It's just that you've reached a turning point of some kind."

Hsiao-yuan thought for a moment, "You definitely didn't squander away the time given to you because Uncle Fu used to praise you a lot. It got wearisome after a while."

"I've never heard you say that!" Hok Leong was surprised.

"There's nothing to talk about," Hsiao-yuan said. "He chose to link everything to you. He wanted to talk you up."

Hok Leong stayed silent. He surveyed the main hall of the gallery. The part that Fu *laoshi* played in his and Hsiao-yuan's relationship was greater than he had imagined. His voice filling with emotion, he said, "The invasion and conquering of China by the Aisin-Gioro clansmen, the fact that one of their descendants wandered to faraway England and later put down roots in Singapore, all of that was designed to bring us together?" He gave a laugh and added hesitantly, "so their historical emergence was connected to us?"

Hsiao-yuan elaborated on the idea, "My parents moving from Xiamen to Singapore, your grandfather moving from Guangdong to Malaysia, and your parents moving from Johor Bahru to Singapore, all that was done to bring us together?"

They fell silent mulling over the conceit. Plangent strands from "The Butterfly Lovers Violin Concerto," the album left behind by Uncle Fu, reverberated around the hall.

Ting Ting and Xuan Xuan ran in from the garden. "Mama! Are we going soon?" they cried. "This place is boring!"

21

The Asian financial crisis erupted in 1997. The crisis had been in the works a long time. People in many sectors and industries didn't know how to react. Steven was especially pessimistic about the situation. The market needed at least a decade to recover from the doldrums, he told Hok Leong. By then he'd be in his sixties. His time was destined to be cut short just like that. It was game over for him.

Hok Leong remembered what Hsiao-yuan said earlier. "I'm getting old too," he said. Steven didn't agree. "You've just started, you know. The coming ten years will leave people like me in the finale stage, but it'll be excellent training for the likes of you as you reach maturity. The future belongs to you."

When Hok Leong shared this exchange with Hsiao-yuan,

she said, "I don't know. I feel old. I don't have the energy to talk about the future."

The Shanghai market was a large one. Competition was fierce. Hsiao-yuan's company had joined the game late, had decided to chase quality rather than market volume. As a result, the crisis didn't affect them too much. Hsiao-yuan also took the opportunity to spend more time at home. She had a chance to entertain Sister Huan and her elder sister when they paid a visit to Singapore. Sister Huan's elder sister was getting ready to migrate to the city state. Sister Huan was piqued by the idea.

Hsiao-yuan was mystified. "Let's practice. I'm an immigration official. This is me examining you at an interview—what's good about Singapore?"

"Stable government, safe environment, food is not a problem," Sister Huan replied, "and you're here. We get to rely on you!"

"Aiyoh, rely on yourself, big sister! I probably need to move to Taiwan to ask for your help!"

Sister Huan said suddenly, "Taiwan has passed its golden age, I think."

For a moment, Hsiao-yuan didn't know how to respond.

Sister Huan returned to the topic at hand. "Nation-states aren't such a big deal nowadays, you know. They've been overthrown by the internet. People in the past used to believe in the mandate of heaven. Subsequently modern science pushed that idea off stage, so rulers everywhere could no longer be the sons of heaven. Then you want me to love the nation-state, but that idea has been taken over by our money-worshipping culture. And now the worse thing is that national boundaries don't even exist on the internet. Everyone knows that nations are an *imagined community*. What are rulers everywhere going to do? How will they coax or deceive the next generation?"

Hsiao-yuan said pensively, "I think about my parents, my

parents-in-law. I think about my godfather who was born a Manchu, and who fetched up in Singapore while still a young man. He never returned to his home in Northeast China. So you tell me. What is homeland or motherland? My parents, my parents-in-law, my godfather—I think those are the two words they most hate to discuss."

Sister Huan shrugged. "Me too," she said.

Hsiao-yuan gave a laugh. "The place that you're weighing up as a potential home, it's always been an abode for people of different ethnicities. By happenstance, they found themselves living cheek by jowl. They developed common values and identified with the setting. If you come, will you do the same?"

"I don't know," Sister Huan said. "How about you? Why did you come to Taiwan in the first place? I'm more interested in that."

Hsiao-yuan gave a facetious reply, "My boyfriend was too sticky and heavy. I wanted to hide away for a while, to find a place to think." She tittered and continued, "Actually, it was no big deal. I just wanted to see how it was like to live in a place that used Chinese as a first language, where you actually think in Chinese."

"You're lucky," Sister Huan said enviously. "You can operate in both English and Chinese settings."

Hsiao-yuan laughed gently. "That kind of duality has its costs, you know. My experience is that every country is like a kind of restaurant. It has its own style, its own set menu. Whether you like it or not you have to accept it. If you don't accept it and want to change the menu, well, you pay an extra charge. I've been paying an extra price all this while. I pay extra for my actions and behaviour."

"You know, I've been thinking about this issue recently, but I use a different analogy," Sister Huan replied. "I think of it as a kind of insurance. Every country is like an insurance company. The insured person has to pay a fee every year to obtain cover, so that he or she can live undisturbed and work happily."

"I agree," Hsiao-yuan said. "I think your insurance analogy is better than mine. It's also more realistic. It's more definite than the idea that people must have common values or they must identity with a place." She added with a laugh, "If you seek my husband's opinion, he'll probably say that it's not so much an insurance payment but protection money."

Sister Huan was delighted with the idea. "That's an even better analogy. An incumbent regime is just a legitimate version of a triad! But why would our *mister electronics sector* talk about protection money? That's not my impression of him?"

"Well, okay, let me share my big news scoop with you. He told me he was involved in a melee fight when was young, one of his friends was later beaten to death."

"Really?" Sister Huan said. "He doesn't look the part. Did he say this when he was courting you?"

Hsiao-yuan nodded.

Sister Huan tittered. "Men always talk big when they're chasing a girl. They say how bad they are, or how valiant and heroic, so that the girl will fall for them. Girls like guys who are a bit bad."

Hsiao-yuan didn't think that Hok Leong was talking bull or exaggerating. She gave a non-committal laugh.

"So, will you change your current restaurant?" Sister Huan asked.

"I don't have many choices to be honest," Hsiao-yuan said. She looked around their locale and gestured at a nearby pond. "You know my Manchu godfather once told me that I'm like the lotus flower, whereas my husband is the lotus root that grows beneath the water."

Sister Huan chortled. "Words of wisdom indeed. Your *mister electronics sector* is definitely a lotus rhizome."

The talk that day ended like that, or something like that, Hsiao-yuan wasn't sure. She later shared the conversation with

Hok Leong but skipped the part about protection money. Hok Leong generally stayed away from <u>ladies talk</u> of all kind. But after hearing what they had discussed, he said, "Didn't you say that Brother Tsao has a girlfriend in Shanghai? Sister Huan can also select Shanghai as a destination, right?"

Hsiao-yuan suddenly remembered. "Yes, that's what I told her as well. She says she wants to be Zhou Li with me," she said, using an erudite term that referred to a sister in law.

"I don't understand," Hok Leong said.

"She asked whether you have any brothers."

Hok Leong guffawed. "It's a pity my nephew is still young."

Hsiao-yuan laughed as well. "She wants a lotus root!"

Hok Leong didn't respond. He went over to the bureau in the room and picked up a book lying open on its back. Thinking that their exchange had ended, Hsiao-yuan also picked up the book that she was reading. "Strange! I just saw it yesterday," Hok Leong mumbled to himself.

"I found it!" he cried after a while.

He read from the book in his hand: "The lotus root helps to cool the body and the blood. It reduces fat absorption, enhances the appetite, aids digestion, and improves one's overall constitution and spirit. It also strengthens the immune system."

Hsiao-yuan was lost for a moment. When she recovered she began to laugh.

5

MARGARET

1

Hok Leong sat in the departure terminal at Shanghai Pudong International Airport, waiting for his flight to Singapore. He was late going back by a day.

The evening earlier he had attended a cocktail party organised by a prominent personage in the electronics sector. He didn't plan on attending at first, but <u>Akita san</u> suggested that he join the event to <u>show face</u>, as they say, so he had changed his mind.

The event was pretty boring. Hok Leong paraded past the organiser a few times to <u>show face</u>. That accomplished, he wondered how he could make himself transparent, the plan being to hang around a bit, check out some exhibits, and then to scamper off or disappear.

To pass time he stood in a corner browsing through the special edition of a magazine that showcased the accomplishments of the organiser. Suddenly the organiser was bringing over someone to introduce to him. He was about the same age as Hok Leong and hailed from Hong Kong. It seemed he was fascinated with the design features of Hok Leong's company office-block in Shanghai. They exchanged name cards. His name was <u>Tony</u>, an architect. No wonder.

For a while they discussed the merits of the office tower in question. Learning that Hok Leong was from Singapore, <u>Tony</u>

said, "My wife studied in Singapore in her younger days. I'll bring her over to say hello."

The guy was descended from money. Hok Leong didn't know whether he would return. He continued flipping through the magazine in his hands. Suddenly he heard Tony calling his name, "Hey Jackie! This is my wife, Margaret!"

Hok Leong raised his head. He was astounded. He believed that he shook a little but quickly steadied himself and held out his hand. "Hi Margaret," he said softly.

Hok Leong believed that Margaret had noticed him before he saw her, and so had time to compose herself, although her smile was a bit forced. She too stuck out her hand. "Hello Jackie!" she said. Her voice even carried a bit of the Hong Kong accent.

Hok Leong felt her hand tremble a little as he shook it. He noticed the jade pendant around her neck with the character engraved in gold denoting the first word of his given name, the word pronounced Hok in the Hokkien dialect and Fu in Mandarin, meaning wealth or fortune. He didn't say too much. His own Titoni wristwatch still laid in his wardrobe in his bedroom, the hands giving the time as 10.27 pm. Hsiao-yuan had asked him about it once. He said his mother gave it to him when he qualified for the university.

Tony saw him checking out the jade pendant. "Margaret's mother gave it to her," he explained.

Again a present from the mater! Hok Leong gave a small laugh. "Yes, that true! These kinds of pendants were really popular when I was studying."

Margaret said awkwardly, "Yes! It was bought in Singapore."

Tony added, "Margaret is Indonesian, she did her secondary schooling in Singapore."

"Oh, really!" Hok Leong answered as simply as he could. He cast around for an excuse to leave but they had just been introduced. "So, do you often come to Shanghai?" he finally asked.

"I come here more often," <u>Tony</u> said. "<u>Margaret</u> comes infrequently. She has to look after our three children."

"Oh! How old are they?" Hok Leong naturally asked.

"My eldest daughter is eighteen," <u>Margaret</u> said. My two sons are fourteen and twelve."

"You're blessed," Hok Leong said to <u>Tony</u>. "My two daughters are only ten and six." He glanced meaningfully at <u>Margaret</u>.

She nodded but didn't reply, signalling that they had exhausted the topic. Fortunately, a saviour appeared in the shape of the event organiser, who came at that moment to pull Hok Leong away, saying that he wanted to introduce him to someone else.

Hok Leong courteously bid farewell to <u>Tony</u> and <u>Margaret</u>.

He studied <u>Margaret</u> as he shook her hand again. She hadn't changed. The only difference was that she had short hair whereas in the past she had long hair; and, also, they were like participants in some weird fancy dress ball, wearing masks that aged them by thirty years or so.

"Hope to see you again," Hok Leong said, wishing her happiness, wishing her well.

"Nice to meet you!" <u>Margaret</u> replied politely.

Hok Leong left with the organiser. He walked a few steps, made like he was distracted, and glanced carefully backwards. He caught sight of <u>Tony</u> and <u>Margaret</u> talking with their heads bowed, the jade pendant swaying gently on her neck. After that he didn't see them again the entire night. They had probably left.

2

The seat next to Hok Leong was taken by an old Caucasian man. The volume on his music player was set so loud that Hok Leong could hear the tune despite the headphones that he wore. Did he have a problem with his hearing? Hok Leong wondered. Two or three tunes later, a song that he knew well began to play:

All my best memories come back clearly to me,
Some can even make me cry, just like before,
It's yesterday once more....

At that time, <u>Margaret</u> was still called Chiu-yun. Hok Leong had just entered secondary two. A new student joined their class. Her name is Lin Chiu-yun, the form teacher said. She's from Indonesia. From now on—everybody—please help her out as much as you can.